TOURMALINE

JAMES BROGDEN

snowbooks

Proudly Published by Snowbooks in 2013

Copyright © 2013 James Brogden

Snowbooks Ltd.
Tel: 0207 837 6482
email: info@snowbooks.com
www.snowbooks.com

ISBN 9781907777967

For Pam, who woke up again.

PART
ONE

PART ONE

*Taken from the Operations Handbook for DCS Field Agents (17th Revised Edition)*1*; Appendix D: Non-Suborned Threats.*

… the araka is an extremely pernicious d-sentient parapsyte which sustains itself on the emotional trauma it causes by compelling its host to perpetrate acts of humiliation, degradation, and beastliness. Infestation is mercifully rare – confined predominantly to the lower-class slums of large conurbations and the ghettoes inhabited by foreigners of known moral dubiety – yet the danger an araka presents to the unwary agent cannot be underestimated.

In its natural state – if indeed it can be said to possess such a thing – the creature inhabits the lowest levels of its host's psyche, close to the threshold of the collective unconscious, which it uses to pass from host to host during sleep; the araka shuns the bright light of consciousness, preferring the crushing blackness of the chthonic depths. Whilst there can, of course, be no objectively verifiable information regarding its appearance, certain commonalities of description have been observed in the insane ramblings of those who claim to have seen one, to whit: writhing multitudes of tooth-lined tentacles proceeding from an integument of horned and overlapping plates. However, in the case of an infected host falling victim to a subornation Event, the araka invariably takes advantage of the Event's protean nature to detach from its host – assuming a form which even to the experienced eye is indistinguishable from the Event's other actants – and hunt for a new host.

Being non-human – and in any event only partially physical within the boundaries of the Event – the araka remains unaffected by the standard arsenal of sal volatile aerosols and tezlar guns. If the agent is fortunate, it may content itself simply with tearing him limb from limb and feasting on the fear-drenched tissues of his brain. If he is unfortunate, the araka may attempt to infiltrate his consciousness completely, turning him into a puppet of flesh for its hideous and abominable appetites.

Thus the advice given to any Counter-Subornation agent who believes he may be in the proximity of such an entity is simply this:

Run.

---

1   *Reproduced by kind permission of the Department for Counter-Subornation*

CHAPTER ONE

SHE SHALL BE CALLED WOMAN

1

Squalling rain chased the young woman up the steps of Birmingham University's Barber Institute of Fine Arts and into the shelter of its wide doorway, where she rested for a moment, shaking the water from her coat and combing back damp hair with her fingers.

Neil Caffrey, nearly at the end of his six-'til-three shift on the main security desk by the gift-shop, nudged his colleague Steve, who was frowning at the Guardian crossword.

'Oi-oi,' he murmured, 'bandits, two o'clock.'

Steve glanced up and then back down at his paper, shaking his head with a smile. 'Don't you ever think of anything else?'

'What's to think about?' grinned Caffrey. 'Man, she is fit.'

'She is a student, is what she is. Don't you like this job, or something? Quickest way to get sacked, mate.'

'Never happen. And even if it did, Christ, it'd be worth it. I want to die between those legs.'

'Yeah, well, you better be wearing flameproof underwear, because you are going to crash and burn, my friend. Crash and burn. Still, whatever,' and he waved Neil on with the end of his biro. 'It's your funeral.'

'Roger that.'

Caffrey put on his best professional security guard smile and sauntered over. The girl was not just fit, he decided – she was gorgeous. Her blonde hair had darkened with the rain, and as he got closer he saw that she had the most incredible sea-blue eyes. Hard to tell about her tits under the coat, but then he liked a bit of mystery.

'Can I help you, miss?' he asked, with just enough emphasis on the "help".

'Oh yes, please,' she replied, looking genuinely relieved. 'I'm looking for a painting.'

'Well you've come to the right place!' he grinned. 'We've got all sorts. Finest collection of French Impressionists outside of the National Gallery and more Pre-Raphaelites than you can poke a stick at.'

'Well it's really only one painting in particular that I'm interested in. *She Shall be Called Woman*, by George Frederic Watts. I understand that it's on loan from the Tate. Could you please tell me how I can find it?'

'I can do you one better than that: I can take you to it myself.'

'Oh no, you really don't need to go to the trouble…'

'No trouble at all, Miss. This place is a bit of a maze.' The layout of the Barber was actually about as complicated as a Wendy House, but a few careful detours would give him plenty of time to work the old Caffrey magic.

'Well, I suppose, if you say so…'

Caffrey led her up the main staircase towards the first-floor galleries, pausing only to leer back over his shoulder at Steve, who mouthed the words *crash and burn* back at him.

2

It didn't take Caffrey long to realise that Steve had been right: he wasn't going to get anywhere with this girl.

He managed to get her name – Vanessa – and the fact that she wasn't a student but had travelled up from London, which didn't make any kind of sense, because why would you travel from London to see a painting that was on loan from a London gallery? Beyond that her answers were monosyllabic and distracted; she kept twisting the strap of her handbag and running on ahead into the next room, despite his attempts to slow it down and draw her out with a bit of chat about some of the artworks which he knew the ladies always went for. Funny how they'd get all excited about a bronze statue of some wood-nymph with her tits out, but stick on a dirty DVD and they slapped you in the face and called you a pig. Just couldn't figure them.

And she was off again. By the time he caught up with her, she was around the corner and too far down the next corridor for him to stop her doing what she did next. The only other person in there besides themselves was an old man on a bench, and he looked like he was asleep, or possibly dead. It wouldn't have been the first time.

The painting that she was heading for was massive – had to be six foot high if it were an inch – and it showed a woman's upper body emerging from a swirling riot of leaves and birds. Flowers bloomed beneath her right hand and a mantle of golden cloud opened around her shoulders and down to her navel as if she was bursting free from some kind of cocoon. But she was cloudy and indistinct: her face thrown back and in shadow, her breasts mere suggestions. It was as if she were awakening fully formed into life without knowing who she was supposed to be.

The impression struck Caffrey so forcefully that at first he didn't realise that the Vanessa woman had stepped over the low brass barrier rail and laid her hands flat smack on the painting. Her head was bowed, and her breath heaved as if she were suffering the world's worst asthma attack.

Caffrey snapped out of it.

'Hey! Er, excuse me, Miss? I'm afraid you can't actually....' He reached out to grasp her shoulder, and his voice died as he saw what was happening.

The paint beneath her hands was moving.

3

Steve McBride looked up in surprise as the rain-soaked woman ran back past the security desk. She glanced at him briefly – a wide-eyed, haunted expression – and was outside before he could open his mouth to ask if she were alright. Standing in the doorway, he watched her run down the campus drive towards where it joined the busy dual carriageway traffic of the Bristol Road, and then she disappeared.

Nice one, Neil, he thought. *A personal best. In what world does 'chat up' mean 'drive screaming from the building'?*

He went back to his crossword.

Ten minutes later, when Caffrey had failed to materialise, he chucked it down again and went to look for him.

Steve found his ID lanyard on the floor at the corner of the Blue Gallery (art 1800 to 1900), in front of the painting which the young woman had been asking after, and there was a strange smell in the air which he almost recognised, but no sign of the man himself. There was no sign of him anywhere in the entire building, come to that. He wasn't lurking outside, having a crafty fag. Steve ducked across the road briefly to the Guild of Students to see if he were taking an unofficial coffee break, mindful that if he was caught leaving the desk unattended it could cost him his job, but Caffrey wasn't there either. Nor was he answering his phone – not his mobile, not at his flat. At the end of his shift, Steve even went around to drop the lanyard off – although it had crossed his mind to keep it and let the silly sod take the consequences of an earbashing from Peterson, their supervisor, for losing his ID – but there appeared to be nobody in. Nobody answered the buzzing intercom, and no lights were on in the window. At which point Steve concluded *sod this,* and went home.

All of it completely drove from his head the trivial detail of the peculiar smell which he'd noticed in the Blue Gallery. It was only long afterwards – after he'd fallen in love with Vanessa Gail, and the horror which she had unleashed had gone too far to be stopped – that he thought back on it and realised what it was: the smell of the sea.

4

The wake which trailed after her through the Institute's doors and down Edgbaston Park Road was picked up by one of the Hegemony's floating sensor buoys, but even if she'd been aware that such things existed, she'd never have noticed it, since it looked just like any other homeless young man sitting blank-eyed and motionless, huddled at a bus-stop, easily ignored on a busy city street.

To the buoy, her wake was perceived as a fading, v-shaped distortion in the meniscus of reality, something like a ripple of heat haze. Beyond that, it was entirely unaware of her existence. In its natural state the creature was something like a large, semi-sentient jellyfish, which swarmed with millions of its kind in shallow tropical waters and grazed on the microscopic fragments of dreamwrack left by sleepers. The detector sense which allowed it to home in on their presence served the Hegemony's needs for a simple, passive early warning system, and they were common enough to be deployed in large numbers throughout most major cities, but it wasn't sophisticated enough to provide any details beyond a simple imperative: *prey here!*

It didn't follow her. That was not its function, since it lacked the necessary autonomy or imagination that might allow it to anticipate a human being's behaviour. However, there was just enough consciousness left in the vessel which carried it to perform basic, well-trained actions.

From within its filthy clothes, it produced a mobile phone and sent a single preset message to the only number the phone could reach.

The call's time and geographical location were logged automatically into a system which routinely received thousands of such calls a day, and it began a slow, upwardly-sifting journey through a series of filters and subroutines designed to trawl through the background chaos of the world and isolate preciously rare fragments of purpose. It was weeks, possibly even months, away from the point where a living, breathing operative might see it – if at all.

But that was the thing about hunting. Sometimes it required a level of patience that was almost inhuman.

5

Caffrey didn't show up the next day either. When Peterson called him into his office and asked if he knew anything about where Caffrey might have gone, Steve confessed his ignorance and produced the lanyard, earning a reprimand which he totted up on his mental account sheet of Shit That Neil Owed Him For. He wouldn't have gone so far as to say that Caffrey was one of his best mates, but they'd worked together often enough to have developed a rapport, which was close enough. Still, Steve had given him a chance; if Caffrey wanted to play silly buggers or had gotten himself into trouble then that was his own lookout.

Equally, if Peterson wanted to call the police and report him as missing, then that was fine too. Steve had learned long ago that the security industry attracted a sizeable proportion of the kind of people whose murky pasts you did not want to get involved with, and if Caffrey turned out to be one of them, he was better off out of it.

It never crossed his mind that it had anything to do with the girl. Caffrey had tried it on with so many others and been shot down so many times that his skin was thicker than his head, and the idea he might have done a runner over her was just laughable.

Then, precisely a week later – and even at the same time of day – she was back. He could hardly miss her; the April weather had turned warm and sunny, and she walked past his desk wearing sunglasses and short blue dress which showed an awful lot of leg.

He followed her upstairs to the galleries, not at all sure of what he was going to say to her. He could hardly accuse her of having kidnapped Caffrey, and anyway there was something a bit off-putting about the relentless way she headed straight for the Blue Gallery. The Barber Institute was a work of art in itself: a Grade 2 listed piece of award-winning Deco architecture which boasted collections from Botticelli to Magritte and one of the biggest collections of ancient coins in the country, and she was walking right past everything (with those very shapely legs), as if none of it were there.

He caught up with her in front of *She Shall Be Called Woman*. She'd taken off her sunglasses and was gazing at the painting – rapt but serene. There was nothing of the haunted panic he'd seen last time. It was like looking at a different woman.

While he was still trying to work out how to approach this, she spared him a moment of her attention.

'Can I help you?' she asked.

'To tell you the truth, I'm not sure', he replied, and faltered. Indicating the painting, he said: 'If you don't mind me asking, what's the appeal?'

'Of this?' She shrugged. 'It's a personal favourite.' As answers went, it told him precisely nothing. 'Is that what you wanted to ask?' There was dry amusement in her voice.

'Well, no. See, the thing is…' he rubbed the back of his neck and looked away awkwardly. 'The last time you were here, you were escorted by my colleague.'

'Neil. He introduced himself.'

I'll just bet he did. 'Yes, well the problem is that since then he's sort of gone missing.'

'That was dramatic of him. No offence to your friend, but he didn't strike me as being that imaginative.'

'And I think you were the last person to see him, and I just wondered if he said anything to you which might shed some light.'

'Not really. Sorry.'

'He didn't – I don't know – *invite* you anywhere?'

'Invite me?' she laughed. He got the impression that she was laughing at the idea rather than him, and found that he liked the sound of her laugh very much. He wondered how a man went about making a woman like this laugh a lot more. Probably not by criticising her taste in art. *What's the appeal?* Jesus. He cringed inwardly. 'I'm sorry Mister,' she peered at his ID badge 'McBride….'

'Call me Steve.'

'…but your colleague didn't invite me anywhere. He came on a bit strong and I said I wasn't interested – several times, in fact – and then he called me a frigid bitch.'

'Oh Christ, I'm sorry.'

She continued quite matter-of-factly: 'Not to my face, of course, but loud enough for me to hear it, so I threatened to complain to his supervisor – *your* supervisor, I suppose – and he stormed off. Look, don't worry about it.' She waved away his apologies. 'I've been called a lot worse. He'll be off nursing his bruised ego somewhere.'

Steve's relief was palpable – it felt like something unknotting itself below his ribs. He should have known it would be something that simple. All the same, if Caffrey had shown his face at that precise moment Steve would cheerfully have punched him in it.

'So anyway,' she added, 'I think I'm done here for the moment. It's been a pleasure to meet you, Mr McBride.'

'I said call me Steve.'

13

'And I said it's been a pleasure.' She held his gaze a little longer than was strictly necessary, and turned to go.

'Can I just say again how sorry I am for all of this?' he blurted.

'Please don't. It's starting to sound a little creepy now, and you made such a good first impression.' Leaving him utterly tongue-tied, those incredible legs carried her out of the building.

It was only after she'd left that he realised he hadn't even got her name.

6

That evening he presented the conversation to his kid sister Jackie for inspection. She was getting ready for her fortnightly Girls' Night Out while he took care of dinner time for her two boys, Mark and Will. Uncle Steve's culinary skills didn't run to much more than fish-fingers, chips and peas, but that was fine with them, being only six and eight years old respectively. They threw food at each other in front of Nickelodeon while he scrubbed vainly at the scorched mess that he'd made of the grill pan, and Jackie drifted in and out of the kitchen, demanding forensic detail of the encounter.

She stopped, fiddling with an earring. 'She said what?'

'That it had been a pleasure,' he repeated.

'And then she looked at you?'

'Yep.'

'How did she look at you?'

'What do you mean, how did she look at me?'

'Well, was it a look or a Look?'

He thought about it. 'I don't know. Maybe it was a Look.'

'And then you said what?'

'Well I didn't know what to say, did I?'

Jackie groaned in despair and whacked him over the head with a spatula. 'You great nurk, that was it! That was the come-on and you missed it!'

'How is a Look a come-on?'

'What did you expect her to do – wrap her legs around your waist and say "Take me now, Big Boy"?' He resumed scrubbing glumly, and she drifted out again but returned a few moments later, hopping on one foot while doing up a shoe – one of her self-confessed 'slut-pumps'. 'Next time she shows, you have to ask her out,' she decided.

'No, I've buggered it now, haven't I? A girl like that – she's never going to go out with a bloke like me.'

'Not if you keep coming out with self-pitying crap like that, she's not.'

'Thank you for your support. I shall wear it always.'

Jackie stopped wrestling with her shoe and seized him in a fierce hug from behind. 'Listen, big bruv,' she said. 'You are a six-foot-one security guard who looks a bit like Ben Affleck in a flattering light, likes kids and can sometimes hold a conversation which isn't about sport. Admittedly you can't cook to save your life, but that just proves you're not actually gay. There are thousands of women in this city who would throw themselves at a bloke like you, believe me. I can still set you up with one of the girls from work, if you like.'

'No bloody fear. I ended up needing stitches last time, remember?'

'Suit yourself.' She gave him a peck on the back of the head and breezed away in a cloud of *Ange Ou Demon*, singing La-Gaga's "Born This Way" cheerfully off-key.

Later, when his nephews were tucked in, he fired up Jackie's laptop and googled She Shall Be Called Woman. It had been painted by George Frederick Watts, who was apparently considered to be one of the greatest Victorian artists, and was supposed to be the central of three paintings depicting the creation, temptation, and eventual repentance of Eve. Steve had no idea how this helped him at all, except that maybe it gave him something to talk about to the woman in the blue dress.

But over the next few weeks he was never able to quite bring it up.

She came by at precisely the same time each Friday, giving him a polite smile and a little nod of recognition as she passed his desk, went upstairs to commune with Eve, and then left. She never lingered to examine any other artworks, and she never stopped to chat, and each time that he failed to start up a conversation with her made it harder the next time. He may well have made a good first impression, but at the moment he was performing a painfully slow crash-and-burn all of his own. This, he was sure, would have continued until the painting returned to the Tate and she disappeared from his life forever, except that she crashed first.

CHAPTER 2

BOBBY BEGINS

1

The raft surged up from the deeps end-first and shot high in a plume of spray before crashing back down with a hard, flat slap which echoed across miles of empty sea. A naked man clung to its leading edge, wreathed in green ribbons of dripping kelp, coughing, choking. Moments later, a small flotilla of debris popped up around the raft, but by that time he'd already passed out.

2

First: the sun.

Filling the sky, hammering blood-red light through his flimsy eyelids, thundering heat onto his exposed back until it seemed that his very bones groaned with the weight of it.

Then: the raft.

Creaking as it tilted beneath him, rough and splintered against his face, sloshing and stinging-wet with brine. He smelled salt and baked wood.

Raising his head, he opened his eyes and immediately regretted it. The sun kicked back a million blinding fragments like a plain of broken glass stretching to the horizon. He groaned, screwed his eyes shut again, and rolled over onto his back, feeling the raft's gentle rise and fall as his motion disturbed it.

He lay there for some time as the seawater dried to a crust of salt on his flesh and the kelp stuck to him like strips of glue-paper. Finally he decided to experiment with the concept of sitting up.

So far so good.

He tried squinching his eyes open bit by bit and found it easier this time.

'Jesus Christ. What is this?'

He was in the middle of nowhere. Three-hundred-and-sixty degrees of complete emptiness, with nothing to break the ocean's monotony or soften its desolation. There were no clouds, and by some trick of the atmosphere not even a clear horizon, so that he found himself staring into a scintillating, featureless void. Where was he – the middle of the Pacific? It might as well have been the bloody Sahara Desert. The absence of anything to fix his sight on and give him some perspective was beginning to give him a weird kind of vertigo, so he gave that up and concentrated on his immediate surroundings.

The raft was just wide enough for him to lie across it spread-eagled, which meant that each time he moved, it rocked alarmingly. It was made of bare planks crudely nailed together and was steaming as the sun dried it out.

He started by peeling away as much of the seaweed as he could reach and examined his body like a confused demon which had mistakenly possessed the wrong host. Not too flabby, but not exactly athletic either. It also looked like he'd been in the wars: a long crescent-shaped scar curved across his left side below the rib-cage. It seemed to be quite old, but not infected, which reassured him slightly but didn't do a thing to allay his confusion over the fact that he had no idea how he'd got it. When something bad enough to produce a scar like that happened, you remembered it. He was no psychiatrist, but he knew that much. Then again, maybe he was a psychiatrist. Maybe he was a bloody yak-herder, for that matter.

It suddenly occurred to him that he didn't know *what* he was. What did he do for a living?

Shit, what was his *name*?

He panicked then and leapt up, screaming for help and scanning around frantically for any sign of human habitation – an island, a boat... even just another plank of wood would be some comfort. He would probably have screamed himself hoarse but then his actions made the raft buck violently – he lost his balance, pin-wheeled for a second, and pitched over the side.

The shock of cold water brought him to his senses. Spluttering, he grabbed for the raft's edge, missing it, arms and legs churning the water desperately until he realised that he was actually treading water. So apparently he could swim. Fairly useful thing to know, given the circumstances. He held his position for a moment, liking the sensation of having control over something, and then struck out for the raft, quickly recapturing it. As he did so, something bumped his shoulder, and his attention was drawn to the surrounding flotsam.

There was all manner of junk in the water with him. Fragments of wood and tangles of rope, seaweed, boxes, buoys, random oddments of clothing, plastic bottles, beach buckets-and-spades, and something which looked bizarrely like half a deck chair. There was no sign of where any of it had come from, but already this kind of thing had ceased to surprise him. The object which had bumped into him was a large travelling trunk of the kind used back in the '30s heyday of grand ocean liners; it was covered in labels and rode low in the water as the contents threatened to sink it. With some careful counterbalancing and manoeuvring, he managed to get onto his raft, but only then did it occur to him to check if it was locked. Sod's Law that he'd gone to all this trouble and then would be unable to open the bloody thing.

To his surprise, the catches popped smoothly, and he tipped the lid back.

He'd been right: it was a gentleman's steamer trunk, though its contents were outrageously archaic. He found shirts, cufflinks, trousers and braces; a dinner jacket and shoes polished to a mirror shine; and a paperback novel called A Tender Death by somebody called Nicholas Brannigan. Never heard of him. Its cover featured a semi-clad femme fatale draped over the hood of an Oldsmobile with all the fins and streamlining of a Flash Gordon rocket, and the inside cover was inscribed in a woman's handwriting: 'To Robert, Armfuls of Love, Adriana' along with a bright red lipstick smooch.

Was he Robert? Was all of this his? It felt like it was from an entirely wrong era, but how could he know for sure?

Underneath everything else he found a shaving kit, some black liquorice, a packet of Craven-A cigarettes which looked like they were smoked by someone out of an Agatha Christie novel, and – bingo! – a small, pearl-handled pen-knife.

Experimentally he lit one of the cigarettes, and nearly choked to death, coughing until his eyes streamed.

'Factoid number two', he gasped. 'Not a smoker.' He tossed the packet – no loss there – but kept the matches. Twenty-seven matches in the box. And how exactly did you light a fire on a wooden raft? It was like that joke about the Eskimo: you can't have your kayak and heat it.

Mostly the clothes fitted him. They made him feel a bit like a shipwrecked Noel Coward, but that sun was still going to kill him unless he did something about it soon, and then he could turn his attention to the trivial matters of food, water, and figuring out where the fuck he was.

3

He managed to construct a crude shelter by jamming a piece of driftwood upright between two planks of his raft and then draping one of the large dress-shirts over it like a tent, anchoring out the shirttails with the shoes. It was only just big enough to shade his head and chest, but it was something. What with all the clambering in and out of the water to fetch things, he'd worked up a thirst which he could do nothing about, and as he lay in its meagre shade he was aware of the prickling dryness in his throat every time he swallowed. It was only going to get worse, but that wasn't the thing that scared him the most.

Every time he stopped working or let his mind wander, it drifted back to the glittering blue emptiness of the world and he found himself slipping into something like a trance. Just staring into the void. It was exactly the same as whenever he tried to remember anything about his life: beyond the last few hours, there was only a drifting blankness which threatened to drown him if he pushed too far into it. Several times already he'd paused in the middle of doing something to find that too much time had passed while he'd zoned out. How much time, he couldn't tell because he didn't have a watch, and this made it worse because he couldn't be entirely certain that it was happening at all. Was the sun lower than it had been? He had no way of knowing.

By this time most of the flotsam had either sunk again or drifted out of reach.

Drifting.

When he looked again, the sun was definitely a lot lower in the sky.

Fuck. Get up, get moving, do something. Don't just lie here, waiting to die. Who cares if you're dehydrating? There's no use conserving energy if you're not going to do anything with it, is there?

He fashioned a crude fishing spear by carving a barbed point into the end of a length of wooden pole, and busied himself unravelling a length of coarse rope, plaiting the strands into half a dozen fishing lines, while for hooks he dug nails out of the raft with his penknife and bent them painfully by hand. The only thing he could remotely imagine using for bait was chunks of liquorice; he just hoped the fish hereabouts had a sweet tooth. He hung them like driftlines from the raft's four sides and on a sudden inspiration peered closely to see what they did. Slowly, all the lines settled at the same slight diagonal.

He was moving. There was no wind pushing him; he was in a current, however weak it was. This meant he now had a forward, a backward, and very possibly a destination.

'Yes! *Yes!!*' Somehow the fact that he wasn't completely dead in the water elated him. He did a little dance – and stopped that in a hurry when the whole raft again threatened to capsize. The sun was setting by now, hanging huge and orange above the horizon. If his guess about the angle of the deadlines was right, he was heading roughly south. Now there was really nothing to do but settle back and wait.

His stomach growled loudly.

'Get used to it, mate,' he growled back.

4

He tried reading some of 'A Tender Death' while it was still light, but he couldn't really get into it and instead found himself returning again to the inscription and its crimson smooch. Several items in the trunk – and indeed the trunk itself – were initialled with R.A.M.J., which he decided stood for Robert

Andrew Michael Jenkins, because why not? Double middle-name, probably from an old family, certainly well-off to judge by the expensive clothing. Robert was a young man, though, given his liquorice, his cigarettes and his penchant for sleazy noir fiction. Bobby, not Robert. Younger son of the family, perhaps given a junior position in the Foreign Office thanks to Daddy's Old Boy network; hence the well-travelled trunk, which was how he'd met Adriana – Russian name – the kind of girl who read books like this and wore bright red lipstick. Definitely not the sort of girl one took home to Mummy and Daddy, and you could bet there was a nice girl at home – most likely the daughter of one of Daddy's business chums – who was waiting dutifully at home for Robert (she would never call him Bobby) to go out and Make His Name, whereas what he was really doing was gadding about the world screwing saucy foreign chicks. Go Bobby, you dog.

Spinning these fantasies in his head allowed him to fall asleep without fearing the blank emptiness which awaited behind his eyes.

5

He woke in the night, convinced that he'd heard somebody walking around on his raft. The sky blazed with constellations he couldn't name, and a half-moon spilled shivering light over the endless desert of water. Under the open sky, the temperature had dropped alarmingly, and he found himself shivering – and listening to something bump and slither invisibly around him. Then his head cleared of sleep fully, and he realised that the sound wasn't coming from around him but underneath him.

There was something under the raft. He froze, listening. Very slowly, he reached for his fish-spear and drew it close. Keeping flat, he crept on his belly to the edge of the raft and peered over.

The sea was alive with movement.

Fish. Millions of fish. Billions, possibly. Shoals, schools, platoons and battalions of fish. For as far as he could see, they seethed and glittered in numbers so vast that he had mistaken them for the surface of the ocean itself. They seemed crammed together so thickly that he fancied he could walk out across them.

He tried to say something, but thirst stuck in his throat like barbed wire and his stomach *going*ed painfully, and he remembered what he really should be doing with them. He hefted the spear.

Never mind that it was night – he could have been blind, armless and chucking the thing with his teeth and still have been able to catch his own body-weight in fish; they were that densely packed. In the end there was simply a practical limit to how much he could pile up on the end of the raft before they started slithering and thrashing off each other and back into the water. Still, gutting and cleaning them in the dark with only a small, blunt pen-knife was a different matter entirely. In the end, the fact that it *was* dark probably did him a favour, because it prevented him from properly seeing what he was eating.

Sushi. Just keep telling yourself you're eating sushi.

It was the first food he'd eaten in nearly twenty-four hours (minus some liquorice), and it went some way towards dealing with his thirst too, and he fell asleep again with a strange feeling which might have been hope.

6

And as he slept, the dream-fish of the Tourmaline Archipelago nourished not just his wounded flesh but also his parched spirit, making him as whole as they could with the fragments they found.

7

Bobby Jenkins was woken up by a godawful racket, stinking of fish guts and feeling generally like shit. For a moment he wondered why everything was so bright and why the bed was tilting to and fro beneath him – had he got drunk and ordered a hammock from the ship's purser? Then he remembered where he was and sat bolt upright. This caused the flimsy shelter to collapse around his head, and in his panic to fight free he very nearly plunged into the ocean again.

'Really must stop doing that, old man,' he admonished himself.

When he pulled his head clear and stood, a cloud of seagulls scattered, protesting, from the pile of fish which they'd been fighting over at the end of his raft. *His* fish.

'Oh no you bloody don't…'

Bobby had never read 'The Old Man and the Sea', because if he had he'd have realised the futility of his actions. Every time he beat one bird away with his spear at least half a dozen more swooped in from a different direction and made off with more of his breakfast, and the only thing he'd achieved by the time they'd stolen everything was to have salvaged a handful of sardines in his pockets, which he guarded fiercely as he retreated to the shelter, watching them squabble over the final scraps.

As it turned out, that was the highlight of his day.

He washed in the ocean and had a shave – because standards were standards even if one was dying slowly of dehydration in the middle of nowhere – but only a few hours after sunrise the temperature was so high that he could do little more than damp down his shelter, curl as much of himself inside as possible, and doze in the heat. He read a little but couldn't concentrate very well; the words kept blurring. If he dreamt, the dreams evaporated upon waking.

By late afternoon, he had a raging headache and his throat felt like it was coated with sand all the way down into his gullet. His lips were cracked dry, and when he tried to lick them, his tongue felt fat and sluggish. At least he was still producing saliva, but without anything to wash food down with, the prospect of eating raw fish was even less attractive than before. When he peed, it was dark yellow and stank. Why was he bothering to prolong his own torture like this? More than once it occurred to him to simply get the whole sorry business over with by jumping into the sea. Oddly, at no point did he consider praying. The fact that he was moving at whatever painfully slow speed now seemed like the final crushing irony rather than anything to celebrate.

He was checking his driftlines for the nth futile time and clearing them of some seaweed when he noticed that at the base of each leaf-frond was a tennis-ball sized flotation pod which sloshed half-full with some kind of sap.

He cut one open and took an experimental sip. It was warm, brackish, and heavy with the taste of iodine, but his parched body was in charge now. He felt the shrivelled sponges of his insides swell and grow blissfully heavy, and he drained three of the globes before he was able to exert enough self-control to stop. Seven left. Probably enough for two or three more days if he was careful. And where there was some, there would be more. He might even be able to dive down and collect some if it weren't too deep in these parts; he might just stand a slim chance of making it to his destination alive.

He was figuring out how to calculate the depth when relief and exhaustion overwhelmed him and he sank into something resembling sleep.

In this manner, another four days passed.

When he woke at dawn of the fifth, a small boy's anxious face was peering upside down into his own.

CHAPTER 3

A REAL WORK OF ART

1

Steve knew that something was wrong instantly when he saw the state of her. She looked like she hadn't slept or eaten for days; there were deep shadows under her eyes and hollows beneath her cheekbones, and she was wrapped in a shapeless coat which made her seem frail and ill, like an escapee from a cancer ward. She staggered in the doorway, and he leapt up to catch her.

'Please…' she gasped, 'Steven, please… take me to her…'

He didn't have to ask who 'her' was.

He half-carried her upstairs to the galleries, shocked by how light she was, as if she lacked some essential substance. It felt like a strong draught would simply blow her away altogether. They shuffled along like this until she came within sight of the painting, at which point she stopped, straightened, and heaved a huge sigh of relief.

'I think I'm going to be okay now, thanks,' she said and completed the rest of the distance under her own power.

Just like Caffrey before him, the thought that she might reach out and touch the painting never occurred to him until she'd actually done it, but Steve was both closer and faster than his missing colleague.

'Ah, no,' he warned, pulling her away with gentle firmness. 'You can't, I'm afraid.' It must have been his imagination, or the sort of optical illusion which happened in the corner of one's eye, which made him think that he saw the paint move under her fingers, because when he turned to look more closely it had stopped. But of course, it had never started in the first place, had it? 'Coffee,' he ordered. 'You and me. Now.'

'But I'm not thirsty.'

'It's not you that needs it.'

2

The Costa franchise in the University's Guild of Students was largely deserted at this time of the morning. Probably, Steve thought, because most of its customers wouldn't be dragging themselves out of bed before noon. Students. He bought her a large slice of carrot cake and watched her wolf it. She still looked haggard but had already regained some of the composure from before.

Nearly finished, she stopped. 'Why are you doing this?' she asked, her suspicion plain.

'Because you needed help. You're welcome, by the way.'

'Besides that.'

'There is no besides that. You were in a state, you needed help. End of. I'm not going to pretend that I'm not curious about whatever's going on with you and that painting – understatement of the year there, but whatever – the point is that you don't know me from a hole in the ground and whatever it is, it's none of my business. Cake. Eat.'

She looked at him as if seeing him properly for the first time. He had a round, open face with hazel eyes which were looking at her in genuine concern, but which also seemed at odds with the tightly-cropped hair and security guard's uniform. 'You are a very interesting person,' she said slowly.

'Except here's the thing. What you did just now, if it happens again you are going to get arrested, and I am going to get sacked. So it's *not* going to happen again, is it?'

'I wish I could guarantee that.'

'Miss, it's not down to you…'

'It's Vanessa. Vanessa Gail. Please use my name.'

'Alright then, Miss Gail. You've obviously experienced some kind of shock or trauma, and the last thing I want to do is add to your troubles, but you need to understand that the next time you turn up to the Barber, I might choose to simply not let you in if you can't guarantee that you're not going to get all happy slappy with the national treasures again.'

'I thought you said you wanted to help.'

He was getting exasperated now. 'This *is* me helping! By rights I should have already called the police.'

She was silent for a long while, absently tearing a paper napkin into thin strips. She seemed to be resolving some inner debate. 'You're right, of course,' she said finally. 'I'm sorry. I owe you the mother of all explanations, despite what you said. But I'm in no fit state to give it at the moment. Are you free this evening?'

His double-take was not entirely faked. 'I'm sorry – for a moment there I thought you'd just asked me out.'

There was playful gleam in her eye despite everything. 'I work an evening shift at the Grange, just around by New Street,' she replied. 'It's going to be a bit busy, but when I'm done I can buy you a drink in return for this coffee and try to explain why a silly painting gets me so worked up. If that's your idea of a date, I mean.'

It turned out it was.

3

Steve didn't think pubs like The Grange existed anymore – certainly not in the City Centre. He'd assumed they'd all either gone bust or been bought up by the big brewers, but this place appeared to have been entirely overlooked by the urban developers and their rampant desire to modernise everything by covering it in chrome and plasma screens ramming twenty-four-hour sport down the customers' eye sockets. This place was narrow and cramped, gleaming with brass and dark furniture which sat unevenly on a sloping floor. There was no concession for the smokers, who stood outside on the pavement with their collars turned up like extras in a wartime movie, and no celebrity-endorsed gastropub menu; he watched men in flat caps tucking silently into steak-and-ale pies while their wives nursed half-pints of stout; the inevitable Lone Weirdo, sitting at a solitary table in the corner, either a retiree widower or a serial killer in training; gangs of tattooed builders jostled pints with salesmen in wrinkled suits, potato-shaped white-van drivers and a handful of students who were either lost, or slumming it, but either way determined to enjoy the place on an ironic level. It was like walking into the middle of a Giles cartoon. Much more his kind of place.

It quickly became obvious that Vanessa was going to be far too busy for any kind of meaningful sit-down conversation. The bar was crammed from one end to the other for most of the evening. Every so often the pub cat would stalk imperiously along between the pumps and the pints, totally unfazed by the noise, just to remind everybody who was really in charge around here. Steve settled himself into a quiet corner and watched Vanessa work.

She had a smile and a bit of chat for everyone, even the Lone Weirdo, and at the same time was able to pull pints with an efficiency which surprised him. There was banter and some good-natured flirting from the customers, but most of them were probably twenty years her senior and none seemed to be seriously hitting on her; he got the impression that they all looked on her more as a younger sister.

Which reminded him. He texted Jackie about his 'date', to which she helpfully responded: *yay bigbruv! jst don't fuk it up ok? ;)*

For a moment the bar was slightly less frantic, and before he knew it Vanessa plonked herself down on the stool opposite with a pint for him and a lemonade for herself. It was obviously hot work; her hair was tied back, and there was a light sheen of sweat on her collarbones which he couldn't help noticing.

'Right,' she said, glancing at her watch. 'Sorry about this. It's utterly manic, but I've got a bit of a break. You've got thirty seconds to tell me your life story. Speed-dating rules apply. Go.'

'Sorry, what?'

'Twenty-seven.'

'You can't seriously…'

'Twenty-five.'

'Okay! Okay!' he laughed. 'Uh, alright then, Steven Peter McBride, born and bred Brummie, big Irish Catholic family, one brother four sisters. Uh, school, not especially clever, decent forward for the football team, fairly okay at Art and Design. Allergic to penicillin…'

'That's not school.'

'You didn't exactly give me a lot of time to plan this!'

'Fair point. Ten.'

He flapped. 'Okay, so, tried to join the police, history of heart disease in the family even though I'm fine, shop jobs…'

'Time's up.'

He sank back and took a well-earned swig. 'Your turn,' he said.

'Ah,' she shook her head. 'What you want to hear can't be told in thirty seconds. Can you hang around until I finish up here? I knock off at ten.'

'No problem,' he said, even though he was beginning to get the distinct feeling that he was being given the run-around.

'Good then.' She flashed him a dazzling smile and returned to the bar.

4

Barry, the head barman, was holding the fort single-handed and tipped her a wink when she re-joined him. 'That your fella then, is it?' he grinned, revealing a mouth which was a stranger to modern orthodontics.

'No!' She swatted him in mock outrage. 'He's just a friend who's doing me a favour, that's all.'

'Oh aye, Vessa, and I know the kind of favour he'd like to be doing to you, alright.'

'You are a dirty old man.'

Barry leered amiably and hip-bumped her as she moved past him to the pumps. He was not a small man – almost as round as he was tall – capable of astonishing violence in defence of his bar but without a malicious bone in his body. He took the welfare of his female staff seriously, juggling shifts as well as he could to let them work around their other commitments. It was a pain in the arse finding decent staff like Vessa these days, for all that you'd think they'd jump at the chance for work in this economic climate, and he did what he could to keep them sweet. Within reason.

'Really, flower, what I need to know is whether or not you'm still going to need that taxi home tonight.'

'Will you shut *up*!'

'No, seriously. I was thinking I might have to re-book it anyway. Need to ask you a favour.'

'Oh, I know where *this* is going.'

Their conversation danced in and out between serving customers, collecting empty glasses from the bar, emptying the drip-trays and the hundred and one other tiny jobs which could be done on autopilot.

'Just 'til eleven. One extra hour. All I'm asking.'

'I don't do past ten, Barry; you know that.'

'Tonight, flower, I don't know any such thing. Everybody else is either away or off sick, and you can see how busy we are. I promise I will owe you big-time.'

'Barry, you know I'm good for weekends, bank holidays, anything like that. But I can't do past ten. I just can't. Sorry.'

'Maybe I can't guarantee you'll have a job by the end of next week.'

'Oh, get real, Barry.'

He flipped the tap off midway through a pint of Stella and turned to glare at her. Vessa mentally kicked herself. She'd overstepped the mark and pissed him off seriously. 'Tell me that was a joke,' she said, worried.

'Vessa, look, you'm a lovely girl and all, but I've got a shift needs covering, and if my staff can't come up with a better reason than missing their frigging beauty sleep, well, this ent a job where employees have too many rights, know what I'm saying?'

'Are you threatening to sack me?'

'I'm saying I don't want to, flower.'

'No choice, then. Fine. I'm going to need a break – I have to explain to my *fella* over there why he's going to have to hang around even longer tonight.'

5

'Hello again!' she said brightly, appearing opposite Steve once more.

'Hi,' he replied. 'Do I know you from somewhere?'

'Very funny. You're supposed to say it's my turn now.'

Steve shrugged. 'Okay, whatever. Your turn.' He'd decided that it was a waste of time trying to keep up with her and to simply go with the flow of whatever this was. 'Although I have managed to fill in a few gaps on my own,' he added, and went on to tell her what little he'd discovered about the painting.

She seemed impressed. 'You've done your homework, I see. Gold star for effort.' She sighed and composed herself, hating what she was going to have to do next because he really was rather sweet after all, and began.

'Once upon a time,' she started, 'I had a very good friend called Sophie. We went all the way through school together, hung out all the time, you know the thing. Or maybe you don't. I don't think boys ever have those kinds of really close friendships that girls have – where you practically live each other's lives. Or do they?

'Anyway. Sophie's home life was not a happy one – understatement of the century, there – and we used to sack off school and go up to London to do the shops, and the museums and galleries. Anything free, basically. So this big old painting of Eve just clicked with her and seemed to comfort her for some reason. She tried to explain it to me once; she said it was like the Goddess of Everything being created, but not from on high – it was like she was making herself. I never really understood that bit.

'And then one day Sophie ran away from home and disappeared. I never saw her again. She didn't write, didn't call – nothing. It hit me hard, I'm not ashamed to say, harder than I thought it would. I started getting anxiety attacks, couldn't go out, couldn't eat, couldn't even pick up the phone. But I found that spending time with the Eve painting and having a bit of a think about Sophie made it easier to cope. Then it moved up here, and so I followed, and then it was now.'

As lies went, it was a work of art in itself. There was enough truth to make her responses convincing and little enough elaboration for him to pick holes in it if he chose. Not that he would. He was sweet and seemed to be genuinely well-intentioned, unlikely to press her on a matter of personal grief even though it came nowhere near answering any of his real questions. To pursue it further would make him crass and insensitive. He'd go back to the gallery, unsatisfied but unable to do anything about it, and she would continue to visit the Goddess as Sophie ordered.

Vessa left Steve inspecting the froth at the bottom of his pint, as if reading tea leaves for a way out of the uncomfortable silence which had fallen between them, and went back to the bar, wondering if her story had worked.

It must have, because the next time she looked up, he was gone. Sophie would have nodded in grim satisfaction, but all Vessa could feel was an unfamiliar, aching disappointment.

6

Later that evening, as she was gathering her coat and bag from the staff hooks by the Grange's delivery door, Barry appeared, grinning with all of his gravestone teeth. He'd torn a notch out of a beermat and wedged it onto the bridge of his nose so that it resembled a ninja throwing star embedded in his face.

'Who threw that?' he asked, mock-surprised, and sketched a little *ta-daa!*

'Sorry, Barry,' she sighed. 'I'm not in the mood.'

'Some big museum security guard, I think,' he continued, taking it off and inspecting it. 'Maybe you can give it back to him.' He tossed it to her.

'What…' she began, but when she caught the beermat she saw that Steven had scribbled something on the back: *Free concerts at the Barber, Tue + Fri 1pm. You owe me cake,* to which he'd added his phone number.

'How long have you been holding onto this?' she demanded, waving it at Barry accusingly.

'Long enough to enjoy seeing the look on your face, flower. Last of the big spenders, your new man, ent he? Just make sure he buys his own condoms, that's all.' He leered, about-faced, and headed back to the bar, whistling cheerfully. But Vessa was too elated to take much notice. She slipped the beermat into her coat pocket so that she could keep hold of it during the taxi ride home.

There was no possible reason for her to notice the homeless old man who stopped rummaging in the bin nearby to gaze after her with curiously blank eyes.

CHAPTER 4

STRAY

1

Bobby yelped.

The boy screamed and fled.

Bobby scrambled up onto his elbows and saw something impossible: the boy was running away across the water. He was wearing only a tattered pair of shorts, and his bare feet kicked up spray as he ran.

When Bobby looked more closely, he saw his mistake, but the truth didn't make much more sense. The boy was running with incredible agility along a thick wooden boom which lay on the ocean's surface. It was made of mismatched timbers and bundles of smaller spars lashed together, which his raft must have bumped into in the night. It had to be at least a quarter of a mile in length, leading towards...

An island. A tiny island, roughly the same size and shape as a circus tent, but an island nonetheless.

'Hey!' he yelled after the disappearing kid. 'Hey wait!' But the kid wasn't waiting. Bobby took hold of the boom and began to pull himself and his raft along its length, slowly towards the island.

There was something odd about its appearance that he couldn't quite pin down. There didn't seem to be any vegetation, but that wasn't it. Closer now, he saw that its shape was more like a giant fried egg: very flat – almost to the waterline – but with a raised centre which at first he'd taken for its entirety. He could make out the scribbled line of a cooking fire's smoke and see tiny shapes of other human beings. People to talk to. People who would know where he was and possibly give him some clue about how he had got here. Maybe even how to get home – assuming he could remember where home was.

He hauled faster.

Soon he saw, coming towards him along the boom, a small boat. Presumably the boy had run to tell the islanders of the strange man who had appeared in their waters, and someone had come out to investigate. He'd like to have thought they were planning to welcome him with garlands of flowers, pit-roasted suckling pig and an army of hula-dancing virgins, but the island really didn't look that big at all, and they were just as likely to see him as a threat. He slowed down, and as the small boat appeared made sure that his fishing spear was close to hand.

It was a shabby-looking affair – clinker-built from overlapping boards of different sizes and with a sail which was a patchwork confection of a hundred different types of fabric, all ragged and sun-bleached. He was unsurprised to see the name painted on her bow was *Tatterdemalion II*. The woman captaining it was powering her craft along the boom using skilful strokes of a long gaff-hook. She had one passenger: a black man wearing a plaid shirt and a fishing hat, who sat in the stern with a baseball bat slung across his shoulders. Muscle in case Bobby turned out to be trouble. Given how weak he was, Bobby would have laughed, but he didn't think he even had the strength for that. The woman's arms were bare, her face a lean and tanned fortysomething under a wide-brimmed hat, and as she got closer, he found himself the subject of a shrewd, narrow-eyed regard from eyes which were exactly the same colour as the hammer-bright sky. She held off a couple of yards, watching.

'I am so glad to see you,' he said, dismayed at the croaking sound of his own voice. 'You have no idea.'

'Some, maybe,' she replied. Her accent was American, somewhere northern, if he was any judge. 'Not a bad job,' she added, nodding at his raft, with its shelter and its neatly coiled driftlines and its little piles of carefully organised salvage. 'How long were you out there?'

'Four days? Maybe five?'

She nodded. 'Mm-hm. Lucky.'

'Not exactly the first word that springs to mind.'

'Maybe. But then by the time some drifters reach us they've been dead for so long that they're basically mummies.'

'Well fair enough then.'

'Sometimes they've just gone batshit crazy from the heat and think they're hallucinating. Sometimes they get violent. You're not going to get violent on me, are you?'

'Absolutely not, ma'am,' he answered.

'In which case I think we're going to get along just fine. I will look after that, though, if you don't mind.' She nodded at his spear, and he handed it over. She gaffed her boat closer and lashed a length of rope between them with quick, sure hands. 'But call me ma'am again and I'll use your nuts for floats, got it? It's Allie.'

'As in…?'

'As in Allie, smartass.'

'Bobby Jenkins. As in Robert Andrew Michael.' He offered his hand, and she shook it, amused.

'Pleased to meet you, Bobby Jenkins.' She indicated the black man, who as yet hadn't said a word or cracked a smile. 'This is Sebastian. Welcome to Stray.'

2

He let her tow him to the island, and he soon realised what was wrong with it. There were no trees, no bushes, no rocks, and no surf. Not even any sand. The boom that they were following ran straight up to a jetty, which became part of the island's structure: timber, driftwood, assorted flotsam, and the jammed-together remains of dozens and dozens of small boats.

Stray was itself one huge raft.

It was roughly circular and must have been a good couple of hundred yards in diameter. Mostly it was flat to the waterline, climbing towards the centre in a jumbled ziggurat of planks and crates, giving the impression that the people who lived here had reached the limit of what they could effectively build and had resorted to simply piling stuff up in the middle to keep it out of the way. The other islanders were standing on the beach – he supposed he should really be calling it a deck – waving and calling. Half a dozen adults and one child – the Jesus lizard kid. *Living* here.

'About now lots of questions will be occurring to you,' said Allie. 'They'll all get answered,' and she added something under her breath which sounded like 'one way or another'. Louder, she continued: 'Everybody will be falling over themselves to make you welcome. But you know how it is on a raft, you have to ration things to survive. My advice? Don't give away too much too soon. And don't be all in a rush.'

They were nearly at the jetty, and people were running forward with ropes and poles and cries of welcome. After nearly a week of trying to keep his balance on something with all the stability of a space-hopper, his legs weren't used to anything which didn't rock, and he stumbled as they helped him aboard. A middle-aged man with a welcome-mat of white belly hair above his explorer's shorts and sandals caught Bobby's arm and steadied him.

'Easy, son,' he said. His accent was Scottish. 'Let's get you under cover and get some breakfast into you.'

They took him to a place sheltered from the sun by an overhead screen of woven kelp fronds which looked just like camouflage netting – underneath, crude benches and hammocks surrounded an open fire supported safely above the wooden deck by an iron grill resting on large stones. Set in the coals was a frying pan roughly the same size as a snow-shovel, and from it sizzled a mouth-wateringly familiar smell.

'My god,' he breathed in wonder. 'How did you get bacon?'

'It's not bacon,' replied the older man. 'It's a fish, like most of everything else we eat here. They taste of all kinds of things. You'd be surprised.'

'What kind of fish tastes like bacon?'

The black man plonked down next to him with a plateful. 'We call him – wait for it – the *bacon-fish*,' he said in a heavy French accent, and laughed. 'Le poisson de la ventreche!'

'Sheer coincidence,' added Allie drily.

'Stuart Lachlan', the older man introduced himself. 'My wife, Marjorie.' He indicated a meerkat-like woman in a wraparound sarong who flapped and bustled about, bringing Bobby a wooden plate heaped with food and a bamboo cup of the coldest, sweetest water he'd ever tasted in his life. There was flat, unleavened bread which he wrapped around the bacon-fish like a big tortilla and topped with a generous helping of something that looked suspiciously like pickled kelp. Never mind the taste; his body craved greens.

'Careful there,' warned the older woman. 'Don't make yourself sick.' But even as she said so she was smiling with maternal self-satisfaction. He wolfed it down and then had two more. 'We have porridge too, if you like.'

'Porridge.' He shook his head in disbelief.

'Made from kelp roots,' explained Allie. 'It's actually more disgusting than it sounds.'

'Allie and Sebastian you've already met,' Lachlan continued. 'And my son Jophiel is around here somewhere. I'll send him along in a bit when you're rested, and he'll give you the grand tour. We don't mean to crowd you. Come on, you lot, chop chop,' he said to the others, clapping his hands. 'There's work to be done.'

'Wait a second,' Allie interrupted. 'What about Sophie?'

'Yes, thank you,' Lachlan replied tetchily. 'I'm sure that Sophie will let us know if and when she's interested in meeting our new guest. Seb, we've got that spar on Down to patch up, remember? Allie, will you please find that fish-brained son of mine and remind him that he has a job to do?'

'Ah,' she replied, 'see there again, you've gone and mistaken me for the nanny. No, it's okay,' she added hastily as he started to object. 'I'll round up your little sprat. I have to get a present for our new arrival anyway.' She tipped Bobby a wink and sauntered off. He wasn't too starved and exhausted to notice that she had a great figure for a woman of her age. Hell, a woman *half* her age. She returned quickly, presenting him with something which he could well understand was a luxury in this place: an orange. He consumed down to pith and rind and finally sat back, feeling uncomfortably stuffed and loving it.

'This place is incredible,' he said. 'Sorry, I don't mean to sound rude.'

'See, anybody but an Englishman would have taken that as gratitude. Do you mean, how can we have flour, fruit, that kind of stuff in a place like this?'

He nodded.

'Rationing, remember?' Her mouth smiled, but her sky-coloured eyes widened fractionally in warning. 'Anyway, I've brought your guide.' She ushered forward the Lachlan's boy, Joe, who was dripping wet and holding an offering of his own. Bobby took it: an oyster.

'Um, thanks.'

'Well open it then!' The boy was bouncing with excitement.

'I, uh, I don't think I've ever opened one of these before.'

Joe tutted, obviously disgusted at a grown-up being unable to do such a simple thing as open an oyster. 'Give it here, then.' He took it back and produced a short-bladed knife which he inserted between the two halves of the shell and levered them apart in a single deft motion, then returned the oyster to Bobby. 'Now, open it!'

Bobby did so, and was astonished to find, nestled in the oyster's flesh, a pearl the size of a marble. 'My God,' he breathed.

'Yeah, he does that a lot,' yawned Allie. 'Says he can smell them out.'

'What do they smell like?' Bobby asked him.

Joe stared at him as if he was an idiot. 'Pearls,' he said. 'Do you like it?'

'In all honesty, it's the most amazing thing I've seen in my life.'

The boy beamed.

'I wouldn't go encouraging him,' she warned. 'Not unless you want to be eating oyster soup for the next month. Anyway,' she gathered up her things and turned to go, 'have fun, you two. Don't get lost or killed.'

'We'll do our very best,' Bobby promised.

3

It took them half an hour to walk the circumference of Stray, with Jophiel stopping every so often to point out something or perform one of the many chores which a place like this obviously demanded. The outermost rim was a wide, flat platform called the Dock; it bristled with jetties, spars, lines, creels, buoys, and a hundred other things Bobby had no name for and whose function he could only guess at. Here, drying on racks in the full open blaze of the sun, were long strands of kelp which Joe explained were used to make thatching for their shelters and cordage for their ropes and lines. It was also the same kelp that produced those sap-filled floats, and he saw dozens of them stored in baskets in the water.

'That's my job,' he said proudly. 'I harvest it because I'm the best diver. It's like a forest under there – you should see it!'

'You are definitely the best diver I have ever seen,' said Bobby, and the boy glowed with pride. 'But I'm going to take your word for it.'

The centre of Stray – which Joe told him was called simply the Hub – rose up in a jumbled construction which looked to Bobby like someone had tried to build a scale model of a Mayan temple out of offcuts from a sawmill. Its flat top was over thirty feet high, and the stepped sides were raucous with seagulls. Amazingly, tufts of wiry grass grew in the caked mess of their guano, some bearing tiny white flowers. All around it, split lengths of bamboo formed an elaborate scaffolding of gutters and downpipes to channel rainwater run-off into wooden barrels, and built up against its lower slopes were thatched-kelp roofs sheltering workspaces, storage, and the Strays' living quarters. Underneath one of them, Allie was sitting with a fishing net spread out in front of her, fixing holes with a large wooden needle and humming to herself. She looked up as they passed.

'Showing you the sights, is he? What do you make of it so far?'

'This place is amazing,' he replied.

'Aw shucks, this ain't nuthin',' she drawled. 'You should see our big place out in the country.'

He laughed.

'Well go on, scoot,' she shooed them off. 'Some of us have got work to do. We don't need being distracted by handsome strangers stopping to gossip.'

As they moved on, Joe said: 'I think she likes you.'

'Really?' Bobby looked back, watching her sure hands working and her long legs gleaming brown in the sun. 'You think I have a chance there?'

Joe shrugged. 'I don't know. I'm only twelve.'

'And how old were you when you came here?'

'Oh, I was born here,' he replied, as if it were of no significance.

'*Born* here?' The Lachlans had been here that long? It was incredible, especially since they must have been in their fifties when Joe was born – not an easy time to become parents under the best of circumstances. Biologically improbable. 'That's a long time for anyone to be stuck here.'

Joe shrugged. 'It doesn't feel like it.' Then, as if moving at the snail's pace of an adult had become too much of an effort, he darted off the left and out onto another of those long booms which stretched into the ocean. 'We've got four of these,' he called. 'This is Up, because it points to where the sun comes up in the morning. On the other side is Down, because…'

'It's where the sun goes down?'

'Right! You'll never guess what the other two are called.'

'North and South?'

'Nope.'

'Left and Right?'

'Nope-nope-nope,' he sang, dancing on the boom.

'I don't know, then. Fred and Ginger?'

'Why would anybody call a boom Fred?'

'Well go on then, tell me.'

'That one over there,' he pointed, 'is Strange, and the last one is Charm.'

'Because that makes so much more sense.'

'You fetched up on Strange.'

'That actually *does* make sense.' The names snagged on a splinter of memory at the back of his mind, but a more obvious question demanded attention first: 'What are they for?'

'They catch stuff that we can use. They have nets and lines hanging down into the water. Mostly it's fish, but there's a lot of rubbish floating around that we use for fixing up bits of Stray, building things, cooking. Boring stuff, you know.'

Far out towards the end of the boom, he could see the tiny shape of a boat, which was presumably where Lachlan and Seb were out making repairs. 'I bet they take a lot of fixing. One storm and a few big waves could do a lot of damage, probably.'

'Oh, we don't get storms here. This part of the sea is called the Flats. There's hardly any wind and no strong currents – things just sort of hang around here. The sea is as flat as a flounder most of the time.'

'So the booms catch food and whatever flotsam drifts your way – and there must be a fair bit of it by the look of things – but where does it all come from?'

Joe shrugged. Clearly it wasn't a question which interested him. 'I don't know. The Islands, probably.'

'Islands.'

'The Tourmaline Archipelago. The Flats is right in the middle of it.' He counted off various points of the compass. 'Drava is that way, Elbaite is way over in the other direction, Schorl is somewhere there, I think, and then further out there's Blent, Lesser Odsae, Greater Odsae, the Carcanet Reefs…'

'Wait – you mean islands with people, and boats, and, well, *people?*'

'Of course! Where do you think all this rubbish comes from?'

'But I thought – I assumed – that you were all stranded here.'

Joe considered this. 'I don't think so,' he said eventually. 'I'm sure if we were, then Da would know and he'd do something about it.'

'Then why are you all still here, for God's sake? Why haven't you got yourselves off this thing and gone to live somewhere where you don't have to drink bloody seaweed juice to stay alive? Why haven't you all gone *home?*'

With the simple, inescapable logic of a child, Joe answered: 'But this *is* our home.'

Bobby squinted at the horizon, but the glare made it impossible to see the shapes of any islands which might be lurking in the distance. He looked up at the Hub. 'How do I get up there?'

Joe looked uneasy. 'I don't think that's a very good idea.'

'I think it's an *astoundingly* good idea. Why, is it dangerous or something? Don't tell me that's your Holy Mountain.'

'That's the Top. Da says that it's dangerous and that I should never climb up there.'

Bobby looked up at the ramshackle height of it again. 'He may well have a point, at that. Look, don't worry. I'm going to be very careful. I just want to see if I can get a decent view of those Islands you mentioned from on top of there.'

'You won't. They're too far away.'

'That may be true, but I'd still like to not see it with my own eyes.'

'But Da said I had to show you around myself.' Bobby watched Joe's gaze crawl reluctantly to the top of the peak and knew that he was genuinely fearful of getting in trouble.

'Well, I won't say anything if you don't,' he promised, lowering his voice conspiratorially. 'Plus I'll be really quick. Up, have a swift look around, and down again before you can say Robinson Crusoe. You keep a lookout. Then you can show me your kelp forest and teach me how to find pearls. Deal?'

With obvious misgivings, Joe agreed.

Climbing the Top should have been easy since it was essentially built like a staircase – albeit one with very high, birdshit-covered steps – and in places access had been made easier to maintain the bamboo guttering. But he was still weak from his ordeal, and by the time he reached the top, his lungs were burning and his limbs felt like seaweed. He could see clearly now the four booms – and thought again: who would give them ridiculous names like Up, Down, Strange, and Charm? – radiating from Stray like the cross-hairs of a gigantic gun-sight, but Joe had been right about not being able to see any islands from the Top. To make matters worse, the siren call of the awful blue void was more intense the higher up he climbed; an attack of vertigo loosened the last strength in his knees, and it was all he could do to get back down safely.

When they had nearly come full circle, Joe pointed out a beaded curtain hanging over an opening which seemed to lead into the very structure of the Hub itself. 'That's where Miss Sophie lives,' he said, and moved on quickly. 'You don't want to go in there.'

'No? Why not?'

'She's crazy. She says that there are monsters living underneath Stray. Plus, she tried to eat me once.'

Bobby nodded as if this made perfect sense. 'Well naturally, trying to eat kids would be a box to tick on the Big List of Crazy, that's true. So the crazy lady gets the only proper cabin on this thing, is that right?'

Joe shrugged and didn't answer. Clearly the whole subject of Miss Sophie filled him with unease. Bobby briefly considered popping his head through the curtain for a quick hello with whomever was inside, but he was still exhausted from his climb to the Top and didn't think he had the mental energy either to cope with any more lunatics. *Rationing*, Allie had said, and it seemed to make sense. He would try not to force himself to cope with any more than three barking mad things before each meal.

He lay in his hammock for the rest of the afternoon, shocked at how weak he was, and trying to make sense of this place.

Chapter 5

Mi Chiamano Vessa

1

During University term time, the Barber Institute of Fine Arts put on free lunchtime concerts, usually by final-year music students, who to Steve's untutored ear sounded as good as professionals. They performed in the ground floor concert hall which had in recent years been restored to its original art deco glory – simple lines and planes of glowing walnut and oak – to small audiences of their friends, colleagues and teachers. When Vessa had completed her customary contemplation before the Goddess (with Steve hovering at a discreet distance), they followed the sound of a solo female soprano downstairs to the concert hall and watched from the doorway, where they could talk quietly without disturbing the performance.

'You'd think,' he whispered, 'that surrounded by all this free art I'd be taking the opportunity to better myself, but the truth is I feel like a dog at the opera. I have no idea what that girl's on about.'

She nodded, considering this, then replied, 'If you're trying to impress me with your cultural credentials, you're doing it very badly.'

'I'm not trying to impress you.'

'I could tell.'

The girl's voice soared over and around them. She was quite small, dressed very plainly in jeans and a university hoodie, seeming too ordinary to be creating such a wide ribbon of sound. Rather, it seemed to be flowing through her from somewhere else.

'She's singing *Mi chiamano Mimi*, from La Boheme.'

'Ah. Yes. Mm-hm.' He nodded sagely.

'Mimi is a penniless seamstress, and she's just met the love of her life, Rodolfo. He's a starving poet.'

'Of course. Is there any other kind?'

'She's trying to explain that Mimi isn't her real name but she doesn't know why people call her that. She embroiders flowers in silk and they remind her of spring, which she loves, but it makes her sad at the same time because the flowers she sews have no perfume. They're beautiful but they're not real.'

'Seriously, though, I can hear that. It sounds like she doesn't know whether to laugh or cry.'

'It's an allegory, of course. All art is an illusion, a fake that can never capture the essence of reality.'

'Nope. Gone again.'

'The problem is,' she continued, 'that it's wrong. Good art – really *great* art – constructs a reality which is just as real as anything else. If Mimi really were a gifted seamstress, she'd be able to smell the scent of her embroidered roses.'

But Steve wasn't thinking about roses – in his memory he was watching the brushstrokes of *She Shall Be Called Woman* coming to life and rippling in response to Vessa's approaching fingertips, as if eager for her to touch it. He thought that if she ever reached for him with anything approaching the same urgency, then his flesh might just ripple too.

'I have a confession to make,' she whispered.

'Whatever you've stolen, put it back, and we'll say no more about it.'

'Not that. I cheated.'

'You cheated?'

'I know nothing about La Boheme. I looked up the concert programme on the internet and everything else on wikipedia. I'm a big fat fraud.'

'You are a perfectly proportioned fraud, if I may say,' he replied without thinking, and turned an instant, furious scarlet. *Somebody please tell me I did not just say that.*

'Why Mr McBride, I do believe you're blushing.'

'I'll just be heading back to my desk now,' he muttered. 'Hopefully somebody's trying to steal a priceless masterpiece, or something.'

She followed him, and as he was about to head upstairs to the upper floor gallery, she called out 'Will you have dinner with me sometime?'

That stopped him in his tracks.

'Give me a millisecond to think about it,' he answered.

'Frankly I'm insulted you should take that long.'

'In that case, yes. Immediately, absolutely, unhesitatingly yes, I will take you out to dinner.'

'Good, then. I'll call you.'

'I'll, um, yeah. That'd be great.'

She smiled – an uncomplicated and unguarded smile of simple happiness which was so staggeringly beautiful that he was glad he was holding onto the handrail of the stairs, because he feared that otherwise he'd actually stumble under in its clarity.

'And thank-you for the free performance,' she added as she left. 'It was very entertaining.'

2

Dinner was at Gustavo's in the Mailbox, the old Post Office depot which had been redeveloped into a complex of high-end boutiques, designer outlets, salons and restaurants catering to those who worked in the shiny office complexes around Wharfside. It was said that Birmingham had more canals than Venice, and judging from the menu, Steve reckoned that it was giving the Italians a run for their money on the costs of things too. He'd taken Jackie there for her birthday a few years ago, and it was a bit beyond his price range for anything except special occasions – which this most certainly was.

'It's kid gloves off, now, Big Bruv,' she'd said when he'd told her about dinner with Vessa. 'Time to wow the pants off her. You've laid the groundwork as a perfectly normal, salt-of-the-earth, non-psycho type, and you've still got that to fall back when you make a total mess of things tonight.'

'This is your romantic pep-talk, is it? How is your work with the Samaritans these days? Make anybody top themselves recently?'

'Shut up and pay something off your credit card, or it's going to be real embarrassing when the cheque comes.'

'Technically she asked me.'

'Technically don't enter into it, babe.'

That said, when Vessa arrived at the restaurant, it definitely felt like he was the one being wowed.

3

She'd chosen a midnight blue dress just short enough at the bottom and plungey enough at the top to showcase her figure without being actually slutty, highlighted by a simple silver necklace and drop earrings. It was the kind of thing that Sophie would never have worn in a million years, but this was her life now. She loved having a reason to dress up and go out, and if those reasons had come few and far between in recent times, well then more fool her for having stayed in the same boring, frightened rut which Sophie had fallen into in the first place. And who knew? Vessa might very well choose to sleep with this particular reason. That idea shocked the Sophie-voice into silence, which was exactly what she'd intended.

'You look stunning,' said Steve, with open admiration.

'Correct. And thank-you. So do you.'

'The tie was my sister's idea.'

'Then I like your sister already.'

They found their table, ordered drinks, and made nervous small-talk about the décor. Gustavo's was a Venezuelan restaurant; Vessa didn't know anything about South American dining practices, but apparently it involved lots of rattan and coloured woven wool.

'I know what this is about,' he said, after a particularly long and awkward silence.

'Oh? Really?' She did her best to sound offhand, despite her racing heartbeat. Where had the air gone, all of a sudden?

'I shouldn't have threatened you last week, about the painting, when we had that coffee. I didn't know that it meant that much to you.'

'Okay…'

'To be honest, I'm not sure I understand it now. Not that I need to; it's your business. I just want you to know that of course there's no question of me ever barring you from the gallery, so if this…' he gestured around at the restaurant, her dress, and his tie '…if this is just a way of keeping me on-side, you don't have to go to the trouble. I just wanted to, you know, get that out there. In case.'

'That sounds just a touch paranoid.'

'Tell me it's not true. Or at least, that it never occurred to you.'

She couldn't. But she reached across and took his hand and said 'Steve, if all I wanted was to keep you on-side I'd have slept with you a week ago. I'm here because you are a sweet, caring, thoughtful man, and I think I'd like to get to know you a lot better. Now can we please order?'

They ordered, and ate, and chatted about anything other than art or their families, and afterwards when he suggested that they go for a drink, she was having such a good time (because someone was interested in her, in *her*, not bloody Sophie for a change), that she didn't think twice about saying yes, so they found a nice canal-side bar which had cocktails and a live band who actually sounded pretty good, and sat out in the warm spring night air looking at the brightly illuminated narrowboats and the lights of Wharfside reflected in the canals, and what with one thing and another she completely lost track of time until she went to the loo and happened to glance at her watch and realised that somehow it had become 11:27.

Shock and adrenalin slapped her instantly sober. How could she have been so stupid?

The Sophie-voice in her head kept a smug, expectant silence.

'Shit.'

4

The next thing Steve knew, Vessa sailed past behind his chair, leaned in to plant a lingering, regretful kiss on him while murmuring 'Sorry, gotta go,' against his lips, and was heading down the brightly-lit towpath, her heels clicking rapidly.

'Hey… wha… *hey!*' He went after her. What was going on? Why the sudden rush? 'I wasn't serious about splitting the bill,' he called.

She ignored his joke and went up the steps to the street, scanning for taxis.

Steve threw some cash on the table, hoping that it was enough, and chased after her.

'Vessa!' he called. 'Where are you going? What's wrong?'

'You wouldn't believe me if I told you.'

'Well I won't be nearly as pissed off as I'm getting right now, if that helps.'

She turned and looked at him as he caught up. All the charm and humour had dropped from her expression, leaving it as serious as a gravestone in the lamplight. 'I have to be home by midnight,' she replied tersely. Then, having flagged down a black cab, she started running towards it.

'Or what? You'll be grounded? Come on!'

She opened the door and was climbing in, but spared him a second to hold it open for him. 'If you want to be a real hero, you can make sure I get there safely.'

'Safely? What do you think is going to happen to you?'

She shook her head and started to close the door. 'Questions on the way, not here. Are you in or not?'

Steve watched the taxi door closing, thinking that there was so much wrong here. Her mood swings, her obsession with that bloody painting, Caffrey's disappearance (if that was even connected in any way), and now this. She Shall Be Another in a Depressingly Long Line of Needy, High-Maintenance Women. What was it about him that always attracted the nutters? But still, she made him laugh; she was clever and unafraid to show it when so many other women seemed to think that dumb was attractive. The fact that she actually *was* attractive certainly didn't hurt, either. No, his hesitation stemmed from the sudden conviction that there was an awful lot more waiting for him inside that black cab than a strange, beautiful, funny woman – and that his journey's destination might be very far away from the world with which he was familiar.

In the end, it wasn't even a choice. He climbed in.

CHAPTER 6

BLESSINGS, GREAT AND SMALL

1

Supper on Stray was a spiced fish stew with some kind of seaweed which tasted not unpleasantly like spinach. They ate from wooden bowls in the light of the fire and a few small oil-wick lamps, chatting and trading news of the day while Bobby listened from the sidelines. There was only one moment of awkwardness when he piled straight into his food and received a warning tap on the knee from Marjorie Lachlan.

'We say Grace, dear,' she admonished gently.

Oops. He waited politely while Lachlan led the prayer and thought he saw Allie tip him a knowing wink from beneath her bowed head. He enjoyed the sense of their camaraderie but was very much aware of his status as an outsider. In the end, Lachlan seemed determined to do something about that.

'So, Bobby,' he said, 'what do you make of us Strays and our little floating village? Don't be afraid to be honest, now. We rarely get newcomers, and it's always good to have a fresh perspective.'

Finally this was something he knew. Lachlan's invitation of an 'honest' perspective was no different from that of any other big-bellied Town Father, and about as genuine. He expected to be praised for his little piece of heaven on earth (or sea), and since Bobby had no idea how long he was likely to be staying, he had no intention of disappointing the man.

'To be honest, sir,' he replied, 'I'm very impressed. To have survived so well on so little, and for so long – I'm no engineer, and I know as much about marine environments as I do about flamenco dancing, but I'd say that some of the solutions you've come up with here are simply ingenious.'

Lachlan puffed up and glowed. Marjorie stroked her husband's arm and smiled adoringly at him.

'Obviously I'm jealous as hell,' Bobby continued. 'I mean, you saw the state my own raft was in when you found me. I'd also like to say to you all, just for the record, how genuinely grateful I am to you for saving my life. I don't know how I can ever repay that.'

Allie tossed him her empty bowl. 'Looks like somebody just volunteered to do the washing up,' she said, and everybody laughed.

'She has a serious point, though,' Lachlan commented. 'It's going to be good to have another pair of hands about the place. We have room and supplies to spare. We don't live like kings, but it's an honest, God-fearing life.'

'That it is, sir.'

Lachlan regarded him for a moment over his mug of rainwater. 'I noticed that you didn't join us in the Grace.'

'Well sir, I'm not much of a praying man, so no I didn't. But I don't have a problem with religion. Faithless but friendly, that's me.'

'We're all very pleased to hear that, I'm sure.' Was he being paranoid, or was there a hint of condescension in Lachlan's voice?

Marjorie got up and began to clear away the dirty bowls. 'Well, never mind,' she said, with the kind of maternal amusement usually reserved for young boys who have just skinned their knees. 'There's still time.'

'It's not really a question of time, ma'am,' he said.

'My wife is a very devout woman,' Lachlan explained. 'She has suffered a great deal of privation here and is thankful for every small gift which the Lord bestows on us. As are we all. When you've been here a bit longer you'll understand.'

Bobby got the distinct impression that he was being rebuked when all he'd tried to do was be polite and respectful, and it was starting to nettle him – as was the assumption that he was set to stay here with them.

'As I said before, Stuart – you don't mind me calling you Stuart, do you? – I am in no position to judge anybody. I meant what I said: this is a truly impressive place. Frankly, I'm even a little amazed.'

'Oh? How so?'

'Joe told me that you've been here since he was born. That's an awfully long time to be living on this kind of diet. I'd have expected to see one kind of vitamin deficiency or another, not to mention just plain old illness and injury, but here you all are – happy, healthy, and holy. I don't know how you do it.' He raised his bamboo cup in salute. *I'm no slouch either*, it said. *Don't you ever go making that mistake, Mr Lachlan.*

'I won't deny that we've had our share of misfortunes. Ours is a hard life.'

'Joe also mentioned something about Islands,' Bobby added.

'Yes. The Tourmaline Archipelago. I'm sure he's explained how it's responsible for the flotsam which drifts to us through the Flats. We also trade with them for certain essentials – medicines and such-like. Please don't get the wrong impression – we're not like the Amish or anything silly like that. We just like to keep ourselves to ourselves.'

But why haven't any of you tried to go home? he wondered, though he suspected that it was a very prickly question indeed. 'Exactly what islands are they?' he asked. 'I've done a bit of travelling in my time, and I've never heard that name before. What ocean are we in? From the climate, I'd say it feels like the Pacific, so maybe it's somewhere in Polynesia, but…' he left it hanging and shrugged.

'He is called the Antaean Ocean,' said Seb. 'The giant with the world on his shoulders.'

'I think that was Atlas,' said Allie. Bobby was pretty sure it wasn't the name of an ocean at all.

'I'm afraid geography was never my strong suit,' Lachlan replied vaguely. 'Alison might have a better idea – my dear, when is the next supply run?'

'Two weeks, give or take.'

Lachlan turned back to Bobby. 'Can you bear to stay with us for a fortnight before we pack you off on your merry way?'

'It'd be a privilege,' he replied, but his heart was dismayed. *Two weeks?* 'I'll try not to break anything while I'm here.'

'Excellent. And who knows? By then you might have come to like this place so much that you decide to become a Stray.'

Marjorie ladled out an extra bowl of stew. 'I'll just go and take Sophie hers, then, if you'll all excuse me,' she said and disappeared in the direction of the beaded curtain he'd noticed earlier.

When she'd gone, Bobby said to Lachlan: 'I take it Sophie doesn't eat with the rest of you.'

'By her own choice. Joe's told you about her?'

'A little. Something about trying to eat him.'

Lachlan grimaced. 'Sad and unfortunate. She was here when I arrived – had been alone for I don't know how long. The stress, the isolation, who knows? There but for the grace of God, yes? Did you meet her on your tour?'

'No. I get the impression she's not keen on making new friends.'

'Well, then. I'm sure she'll introduce herself before too long. Try not to…' he faltered. 'Try not to judge the rest of us too harshly by what you see of her, yes?' There was something in Lachlan's expression – some uncomplicated, basic plea for compassion – that made Bobby soften his attitude to him. Lachlan was right; he shouldn't judge these people so quickly. They'd had to cope with living conditions which would have killed most people, or at least driven them insane. He didn't like to think how he'd have coped in their place.

But you are in their place now, aren't you Bobby? he told himself. *At least for the next fortnight. Who knows what kind of state you'll be in by then?*

The conversation broke up and people drifted away as night deepened. It turned out that they hadn't been joking about him doing the washing-up.

2

Seb found him just as he was settling down to sleep, and with many secretive hushings led him to the other side of Stray, where Allie was sitting by a small but elaborate construction of rubber pipes and metal tubing. She was fiddling with it, turning a small tap; there was a gurgle of liquid, and she took a tentative sip at something in a bamboo beaker. She gasped and said something extraordinarily rude.

'Try this,' she whispered to Seb, who sat down beside her.

He took a sip. '*Merde-alors*,' he grunted, and passed the beaker to Bobby. ''Ere, this will put the hairs on your chest.'

'What is it?'

'About eighty per-cent proof,' Allie gasped. 'Jesus that's rough.'

It was a still. They were making hooch. 'Outstanding,' he said, and joined them.

'We though maybe we wait for you to get more better,' said Seb. 'Then we figure, pfft, fuck it, eh?'

Bobby sipped cautiously. He'd been caught out before by getting too blasé about the homebrew offered by friendly natives, but even so, what hit his mouth came as a shock. It tasted like salted antiseptic with a petroleum chaser, after which somebody had tossed in a lighted match.

'Fucking *hell*,' he croaked. Seb was grinning and nodding insanely, while Allie lay on her back and blew cigarette smoke at the stars. 'Seriously, what is this?'

'Is a kind of vodka, we think. We make him from whatever come to 'and – fruit peel, mostly seaweed. He has something of a kick, eh?'

'There are laws against this kind of thing, you know.'

'But now,' Seb hunched forward, becoming even more animated, if such a thing were possible, 'now we 'ave you and your liquorice. Very clever, my friend, liquorice for bait. We can make Ouzo! Yes?'

'Sure, ouzo, why not? It might do something about the aftertaste. You know, you really can taste the kelp.'

They passed the beaker around again. Allie offered him a drag on her cigarette, but he declined. 'More for me,' she shrugged.

As the burning in his throat subsided he said: 'Don't get me wrong, but it seems to me like the Lachlans wouldn't be very approving if they knew about this, would they?'

'Oh, they know,' Allie answered. 'They must do. You can't hide something like this in a place so small. We pretend to hide it and they pretend not to know and everybody's happy.'

'Until you turn up for work shitfaced and hungover.'

'Ah,' she shook her head sadly. 'Therein lies the greatest tragedy of our weird, floating existence, my friend. We do not have enough fresh water to spare for distilling the amount required to get shitfaced and hence hungover. We only have enough for the occasional nightcap.'

'A snifter,' added Seb. 'It is a word, yes?'

'It is a word,' she confirmed sagely. 'And also, to toast the arrival of new weird floaters. To our new friend Bobby Jenkins.' She held the beaker aloft. 'God bless him and all who sail in him. Chin chin, old bean.'

'Salut!'

And the beaker went around again.

After a while the nerve-endings in his mouth and throat became too traumatised to communicate the full horror of what they were experiencing to his brain, and he got quite a nice little buzz which followed him back to his hammock and into sleep.

CHAPTER 7

THE CINDERELLA CURFEW

1

As Steve slipped into the taxi seat beside Vessa, she was already giving her address to the driver, and they pulled away.

'So you need to be home by midnight,' he said. 'A bit like Cinderella, then.' As much as anything else, he wanted to distract her from her evident anxiety – repeatedly checking her watch and peering ahead at the traffic – no matter how inane his chatter.

'Not really. Cinderella had to leave the ball by midnight. This is an entirely different thing.'

'I'm listening.'

She glanced at him warily.

'Honestly. You asked me to help. This is me helping. I listen.'

'One joke and I will kick you out of this thing, I swear.'

He said nothing.

'Okay then,' she relented. 'At midnight I fall asleep. Every night, like clockwork, no matter where I am or what I'm doing. Spark out, like that.' She snapped her fingers. 'Which, as you can imagine, caused a few awkward situations before I worked out what was going on. Then, at six o'clock the following morning,' she snapped her fingers again, 'Good Morning Britain. Just think of it as a weird kind of epilepsy, if you like.'

'Wow,' he said quietly.

'Yeah. Wow.'

'Why didn't you mention anything earlier, like at dinner?'

She cocked her head on one side and looked at him.

'Okay, stupid question. Sorry.'

11:31

Streetlights and headlights threw mutating oblongs of light across the cab's ceiling as they drove south out of the city centre towards Selly Oak, the University, and student country. Each time they had to slow for traffic or signals he found himself getting edgier and edgier on her behalf.

'Oh, one other thing,' she said suddenly, digging in her handbag. 'I know you're all capable and manly and everything, but seeing me flop is likely to freak you out, so,' she was scribbling on a scrap of paper, 'I want you to promise me something.'

'Anything.'

'No emergency services. No matter what you see, unless I am actually physically dying, no 999, no doctors, no hospitals.' She held out the piece of paper but didn't let him take it yet. 'Got it?'

'Do I get to know why?'

'Let's just say that I've seen enough hospitals to last me several lifetimes over. If you need to call anyone, call this, but only in an absolute emergency. He'll be pissed if you phone because you're feeling a bit wibbly, and this is someone that you really don't want to piss off.' She handed him the piece of paper; on it she'd written a mobile number and a single name: *Ennias*. 'He'll be pissed that I gave you his number anyway, but what the hell.'

'Family doctor?'

'Closer to just family. Sort of. Only in an emergency, remember?'

'No problem.' He pocketed the scrap.

11:39

Road-works began to pile up, part of the never-ending scheme to bypass traffic around where the traffic wanted to go. Cones funnelled two lanes into one, and they slowed to a crawl.

11:42

'This is ridiculous,' she said.

'You want to risk walking it?'

'I don't know. Maybe. It's only a couple of streets from here.' She looked at her watch and bit her lip, calculating. If she'd been on her own, then the answer would have been no, better to pass out in a taxi which could take her to hospital rather than on the streets where anything could happen. But Steve was with her, and she felt an unfamiliar fluttering sensation at the thought. Steve was by her side.

Yes, but don't you remember? whispered the Sophie-voice slyly. *You wouldn't even be in this mess if it weren't for him.*

Decide. Now.

'Yes,' she said, threw a tenner at the driver and jumped out.

2

Steve was surprised by the ferocious pace which she set. He liked to think of himself as a tolerably fit man – he played a bit of pub football with the lads and went to tae-kwon-do class every week, and not just because it looked good on his CV – but rather than 'escorting a young lady home' he found himself hard-pressed to keep up. It didn't allow much by way of conversation but then she was too preoccupied with the time anyway; checking her watch and then pressing on with greater urgency than before.

She was renting a bed-sit as part of a terraced student house only a few streets away from the University, but with it being the Easter break, the other inhabitants were presumably at home for the holidays getting their laundry done, because when Steve and Vessa got there, it was locked and dark.

He checked the time again. It was either dead on midnight or so close to it that he couldn't tell the hands on his watch apart. Not bad going. She was fumbling for her keys.

'I think that might be something of a world record,' he said, trying to lighten the mood. 'What do you say you and I enter the next...'

'Goodnight Steve,' she said rapidly, even as she was opening the front door. 'And thanks. I'm a mad, ungrateful sod, I know, but I swear I'll make this up to you.'

She gave him a quick peck on the cheek and closed the door in his face. Through a panel of corrugated glass he saw a hall light come on and her wavering shape receding.

For a moment he stood looking at the brass doorknocker.

'Night then,' he replied to it and turned to go. She Shall Be Called Mad as a Box of Frogs and Yet Strangely Attrac...

There was a heavy thud from just inside the front door. The kind of thud which might be made by a human body falling to the floor.

'Vessa?' he called.

Nothing.

Worried, he cupped his hands around his face and pressed his nose up against the glass. He thought he could make out what could have been her, lying on the lower slope of a staircase.

'Vanessa, can you hear me?' Thoroughly alarmed now, he shoved at the door but wasn't surprised when it didn't move. Nor did her shape. If what she'd told him in the taxi had been true, she'd probably just passed out, but equally she could have bashed her head or broken something when she'd fallen. What if she were bleeding?

'Vanessa!' he yelled, banging on the door. This did no more good than before, nor did it awaken anybody else who might have been in the house. It crossed his mind to dial 999, never mind her barmy instructions to the contrary, but ultimately he wanted to be sure that he had absolutely no other choice before he did something which alienated her from him.

Bracing himself, he booted at the door. He was expecting it to be a lot harder than it was on TV, and if Vessa had taken the time to bolt the door as she usually did, it would have been, but only the Yale latch held it and that burst free easily. The door slammed open and he fell into the hall.

She lay at the foot of the stairs, unmoving. He quickly checked her over, discovering in a flood of relief that she was breathing easily, and her pulse was steady – steadier than his own, in fact. He told himself that you didn't call an ambulance every time an epileptic had a seizure, as long as they were safe and unhurt, so he put her in the recovery position and then hovered indecisively. Her keys lay a few inches from her outstretched hand, but he found that he didn't want to leave her for even the few minutes it would take to find out which of the upstairs rooms was hers. She seemed to be as comfortable as he could make her, but he had no guarantee that she wouldn't stop breathing or have a seizure or something like that. He hesitated, weighing the probabilities.

'I'll be back as quickly as I can,' he promised, grabbed the keys and ran upstairs. After a frantic bit of trial and error he found the right door and then returned to carry her as gently as he could up to her room. It was a narrow Victorian terraced house on three floors, and as Sod's Law would have it, her room was on the topmost, overlooking the street.

With Vessa deposited safely on her bed, he looked around for somewhere to sit. No way was he going to leave her unattended.

There was just enough space for a bed, a dresser, a small armchair covered in glossy magazines, and a tiny sink-and-stove unit next to a fridge which made hotel minibars look generous. Under the window was a paper-strewn desk, along the back of which was stacked a row of textbooks. He expected to see that she was studying something pretty but useless like English or Art History, but found instead that they were quite random – they looked like the result of someone running blindfold through a second-hand bookshop with a butterfly net. There was a biog of George Fredrick Watts, of course, and a few books about art, but also lots of crystal-clutching silliness about chakras, dreams, demons and angels (Befriend Your Guardian Dolphin Spirit!), plus secondary school revision guides which were completely out of place next to some hardcore-looking textbooks about mental illness.

He couldn't dismiss the possibility that he was completely wrong about all of this, but she said she'd be awake at six, so he decided he'd watch over her until then, and if she didn't he'd be straight on the phone to this Ennias person, whoever that was. He saw her eyeballs roving behind their lids as she slipped into REM sleep and started dreaming. He'd have given anything to know what she was dreaming about. *Just think of it as a kind of epilepsy*, she'd said.

Clearing the armchair of its magazines and settling himself into it as comfortably as he could, he set his phone alarm for a quarter to six and tried to catch a few hours' sleep.

3

And in the dream-thronged darkness behind her eyelids, something battened on them, and grew strong.

4

He awoke to the smell of frying bacon and a savage cramp in the side of his neck. It was nearly seven.

'Shit,' he groaned and struggled up. His stomach grumbled in agreement.

'And a good morning to you too,' Vessa replied. She was standing at the tiny one-ring stove, pushing pieces of bacon around a frying pan which was approximately the same size as a table-tennis bat, with the window open on a clear spring dawn and the radio burbling. Her hair was damp, she was dressed in plain jeans and an ancient Rage Against the Machine t-shirt which read "Fuck You, I Won't Do What You Tell Me", and if anything she looked even more beautiful than last night.

'My alarm was meant to go off.'

'It did. It was going when I woke up. Very annoying sound. I turned it off – hope you don't mind. You looked like you needed the sleep.'

Steve hesitated, not quite sure whether he should mention the events of the previous evening. 'Are you, you know, is everything?'

'Me?' she said in surprise and turned a radiant smile on him. It seemed impossible to square this picture with the anxious woman he'd found unconscious on her own stairs. 'I'm absolutely fine! I said I would be. But you stayed anyway; that was very sweet of you. Would you like some breakfast?'

Before he could reply, she tossed the spatula aside, snaked her arms over his shoulders and planted a deep kiss on his very surprised mouth. Her shampoo smelled of apples. 'Or would you prefer something else?' she murmured against his lips.

By the time he arrived late to work, he was still starving but grinning from ear to ear.

CHAPTER 8

SOPHIE

1

It was the birds that told Bobby about the dead man.

Lachlan had put him to work on the most menial of maintenance chores first, since nobody knew what he could do, which involved cleaning off the worst of the caked seagull shit from the Top and the bamboo guttering, and collecting it all in wooden boxes which Marjorie optimistically called her 'kitchen garden' – optimistic in the sense that nothing apparently had ever grown in it. Over the years she'd tried collecting seeds from their food scraps and sowing them in what should have been one of nature's best organic fertilisers, but something – either the salt in the air or the quality of the water – conspired against her, and though wiry sandgrass sprouted stubbornly on Stray's higher reaches, no touch of green ever rewarded her efforts. Still, she was philosophical about it. 'The Lord will provide when he chooses to provide', she would say, but it seemed to Bobby that so far all the Lord had chosen to provide was other people's crap for them to live off.

While he was up there he avoided looking at the view too much, but he couldn't help keeping an eye on the southern horizon; low down, a hazy line of cloud had appeared, which Lachlan predicted would bring rain sometime in the next few days. Also, a knot of seagulls were diving and fighting over something several miles out. It reminded him of the way they'd squabbled over his raw fish breakfast, and he wondered if maybe it wasn't another raft, bearing another castaway.

He hurried back down to raise the alarm.

It did indeed turn out to be a raft – of much the same dimensions as his own – but its passenger had been nowhere near as lucky as Bobby.

What was left was so badly decomposed and damaged by the scavenging birds that the only way they could tell it had been a man was from the tufts of beard on its hollow cheeks. A few pathetic remnants testified to the desperate soul's last days: a plastic bottle half-full of urine and some scratches in the wood which might have been an attempt to keep track of the time or write a final message.

The Strays broke up his raft for firewood and tipped him into the sea with a prayer for his soul – and even though Bobby didn't join in, the knowledge of how close he had come to ending up like that made him want to be grateful to someone or something, so he made sure that he did a bloody good job on that guttering.

2

When Bobby managed to find any spare time, he bored a hole through the good-luck pearl which Joe had given him and threaded it on a piece of string around his neck so that it wouldn't get lost, and then he busied himself carving a toy for the child out of a piece of driftwood. He felt sorry that the lad had no friends his own age to play with, and try as he might couldn't get his head around why, if there were inhabited islands within reach, his parents kept him isolated out here. It seemed totally unnecessary – more than that, it seemed cruel. The boy deserved things like friends and girls to chase and an education. Not pearl diving and gutting fish.

The toy was a swimming man with rotating arms on an axle through the shoulders wound up with a rubber band, so that when it was let go it *splish-splish-splished* along on its own. Joe was speechless with delight when Bobby presented it to him.

It was one suppertime, and only because of the firelight, that Bobby noticed the oddness of Joe's eyes. During the day, he wore the same kind of wide-brimmed sunhat as everyone else, which kept his face in shadow, but that evening the boy reached past him to a second helping of fish stew, and Bobby caught a strange, iridescent glimmer in the sclera of his eyes. What should have been the 'whites', except that they weren't really white at all. They looked more like mother-of-pearl. He spent a lot of the next day sneaking covert glances at them, not wanting to cause embarrassment by drawing attention, and once he was looking for it in broad daylight it was unmistakeable. Outside the blue of his irises, Jophiel's eyes were shot through with nacreous, rainbow swirls.

He couldn't not mention it to someone. Seb's response was typically phlegmatic: 'Sure, it's weird, but so what?' he said. 'Maybe he eats the pearls. Who knows?' Apparently this was one of Stray's mysteries which wasn't worth the trouble of pursuing, so he let it lie and concentrated on his chores and the more urgent problems of survival.

He quickly recovered his strength and even put on a little muscle. The combination of fresh air, hard physical work and a spartan diet did more to undo his doughy pallor in one week than months in the gym had ever achieved. The others noticed, Allie especially.

'Looks like our lifestyle is starting to agree with you,' she said to him one day, and in passing let her hand trail appreciatively across the planes of his bare shoulders. No question about her coming on to him there, he thought. But how could it ever work in a place like this? He was set on getting away to those Islands as soon as possible, so he ignored it.

Meanwhile, the clouds continued to build.

3

Two days later he was promoted to Assistant Kelp Harvester, with twelve-year-old Jophiel Lachlan as his mentor and boss. They worked from his raft and Joe's little coracle out in the quadrant between the Up and Strange booms, using baskets of rocks to carry them down to the seabed thirty feet below, where great strands of kelp with stems the thickness of Bobby's arm clung to rocky outcrops. Joe showed him how the baseball-sized flotation cysts – each with its reservoir of filtered seawater – grew at the base of each leaf and kept the plant growing towards the sun thanks to the desalinated water's lower density, and how to cut them free from the stem.

Bobby found the gloomy submarine forest utterly compelling. He wanted to be able to go off and explore its dark groves for hours. Joe showed him which kelp plants were being harvested and which were being left to regenerate, and warned him of his father's injunction to never, under any circumstances, swim directly under Stray itself. The kelp there grew thicker than anywhere else, right up to the raft's underside, and he could well believe that there were all kinds of lines and bits of netting which would entangle and drown a careless swimmer, without the need to make up stories about monsters living there. At the edges, fish in all manner of shapes and sizes darted amongst the waving fronds like birds and made their homes in the conical trunks of the kelp's root holdfasts. They swam around him, entirely unafraid, as if inspecting his handiwork.

But enjoyment bred complacency, and he got sloppy.

The knife was so sharp that at first Bobby wasn't even aware that he'd cut himself. There was a sudden blossoming of red around his left hand, and he had time to think *That's weird, it looks just like…* before hot, stinging agony burst there too, made all the worse for being in salt water. His yelp of pain escaped in a stream of frantic bubbles, and he kicked for the surface.

He clambered back onto his raft, smearing red everywhere, and yelled over to where Lachlan and Seb were working on one of the booms. While they were rowing over, Joe surfaced nearby.

'Are you okay?' he called, treading water.

'Sliced my hand,' Bobby grimaced. 'Silly wanker.' There was a long, deep gash across the fleshy pad at the base of his palm. And though he gripped it tightly blood dripped steadily from his clasped hands into the water.

'Oh wow!' Joe was peering down at it, fascinated. 'Look at your blood! Look what it's doing!'

'I can see what it's doing,' Bobby muttered through clenched teeth. 'It's bloody *leaking*, that's what it's doing.'

But that wasn't what Joe meant.

Where Bobby's blood dripped into the water, instead of diffusing into a red cloud as it should have done, the drops remained round crimson beads falling slowly through the water like a broken string of ruby-red pearls. They were being gobbled up by three large fish who followed them to the surface, fighting over each new one as it fell.

'Yeah,' he said. 'Bizarre.'

Blood should definitely not do that. What was wrong with him?

They took him in, and Marjorie strapped him up with little sympathy since he'd effectively rendered himself a useless burden on them through his carelessness. He spent the rest of the day morosely trying to descale fish single-handed, watching the clouds massing with agonising slowness and wondering when it would rain, if ever.

4

That evening, when Marjorie took Sophie her supper, she came back to the fire with an oddly worried expression.

'Bobby,' she said, 'it seems that Sophie wants to talk to you.'

Silence fell over the meal. The Strays were looking at him expectantly.

'About what?'

'She wouldn't say. I simply mentioned that you'd cut your hand, and she said she needed to see it for herself.'

He looked at the blood-stained bandage and flexed his hand painfully. 'She's more than welcome to come out and have a good old point-and-laugh like everybody else, if she really wants.'

'Best if you just go in and see her, son,' suggested Lachlan.

'Fine.' He tossed his bowl down and stomped off grumpily to humour the crazy girl.

Past the beaded curtain, he found that the hollow interior of the Hub was larger than he'd expected. Much of the space was filled with the beams and struts which held it up, but there was still enough room for him to stand up straight. In the open space at the very centre was a square hole in the floor, and barely a foot below that, water. The core of Stray was open to the ocean's surface. It reflected the light of a single reed-wick lamp which burned next to where a young woman sat in a nest of bedclothes, staring at the reflections as if hypnotised.

She was younger than he'd expected – for some reason 'Sophie' sounded like an old woman's name – dressed in ragged jeans and a t-shirt of the same ubiquitous shade of sun-faded grey as everything else, but under a lank fringe of mousy blonde hair her eyes were deeply shadowed. He couldn't decide whether she looked rapt with concentration or just exhausted.

'You wanted to see me,' he said.

She looked at him, and then down at his hand with small frown of concern. 'You cut yourself,' she replied simply.

'I'm a silly bugger, I know.'

'May I see?'

'It's not very pretty.'

'Please. I have some experience with injuries. I'm what you might call the workplace's designated first-aider.'

He hesitated, plainly suspicious.

'I'm sorry that we haven't spoken much before now,' she continued. 'I sometimes find it hard with new people. It's funny – we're surrounded by all this emptiness, and yet somehow it feels so claustrophobic, you know?'

'I know.' He gestured around at the encompassing timbers. 'Still, bit of an odd place to sleep for someone who doesn't like enclosed spaces, isn't it?' He found himself relenting somewhat. She seemed to be genuinely sympathetic – or at least interested. Either way, he reasoned it was the best opportunity he had to find out more about her. He trusted his gut with first impressions much more than rumour and hearsay, and he wasn't convinced of what the others had said about her.

'Lachlan tells me you were the first one here. That you were on your own for a long time before anybody else arrived.'

'I wouldn't say that. There have been others here. Some left for the Islands. Others just sort of gave up. You have to be very strong to stick this place out for any length of time – but I suppose it suits Stuart's sense of self-importance. That man has to be the alpha and omega of his own little floating family. You can't blame him, though. This is a hard place to survive, and each of us finds their own way.' She fixed him with an expression of surprising earnestness. 'You should leave too. Soon. It's not safe here.'

'Oh, don't worry about that,' he reassured her. 'I intend to make my way back home as soon as I possibly can.'

That seemed to please her, and she relaxed. 'Good. So, are you going to let me look at that hand?'

He crossed to her side of the pool, sat beside her, unwrapped the bandages and showed her his wound.

'You going to tell me my future, too?' he joked.

'I could do,' she murmured absently. Her hands were calloused and her nails chewed ragged, but she probed his wound with exquisite gentleness. 'It seems clean enough. Salt water will hurt like a bitch, but it'll do the trick. Do you know what haematomancy is?'

'Um, no.'

'Divination by blood. I'm not going to do anything to you but this may seem a little… odd. Some people are so squeamish. Usually it's the boys.'

'What…'

Where her fingertips had come away bloody, she put them in her mouth and sucked. He was about to tell her that he didn't think that was a very good idea at all – there was no telling what kinds of bugs might be in his blood – when he saw the manacle encircling her wrist and the heavy chain which trailed from it and into the water.

They had her chained. *Crazy*, Joe had said. *Violent*. Monsters under Stray. She had her eyes closed as she tasted his blood, as if concentrating hard. Or maybe just enjoying the taste.

Slowly, like a man stepping off a landmine, he disengaged himself and edged away. She didn't seem to have noticed. She was frowning slightly.

'All here,' she murmured. 'You're all here.' She opened her eyes and looked at him, puzzled. 'How can you be all here? That doesn't make any sense.'

But by that time he'd ducked back out through the doorway and into the fresh night air.

5

Bobby picked at the rest of his meal in silence, carefully avoiding eye contact with the others while he tried to make sense of what he'd just seen, and failing miserably. Sod waiting for the supply run. He'd leave it until everybody was asleep, load Allie's fishing skiff with whatever was closest to hand and take his chances on finding the Tourmaline Archipelago. Starvation at sea now actually seemed preferable to spending another day with these lunatics. It was a shame about Allie, though.

When he judged that he'd left it long enough to avoid drawing suspicion, he gave an exaggerated stretch and yawn. 'Well, that's me done, folks. I'm knackered. Going to turn in, I think.'

As he turned to go, Lachlan said: 'Bobby.'

Bobby stopped. 'Yes?'

'Just ask the question.'

'Sorry? What? What question?'

Lachlan sighed. 'You know for someone who claims to have a consular background you're about as subtle as a baboon's arse – which is also what you're currently making of yourself. Sophie has had one of her little chats with you, hasn't she?'

'Yes, why?'

'Well then. Ask the question.'

Bobby squared himself. 'Alright then. What has she done to deserve being treated like an animal? Why have you got her locked up? What are you people doing to her?'

'We haven't. We aren't. She does it of her own volition. She's got the key on a piece of string around her neck – you can go and see for yourself, if you like.'

'But why would anybody do something like that?' he objected. 'That's crazy.'

Seb threw his hands up in celebration. 'Hallelujah! Finally! 'E gets it!'

'Bobby,' there was an earnest sincerity in Lachlan's voice which he couldn't deny. 'I tried to tell you before: we're not hiding anything from you. This place is too small for secrets. I'm not saying that each of us isn't a basket case in our own way, but there's nothing malicious going on here. We have to live with some very strange compromises in order to survive here, but we're not bad people.'

'But if that girl is sick, she needs help, surely. You have to get her to the Islands – she needs a hospital!'

'There are no hospitals in the Archipelago,' said Allie. 'At least, none you'd recognise as such. The islanders wouldn't have the faintest idea how to cope with Sophie. Taking her there would only do more harm than good, and she wouldn't want to go anyway.'

'I hardly think she's capable of making that decision for herself.'

Allie stared hard at him with narrowed eyes. 'Nice bit of holier-than-thou you've got going there, Bobby Jenkins. Tell you what, when you've got us all worked out, and you know what's the best for everybody, why don't you go and stick it right up your ass. In the meantime,' she added, with a bright fuck-you smile, 'Good luck with not dying, okay?' And she stormed out.

'Allie, wait…'

But she'd gone.

'We are caring for Sophie the best way we can,' explained Marjorie. 'We feed her, keep her clean, and try to stop her from hurting herself or others. We tried to take the chain off her once, but the poor child became so very distressed. It was awful. Her head's full of paranoid delusions about things underneath the raft that only she can deal with. She's just a girl, and she's suffered so much; we're the closest thing she has to a family.'

Bobby sat back down, shamefaced and feeling stupid. 'I think I owe you all an apology.'

'Not necessary,' said Lachlan. 'I know how this must look to an outsider's eyes. You might want to try that apology on Alison, though. She and Sophie – I don't know; they have some sort of understanding.'

'Come!' Seb clapped an arm around Bobby's shoulders and hauled him to his feet again. 'We will unruffle her feathers with great quantities of the finest Ouzo, and your baboon's ass will be all hers.'

6

A single crimson pearl of Bobby's blood, having escaped the fishes' voracious attention, drifted to the ocean bottom close to the wild thicket of uncultivated kelp which grew right up to the underside of Stray – where Stuart Lachlan had with good reason told his son never to swim, ever, under any circumstances.

Something thin and black and whiplike uncoiled slowly from within the shadowed holdfasts – something which might have looked like the tentacle of an octopus, if instead of suckers it had possessed rows of lamprey-like teeth. It was only one of many which drifted, vegetative and blind, amongst the kelp, swaying in the currents around Stray. Its tip grazed the blood-pearl and drifted past.

Then came back.

It quested around, as if sniffing.

It located the blood, coiled around it eagerly and withdrew into the darkness.

Deep amongst the kelp holdfasts under Stray, and as far from the painful light of the upper shallows as it could get, the araka awoke.

It was emaciated and starving, as close to death as it was possible for a deathless thing to be, but something had roused it. Some taste. It had not been aware of feeding; its tentacles responded to smell and movement out of instinct alone, like a drowsing man swatting sleepily at a buzzing insect, except in this instance it had chanced on something edible. Utterly unlike the pain that was its normal diet, this was heavy, rich, solid, and fleshily corporeal. It trickled through the araka's wizened veins like hair-thin threads of lava, jerking it into wakefulness, and with that the awareness of how appallingly hungry it still was. It had never tasted anything physical before – it had never *been* physical before. As far as it knew, it was the only one of its kind which had been forced into existence in either world. There were no precedents for this sort of thing.

It only knew one thing for certain: it wanted more.

Slowly, painfully, the araka began to explore the limits of its confinement.

CHAPTER 9

THE NIGHT THE RAINS CAME

1

'Steve,' said Vessa, as they lay together in bed at her place. 'I've been thinking.'

'Always a bad idea,' he murmured. 'I try to avoid it, myself.' He was staring at the pages of a book on the Civil War without really taking any of it in; just marking time until her Cinderella curfew kicked in and he could sleep knowing that she was safe.

'I want to try and stay awake after midnight.'

That got his attention. 'But I thought you said you'd tried everything and nothing had ever worked.'

'Well, almost everything,' she smiled and snuggled closer. Under the covers her hand reached out to curl around his cock. 'I'm thinking that it might not be so easy for me to drop off if you're keeping me busy.'

He'd been involved in enough short-lived relationships to know that in the first flush it was possible to ignore all manner of peculiar personality quirks, and so the issue of her curfew didn't bother him overmuch. He'd gone out with snorers, vegetarians, smokers, and even one girl who had a thing about seagulls – which had, incidentally, made his spontaneous romantic surprise of a weekend in Great Yarmouth a bit of a disaster – and as long as he remained on day shifts at the gallery, the curfew wasn't a problem. True, she was spending more and more time at his flat rather than her bedsit, if for no other reason that he had more space, but it wasn't as if they were moving in together. Not yet, anyway. And here was the funny thing: getting used to whatever baggage your new girlfriend brought with her on the journey was nothing compared to the awkward undercurrent of the fact that ultimately he was looking for someone to settle down with, and in his not entirely limited experience women were just as commitment-phobic as men.

But still, if the lady insisted; and her hand was so very insistent. After their earlier lovemaking, he'd thought himself done, but apparently not.

'Sounds like a reasonable theory,' he said. 'I say we give it a shot.'

With the simple, urgent certainty of him inside her, his mouth on her breasts and her thighs gripping him tightly, Vessa watched the minutes on his bedside clock mount inexorably towards midnight, wondering what would happen if it wasn't enough – if she went away again. She'd thought that the way to be rid of Sophie was to paper over the cracks with new certificates and qualifications in her own name, but here and now, with her man loving her (*her* man, she told herself again in delight), it was Vessa's body and skin and nerves which were coming alight, not Sophie's. Hers now, regardless of who had been born in it, and Sophie was going to have a fight on her hands if she wanted to reclaim it.

She urged Steve on harder and faster with her teeth on his neck and her nails on the muscles of his back, and whether it was his increasing heat or her fear and anger fuelling it, she climaxed suddenly in a great formless iridescent explosion as if the entire world had turned to mother-of-pearl and spiralled back down into itself like the depths of a gigantic conch shell.

As the waves of it washed away, Vessa looked at the clock again. It was 00:01.

Fierce pride filled her then, and love for the man who had helped her, and she turned her attention outward to him; kissing him, biting him, feeling his urgency mount.

And suddenly she couldn't breathe.

2

Sophie was screaming.

Its banshee sound cut through entire worlds of sleep – even the araka on the sea-bed beneath Stray shifted uneasily – and brought everyone running.

When Bobby got into her chamber he found Marjorie attempting to console the girl, who was deeply distressed, but every time the older woman came near, she lashed out, the chain around her wrist thrashing, and screaming a confused babble with a single hysterical phrase repeated: 'She's not here! She's left me! She's not here! She's left me! She's...'

Lachlan strode in. 'What in God's name is happening?' he demanded.

'Your guess is as good as mine,' Bobby replied.

'P'raps she is having some sort of grand mal,' suggested Seb, who appeared behind them, rubbing the sleep from his eyes.

Far from calming, Sophie was becoming more agitated. She started pounding her head against one of the wooden beams, shrieking 'Vessa's gone! Vessa's gone!'

'Bugger this.' Bobby edged forward. He wasn't sure what you did when someone had a screaming fit like this, but he was pretty certain you didn't let them bash their own brains out. He grabbed for one of her flailing arms, the one with the chain, catching it on the third attempt. Seb caught the other – and she bent and sank her teeth into his hand. He yowled and dropped her. *That's it*, Bobby thought. *Crazy girl or not.*

'Sorry, love,' he said, and punched her in the face. She collapsed, senseless.

3

Steve was close, so close, with Vessa's nails raking his shoulders in that animal way which drove him absolutely crazy for her. Except now she wasn't just scratching but pushing, shoving him away, twisting her body out from underneath him and shouting 'GetoffmegetoffmeGETOUTOFME!'

He fell to the edge of the bed, staring at her in shock. 'What...?' he panted. 'Vessa, what the...?'

'Vessa?' she spat. 'Oh of course there'd have to be a *man* involved, wouldn't there? Does she really think it's that easy?' She drew her knees up to her chin and dragged the bedclothes over them, glaring at him over the top with undisguised contempt. 'You tell that faithless bitch next time you're fucking her that we had an agreement, and if she ever tries this shit again I'll make her wish she'd never been born.' Something about this seemed to strike her as funny, because she began to laugh: a thin, hitching sound so completely unlike Vessa's that it raised gooseflesh all over his naked, unprotected skin.

Somehow – he couldn't imagine how – this wasn't his girlfriend. Someone else was here.

'Sophie?' he whispered.

'I was here first,' she said sulkily, like a petulant child. 'Don't either of you forget that.' She was nodding now, suddenly drowsy.

'Where's Vessa?' he demanded. 'What have you done with her?'

'If she won't do her job,' she muttered, head on her knees, 'then she'll have to do mine, won't she? Can't let it go, Steven. Sorry. So tired.' She yawned hugely.

'Let me speak to her!'

'…so…'

Then she was gone, and her body slumped into the bedclothes, too deeply asleep to rouse.

4

Bobby and Seb were lowering Sophie's unconscious body gently onto her cot when she started to come around. Marjorie ran forward with a damp cloth to wipe the blood from her battered and swollen forehead while the rest of the Strays watched from a cautious distance.

'Oh my dear,' the older woman shushed. 'My poor, poor dear. What's happening to you, hen? What's happening?'

'I'm getting rid of this stupid bloody chain for a start,' Bobby declared and reached for the key which hung from a piece of string around her neck. Woozily, her free hand swatted his away.

'No,' she slurred. 'Can't let it go. My job now.'

'What's your job, Sophie hen?' asked Marjorie gently.

'Not Sophie. Sophie's not here any more. She's asleep. I'm Vanessa.'

Steve threw some clothes on and paced her bedsit in a panic of indecision. No hospitals under any circumstances, she'd said. Not unless she was actually injured or suffering a serious medical emergency.

'Well what the fuck do you call this?!' he protested to the empty flat. Once again her breathing and pulse were completely normal; she hadn't banged her head or cut herself. 'Oh no, nothing major. Just, you know, completely switched fucking personalities!' He desperately needed to talk to Jackie but couldn't bring himself to call at this hour. The only alternative was the phone number Vessa had given him on their first date – the one with the single name: Ennias. He still had the battered slip of paper in his wallet, but no better idea who that was after all this time. Vessa had never spoken of him since. Steve had absolutely no reason to trust that this Ennias person could be any more use to him than a qualified doctor. *Except that she trusted him,* said Jackie's voice in his head. *That should be enough for you, if you really want to help her.*

'Oh bloody hell,' he moaned, and with great reluctance dialled the number. *If it rings out,* he told himself, that's it. *I'm dialling 999.*

It was picked up on the first ring.

'This better be good, whoever you are. It's late.' A man's voice, inflected with a European accent he couldn't place.

'I'm a friend of Vanessa Gail's. She gave me this number in case of an emergency. Are you Ennias?'

There was a long pause, during which he could hear the other man breathing and what sounded like traffic noises in the background.

'Where are you?' Ennias asked eventually.

'Who exactly are you, and why would she…?'

'Shut up and listen to me. If you don't know who I am, then she's told you sod all about anything, so you're not setting the terms here. Tell me where you are, and I'll come and make sure she's alright. Or not. Whatever. Has Sophie spoken to you yet?'

'How do you know about her?'

Ennias sighed heavily. 'Listen, boyfriend. It's been a long night, and I don't have the energy for this. The fact that you have called me indicates that, from your perspective, some fairly weird shit has just happened, and you have no clue what to do about it. The fact that you are still alive and breathing indicates to me that so far you have been very sensible and not done anything idiotic like taking her to the authorities. Your instincts so far have been correct. Listen to them. Tell me where you are.'

It all sounded a little bit too much like a threat for Steve's liking. He'd wait until Vessa – or Sophie, or whoever was asleep in there – woke up, and ask her for himself.

'I don't think so.'

'You stupid …'

But Steve had already hung up.

6

'Vanessa?' Bobby crouched beside her nest. Seb had been whisked away by Marjorie to tend his bitten hand, and Joe along with them despite his complaints; Stuart and Allie hovered in the background, watching warily. 'Is that your name?'

He wasn't sure that she could hear him properly. She seemed to be semi-conscious, twisting in her blankets like a child fretting in its sleep. 'Off!' she cried out. 'All of you… have to get off… kill you all…'

For a brief moment, she opened her eyes and looked at him. 'I know you from somewhere,' she said.

'Yes, just the other day. You looked at my hand.'

'No,' she frowned. 'No, somewhere else. I can't remember. There were paintings. Why can't I… *Neil*, that's your name. You were rude to me.'

Bobby felt like someone had just tipped a jugful of ice-water down his spine. He leapt up and away from her, his skin crawling, mind reeling. The crossed timbers of her chamber were suddenly pressing in on him like a coffin; there was no space. Fragmented memories – barely even that; not much more than vague impressions – of falling, drowning, surfacing. His vision blurred; the woman below him looked like she was bursting out of a golden cloud of leaves and birds and someone close by was saying *Crash and burn, my friend. Crash and burn.* Who had that been? He couldn't breathe. He had to get out. Most especially he had to get away from *her*.

He barged past the others and out into the open air.

'Bobby?' Allie ran after him, concerned. 'Bobby, are you okay?'

Lachlan was left with Vanessa, but he hovered by the doorway, unwilling to get any closer than he absolutely had to. 'What do you want with us?' he pleaded.

She smiled grimly. 'Me? Nothing. Nothing at all. I just work here. She warned you, though, didn't she? About what would happen if you stayed?'

He followed Bobby's example and fled.

7

Half an hour later – after Steve had made himself a cup of coffee and settled himself in the armchair to watch over her until six, or else call an ambulance and damn the consequences – a heavy thumping sounded on the bedsit door, making him jump. He tiptoed across and peered through the door's security peephole.

A man of indeterminate Slavic appearance, dressed in dark clothes and a long leather coat, was standing outside. As Steve watched, he took out his phone and dialled. Steve's phone rang.

'Shit!'

Ennias stared right into the fish-eye lens and gave a little wave.

Steve opened the door but kept it on the chain. 'How did you find me?' he demanded.

Ennias simply shrugged. 'Oh, the apps one can download these days, if one knows the right people,' he said cryptically, putting his phone away. 'Aren't you going to let me in?'

'Just answer one question for me. How do you know Vessa?'

'Do you really want to know?'

'It's the only way you're getting in.'

'Okay then. She contacted me after escaping from a high-security psychiatric institution acting as a front for a world-wide conspiracy which abducts and imprisons refugees from an alternate reality. I work for an underground organisation which helps those refugees create new lives in this world.' He said this with an absolutely straight face.

Steve looked at him.

Ennias laughed. 'No, I'm just messing with you. I'm her ex. Can I come in?'

'Sure. Why not?' If the man had said anything remotely normal, he didn't think he would have believed him. Steve opened the door.

After Ennias had apparently satisfied himself that Vessa was sleeping normally – whatever that meant these days – he began mooching around her bedsit, picking things up, examining them, and putting them back again.

'I won't ask how you know her,' he said to Steve. 'I think "biblically" is the word, yes? I would say you are a brave man involving yourself with her, but I also think that you have no idea what you're getting into, so let's not get carried away.'

Steve didn't like the way this strange man was rummaging through her things. 'Do you mind not doing that? Seriously, what's your connection here? What's wrong with her?'

'Oh the size of those questions, and they come out of your mouth as if they're nothing at all! What are these books for?' Ennias waved a Biology GCSE textbook at him.

'She's, uh, she's studying.' He was having trouble keeping up here. 'When you said psychiatric institution, you were joking, right?'

'Do I look like I'm joking?' In truth, he had the eyes of a man who looked like he slept little, if at all. 'Studying. For examinations? Qualifications?' He was digging through the rest of the paperwork on her tiny desk, peering at documents and tossing them aside carelessly.

'Yes. Look, I'm just going to, uh…' he edged away, digging out his phone, ready to call the police. He found that his phone had no signal, which was odd, but it didn't make any difference; you could still dial 999 without a network signal. He did so – and heard nothing. No dial tone, no recorded message. Just blank white noise.

'Apps, remember?' said Ennias absently, waving his phone at Steve while he continued to dig through Vessa's things.

'Hey, I warned you. Leave her stuff alone.' Steve crossed the room and moved to grab Ennias' arm, but before he made contact Ennias extended the forefinger of the hand that waved his phone and planted it squarely in the middle of Steve's chest. Steve stopped dead as if he'd just run into the end of a construction beam and saw the front of his torso ripple in concentric circles where he was touched. He staggered back, gasping for breath.

With his other hand, Ennias waved a piece of paper in his face. 'This looks like a driving licence application form to me.'

'So what? What the fuck did you just do to me?'

'And this appears to be an application for a Marks and Spencer store card.'

'So?'

'So it looks like our girl is trying to make herself real without having even the basic sense to use the false ID she was given. Honestly, I'm amazed that the Hegemony hasn't caught up with her yet. She must have finally gone wampy; how can she think they don't know about her? You tell her, when she comes back, that when I agreed to help out in an emergency I didn't think she'd be doing everything in her power to get caught again, the silly bint. I'm off.' He tossed the papers to the floor in disgust and headed for the door.

Steve made a half-hearted attempt to bar his exit. Ennias looked surprised. 'Really? Make up your mind, Mr McBride. Do you want me in or out?'

'Out. But only in the back of a police van.'

Ennias raised his hand as if casually inspecting his nails. 'Mr McBride, you've seen what I can do with just one of these. How curious are you to see what I can do with five?'

Not very, as it happened. Steve let him go. 'You're not really her ex-boyfriend, are you?' he asked.

In the hallway outside, Ennias paused and looked back. 'You might not be so quick on the uptake, but you seem like a decent fellow, for what it's worth. My advice to you? Walk away. She'll drag you down with her like a sinking ship, Mr McBride, whether she loves you or not. She won't be able to stop herself.'

Then he was gone, and Steve was rubbing the centre of his chest, where a large bruise was starting to appear.

8

Allie took Bobby to her bed on the night that the rains came.

There was nothing especially dramatic about it – no sudden torrents of passion or burning, savage embraces – and afterwards, no embarrassment or awkwardness. In the end, neither of them could clearly remember who had made the first move. It seemed that with the opening of the clouds, some unspoken consensus had been reached, an agreement made on a level so removed from their conscious thoughts and feelings that it was absolutely authoritative and unquestionable. It was as if they'd done this a million times before and only temporarily forgotten about it.

He'd been brooding over the contents of the chest which had been rescued from his raft – the cuff-links, the shoes, the book with its inscription from a woman he had no memory of – while half-listening to the music of Stray shifting against itself in an atonal chorus of creaks and subsonic groans, like whale-song. Was any of this his? Or if not his, then whose? He was so wrapped up in his own spiralling uncertainties that he didn't realise she was standing by his hammock until he felt her warm, dry hand reach to take his own.

He rose. Before he could say anything she laid a long finger on his lips and just looked at the shadow of him, liking what she saw. She led him a short way along the Charm boom, completely sure-footed in the dark, to where her boat was moored, and on a bed of sailcloth and fishing nets she took him to herself without saying a word, communicating what she wanted with her hands, her legs, her mouth. As the first older woman he'd ever slept with, she was stronger than he'd expected and nowhere near as soft or passively yielding as the diplomats' daughters he'd bedded – she took what she wanted from him without apology and encouraged him to take her in return. He had enough presence of mind, at the end, to force himself to pause and say 'I don't want to… you know… get you…'

'You won't,' she whispered, her eyes dark, drinking him in. 'You can't, not on Stray.'

So he finished inside her, and in the end there were no doubts or questions or fragments of other people's thoughts cluttering his brain. Just the absolute certainty of her: the taste of her skin, the smell of her hair, the sound of her quickening gasps as she came a second time in response to him.

Later, without thunder or lightning or even a strong breeze, it began to rain. They gathered their clothing and dashed back for the shelter of Stray, laughing as clean, fresh water streamed from their naked bodies.

CHAPTER 10

DEGAN

1

The wake caused by Sophie's intrusion from Tourmaline was large enough to be detected by every single one of the Hegemony's buoys within a two-mile radius of Vessa's bedsit; compared to the v-shaped trail which had followed her out of the gallery, this looked like the result of a hand grenade being thrown into a swimming pool. The cascade of notifications bumped the incident straight out of the Hegemony's autonomic data-trawling systems and onto the desktop of an actual live, human supervisor, who farmed the process of putting a name and a face to the disturbance out to half a dozen operatives.

Very few of even the most paranoid conspiracy theorists had any clue about the Hegemony's existence, and contrary to some crackpots' Hollywood-inspired imaginations there were no massive high-tech bunkers or central control rooms with large banks of gleaming computer consoles. Working from phones and laptops in their homes, on trains, park benches, school classrooms and government offices, these Hegemony operatives – who in most cases didn't even know that this was what they were – proceeded to electronically scour the immediate geographical vicinity of the disturbance through a number of legal and semi-legal information systems ranging from Tesco Customer Services and the Yellow Pages up to the Inland Revenue, the police's own Holmes2 criminal database, and even the Global Terrorism Database; for the Hegemony, even international terrorism was merely one of many tools of governance.

Within twenty-four hours, the result was delivered to an individual whose name would not have appeared in any newspaper, Hansard archive or police report, and who was, at that very moment, holidaying on a beach in Montenegro, allowing an extraordinarily expensive Russian prostitute to massage sunscreen into his back. The report was pinged to his phone using an intelligence service app which would have made civil libertarians run screaming for their lawyers. It read simply:

```
> vessel pn07139/cond.7 — marchant.sophie.r
(alt: gail.vanessa)
> manifest: araka (cat.: d3)
> status: abscondment/fac.uk249/reacquisition
pending
> prosecute? y/n
```

He pressed Y and settled back with a satisfied sigh to let the Mediterranean sun soak into his flesh; it was always pleasing to account for one's wayward charges. He briefly considered bringing forward his return flight to the UK but dismissed the idea. It was only one girl, after all, and Maddox was more than capable of dealing with it. He let the call-girl's talented fingers work their magic on his scapulae and dozed.

2

After her curfew had passed the following morning, Vessa tried to explain.

'I told you once that She Shall Be Called Woman was a favourite of Sophie's when she and I skived off school to visit London together.'

'Yes, I remember.' Steve's tone was guarded. He'd made it clear that whatever explanation she was about to give, it would have to be full and honest; he would have to be able to ask her anything about it, or he was gone. Surprising herself, she'd agreed.

'The first time, Sophie was on her own. I think I also said that she had a terrible home life. Her parents did really awful things to her – the kinds of things for which people get locked up for the rest of their lives – so she stopped sleeping when the nightmares became too much to bear. Simply stopped altogether. The doctors tried giving her drugs and shocks and all kinds of different sleep therapy, but she just refused to sleep. The problem is that the human brain isn't designed to survive without sleep; chronic permanent insomnia will kill you in about two weeks. One day she escaped the hospital where she was being kept and ran away to the Tate, where the painting is normally kept, and she sat there looking at it and just cried and wished that there was someone who could look after her – somebody older and wiser, somebody more capable, who could sweep in when things got too rough and take over so that she could hide away from what was being done to her. She wished so hard, with all of her pain and loneliness fuelling it, that I came.'

'What – you mean you found her there?'

'Sort of. One moment I didn't exist, and the next I did. Her mind simply wasn't strong enough to contain all that it had to cope with, or what it needed, so it spun off another person who could. Me. I am what the psychiatrists dismissively refer to as a "secondary personality".' She hmphed in disgust. 'As if Sophie is more worthy simply because she came first.'

She could see Steve struggling with this, having to rearrange assumptions and re-evaluate countless tiny details of things she had said and done while they'd been together. She let it be.

'So,' he said eventually, 'you're one half of a split personality?'

'No!' her anger flared up instantly, frightening them both. 'I'm not half of *anything*! I am *me*! I have my own thoughts, my own memories, feelings, ambitions, hopes, fears, everything – none of which she shares! I don't need her! She may have been born in this body, but it's *mine* now.'

'Okay, I'm sorry – I didn't mean to offend,' he said, backing off, hands in the air. 'It's just… I don't know the right words. I've never… you have to admit that from my point of view, this is pretty weird.'

'I do, I know, and I'm sorry. I didn't mean to blow up at you. But it's not easy for me either. For ages I've done what needs to be done, including sleep for her.'

'The curfew?'

'Exactly. It's the one thing I have no control over – and believe me, I'm working on that. At first Sophie was happy for me to take over in stressful situations, and mostly that was okay, but sometimes it pissed me off. I sat all her exams, for example, and the certificates were all awarded in her name. Can you imagine how unfair that feels?'

'That's why you're studying,' he realised, another piece of the puzzle slotting into place.

'And after a while she found it easier to let me take over pretty much everything. She came out less and less and eventually stopped altogether. She hasn't been conscious for over a year now.'

'She's unconscious.'

'Yes.'

'In you.'

'In this body,' she corrected him.

'Hmm.'

'Think of it as a pilot and co-pilot of a plane. The pilot has fallen into a coma, and the co-pilot has been left to fly the plane single-handed. How long does the flight have to last before ground control acknowledges her as the new pilot as opposed to the useless lump of meat sitting next to her?'

'Interesting point,' he said. 'Am I ground control in this analogy?'

She stroked his cheek. 'If anything, you're a frequent flier. The painting is important to me because it's the first thing I ever saw. When I'm feeling wobbly or out of control, seeing it helps me strengthen my sense of myself. Touching it is better, but we both know how that goes.'

He thought about this, remembering how stressed out she had been the third time she'd come to the gallery. There was also that nagging memory of the painting seeming to have moved in response to her nearness, but of course that could never have happened, just like the incident with Ennias could never have happened. That must have been some kind of martial arts thing, the kind of thing that Caffrey knew all about. That wasn't what was really nagging at him, however. It was something she'd just said – something small hidden away behind those huge revelations.

'So,' he said, 'are you on any kind of medication for it?'

'Am I on drugs, do you mean?' she bridled again. 'Are you afraid that you're taking advantage of a mentally ill person or just that I'm going to turn psycho on you?'

'Come on, Vessa, that's not fair. Can you really say it's an unusual thing to ask, given that little bombshell?'

'I'm not the one who's ill. Sophie is. She was on beta-blockers for anxiety attacks, but they ran out a couple of weeks ago. I can't get a prescription for myself because I don't have a doctor, and I can't get a doctor because I don't have the right kind of ID. Yet.'

Ennias had said something about a fake ID being given to her, which presumably she was refusing to use because it wasn't *her*, Vanessa Gail. The older and wiser friend that Sophie Marchant had called into being to help her cope with the un-cope-able. The one who had dealt with all of her stressful situations – like sitting exams.

That nagging suddenly ballooned into a vast, horrifying suspicion which filled his chest and made it difficult to breathe. 'Vessa,' he asked slowly, 'you know how you told me that you're twenty-three years old?'

She stared at him without reply, waiting for him to ask the rest. Daring him.

'How old is Sophie?' he finished.

'Why do you care?'

'How old, Vessa? And don't lie to me. It'd be so easy to find out.'

'You think I'm lying to you? How dare you!'

'Don't change the subject. How old?'

'You're not sleeping with her. You're sleeping with *me*.'

He slammed the table. '*How old?*' It was his turn to be angry now – angry at her evasiveness and at the fear that this might not be the only thing she had been lying to him about during their short time together.

Defiantly, Vessa raised her chin and replied, 'She's eighteen.'

The balloon inside his chest burst, but it wasn't filled with air – it was filled with toxic gas; heavy yellow poison which clouded his head so that everything swam, and which corroded his limbs so that when he tried to stand up, he staggered and had to clutch the chair for support.

'Oh Jesus,' he moaned to himself. 'Oh Jesus Christ, no. You stupid son of a bitch. You stupid, *stupid*…'

'I don't see what your problem is,' she protested. 'It's not as if it's even illegal.'

'*Illegal?*' he yelled at her. 'You think I give a shit about whether or not it's *legal?* You're a *teenager!*'

'*I am not Sophie!*' she yelled back at him.

'Maybe in your own twisted, fucked-up head that's true, but not as far as the rest of the world is concerned – not as far as *I'm* concerned! How could you not mention this? How could you think that it wouldn't matter?'

'Because for one stupid, idiotic second, I actually thought you were different!' She laughed bitterly. 'But you're not, are you? You're just like all the rest.'

He shook his head in angry denial and began gathering up his coat. 'I don't know what else you could have expected. For someone so smart you're unbelievably naïve.'

'Well what do you expect from a fucking *teenager?*'

He slammed his way out of her bedsit so hard that the door bounced halfway open again, and her shout echoed after him as he lurched like a drunken man down the stairwell and out into the street. He was so angry that he didn't notice how many people on the street weren't moving at all, but simply watching the house with expressionless eyes.

3

The Passenger from Elbaite stared morosely through the hotel window's chintz curtains, waiting for his captors to return. Below, past the hotel's truncated grounds and the cliff edge beyond that, the Channel's grey swell wandered up and down a rubble beach as if it couldn't be arsed to summon up the strength for a decent wave, and seagulls wheeled like windborne litter in a sky the colour of lead. This wasn't what he'd been promised. He was going to have words.

The old Park Royal hotel – known simply as the Park to its desperate inhabitants – was one of the few remaining buildings in the village of Lyncham, a village which didn't exist on maps any more, perched on a crumbling lip of Dorset coastline with a dark tangle of woodland separating it from inland and nothing ahead until France except the crawling shapes of distant, unreachable ships. Most of the rooms above and around him were empty, but enough were inhabited for him to know that he was not the only castaway to have been caught. He heard the screams and the noises they made at night, which also told him that not all of them were human, despite their outward appearances. The Tourmaline Archipelago was very wide – some said endless – and if half the stories he'd heard about the nightmarish creatures of its furthest islands were true, then he shuddered to think what lived in those rooms. Below, one of them shambled along the scree-shore, set to guard this shabby gulag from intruders. It felt like being in a zoo. He'd seen a zoo once, while on shore leave at the Royal Gardens on Blent, and the memory made his heart lurch with homesickness for turquoise waters.

He squashed it. That kind of thinking was apt to drive him insane. Sometimes they let him go walking on the beach, and he collected fossils which he lined up on the windowsill: ammonites and trilobites and echinoids, oh my. Things that had once been alive but were now stone. Like him.

Time settled in flakes of dust on his windowsill. He couldn't tell where the sky ended and the sea began; the world was a continuum of grey. Even the man he'd surfaced into had been a passionless button-pusher. Sometime he thought he could feel that man, deep inside, struggling and screaming to be free, but mostly he was silent, as if he knew that even this state was preferable to what his life had been before.

The Passenger heard it, then: the faint rumble of lift doors opening, footsteps on thick pile carpet, the jingle-slap of keys being tossed and caught.

Maddox, the Custodian.

Keys rattled at his door, and it opened.

'Good afternoon, Mr Simkin,' said Maddox. 'Ready for another outing, are we?'

The Custodian was a large, genial-looking man, well fed without being overweight, and always impeccably groomed. He gave the impression of having risen through the ranks of a career which had once involved the frequent application of physical violence, and that even though it wasn't part of his job description anymore, it lay close beneath the surface, like a reef under shallows. It was in the way his eyes flicked quickly around the room's interior before he entered, and the way he twirled a large bunch of keys around his forefinger, letting it thump heavily into his palm with each revolution. The Passenger had learned to be wary of Maddox the hard way.

'My name is Degan,' he replied. 'I am a naval rating aboard the Elbaite frigate *Suzerain*. How many more times?'

'As many times as it takes. Thanks, by the way – I'd love a cup.'

Resigned, Degan filled a kettle in his tiny en-suite and set it to boil, while Maddox poked and prodded with lazy insolence amongst his belongings. He picked up a piece of driftwood which Degan had been carving into a likeness of the Suzerain's winged mermaid figurehead.

'Been keeping busy, I see.'

'It bides the time.'

'There's only so much wanking a man can do, I suppose.' Maddox laughed – easy, friendly. *We're all mates here*, that laugh said. *All in the same boat together*. But flick-flick-flick went his eyes, looking for anything out of the ordinary. As if anything here could be. Maddox turned the carving over in his hands appraisingly. 'I suppose this must be what they call "outsider art", then. They don't come much more "outsider" than you, do they?' Degan was surprised at the sudden anger which flooded him, seeing Maddox pawing the likeness of his ship's goddess – a man like that wouldn't have lasted a day under Elbaite naval discipline. Afraid that the anger would escape him, he busied himself with mugs and milk.

'This is against regulations, you know that, don't you?' asked Maddox.

'Yes, sir.'

'Carving, paintings, stories, poems – anything about where you lot come from. You do know that.'

'Yes, sir.'

Maddox glared at him. 'Insolent little fucker, aren't you?'

'Yes, sir.'

The Custodian turned away and replaced Degan's carving on the windowsill. There might have been a smile curling the corners of his mouth, but when he turned back, it was gone.

The thing with the tea, Degan knew, was not just some kind of power game designed to remind of his place, and it definitely wasn't just a random pleasantry. Degan knew about tea because Roger Simkin – the accountant whose body he inhabited – knew about tea, just as he knew about hotels, and driving cars, and everything else about this grey, hollow world. But the more that Degan dwelt on thoughts of home, the less able he was to make use of Simkin's knowledge, and that made him useless to the mysterious Hegemony for whom Maddox worked. On the other hand, the more mired he became in Simkin's mundane existence and further away from Elbaite, the weaker became the powers which bled through from home. Credit where credit was due: the Custodian understood very well the balancing act which his assets like Degan had to tread.

And Degan liked his powers. On the Suzerain he'd been nothing more than deck-swabbing grunt, and even though he was a freeborn man, he was treated not much better than one of the galley slaves, but here... oh *here*, the things he could do. The things he had done – and willingly so. It felt good to be able to dish back a little of what he had to swallow here, even though it did nothing for his homesickness. Still, there it was: a winged mermaid or a cup of tea. Servitude whichever way you looked at it.

'You mentioned an outing,' said Degan, eagerly.

From an inside pocket Maddox brought out a large envelope which he tossed onto the bed. 'Chauffeur and retrieval duty,' he said. 'Nothing messy this time, you'll be disappointed to hear, unless you fuck it up. Go to the address, pick up the girl, bring her back. Easy as.'

'What kind of Passenger are we talking about?'

'Read the file. That's what it's for. In the meantime get that brew sorted, and I'll introduce you to your muscle in case you *do* fuck it up.'

Mugs in hand, they walked down the hallway towards the lift, which took them up a floor to where the 'muscle' was being held.

The zoo. Up here, no effort had been spent on maintaining the décor to a standard fit for human habitation. The carpet was filthy, the wallpaper peeling, and both carried the marks of damage caused by the Passengers that lived on this floor. Smashed plaster. Claw marks. Bloodstains.

'You ever see a hradix?' asked Maddox.

'No, sir.'

'Vicious, clever fuckers. Reptiles, but they live in trees. Think chimpanzee crossed with velociraptor, and you'll get the idea.' He stopped by a door, keys in hand, and looked back. 'You haven't got kids, have you, back where you come from?'

'No. Why?'

'Good. Some people have... trouble with this. Take a look.'

Degan peered through the fish-eye lens, which, as in all the doors on this floor, had been inserted back-to-front so that the exhibits could be inspected safely. It was gloomy inside; tatters of curtain were nailed across the window, but he could just about make out...

'Sweet Lady of the Islands,' he breathed, horrified and fascinated in equal measure.

It was a boy. Or at least, it had been a boy, once upon a time. Its hair was matted and unkempt, the hair of an animal which had long since ceased to tend itself properly – or, if Maddox was to be believed, didn't possess any in its natural state – and it was dressed in the remains of a public school uniform so filthy that it was impossible to tell what school it might have been from. Its mouth was a ravening, tooth-filled hole from which came a low animal growling. This rapidly escalated into a high yowl as it lunged at the door, only to be checked by a length of heavy chain anchored to the wall. It knew they were outside.

'Yeah,' grimaced Maddox. 'It's passengered in a ten-year-old kid. Having his tonsils out, would you believe it? Must have been dreaming about jungles and ended up close to one of the fuckers while it was hibernating, or something, when they brought him out of the anaesthetic. And here we are spending millions of pounds and thousands of hours trying to engineer just this kind of thing. Dumb fucking luck.'

He unlocked the door, and Degan gagged at the smell – the ripe, fetid stench of rotting meat. The creature went into an agitated frenzy, thrashing on the end of its chain and snarling at them.

Maddox took out a packet of extra-strong mints and tossed one to the hradix. It snapped the mint out of mid-air and crunched it down in two gulps, calming immediately. 'There's still enough of the kid left in there to be bribed with sweeties, though,' he added. 'How messed up is that?' He passed the packet to Degan. 'You might want to stock up on those.'

The hradix's eyes glittered with savage intelligence as they darted between the two men. Degan wondered if it understood what they were saying.

'What's his name?'

Maddox glanced at him sharply. 'Never you mind what its name is. All you need to know is that it's your insurance policy in case things go pear-shaped. We'll have it cleaned up while you sort out something from the car pool.'

'I thought you said this was a simple chauffeur job,' he said. 'Why am I going to need this thing?'

'The thing passengered in the girl you're going to pick up isn't from anywhere in either your world or this one. It's from Between. At the moment we believe it to be dormant. Dennis the Menace here is your last resort in case you're stupid enough to wake it up. Because it might just turn out to be even worse.'

PART TWO

CHAPTER 11
Berylin

1

Half a world away from Stray, as Bobbie and Allie dreamed of rain, Officer Berylin Hooper of the Oraillean Department for Counter Subornation stared up at the shabby red-brick façade of an ordinary-looking tenement building and tried to gauge what manner of nightmare was occurring inside.

The subornation Event at 473 Willoughby Terrace to which she had been called should have been small, localised, and essentially harmless – if the clatter reports from the Carden Constabulary were reliable – but she knew that this was extremely unlikely to be the case. Far from exaggerating the details, or even making them up in a superstitious panic like the rural authorities were likely to do, the city plod were so phlegmatic in the face of such things that they were liable to underplay its seriousness – mostly because they thought they'd seen it all before (which they hadn't, not by a long chalk), but also, she liked to think, because the DCS were that good at putting the genie back in the bottle. Which was why she wasn't going to take any stupid, complacent chances with one even as small as this.

She'd already ordered the tenements on either side to be evacuated, for a start. From the cynical smirks on the faces of the constables, she knew that they thought she was overreacting; either that or ordering them around simply because she was a woman and she could. She knew that she didn't impress them; she wasn't all that physically imposing, with her hair cut short rather than in the fashionable ringlets of the pretty young things one saw perambulating in Alexander Park, and her gentleman's trousers rather than a more respectable bustle and skirt. Well, let them smirk. There'd been few deaths in any of her cases, and only a handful of imbecilements – and that was a damned good track record for anybody.

The Carden fire brigade were standing by at close quarters in their red uniforms and shiny brass coal-scuttle helmets, with their big drencher chuntering away as it got up to pressure. So too the Beldam Unit. They were a bit more discreet, but no less capable for their stove-pipe hats and padded waistcoats; these were seasoned ward orderlies who dealt regularly with some of the most violently unstable patients in the Kingdom. The three groups of men had staked positions on three separate street corners as if preparing for some kind of bizarre three-way tug-of-war. Behind them, of course, strained the inevitable crowd of gawkers.

But neither fire nor insanity scared her half so much as the third danger for which there was no adequate preparation other than dogged, meticulous protocol, and so she called Sergeant Bloom over one last time.

'I'd like to double-check the residence status again,' she said.

'Double?' The Sergeant's boot-brush moustache corrugated as he sniffed sceptically. 'We've already been through it twice, ma'am. I think if anybody'd got in or out in the last half hour, we'd've seen 'em.'

'They say the third time's the charm, Sergeant. So charm me.'

He sighed and flipped through a sheaf of onionskin census forms for the tenement. 'Apartment 473,' he read. 'Drabble, Hugo Marthen, twenty-nine years of age, mechanist. Wife, Margaret, twenty-seven, lady's domestic. No elderly dependents, lodgers, or pets. Two minors; boy, Clive, eight; girl, Daisy, eleven.'

'The husband is at work?'

'No, ma'am.'

'No?'

'No – he's over there, lookin' a bit upset. Can't say as I blame him, meself.'

'Yes, of course. Let's have a word with him, shall we?'

Hugo Drabble was allowed forward from the cordon. He was pale, thin-faced, and grimy with soot and oil; a gawky denizen of Carden's labyrinth of back-to-back streets who had probably never ventured further than a few city blocks from where he was born. His eyes were red with worry. 'Are you the tezzer?' he asked hopefully.

She let the slang pass. 'Yes, sir. That I am. I want you to know that I am going to do absolutely everything in my power to get your family back safer than sound.'

'Oh, bless you miss,' the man snuffled, knuckling tears from his eyes with both hands so that they made cleaner streaks like drooping pigeon's wings down his cheeks. 'Thank you so much.'

'But I need you to help me.'

'Anything! Anything!'

'I need you to be as clear as you possibly can about exactly who is in your apartment. If it's just Margaret and the boys, and nobody else.'

'Meggie, miss. She's my Meggie.'

'Meggie, then. Is it likely that she would have taken the children out anywhere today – to the park, possibly, or a friend's for supper?'

'No, miss.'

'To your knowledge, was she expecting visits from any cleaners, tinkers, or any type of tradesman?'

'Not that I know of, miss.'

'Very good. You are being marvellously helpful so far, Mr Drabble. Please forgive what I am about to ask – I am neither a police constable nor a priest, and I am not in the business of condemning anybody legally or morally – but I also need to know if you have any lodgers or relatives living with you not counted in the official census, or children unregistered by birth, or whether it is likely that your wife may be receiving visits from other men, or women for that matter. In short, Mr Drabble, for the safety of all concerned and for no other reason, can I and my partner expect to find any other people in that apartment at all?'

'Why, of course not, miss.' The man plainly couldn't decide whether to be shocked, insulted, or just confused by her insistence – but then, he wasn't the one who was going to have to decide whether he was pointing his gun at a phantasm or a suborned human being when he got in there. She searched his face and watched his hands carefully for any signs of deceit and, finding none, nodded gratefully.

'Thank you very much, Mr Drabble.'

The husband was escorted back to the police cordon, and Berylin returned to her carriage, where Runce was unloading their gear.

'Typical plod,' he grumbled, hefting down a crate. 'No bloody help with the heavy work.'

William Runceforth was a dour forty-something, grey from the thinning pate of his angular head to the army issue socks on his feet, but what he lacked in youthful vigour – or human warmth – he more than made up for with two qualities she prized highly. The first, and most surprisingly for a man of his military background, was that he'd never exhibited any qualms about taking orders from a woman. The second was an almost total lack of imagination. Runce was a literalist to a frightening degree. Poetry, art, allusion, metaphor – all bypassed him completely, leaving him fiercely insistent on what he referred to as 'the bare bones, ma'am, just the bare bones', and even though it meant he was certain never to be promoted higher in the DCS than assistant investigator, his indefatigable pragmatism had more than once saved her life in the hazy flux of a bad subornation Event, when she couldn't distinguish between nightmare and reality.

'That's why I have an assistant, Runce. Don't be too hard on them – they're probably scared to bits of touching it. I would be, if I were them. And please mind your language. We're in public.'

'Beg pardon, ma'am.' He straightened up and flexed the small of his back.

'Are we set?'

'Yes, ma'am. Mirror stations are established, and the perimeter is holding at a steady eighteen kay-vee, tezlars are fully charged, and Buster has been fed.'

'Where is he? Here boy!'

Down from the carriage jumped a beagle, all flop-eared and loll-tongued, who sniffed eagerly around their feet and the equipment crates, pausing only for a quick pee up one of the carriage wheels. Berylin ruffled Buster's ears and clipped on his leash. 'Going to catch some ghosts, aren't we boy? Aren't we?' Buster grinned and licked her nose.

Runce humphed. He busied himself with a large satchel-like affair which gleamed with dials, grilles, bulbs and meters; fine-calibrating their settings. His job would be to monitor the extent to which the laws of physical matter had mutated within the subornation Event, as well as the speed and scale of any further change – what was referred to as the Event's protean vector, or simply its *pv*. It was crucial to know how inimical were the conditions inside and how apt they were to change. For her part, Berylin strapped the heavy battery pack of the tezlar pistol to her belt, ensuring that the flex cables swung freely. Only ever one tez per team; too many investigators had been killed or maimed hideously as a result of friendly fire from a partner who had panicked and mistaken them for a phantasm. Fire-retardant coveralls, thick goggles and rebreather masks completed their protective gear. Both gave their canisters of atomised *sal volatile* a few quick squirts to clear the nozzles and, looking like a pair of deep-sea divers, approached the door to the tenement building.

2

Runce, efficient as ever, stopped to check the mirror station by the main door, even though it needed no checking. In a handful of cases where a phantasm had been cornered and the investigators too slow to tez it, it had tried to make a break for freedom – not that it could survive long outside the subornation zone of its own creation, but it had caused significant damage and distress all the same. A circuit of mirror-stations – highly polished reflective metal plates carrying the same electrical charge that their tez-guns fired – prevented this, based on the well-documented observation that phantasms could not bear the sight of their own reflections. Nobody knew why. So much was unknown, and it frustrated Berylin because more and more often she felt like all she was doing was cleaning up the mess and not getting to the root of the problem.

They heard it as soon as they entered the ground floor lobby: the squeal and groan of a building's frame protesting at the stresses that were being caused by whatever the subornation Event was doing to the laws of physics up in apartment 473. Hairline cracks spiderwebbed the walls. The lobby and stairs were scattered with belongings dropped by the other tenants as they'd fled: clothing, toys, photograph frames. Buster sniffed at them and moved on. Broken glass crunched underfoot as they climbed steadily.

By the time they reached the fourth floor, those sounds had been joined by others, dim but distressing: screams, shouts, and discordant music. The lines of the hallway were subtly twisted out of true, as if perspective, or light, or gravity itself were being drawn to the door of 473.

'PV?' she asked Runce.

He checked the readings on his console satchel and so-so-ed. 'Maybe point-oh-four. Seems to be contained in the apartment.'

Good. No spillage. Nice and neat.

Buster had set up a low, insistent growling. Berylin wasn't alarmed; he was well-trained and knew that the noises didn't yet indicate a threat. It was simply the canine equivalent of a man muttering under his breath: 'Steady now, steady…'

They took station on either side of the door. From inside she could distinctly hear scratchy, echoing music – the kind of mindlessly cheerful burbling that bands played on Sunday afternoons – voices, like platform announcements, and a distressed shrieking which rose and fell. She raised her eyebrows at Runce. *Ready?*

He nodded.

She counted down with her fingers: 3… 2… 1…

He booted the door open and covered her as she went in. She would be vulnerable in the first few moments as her senses adjusted to what was inside, and he was ready to haul her out again if necessary. She'd do the same for him, and so they'd leap-frog each other into the madness.

a dizzying moment of disorientation, like coming off a carousel too fast while the world twisted around her in opposite directions, perspective contracting and expanding simultaneously, and a fragmentary glimpse of a perfectly ordinary sitting room before

It was a hospital, but like no hospital she had ever seen. Instead of the comforting glow of rose-coloured tiles under naphthene lamps, the walls were concrete and a sickly pale green. Lit garishly by glass tubes which spat and fizzed, many of them broken while others dangled from the ceiling, it looked more like an abattoir. The only reason she knew it was a hospital was because of the empty gurneys ranked along the corridor – evil-looking contraptions of levers, wheels and shackles which looked more like torture devices of the Hadrine Inquisition. All were empty except one.

It was impossible to tell whether the patient was male or female, young or old, because every inch of visible flesh was encrusted with barnacles. He or she was singing in a high, fluting voice more like that of a bird, nonsensical words ('I'm a mellow yellow jello fellow') which she didn't bother stopping to listen to. There was nothing to be gained by trying to make sense of anything in a subornation – the only thing that mattered was ending it. She kept a bead on it with her tez-gun and let Buster off the leash.

He ran over, sniffed the figure, and gave a couple of excited yips. She motioned to Runce. 'Salvol here.'

Runce took his canister of smelling salts and gave the figure a brief squirt, enough to make it jerk sharply. For a moment it flickered enough for them both to see the figure of a young boy lying on a settee, staring up at them with suddenly bewildered eyes.

'Wha...?' he said, and then the subornation closed in again, and the barnacled figure was back, fluting softly. Berylin decided he could be left safely – just so long as underneath it all he stayed awake, it would be fine. A subornation in daylight was generally not too much of a problem. At night, when the victims were almost all asleep, it was imperative that they all be roused, because the thing that scared her the most – more than death, fire, or insanity – was the danger that if any of them were asleep when the subornation was dispelled, they would be carried off with it and out of the world altogether. It was rare, but it happened. Once there had been a massive Event which had encapsulated an entire city block, and even though the census records were a reliable enough guide to whom should have been resident in any given place, there had been no possible way that the DCS were able to keep track of all the visitors, passers-by, and general transients in such a large area; the missing persons tally had finalised in the dozens. Dozens of living souls plucked straight out of reality and into Reason-knew where.

'Clive, the son,' she confirmed.

'Which just leaves the daughter and the wife.'

'Not to mention the phantasm.'

'Silly me,' he replied drily. 'There was me forgetting all about the one responsible for this. PV plus point seven inside.'

'Noted.'

What complicated matters was that in the protean flux of a subornation, it was impossible to tell the difference between the innocent human victims and the incorporeal entity which had created the event. Nobody knew what they were, where they came from, or even what they looked like, and some in the DCS believed that they didn't originate subornations at all but simply rode in on their wakes like sharks following boats. Berylin believed otherwise. She'd seen enough to know that they might not always be in control of what happened, but they were certainly responsible. One thing everybody agreed on, however, was that a good solid couple of thousand volts from a tezlar pistol was enough to send them packing. It was also enough to kill a person several times over, hence the absolute necessity to be sure with the salvol and a good old-fashioned sniffer dog like Buster.

She put him back on the leash, and he trotted on ahead.

3

The corridor ran straight towards a pair of large swinging doors, which, if this were a hospital, looked like they might belong to an operating theatre. Building specs put it analogous to the apartment's main bedroom. From inside, a voice was shouting something about angels, but it was hard to tell with the tinny muzak.

Something beeped on Runce's console. 'PV spike,' he warned.

They braced themselves for anything from a sudden rush of cold air to a total gravity inversion.

The air became opaque, blurring in drifting colours – umber, bruise, kaleidoscope – as if gauzy veils were drawing across ahead of them, and the corridor which had been straight now twisted and crouched in feral geometries so that as Berylin and Runce moved forward cautiously they were walking one moment, climbing the next, and sliding after that.

'It's no good, you know,' giggled a voice behind them. 'They'll never let you in dressed like that.'

Something which looked like a monkey's head on the body of a wooden toy train was goggling at them from halfway up the wall. It stuck its tongue out and crawled off, caterpillar style, at a fair speed. Giving chase, Berylin managed to get off one good dose of salvol and watched with satisfaction as the creature squealed and fell, flickering into the form of a young girl running away down a perfectly ordinary hallway. Then the hospital settled back around them like heavy canvas.

'That's the children accounted for, then,' Runce observed. 'Somehow it's worse with the little ones.'

'It's worse with everyone. Let's find Mrs Drabble and put an end to this.'

As they approached the operating room doors, they were able to clearly make out – between sobs and shrieks of insane laughter – a voice screaming over and over again: 'Angels in my head! They're putting angels in my head!'

Then, somehow, without knowing quite how it had happened, they were through and inside the operating theatre, and the scene which presented itself stopped her breath. Buster was barking continuously, furiously. Even Runce, who was about as superstitious as a piece of toast, shrank back against the wall, muttering 'Holy Mother and all the saints in Heaven.' In her short but shining career in the DCS, Berylin had witnessed scenes ranging from the most brutal atrocity and orgiastic licentiousness to those verging on holy revelation, but never anything which seemed to combine both in such a disturbing manner.

A man, the patient, lay shackled and screaming to the operating table, while over him towered a female figure of skeletal, ravenous appearance. Its limbs were so long and spindly that it had to crouch to being itself level with its 'patient', and even then its knees arched high up above its head like a spider. It had twin rows of wizened, pendulous teats from which a bitter fluid dribbled, battened upon by a crawling swarm of pale, blurred things which Berylin's eyes refused to acknowledge. But worst of all was what it was doing with its hands. It had six arms, two of which were restraining the writhing man while one fed handfuls of the pale things into a meat grinder socketed in his forehead, and another turned the handle, while the stinking juices of their entrails ran down the side and over his face like tears as he screamed 'Angels in my brain! They're putting…'

'Enough!' bellowed Runce. He snatched the tez-gun from Berylin's holster, aimed it at the towering monstrosity and fired.

'Runce, no!' She shoved the weapon aside as a jagged beam of purple-white fire raved from the barrel and scorched a smoking black trench along the wall (which, for just a second, was perfectly ordinary wallpaper). He stared at her, aghast. She reached for her salvol.

But they had caught the creature's attention. Roaring, it unfolded two impossibly long arms. One hand clamped itself around Runce's throat while the second slapped the spray canister from her hand and returned for her eyes, fingernails hooked into claws. She ducked, rolling, grabbing at the gun flex and reeling it in. Claws raked at her face, yanking away her rebreather mask. She gagged on the stench of rotting flesh and ammonia-like disinfectant. Acting on the crudest instinct, she aimed her tez-gun at the patient on the table and fired.

Energy seared through the air, frying it to ozone and igniting the man. For a moment he burned like a star and then just as quickly collapsed into blackness as if falling down a well, taking everything of the hospital with it.

Reality flooded back in a sudden restoration of normal air pressure which blew out every window in the apartment and would have burst Berylin's and Runce's eardrums had it not been for their earplugs. They were left slumped against the wall of a perfectly normal bedroom: paisley wallpaper, candlewick bedspread, wardrobe a-teeter with boxes – and a very dazed-looking mouse of a woman standing by the bed looking around in confusion.

'Ooh, I say,' she murmured. 'I do feel peculiar,' and fainted dead away.

CHAPTER 12

TO THE ISLANDS

1

'I swear those fish are following me,' said Bobby, peering over the side.

He and Allie were a day out from Stray, en route to the Islands for supplies. The Tatterdemalion II – or, as Allie affectionately nicknamed her, Tatters – was a single-masted fishing skiff so thoroughly patched and repaired that probably not a single one of her boards was original. Astern of her threadbare sail was a tarp cover which gave just enough shelter for two people to sleep, sit and eat; in the bow was cargo space currently stocked with their food, water and sacks of oyster shells, their mother-of-pearl being a highly tradable commodity. Most precious of all was the small bag of pearls which Allie kept on a string around her neck.

'Mm-hm.' She was on the tiller, apparently dozing. Her sunhat was pulled far over her face, and she looked like he imagined Snufkin would appear in a film if he was a she and played by Meryl Streep.

'No, seriously,' he insisted. 'It's those three from when I cut my hand. They've been following us since we left Stray.'

'Don't be silly,' she murmured. 'Fish don't track boats. Unless they're sharks. You haven't been upsetting any sharks, have you?'

'They're definitely not sharks. Truth to tell, I don't know what they are.' He peered closer. It was definitely the three fish which had made such a feast of his blood. The smallest of the three had protruberant eyes and looked like some species of blenny; the next possessed a flamboyant collection of fins and tail, which reminded him of the outrageous outfits of Carmen Miranda, and the third was a monstrosity from the lightless depths which was all jaw and fangs. 'I'm not even sure that one should be alive this far up,' he said. Igor, that was it – Professor Frankenstein's hunchbacked assistant. Blenny, Carmen, and Igor. The Three Fishketeers. But why were they following the boat? 'They're not tracking the boat,' he realised. 'They're following *me*. I think they want some more of my blood.'

'Oh yeah,' she nodded drowsily. 'Because that makes much more sense.'

'Watch.' He pricked the end of his finger with a knife and squeezed several ruby-red droplets into the sea. Just as before, they see-sawed lazily down through the water like pearls rather than diffusing in clouds, and the Three Fishketeers dashed to gobble them up. Apparently satisfied with that, they flashed away into the depths. 'See?'

'Mm-hm,' she replied, plainly not at all interested. From time to time she consulted a small plastic compass which looked like it had come out of a Christmas cracker – but he knew that her navigational instincts were razor sharp all the same. The boat was a miniscule speck in the immense, glittering blue desert of the Flats.

'Hang on a minute,' he said, taking back the line he'd been splicing before the fish arrived. 'Let me get this straight. Normally it's you and Seb on the supply run, yes? Because it takes two people to get back to the Stray.'

'Yep.'

'Because there's bugger all wind out here, and when the boat's fully loaded you have to mostly row back.'

'Got it in one, old sport.'

'So here's my question. I've told everyone that my plan is to find someone on Danae who can get me back to civilisation. I've made my goodbyes. I'm not coming back to Stray.'

'That's not technically a question,' she pointed out.

'Smart alec. Don't avoid the subject. My question is, how are you going to get back on your own?'

She raised the brim of her hat and tilted a dangerously bright eye at him. 'What – you think I can't look after myself just because we've fucked a couple of times?'

He winced. 'You know I don't like it when you talk like that.'

She flapped dismissively. 'Ya big baby.'

'And in any case, that's not what I meant.'

'Damn straight it isn't.'

'I meant, you're going to row it all back by yourself?'

'Meh. So it'll take a little longer, that's all. It's worth it to have you to myself for a couple of days.'

'I'm flattered.'

'You should be. I'm a fine lookin' woman.'

He grinned and went back to splicing his line.

'This civilisation of which you speak,' she said, after a while.

'What about it?'

'I don't mean to be blunt, and try not to take this the wrong way, but you know it ain't there any more, don't you?'

'Ah.' He nodded sagely. 'Very philosophical. Very zen. If a tree falls in the forest and there's nobody to hear it, and all that.'

'No, what I mean is, whatever home you're trying to get back to, it doesn't exist. You won't find it.'

'Is this supposed to be some kind of riddle game? I hope it's better than I-Spy. That got old fast. Something beginning with W, you say? Hmm, let me see. Ah yes, water!'

She sighed. 'It's okay. I don't really expect you to believe me. I'm telling you now because when we get to Danae, the first thing you're going to find is that there aren't any phones and no internet access to contact the "outside" world. There are no radios, no TV, and the one newspaper which does the rounds out here will tell you about wars and crimes in countries which you've never heard of but which sound kind of familiar all the same.

'You won't find anything remotely like a British embassy, that's for sure. Come to that, you won't find any Brits, or Americans, or Outer Mongolians, no matter how many of the tavernas you go into. You won't find anybody who even *knows* a Brit or an Outer Mongolian.

'So you're going to think fine, screw these insular hicks, and you're going to want to pay for passage on a fishing boat, but you won't recognise the names of any of the nearby places – even if you can find a map, and I'm pretty sure there aren't any on Danae – and the skipper won't recognise the name of anywhere you're trying to get to – Tahiti, Vanuatu, Fiji, whichever. Doesn't matter. It won't stop him taking whatever you can pay, of course, and he'll get you to the next island – probably Aura or D'unjin – and there the whole sorry situation will play itself out again.

'I'm betting that you'll have popped long before that, though. At some point you're going to lose it completely and go postal on the natives; you're going to start running around making a big fuss about why you're stuck in the middle of nowhere and how you just want to go home and what kind of fucking conspiracy is this anyway. Trust me. I've been there.

'Here's my point, Bobby: I don't need that shit. The locals don't like us Strays too much as it is because we don't belong here – we're *wrong* in a way I don't understand, but it's there all the same. We need to trade with them to survive, and I can't have you jeopardising that. I'm telling you all this so that when it goes down I'll be standing right by your shoulder, and you'll look at me and remember we had this conversation, and hopefully we'll all get to eat for the next month.'

Bobby thought about all of this as Tatters dawdled through the Flats, and there was nothing but the creaking of wood and lapping of water to fill the silence.

'If all of that is true,' he said at last, 'then where exactly are we?'

She looked at him full on for the first time. 'Let me ask you something else. Why has it taken you so long to ask that one simple question? I would've though it would be the first thing out of your mouth. You got close to it that first night, but never since. Why do you think that is?'

He frowned, puzzled. 'I don't know, now that you mention it. That's very peculiar.'

'Have you considered that it's because part of your mind simply doesn't want to know and is afraid to ask?'

'Alright then.' He faced her squarely. 'Where exactly the bloody hell am I?'

She shook her head, smiling. 'Oh no. You don't get that until I'm even halfway sure that you believe me. Until you go pop, anything I tell you is only going to do more harm than good. Rationing, remember?'

'Bloody rationing!' He threw down his half-spliced line in annoyance. 'Isn't there anything around this place I get for free?'

She cocked her hat at him again, but the gleam in her eye was different this time. 'Oh, I can think of something,' she said and reached for him.

2

It was a relief when Berylin finally received the summons from Director Jowett's office. A week's recuperation leave might be the prescription of the DCS' psyrgical department, and though in truth it helped her get over the immediate shock, it did little to alleviate the underlying problems, which had nothing to do with her job. Too much time spent rattling around in a house with too much space, that was the problem. Space which should have been a nursery or filled with the sound of male company. But Stephen was gone these ten years, finding it easier to blame her barrenness than admit his own inadequacy in the face of her more successful career. She'd had her dalliances then, to be sure, and asked for nothing from them except company and an assurance that the world was basically right and normal (even if she wasn't), but still, an empty house in autumn was a sad thing.

So when the call finally came, she was waiting in the office of Director Jowett's secretary half an hour early, trying not to notice the other woman's half-fearful glances as Berylin accepted tea and biscuits. The ritual completed, she was shown in.

She'd only ever met the head of the Kingdom's Department for Counter-Subornation a handful of times: once upon earning her warrant card, and twice more after having rescued important individuals from some nasty Events – those occasions having been attended by a certain amount of pomp and ceremony, in which she felt awkward and uncouth, and so it was even more of a relief to find that behind his doors he was thoroughly plain, modern, and down-to-earth. Timothy Jowett eschewed a politician's traditionally impressive moustache and ostentatious display of wealth in favour of a cleanly-trimmed goatee, conservative suit, and an office furnished along Modernist lines – all geometric patterns and plain, well-crafted furniture.

'Ms Hooper, isn't it?' He rose and shook her hand as she took a seat.

'Yes, sir. And thank you.'

'For?'

'Not calling me Miss.'

He smiled. 'Quite. You are recovering from the Event at Willoughby Terrace, I trust?'

'"Recovering" may be a little optimistic, sir, but I am – reconciled. Satisfied that the job was the best I could do.'

'An impressive one at that,' he replied, leafing through some papers on his desk which, she assumed, contained her report and those of the other emergency services which had attended the scene. It was a thick folder. 'This looks to have been a fairly straightforward case.'

'As far as such things go, yes, sir.' Straightforward. The man had no idea.

'Quite. I have only a few questions, and then I'm happy to sign it off.'

'What would you like to know, sir?'

'In your report you say that Sergeant Runceforth's first reaction was to tezlar Mrs Drabble, who had been suborned as a manifestation of...' he flicked through the papers, briefly at a loss.

'Lilivet, sir. A cannibalistic demon-goddess from Suva-Naheli, who dispenses wisdom but also kills indiscriminately. Children, usually.' She saw again the patient screaming *Angels in my brain! They're putting angels in my brain!*

'Charming. Sounds like she'd get along famously with my Aunt Phyllis. My question is, how did you know that this Lilivet was not the dreamer? Plainly it was the agent controlling the subornation – or at least Runceforth believed so.'

'Sir, Runce is the most experienced assistant I have ever...'

'Oh do calm down, Hooper. This is not about him. Though your loyalty is commendable.'

She relaxed somewhat. 'It was the hospital scenario, sir. I've never yet come across one where there wasn't some kind of torture or persecution involved. In such cases the phantasm is as much a victim of their own dream as the innocent bystanders who get caught up in it.'

'If I didn't know better, Hooper, I'd say that you were in danger of feeling some sympathy for them.'

'Not at all, sir. It was simply an observation. The balance of probability lay with the phantasm being the figure of the patient.'

'Balance of probability be damned,' he snorted, though not unkindly. 'It was a snap decision, a matter of instinct. You followed your gut reaction, and your gut was right.'

She fidgeted. 'Forgive me sir, but I don't see where this is leading.'

He fixed her with a regard which was uncompromising in its frank appraisal. 'You have a feeling for this sort of thing. One might almost say an affinity. That makes you uncomfortable, doesn't it?'

'Honestly, sir? Yes. It does.'

'Good. Victims of their own dreams or not, these things are abominations. For some reason you seem uniquely equipped to sniff them out, which is why I'm so annoyed about this.' He opened a drawer and took out a thick file, which he tossed in front of her. 'A few days ago the External Bureau was approached by an ambassador from the Amity – you are aware of where that is?'

'An alliance of island states in the Tourmaline Archipelago, I believe. There was some talk of war with Elbaite a year or so ago, but nothing came of it. Why are they interested in me?'

'Quite. Nothing came of it because something occurred in the middle of the ocean between Elbaite and the principal Amity island-state of Drava which rendered navigation impossible, and hence invasion, and so the Amity have been very happy to let things stay that way for the time being, thank you very much.'

'Are you talking about a subornation, sir?'

Jowett nodded grimly.

'But that's impossible. They must be mistaken. The longest Event ever recorded lasted only for a matter of hours. You're talking as if…' she trailed off, horrified at the implications.

'Months,' he confirmed. 'Possibly years. The details are sketchy.'

'Why in Reason's name didn't they do something about it?'

'In part because they lacked the technical expertise, but mostly because until now it has been politically expedient of them not to do so.'

'But if a ship should stray into it…'

'Well that's precisely it, isn't it? That's been the deterrent stopping Elbaite from launching its armada up to now.'

'Even so, sir, with the ocean being so large, it should be a simple matter to navigate around it.'

'Hooper, we're dealing with something a bit larger than an apartment, or even a city block. This Event is huge. It is miles across, and it is *moving*. It drifts across the ocean with the prevailing winds and tides, making predictions of its position all but impossible. Not only that, but it is also growing.'

'*Growing?*'

'It is starting to affect the Amity's own territorial waters, damaging their trade and their fishing, which is why after all this time they have come to us for help, and why your name is currently being spoken of in very high circles as the woman for the job.'

'Well, I'm flattered, of course, but there must be better qualified and experienced agents that you can send. Why, I've never been abroad, not even for a holiday. I can't believe that I'd be much use as a foreign consultant, or whatever the proposed role is. Surely one of the Collegium's researchers…'

Jowett looked disappointed. 'Please, Hooper, spare me the fake humility. This isn't a Ladies' Brigade meeting; nobody's going to turn their nose up at you for admitting what we both know: that you're damn good. I was asked to recommend a name. I recommended yours. Are you telling me I was mistaken to do so?'

'No sir.'

'Well then, let's have less of the mimsying around, if you please.'

'Yes sir.'

'You'll note that this is not being put to you in the form of a request. The External Minister and the Amity ambassador went to Charford together, and we all know how the old school tie network operates.' He made a face as if tasting something disagreeable. 'But I wanted to do you the courtesy of letting you know exactly how the wind blows, so to speak. The Amity have no desire to see this monstrous subornation abated – after all, it has kept a powerful adversary at bay for some time. What you are being tasked to do is investigate its expansion and find some way of halting it so that it does no further damage to their own interests.'

'You mean I'm…' she struggled to articulate the idea. It was so aberrant, so wilfully and appallingly wrong that her voice almost refused it expression. 'I'm to find a way of *preserving* it?'

Jowett nodded grim agreement. 'You will be given every possible assistance in this matter – equipment, personnel – simply list your requirements.'

'But sir!'

'And before you attempt to harangue me like my wife,' he overrode her, 'be assured that there is no way this Department will allow such a state of affairs to exist. Not while I sit in this chair, at least.'

'I don't understand.'

'Between these four walls, Hooper. Between these walls, understand? The Kingdom of Oraille will not sit idly by and allow a third-world nation state of fishermen, pirates and ex-slaves to militarise the subornation of reality, no matter how peaceful and defensive their intentions, nor how many times the External Minister let himself be buggered in the dorms by one of them. You will smile politely, complete your investigation with all possible diligence and thoroughness, but be compelled in the end to inform them sadly that there is nothing you can do, and, with great reluctance, you will destroy the abomination and allow war to take its natural course.'

'When you put it like that, sir, how can I refuse?'

'Hmm. Indeed. You may see Miss Fortescue outside for all the necessary files and requisition forms.'

'Very good, sir.' She stood to leave as he returned to his paperwork.

'Oh, and Hooper?' he added, without looking up.

'Yes sir?'

'That smirk on your face.'

'Smirk, sir?'

'Yes, the one that appeared during my rant about the buggering of senior court officials.'

'What of it, sir?'

'It was most unladylike.'

'Yes, sir, I daresay it was, sir.'

'That will be all, Hooper.' It was hard to tell, but he might have been smiling as she left his office.

3

On a blustery May morning in the twenty-seventh year of the reign of King Alexander VII, the tramp steamer *Spinner* set off from Jubilee Wharf in Tinmouth for a twelve-week scientific survey of the Tourmaline Archipelago. According to Berylin's paperwork, the *Spinner* was an unexceptional vessel: a converted fishing trawler of a type built by the thousands in the Coronsay shipyards, and to be seen in every port, large and small, from one coast of Oraille to the other. Almost the whole front half of her deck was wide and open with large hatches to the holds below for landing catches, while a wheelhouse stood amidships. From that, the superstructure and cabin housing extended back towards the stern, where a small wooden dinghy stood ready to transport her crew to and from shore. Just behind the wheelhouse rose a tall smokestack; the *Spinner* was powered by a seventy-nautical-horsepower, three-cylinder engine and boiler capable of getting her speed up to a respectable twelve knots in good weather. She'd seen some service during the Jassit Peninsula War, primarily as a support craft for hauling away the wreckage of destroyed cruisers, but with a short and exciting career as a minesweeper, and the military conversions which had been completed to her twin trawler booms made her perfect for Berylin's needs.

Officially she was being chartered by the Collegium for the purposes of collecting volcanic ore samples from many of the outlying islands in the archipelago, with a view towards identifying fuel reserves or deposits of precious metals for the hungry wheels of industry, and so the loading of many crates labelled simply 'scientific equipment' didn't raise any eyebrows. And if the behaviour of her crew did... well, that was scientists for you. The sound of hammering from belowdecks was so commonplace on a shipyard as to be completely unnoticed, and even the strange purple light glowing from the portholes was easily attributable to specialist welding gear. Space was even made for Buster, who accepted his promotion to the position of ship's mascot with sober diligence, sniffing every inch of the ship from bow to stern before pronouncing it seaworthy.

The Spinner made good time east along the coast, past toy-sized seaside towns and villages, weaving between the ketches and tugs which plied their busy trade back and forth across the Gulf of Kurra, between Oraille and Jassit – because people's memories for past grievances grew shorter as the chance for profit grew bigger, it seemed – and then out and north-east across the Dawn Sea towards Carax, with its granite headlands rising like the foreheads of giants. She took on coal and water at Vairstock, in the shadow of a steeply cloven fjord whose cliffs had been carved by ancient hands, so that when the frozen southern gales blew across it, they boomed and hooted like a mountain-sized pipe-organ made of stone. Further stops at Mardis, Rosburg, Dauncette, and Zana of the Seven Arches saw her journey ever northwards into increasingly balmy and humid weather, and she began to be escorted by families of Nederi: large intelligent fish who would leap out of the *Spinner's* bow-wave and glide for yards on vast fin-wings while calling to each other and those on deck in wordless song. They appeared to enjoy teasing Buster especially, who barked at them until he was sent to his kennel in disgrace. Some of the crewmen who were more adventurous – or superstitious, depending on your perspective – jumped in and swam with them, later claiming that they had been told their fortunes. Runce grumbled that the only prediction which a petitioner might believe of such 'oracles' was that he would die in a stupidly inevitable drowning accident, a point for which he was not thanked.

Crossing the equator into the northern hemisphere was marked by a celebration of bacchanalian drinking, cross-dressing and general lewdness which was in no way restrained by the presence of a woman on board, but nobody really felt that they were in the wider ocean until they passed the Babel Reefs.

These were a maze of beautiful but navigationally perilous coral reefs which rose into thousands of shimmering pillars, as if the microscopic creatures which built the coral had one day simply decided to build up towards heaven rather than along towards their fellows. All were busy with wheeling, screaming seabirds, and the same adventurous crew who had swum with the Nederi braved the gulls' sharp beaks to climb up and plunder their nests for eggs, which made a welcome change from the powdered variety. In this more rational age, the Babels were taken as a sign of how much higher the sea level had been aeons ago – some scientists even theorising that once upon a time the entire world had been underwater. Whatever the explanation, it was agreed that they were still growing. Some had tumbled and looked like the broken pillars of a long-dead civilisation. Others were carved by wind and weather into fantastical shapes: spindles, honeycombs, twisted and ribboned columns, or balanced gnarled globes on thread-thin necks. Ancient sailors, believing them to be set as a boundary to the curiosity of mankind, would sail no further for fear of inviting divine punishment.

Captain Mair guided his vessel with expert hands through the treacherous channels and out again into the open vastness of the Antaean Ocean. Nothing now lay between them and the Tourmaline Archipelago but another week of wide, empty horizons.

CHAPTER 13

FIELD TESTS

1

Runce found Berylin on the *Spinner's* high foredeck, gazing out at the approaching immensity of the Antaean. For a long while they simply stood together, feeling the thrum of engines through the steel and the spray of the bow-wave blowing back in their faces.

'You've been quiet the last few days,' he observed.

'Thinking.'

'Ah.' He nodded slowly. 'Thinking. Bad business, that. Best avoid it if I were you.'

'An easy thing for you to say, military man.'

He scratched his nose.

'Tell me, Runce, when you were in the army, where was the furthest you were ever stationed?'

'Pirogue, ma'am. Three months. Bloody horrible place. Everything made of bamboo, and the food went straight through you.'

'Thank you for that intimate portrait. Your wife must be a very remarkable woman, seeing you sent off into danger in all manner of places like that.'

'Mrs Runce is an army wife, ma'am,' he replied, elaborating no further, having obviously explained all that needed saying.

'Well, nevertheless, I wish I had taken the time to thank her before we left.'

'You'd only have embarrassed her.'

They stood awhile longer. Presently Netto, the ship's cook, appeared from the galley amidships and began tossing scraps of leftovers up into the air for the gulls that wheeled and dived overhead. Buster eyed them disdainfully from the shade of his kennel, having learned the wet and cold way that there was no catching them.

'You know,' she said, 'this is the furthest I've ever been from home.'

Runce frowned, and replied: 'I had a Sarnt Major who used to say "the further you are from home, lads, the less there is to see looking back".'

'Wise words.'

'Possibly. He was a complete bastard the rest of the time.'

She laughed. The continents of his craggy face drifted into an expression of mild surprise, as ever when he'd said something unintentionally funny – and it was always unintentional. Runce could no more crack a joke than a gun could play reveille. That was part of his charm: that he could always somehow manage to cheer her up without meaning to, and usually by being a humourless sod.

'I really only came to tell you that Harcourt says he *thinks* he's got the device finished.' Runce's disdain for the young Collegium engineer was evident.

'Excellent. Let's see what our pet boffin has created for us, shall we?'

2

A vessel like the *Spinner* normally slept sixteen crew: Skipper, mate, bosun, chief engineer, second engineer, two firemen, half-a-dozen deckhands, apprentice, clatter operator and cook. With so many people on board, secrecy was an impossibility, and so Berylin had left none of them in any doubt as to the expedition's true purpose – though maybe not the politics behind it. Not, she suspected, that Captain Mair would have cared a hoot either way. While she'd been happy enough for him to choose his own crew, she had engaged the additional services of a young engineering savant named Denton Harcourt who was attached to the DCS' technical support division. This had ruffled a few privileged feathers amongst those in the External Bureau who had their own nepotistic preferences for the position, but since Harcourt already knew the technology, he was probably one of the few engineers in the Kingdom she trusted not to blow them all to smithereens with some ambitious and cock-eyed contrivance.

The young man was a normally pale southerner whose sunburnt skin now glowed a painful red, and instead of the traditional savant's multi-pocketed grey coveralls he was dressed in short britches and a loose floral shirt of the style favoured in Zana – but despite his comical appearance he busied himself proficiently with attaching a network of fat electrical cables around the outside of the *Spinner*, while the deckhands put together and heaved overboard a large floating target tethered from the stern. Around the target was arranged a loose circle of fifteen fishing buoys, all heavily customised with mirrored panels, copper coils, capacitor blocks, and other technological encrustations at whose function Berylin could barely guess.

Its appearance was greeted with laughter from the rest of the crew, and even she was forced to suppress a smile. Someone had painted on it a crude but accurate portrait of Runce looking suspiciously like an intimate part of the male anatomy.

He grunted when he saw it. 'Someone's a proper bloody artist, aren't they?'

Harcourt took off his glasses and polished them in embarrassment. 'They threatened me,' he explained, indicating the sniggering deckhands.

'I'm sure they did.'

'You asked for something to contain a subornation at sea,' Harcourt said to Berylin. 'Obviously the electrical conductivity of the water itself proves the most significant obstacle, but what you see here is, on a small scale, something which should suffice.'

'Does it work?'

Harcourt considered this, seemingly for the first time. 'It works in theory,' he ventured.

'Let us see if reality agrees, shall we?'

The young engineer relayed orders to the engine room, who put on more steam, powering a large dynamo which in turn fed the capacitors on the buoys. His hand hovered near a large switch as the charge built, and a deep humming of electrical energy grew in volume, like the swarming of a million wasps under their feet and in the air all around. The crew glanced at each other nervously. Buster whined and disappeared below. Glowing candles of St Elmo's fire sprang into life at the point of each spar and strut.

'Do you think…' started Berylin.

'Wait!' Harcourt was peering intently at a bank of instrument meters, whose needles were trembling disturbingly close to their red sections. 'Almost there,' he murmured.

The buzzing, now very loud indeed, was attended by a crackling which sounded like the air itself as about to catch fire, and she felt her hair begin to stir and rise. She was about to order him to turn the thing off before it killed them all, when he shouted 'Now!' and threw the switch.

Purple lightning arced from one buoy to the next, burning away the insulation from the cables and destroying several of the mirrored panels in a series of explosions which sent the onlookers ducking for cover from flying shards. These were followed closely by a fine rain of seawater and blackened fragments of electrical equipment pattering to the deck.

Cautiously, Berylin raised her head.

The water inside the circle was steaming, but the circle itself was no longer intact; several of the buoys were nothing more than blackened cinders, and two had exploded completely. The wooden target was undamaged, except by debris. As she watched, a dozen dead fish floated to the surface.

'Cheer up, son,' said Runce, patting the stricken-looking Harcourt on the back as he headed below. 'At least you've caught us dinner. And cooked it, too.'

3

'This is absurd,' said Captain Mair, as they ate a forlorn supper in the officers' mess that evening. 'Even if you could get it to work – which I'm sure you will,' he added hastily, seeing Harcourt turn a deeper scarlet than he already was, 'how big a device would you need? We've been told that the subornation zone is miles across. *Miles.* You'd need thousands – maybe dozens of thousands – of those buoys, and there's no possible way they could be kept functioning. The cost in man-hours alone would be huge. The

Amity must know this. They might not have our level of know-how, but they're not stupid.'

Harcourt shook his head. 'I can't believe that they would simply waste time and effort on such a futile undertaking. It must be possible.' He'd barely touched his fish and was absently doodling equations on his napkin. The officers' mess was small but well furnished; they were dining off decent crockery and white linen and drinking a clear white Rozelle from actual glasses. Mair had done well for himself out of the contacts he'd made during the *Spinner's* requisition as a minelayer, and he'd taken full advantage of Berylin's DCS expense budget, it seemed.

'You assume that the point is to succeed,' said Berylin.

'Why on earth would they expect us to fail?' demanded Mair.

'I have a suspicion that neither success nor failure are anywhere near as useful to them as the sight of an Oraillean survey vessel steaming around in contested waters, flying their colours.'

Harcourt looked shocked. 'You think this is political? That they would use an Event like this for nothing more than cheap point-scoring?'

Runce spoke for the first time that evening. He'd forgone the crystal and was sipping wine from his battered army-issue tin mug. 'I'm assuming you were bullied at school.'

'What does that have to do with it?'

'Just that you should know better than anyone that when you're little, becoming chums with the big boys is a very good tactic for keeping the bullies away. Or provoking them into doing something stupid.'

'Dear Reason,' the engineer murmured. 'They might very well be *that* stupid.'

'But Elbaite will never believe that Oraille will take sides in another regional dispute,' protested Mair. 'Not after Jassit.'

'Of course they won't,' she replied. 'The Amity knows this. And Elbaite knows that they know, and so on, ad nauseum. It's called brinkmanship – they're flicking each other to see who flinches first, not because they actually think the other will do anything about it, but so that each Minister of War can outface the rivals in his own court. It doesn't matter who you're at war with, just so long as you are at war.'

'Not if you're one of them as is doing the fighting,' put in Runce, darkly.

'Exactly. Regardless of who wants what from whom, there are innocent people caught up in the middle of this – in the middle of that subornation – and they're our first priority, no matter what their nation. As far as we possibly can, we'll be nice and polite and play everybody's games by their rules, but here's the bottom line: our job is to ascertain the extent of whatever is out there in the Tourmaline Archipelago and put a stop to it. Nothing can be allowed to compromise that. *Nothing.*'

The change which came over her expression was startling. The lines of her face had hardened around an intense glare which seemed focussed on something far beyond the walls of this room; the expression of something relentless and implacable scanning a distant horizon. Something predatory. The three men shared an uneasy look and finished their meal in silence.

CHAPTER 14

DRAVA

1

Four days out from the Babel Reefs they saw smudges of land on the north-eastern horizon and passed the first Dravanese fishing boat. The fisherman stopped to gawp at the approach of the great steel-hulled monster which chuntered past, billowing smoke and steam and making his tiny single-masted ketch bob like a cork in its wake.

Only a few island-states of the Tourmaline Archipelago possessed the werewithal or the inclination to sustain steam technology; the absence of significant coal or iron reserves – as opposed to an abundance of wood – making it prohibitively expensive to maintain. A handful of powerful individuals ran such vessels, purely as status symbols, but steam ships were still rare enough for their appearance to cause small children to run screaming into their mothers' skirts, for old people to mutter that no good would come of such things, and for the hearts of young men to quicken with the excitement of adventure and distant lands. One of the deckhands was overheard to remark to another that by the time word of their arrival had reached Drava, the tale would have each of them with two heads and the Hooper woman swinging bare-breasted from the rigging – for which he earned a tirade from Captain Mair and a day's duty in the bilge.

They passed dozens of small islands before they even came in sight of their destination. Some rose in steep, forested slopes with villages clustered safely at the edges, to forbidding peaks which smoked ominously and were wreathed in clouds of their own vapour. Others were labyrinthine eyries of limestone arches and stairways where people lived in houses carved directly into the cliffs. Many were uninhabited – little more than strips of sand and jungle a few feet above sea level – but even so they saw villages built on stilts over less ground than that, apparently rising straight out of the crystalline waters. By no means were all of them mapped. Not all of them could be. Some had coastlines which changed with the seasons or phases of the moon. Some were nomadic, floating on a bedrock of pumice at the mercy of tide and weather. Berylin even saw one island which appeared to be floating in the sky – by which miracle of Natural Law she couldn't begin to imagine – and tethered to its earth-bound cousin by cables and rope ladders which the inhabitants used to climb up and down on their daily business.

But it was the ocean itself which was the most wondrous sight by far. She had never seen such colours, nor imagined their existence. A childhood spent in drab, rainy Oraille, with the occasional family holiday outing to grey seaside resorts like Trowsby or Codmaston, had left her unprepared for the overwhelming variety of hues which gave the Tourmaline Archipelago its name. She lost hours staring at the shimmering turquoise water shot through with shoals of opalescent fish, and in the shallows where the underlying sand changed it to watermelon and citrine. In several places she swore she could see gold coins strewn all over the sea bed; 'nixie gold', Mair called it, explaining how the first explorers had lost so many men to drowning in pursuit of it that for centuries thereafter mariners believed it to be a trick of mischievous water sprites. Harcourt theorised that it was more likely due to a combination of light refracting through sea-water and reflecting from some peculiar arrangement of mineral crystals in the sand, and doubtless he was right, but something in her mourned the loss of 'nixie gold' as an explanation.

Above all, she longed to swim in these waters – to immerse herself in their pure, crystalline beauty – and more than once gave serious thought to abandoning the rules of propriety which forbade it and simply diving right in. But the Captain warned that his men, though basically decent and well-mannered, had spent nearly three weeks at sea, and the sight of a bathing woman would be a challenge to ship's discipline which he wished to avoid if at all possible. She couldn't have cared tuppence for his prurience, but when he also pointed out the black, triangular fins which were often to be seen in these waters, she resigned herself to staying high and dry. Slapping a cheeky sailor was one thing; she didn't think it would be so effective with a shark.

2

Berylin and Captain Mair were in the high wheel-house, looking at their somewhat sketchy charts of the region and discussing likely areas for the subornation to be drifting, when Runce appeared.

'Welcoming committee,' he said simply. 'Dravanese patrol.' And left.

On deck, they found that the *Spinner* was being hailed by a sleek and swift-looking two-masted war sloop. She flew Amity colours: twenty-three stars of the island states against a blue field, topped by the crown-and-nederi crest of Drava. Marines in azure uniforms aimed long muskets at them, and the gun-ports on her single row of cannon were open.

'Ware, foreign vessel!' hollahed an officer. 'State your intentions in these waters!'

'We are a survey ship out of Oraille, come at your country's request,' called Berylin in reply. 'I was told that you would have orders expecting us.'

There was a moment of consultation aboard the sloop before the officer reappeared. 'It is so. You are most welcome, friends from Oraille. Please allow us the honour of escorting you safely to harbour.'

Runce murmured: 'That's the most polite way I've heard anybody say "keep your hands where I can see them and don't try anything funny". They've got manners, this lot, at least.'

3

On their charts, Drava looked a bit like a knight on a chessboard, with a long spine of mountain range running the length of the mane and around the base, sending out spurs of lower ranges into the forested foothills and arable lowlands of the horse's head and chest. A wide river flowed into the bay where these met, and at its mouth was the city of Bles Marique, built on the many rocky islets of the river delta and linked together by arched bridges and causeways. It was a city of towers and tall houses, steeply winding streets and precipitous stairs. Dozens of ships rode at anchor or were moored at the long fingers of stone quays, with scores of smaller, flat-bottomed boats poling around between them, ferrying cargo and people under the bridges and around the city islands. In one part of the harbour – heavily protected by ramparts, towers, and a great sea-chain – they could make out the tall masts of many war vessels.

As they approached, there was a terrific plume of black smoke from amongst the warships, and steaming out from their midst came the heavy bulk of an ironclad. Plainly it was the pride of their armada and sent out to both greet and impress the visitors, even though its massive riveted plate armour and paddle-wheel propulsion were decades behind Oraillean technology, and it was jarringly ugly compared to the streamlined grace of the other Dravanese sailing vessels. On its deck, ranks of marines stood at attention with their steel breastplates gleaming mirror-bright and their long muskets at order arms.

At their head stood a flamboyantly dressed civilian in a frock coat, pantaloons and broad-brimmed hat, which he swept from his head in a gesture so extravagant that, had it been fitted with any sort of a blade, would have surely caused dismemberments and decapitations amongst the nearby soldiers.

'Welcome!' he called. 'A thousand times welcome to our most excellent friends and allies from the south. I am Matalo Cheyne, cultural liaison to the Conclave of Drava and the Union of Amicable Island Territories, on whose behalf I am sent to extend to you the freedom of our city and invite you to a feast this night in honour of your arrival. Might I know if I am addressing the esteemed Sir Berlin Hooper?'

Berylin sidled up to where Harcourt was watching proceedings from the ship's rail, and nudged him. 'Over to you, Sir Berlin,' she said under her breath.

He jumped and stared at her in terror. 'What – *me*?'

'They're expecting a man. Don't worry, I'll put them right, but I'm not going to embarrass this fellow Cheyne in front of his subordinates. Nice and polite and playing by their rules, remember?'

'But I'm not... I don't...'

He spluttered through some polite formalities which Berylin fed him from aside, and if Cheyne found anything jarring about the behaviour of the stammering young man he was, of course, too courteous to let anything show. Presently the Dravanese ironclad withdrew and moved to escort them on the other side from the patrol sloop as they entered the harbour.

In the meantime, a very different sort of welcoming committee had formed on a neighbouring civilian quay: fishermen, merchants, goggle-eyed children, and a flock of whores who cooed and flashed their glitter-painted breasts at the crew. It was a testament to Captain Mair's discipline that he was able to control the men long enough to get the ship moored properly. When he finally had them lined up, agitated and grinning, he scowled at them thunderously.

'Right,' he growled. 'You know the rules. One: end up in jail and nobody's coming for you. Two: whores only. No civilians, or I'll fucking geld you myself. Got that?'

'Yes, sir!' they chorused.

'Fine.' He waved them off. 'Go, enjoy the sights of this exotic land.' He turned, found Berylin listening to this, and blushed scarlet. 'Begging your pardon, ma'am. My language just then...'

'It's quite alright, Captain. I find your concern for your men's well-being touching. But will you not be going ashore too? I mean, obviously not for the same, ah, that is...' Now it was her turn to blush.

'No, ma'am. I'll stay here and keep an eye on the old girl until things die down a bit. When the lads have got it out of their system, so to speak, I'll be able to go and have a quiet drink somewhere.'

They were both rescued from this conversation by the official armed escort, which arrived and began breaking up the crowd by the generous application of musket-butts, opening a space for the widely beaming visage of Cultural Liaison Matalo Cheyne.

4

Berylin had brought precisely nothing resembling the kind of evening dress she imagined one might wear to an ambassadorial banquet. Rather naively, she had assumed that her interactions with Dravanese officialdom would stretch no further than the scientific and investigatory – it simply hadn't occurred to her that there would be a diplomatic dimension, and while she liked a pretty dress as much as the next girl, she detested official functions and positively loathed being the centre of attention at them. Reluctantly she prevailed upon Cheyne to provide her with assistance for such a purchase – what in the upper circles of Oraillean society would have been called a dress maid – in response to which he sent along his younger sister Meria, who was so deliriously excited by the whole affair as to be practically inarticulate half the time. Berylin began to allow herself the tiniest guilty thrill at being treated like minor nobility, and together they toured the dressmakers' establishments of Bles Marique's more fashionable quarter.

There were no department stores such as she was used to along the traffic-thronged thoroughfare of Bertram Street back at home in Carden. Merchants conducted their business over long counters opening directly from their ground-floor workshops onto the street, so that in the case of dressmakers, she could watch the seamstresses at work and marvel at the rich profusion of colourful fabrics which were stacked everywhere in rolls and bolts.

Trying a dress on was in itself an exciting novelty, conducted in a small room off one side of the workshop. The concept would have been scandalous in Oraille, where one took one's purchase home, tried it on in respectable privacy, and if it proved unsatisfactory had the proprietors send a boy around to collect it. She couldn't deny a certain exhibitionistic thrill at undressing in a strange room, which was enhanced by the cut of the garments themselves. They were looser and freer in this much warmer climate, low in the neckline where Oraillean dresses were high, fastened with laces and ribbons instead of clasps and buttons. She let herself be guided entirely by Meria as to taste, and settled on a moderately conservative gown of a material called seasilk which shone like opals and flowed along what curves she had before descending to a short train. It felt wonderfully like she was wearing a waterfall. More than happy with the result, she returned to the apartments which Cheyne had arranged and thanked her for a lovely day.

'Oh no, my lady,' Meria objected. She had steadfastly refused to use Berylin's first name all day; it was unthinkable, she'd said. 'Why, we haven't even begun to think about your hair!'

5

As it turned out, the banquet was every bit as lavish and exotic as anything her imagination could have furnished, and she felt that she acquitted herself rather well – that was, up until the end.

There were dozens of dishes, mostly different permutations of fish and fruit, all of which she was able to heap praise upon quite honestly – even the ones which she found too spicy for her southern palate (what was it about hot countries that they felt the need to make their food hotter still?) but which Harcourt said he preferred. She'd dragged him along in his best savant's robes as much for moral support as to satisfy the expectations of her hosts, and it was hard to say which had alarmed him more: the enforced bonhomie or the prospect of being her 'plus one'. Fortunately, the other guests took his awkwardness for gravitas and nodded respectfully at his every utterance. There were sincere and fulsome speeches praising the long friendship between their two nations, et cetera, and she was able to reply courteously enough to avoid provoking an actual war, so that was good. It was only when conversation began to relax between neighbours, after the third dessert and before the first of the liqueurs, that she ran into trouble be being asked to hold forth on a subject which, ironically enough, she was most qualified to speak: the nature of subornation. Her interlocutor was the Dravanese First Minister – a large man called Lidan, who in his prime would have been athletic but now simply sprawled. He was also extraordinarily hairy, with black wiry curls of it peeping at cuff and collar as if he were losing his stuffing. At first, he had directed his questions at Harcourt.

'I am curious, sir,' he boomed, 'as to the Oraillean understanding of the phenomenon of Visitation – what you would call *subornation*.'

In reply, Harcourt had simply tilted his glass at Berylin and said 'My apologies, sir, but Officer Hooper is your expert there.'

'Really?' Lidan turned to her in great surprise. 'I had no idea that the women of your nation were so learned.'

'More than learned,' she responded. 'Don't tell him this, but I actually outrank him.' She'd been aiming for a tone of conspiratorial levity, and sure enough Lidan laughed, but something about the indulgent sound of it annoyed her. When he answered 'A fair jest from a fair lady, to be sure,' she understood why: he'd not been laughing at her but at the idea that she could be Harcourt's superior – or, presumably, any man's.

'What fascinates me the most about it,' she continued, as if he hadn't said anything, 'is the wide variety of terms used to describe the same thing: subornation, geopossession, haunting. Take *visitation*, now. Not a word that's heard very often these days. I would never have pegged the First Minister of so large and flourishing a nation for a mystic.'

'You find it hard to believe that a man of God can also be an effective administrator of worldly affairs?'

'No more so than that a woman can be an effective investigator of otherworldly ones,' she countered.

He acknowledged the point well scored. 'Or indeed a debater. My apologies if I have caused offence. If I spoke out of turn, it was simply from surprise, for in Drava a beautiful woman will have armies of men falling over themselves to provide for her, while a clever woman will have them working under her – it is not common in my experience to meet a woman who is both.'

She accepted with a gracious nod and a small smile.

'But there,' he continued. 'An interesting word of your own. "Investigator". Such a cold, procedural term for dealing with something so esoteric.'

She laughed. 'Well, I must congratulate you on having found possibly the best understatement I've ever heard to describe it. You are correct, though – it is procedural. A hundred years ago, my job would have been done by a priest with bell, book and candle rather than electrostatic technology, probably killing as many innocents as he saved. Did you know that they used to burn entire villages to eradicate cases of what the Hegemonic Church called "demonic infestation"? Is that what you mean by "esoteric", perhaps?' This was possibly a little harsh, but at least it wiped the condescending smile from his face. He seemed to look at her properly for the first time.

'What I mean, my lady,' he answered carefully, 'is that the phenomenon of subornation, as you choose to call it, is an ineffable mystery of God's universe, which – though we may deplore the injury done to innocent lives – no amount of steam-power or lightning guns will ever truly penetrate.'

'I have no desire to penetrate anything, my Lord Lidan. I am not a savant or a theologian. My job is simply to make bad things go away.'

To her immense surprise, Harcourt interjected: 'The procedure, steam-power and lightning guns with which she does so are the fruits of our nation's Great Mechanisation, which has been achieved, in part, by casting aside the medieval superstitions of our forebears.' She winced.

'Then I come back to my original question,' replied the First Minister. 'If these subornations are not demons, then what are they? Please, you would flatter a superstitious medieval man with the benefits of your great mechanised wisdom.'

She caught the dangerous undertone in his voice and tried unsuccessfully to warn Harcourt, who ploughed in, oblivious.

'Are you familiar with the psychodynamic theories of Professor Falaise?'

'A little, in passing.'

'He was a psyrgeon at the end of the last century, working to help victims of subornation recover from the trauma of their experiences – you must understand that the therapeutic methods of the time were extremely barbaric. Patients were subjected to forcible restraint, had holes drilled in their heads and even parts of their brains cut out – all sorts of horrible things. Anything the patients said about their experiences was discounted as nothing more than insane babbling – the nightmare reactions to an unspeakable horror – but Falaise was the first to take the obvious step of entering an active subornation zone to see how much of their testimony could be verified. When one reads his early case notes, one cannot escape the impression of reading the diary of an explorer discovering an entirely new continent – and in many cases this was literally the case. The dangers which Officer Hooper and other members of the DCS face – with all of their equipment and support – he walked into willingly, armed with little more than a notebook and a stopwatch.'

'You sound like you admire him a great deal.'

'I do. His bravery and tenacity in the face of received scientific wisdom telling him that he was wrong. Because it was all true – every word of the patients' accounts. The nightmares and dreamscapes which they described were not trauma-induced distortions but accurate recollections of events in which they had been forced to participate. Somehow, by a mechanism we still don't understand, certain people's dreams impose themselves on areas of waking reality in such a way as to incorporate the people and places within those areas into the dream's narrative – effectively suborning them for its purposes, hence the term.

'Falaise identified a range of typical narrative building blocks that he called *tesserae* – which combine, recombine and mutate to give the dream narrative its often chaotic structure – and the *actants*, who are the character functions that the victims are suborned into performing. He developed the protean vector scale to measure the speed and extent to which these dream features change. Also, every dream has a *phantasm* who is responsible for the conditions within the subornation, though there are conflicting theories as to whether or not they have conscious control over what happens.'

'What do you think, Miss Hooper?' asked Lidan

'When you are caught up in the shifts of a subornation it is impossible to tell whether any given figure is the author of the Event or a suborned victim,' she explained. 'In my experience the phantasm is almost never aware that he or she is dreaming at all. In many cases it is actually as much a victim of its own nightmare as the people caught up in it.' Clear in her memory was an image of the man with worms being ground into his skull. *Angels in my brain! They're putting angels in my brain!* She shuddered and gulped more wine.

'I note that you refer exclusively to nightmares and fear, and the trauma of being overtaken by another person's dream,' he observed. 'But there must be more positive dreams, must there not? Dreams in which miracles occur? In which we may fly or see our departed loved ones or converse with angels?'

'They are dreams, to be sure, but daydreams – nothing more. They are nothing like the awfulness which grins and dances behind our eyelids while we sleep.'

'That is very poetic, if somewhat grim, for someone who claims to be a mere functionary. I do not think that you are as coldly materialistic as you would like to appear.'

'Thank you for the compliment – I think. Hegemonic Church doctrine would once have had us believe that they are visitations from the powers of heaven and hell and pinned the blame for them on the sinfulness – or otherwise – of those who were afflicted. There is an emerging Rationalist school of thought at home which contends that they come from human dreamers in an entirely separate world existing alongside our own called the Realt. Savant Harcourt holds to this view, don't you?'

Harcourt blushed, as if having had some secret vice exposed. 'It explains much of the observed phenomena which cannot be accounted for by orthodox...'

She waved his sputtering away, though not unkindly. 'But to my mind that's just as mystical and unnecessary an explanation. I'm sorry, my lord, I have seen too much real pain and injury inflicted on too many real people to be under any illusions as to the nature of subornation; what you hear as poetry is nothing more than simple outrage. I loathe and despise the authors of these Events for the way they arbitrarily impose themselves on people's lives and the things they force them to do – wherever they're from. It is a violation, my lord, as plain and brutal as that, and I cannot abide it. I *will* not abide it.' She drained the remains of her wine and put the glass down a little too heavily. The air seemed very thick and warm around her.

The First Minister topped up her glass again. 'You are convinced, then, that such subornations are entirely injurious. Nothing more.'

'I have yet to see evidence to the contrary, my lord.'

Lidan considered this for some time. 'I wonder,' he said eventually, 'if you would be interested in seeing how a small nation such as Drava cares for the victims of its own, ah, violations.'

'Please,' she shook her head. 'You are very polite, but I am sure that the last thing your people want is an arrogant Southerner like myself poking around, trying to hide her condescension at your supposedly primitive psyrgical methods.'

'Oh, I think you'll find that we are not so thin-skinned as that, Miss Hooper.'

She blinked, taken aback, and kicked herself for allowing the wine to dull her wits. How had she managed to offend him? 'I'm sorry, my lord, I didn't mean…'

'Yes you did,' he interrupted, though not ungently. 'To expect otherwise would be unreasonable – and undesirable. Careful politeness may suit us diplomats, but for those like you, who are trying to shed light into the dark corners of the human soul, it is worse than useless. Were you not so forthright, you might not be so able. Jowett's recommendation was well made.'

'You are too generous.'

He laughed. 'Oh don't spoil it now, I was just beginning to like you!'

'Very well then.' She straightened up and fixed him with her most arch look. 'I would be delighted to accept your kind invitation, First Minister. I am indeed extremely curious to see how the rest of the world copes with the curse of subornation – and rest assured, I shall be as patronising and supercilious as everybody expects. I wouldn't want to disappoint my most gracious hosts, after all.'

'Excellent!' He beamed, and she caught a tantalising glimpse of the handsome man he must have been in his youth. 'There is a sanatorium in the mountains a day's ride from here; the Hospice of Bles Gabril. I shall have Cheyne arrange transport and send for you tomorrow morning, if that is convenient.'

'That will be perfect. It will take my crew more than a few days to supply for our journey to the Flats, and I shall leave Savant Harcourt here to liaise with your people regarding the necessary technical details.'

Talk turned to other, more frivolous matters, and at the evening's end, they bowed and parted amicably, but as she and Harcourt returned to the *Spinner* along the lantern-lit boulevards of Bles Marique, he said 'So what exactly happened between you and the First Minister? Did we just make an ally or an enemy?'

'I'm not sure,' she replied. 'He's offered to show us how the Dravanese deal with subornation.'

'Then I'd say take Runce with you and pack for trouble.'

'But subtly.'

'Subtle trouble?' He tugged at his formal collar uncomfortably. 'Politicians,' he muttered. 'Give me mind-eating demons any time.'

CHAPTER 15

THE MIRACLE OF BLES GABRIL

1

Berylin, Runce, Matalo Cheyne, and a small retinue of liveried servants set out on horseback from Bles Marique at dawn the next day. Runce had packed his pv-satchel and the fully-charged tez gun carefully out of sight.

The sun lifted veils of early morning river mist over the city's rooftops in gauzy plumes which quickly burned away, and choruses of crickets shrilled in the dry grass on either side of the main road which followed the broad sweep of the Barra River, out through patchworked fields, vineyards, olive groves, and up towards the island's mountainous interior. As the day grew, so did the temperature, and Berylin soon began to wish that she'd dressed in the loose silks that Dravanese women favoured, rather than the heavy cotton of her customary travelling clothes. Yellow dust from the sun-baked road hung in a perpetual haze about them. Buster trotted happily alongside, tongue lolling, delighted to be able to exercise his legs on solid ground for a change.

They passed through many riverside towns bustling with farmers, fisherfolk, and the crews of huge log rafts being poled downstream to feed Bles Marique's insatiable demand for ship timber. Similarly to its warlike rival Elbaite, the island of Drava was large enough to boast a variety of natural resources such that she could be self-sufficient if necessary. Fishing villages along the coast, and small market towns in the agricultural hinterland behind them, fed mining and logging towns higher up. The Barra's tributary streams – some of which were large enough to be rivers in their own right – were crossed by stone bridges with high, vaulting arches, and at one of these they left the Barra to follow a stream which soon led them up and out of the cultivated river valley, foaming as it tumbled out of the forested uplands. The trees were strange to Berylin. They had coarse, dagger-like leaves and a peculiarly pungent smell, and their bark hung in tattered strips from the trunks as if even they found the heat intolerable. She guessed they were eucalyptus, though had never seen one in real life before. Buster bounded to and fro, gleefully stuffing his nose full of as many new and exotic odours as he could.

For a road which seemed to be heading away from civilisation, it was in better kept condition than the main river-road which they had just left. Not paved, but oiled and hard-packed earth with few ruts or potholes, clear drainage channels on either side and steeply-roofed shelters every mile or so, beneath which she saw travellers resting from the heat. Though there were fewer carts and goods wagons, this road was no less busy; there seemed to be just as many travellers on foot, and all heading in the same direction as Berylin's party. Most were sick, injured, or crippled in some fashion – some so badly that they had to be carried by their companions or else drag themselves as best they could through the dust. Though she was more used to the sights of pain and suffering than most, she nevertheless found the spectacle disquieting and voiced her concern to Cheyne.

'Why build a Hospice so far away?' she asked. 'Surely it would make more sense to be located in a large population centre.'

'The Hospice is centuries old,' he explained. 'It was originally constructed as a Romish villa, close to a pool fed by underground springs where it was said that the Blessed Gabril once appeared to heal a blind woodcutter's boy.'

'And so the most severely afflicted of your people must crawl for miles into the hills because of a fairy tale? Forgive me, I speak only as an arrogant imperialist,' she added wryly.

'Many of our sick and infirm find their way to the Hospice of Bles Gabril for healing. Most will donate coin, however little. Some from the wealthier merchant or noble families will donate a great deal for the upkeep of this road, amongst other things. The rest – the beggars and the destitute who have no choice but to travel on foot and might not have even those – are looked after by the prentice healers. Look more closely.'

She did and saw that those whom she had taken to be the companions of the afflicted all wore about their necks the same sky blue chasuble embroidered with a white hand cupping a red heart. They patrolled the Hospice Road in pairs, helping the least mobile to the nearest shelter and moving on again. It appeared to be a simple but effective system.

'Whether you believe or not,' Cheyne continued, 'the springs themselves have medicinal qualities. There is some pragmatism buried in our hopelessly superstitious hearts.'

They watered their mounts at the next shelter, where wide troughs were fed from a well, and rested in the welcome shade, eating nuts and dried fruit.

'I once worked in a place similar to your Hospice,' Berylin told Cheyne. 'The biggest asylum in Oraille: La Belle Dame de Merci. We call it Beldam for short. My father was a doctor and lucky enough in his early career to have studied under Savant Falaise himself, though the great man was quite old by then. But father was ambitious, and subornation was not a subject fit for polite dinner table conversation, so he never pursued it. I, on the other hand, having eavesdropped on the conversations he had with his colleagues about dreams spilling out into reality, couldn't think of anything more exciting, so as soon as I was old enough, I took my nursing certificate and obtained a position at Beldam.' She stopped. 'What? You are laughing at me!'

Cheyne shook his head. 'By no means. It is just that I find it a little difficult to imagine you as a nurse.'

'You don't know the half of it,' grunted Runce.

She humphed. 'As it happens, so did I, but since there was absolutely no question of me pursuing a man's profession, nursing was the best I could do. And it was good, noble work, please don't mistake me. I was able to help people overcome the trauma of their subornation, many of whom were able to go back into the world and resume something like their old lives. Doubtless I would still be there today.'

'Except that something happened, clearly,' prompted Cheyne.

'An Event occurred inside the asylum itself. It was not particularly extreme as such things go, but it had a devastating effect on the patients – even the ones who were not directly caught up in it. The asylum should have been the one place in the world where they were safe, but it wasn't. Four of my patients committed suicide as a result. Shortly afterwards, I applied for a position in the Department for Counter Subornation, never mind what my father or anybody else said, because I realised that there were far worse things in the world than the petty prejudices of men.'

'Or women,' he added.

'Indeed. So I hope you will forgive my bluntness, Mr Cheyne. I am no diplomat. I care nothing for nation or sex or religion in the face of this scourge. I care only that it is gone.'

As they packed up to move on once again, Runce took her to one side, a frown of puzzlement on his face.

'What is it?' she asked.

'Well, ma'am, I was packing up just now and I noticed something odd on the PV.'

'Odd how?'

'Chronometer's reading a lag of point oh-nine-seven seconds.'

'Everything else? Temperature? Gravity?'

'All as should be. It might be a calibration glitch, but I thought to mention it just the same. Because if it ain't…'

'…then time is moving about a tenth of a second more slowly for us here.'

'We couldn't've passed through an Event boundary without realising it, could we?'

'If we have, it's incredibly weak. Keep an eye on it, and if anything spikes, let me know.'

'Oh don't you worry about that, ma'am. I'll be yellin' fit to beat the band.'

They rode on. The day lengthened toward evening while the road climbed higher into the foothills, and the tumbling stream on their left dwindled as they crossed the numerous small creeks and gullies which fed it. The bushland was now a thick forest of tall, mottle-barked eucalypts, whose crowns opened into green clouds. Up in this canopy, flocks of brightly-coloured birds flashed like tropical fish in the air and others called out in voices like high, tiny bells. Finally, a pair of great sandstone columns signified their arrival at a high, wide clearing with a commanding view of the island, and Berylin saw the Hospice of Bles Gabril.

It retained much of its ancient Romish architecture: a steep terra-cotta roof and many high arched windows in its two storeys which glowed in the late afternoon sun, enclosed by a large, walled courtyard which was in turn surrounded by fields and orchards. There were some Church modifications from more recent times – a modest chapel and recessed statues of the Hegemonic saints dotted around the courtyard – but at least here in Drava they hadn't razed it to the ground as had happened to so much of the beautiful ancient structures in Oraille. They rode through a small hamlet which spilled away from the outer wall; not much more than an inn, a smithy, and a cluster of shingle-roofed cottages which were homes to the Hospice's labourers and servants – and then they were at the gates of the great courtyard itself, which stood wide open to accommodate the steady stream of travellers who passed in and out. Grooms took their mounts, and they found themselves in an immense herb garden planted out in an intricate knot pattern, busy with bees and robed figures collecting cuttings in wicker baskets.

Runce nudged her. 'Point four-seven-two,' he whispered. If it was a subornation, then it was the most peculiar she had ever experienced. There were no outward signs of anything unnatural or even remotely protean. She knelt down by Buster and ruffled his floppy ears.

'You don't smell anything odd, do you boy?' she murmured. Buster licked her hand and grinned his doggy grin. Apparently he didn't.

News of their arrival had undoubtedly preceded them, because within moments the Hospice's chief psyrgeon appeared to meet them, he and Cheyne greeting each other with the warmth of old friends.

'Miss Hooper, it is my very great honour to introduce you to Gevon Corlys, the Frada of this establishment as well as one of Drava's pre-eminent medical minds.'

Frada Corlys sported a neatly trimmed beard but was otherwise completely bald, the planes of his skull gleaming like the facets of a gemstone. He winced a little at Cheyne's words. 'The only talent I'll lay claim to is knowing when this old rogue's flowery tongue becomes a danger to himself and others,' he remarked.

'Pah!' scoffed Cheyne. 'This is what living in the middle of nowhere will do to you – it gives you a false sense of modesty. Well then, may I present to you Ms Berylin Hooper, of King Alexander's Department for Counter Subornation. She has been kind enough to take an interest in how we cope with Visitations.'

This seemed to surprise the Frada. 'I'm sorry, I had not realised that this was your area of expertise.' He raised questioning eyebrows at Cheyne, who shrugged.

'The fault is mine,' he admitted. 'A simple oversight; in all the excitement, I neglected to send a messenger ahead. If any awkwardness…'

'Oh do shut up, Matalo,' Corlys interrupted, clapping Cheyne amicably on the shoulder and turning with mock-weariness to Berylin. 'I don't know. Politicians, eh? Always thinking three moves ahead of the game but not bothering to tell the little people anything about it. Never mind. If it's the after-effects of a Visitation which you've come to see, we may be able to accommodate that tonight, with luck.'

'With *luck*?'

'Of course! How else would you describe being healed by a saint?' In response to her look of blank confusion he added. 'Dear me, the good councillor here really did tell you nothing, didn't he?'

'It would seem so.' She regarded Cheyne coldly.

'Every few nights or so, our humble community is visited by the Blessed Gabril himself. He appears in a grove by the waterfall at the head of this valley for a precious few minutes, and in that time we present as many of our patients for healing as we are able. They then, of course, return to their homes. So you see, even though we currently have no patients who have experienced a Visitation, all of them hope to, and if you are fortunate you are of course perfectly welcome to ask them whatever questions you like, if it would assist your investigations.'

'In your terms,' added Cheyne, 'you might say that it is someone having a recurring dream of being Bles Gabril, rather than the saint himself, but the end result is the same.'

Berylin could scarcely credit what she was hearing, but she tried not to let her alarm show. 'Do you mean to say that you deliberately put sick and injured people within the range of an active subornation Event?'

'If you choose to put it that way.'

'Do you not think it slightly dangerous?'

'Be assured, Miss Hooper,' said the Frada earnestly, 'no harm has ever come to one of our patients, not in all the time that we have enjoyed Bles Gabril's presence. Not once.'

Runce grunted sceptically. 'A wild dog that eats from your hand today is no less likely to bite you tomorrow.'

The other men reddened, and suddenly it seemed as if the whole courtyard had stopped to listen to their conversation, even the bees.

'Runce,' she murmured, laying a hand on his arm, 'Please would you go and see to our rooms? Then you may conduct some further readings around the hospice.' Once he had disappeared with their baggage, she turned to the Frada. 'I must apologise for him. He is a soldier, and this is an unusual situation for us, to say the least.'

Frada Corlys bowed. 'Think nothing of it. I hope that by tomorrow morning we will have been able to allay all your fears and provide you with one or two useful insights. Or at the very least a decent cup of tea. Come, you must be parched.'

2

She was shown to quarters which were small and plainly furnished, but they were clean and had a magnificent view of the mountains, where she was able to change out of her travel-stained clothes with the delicate sound of bell-birds chiming outside. Elsewhere she could hear the murmurous activity of the hospice's inhabitants going about their business and an occasional air of music drifting by. There were none of the shrieks and cries she had come to expect from her time at Beldam; the distant noises of distress which no number of stone walls or iron doors could ever properly muffle. It was unexpectedly peaceful here.

She didn't trust it one bit.

When Berylin had rested, Frada Corlys returned to give her a tour of the infirmary, and she found that the same peace and calm was evident everywhere. To be sure, there was sickness and injury, and even though many of the healing methods she saw being employed would have been dismissed by Oraillean doctors as laughably antiquated, the Dravanese plainly knew the virtues of hygiene and quarantine. But still, it was all purely physical. She found nobody who seemed to be suffering from the mental derangements typical of exposure to subornation. If it weren't for the pv-detector's ambiguous readings indicating that something somewhere was amiss, she would have assumed that she had been brought to a perfectly ordinary Church infirmary by mistake.

'Forgive me,' she said to the Frada. 'I am appreciative of the time you have taken to show me your admirable work, and I do not wish to be churlish, but this is not quite what I was expecting. Are these people really all hoping to be suborned? Do they know what they might be letting themselves in for?'

He smiled. 'Miss Hooper, we understand your concern. It is perfectly reasonable, given your profession. And I will not deny that my hope in bringing you here is to show you that in Drava we have, in some cases, learned to live with the effects of subornation – not all of which are destructive.'

A sudden realisation hit her: this wasn't about sick people at all. It was about the Flats. They knew exactly what the Oraillean view of subornation was and probably that given half a chance she would destroy whatever was out there in the middle of the ocean, and they were trying to convince her that they had it under control. That they – dear Reason – that they'd *harnessed* it. The reckless arrogance of it took her breath away.

'Please ask yourself,' Frada Corlys was saying, 'would the sickest, frailest people you can imagine flock to this place in their thousands if so much as a hint of violence had been visited upon them? We have no secrets here. You are free to come and go as you please and talk to any of our patients. Ask them anything. Ask them why they have come and what they have heard, and if you remain sceptical, then I hope you will accompany us tonight and see for yourself, should Bles Gabril choose to appear.'

'I will certainly do that. I can't promise to be convinced, no matter what my eyes see, but thank you for your openness at least.'

The Frada bowed.

'Here,' said Cheyne. 'There is one patient at least who I think you should meet.'

He led her to where an exhausted-looking mother was sitting by the bedside of her adult daughter. Each bore the fading bruises and abrasions of a violent attack, but while the older turned to watch them approach with pain-haunted eyes, the younger simply lay and stared glassily at the ceiling like a waxwork. It was a look Berylin had seen all too often: the outward face of a mind which had seen something so appalling that it had chosen to abandon awareness altogether.

When the mother spoke, her voice was a dead, dry husk. 'Will the saint come tonight? My Soolie – she grows weaker every day.'

'We can only pray,' said Cheyne, clasping her hands in his.

Knowing that she was going to regret it but powerless to stop herself all the same, Berylin asked, 'What happened to her?'

'To us both,' replied the woman. 'Raiders from Elbaite. They attacked our island. We were only small, just one village. We had no garrison, no ships – they had no *reason*. What threat were we to them? When the men were dead – my poor, brave Bero dead, he was floating, just like he was looking for oysters, I remember that – when they were done, they turned to the women, and they… well, I'm old, so they didn't… but Soolie, oh my precious, precious Soolie,' and she collapsed into dry, heaving sobs while all Berylin could do was be a mute and helpless witness to her grief.

3

Later, when they were safely back in her chambers, she railed at Runce.

'The arrogance of that man! It's incredible! To wave that poor woman's pain in my face as if to say "Don't judge us, Southerner, you have no idea what we have been through." Does he think that

I don't know? Does he think I haven't seen that a dozen times over, and worse? Reason defend us! I wanted to shake him until his eyeballs rattled and tell him that I'd seen parents forced by subornation to do that to their own children and ask him what he thought of that! They ask for my expertise, and then they resort to the crudest forms of emotional blackmail – they're not listening to a single thing I've been telling them!'

'It's obvious you've never been in the army,' Runce observed calmly. He was cleaning the copper contact relays on the tez gun rig with a small wire brush and cursing the road dust for getting into everything. 'Though there is one ugly possibility which occurs.'

'That being?'

'What if they're right? That many people don't come this far for nothing. And not for something that's as liable to kill as cure 'em.'

'These are people of faith, Runce,' she retorted in disgust. 'Who knows what they'll do to themselves?'

He cleaned in silence for a while, letting her calm down. Presently he said, 'In other news, I went for that walk you suggested. You'll never guess what I found.'

'The chrono-variance is getting stronger?'

He nodded. 'I went for a bit of a wander up the valley, following the stream. Apparently there's a pool up there where their Blessed Gabril is supposed to have appeared and done his magical act. Well, I didn't see no saints or angels or anything else like that – just a pretty spot with a waterfall and some flowers and whatnot – but there's definitely something up there, because the closer you get, the stronger the variance. I was only gone for half an hour.'

'But that was three hours ago!'

'It's exponential and centred on the site. They're all off up there at dusk, you know.'

'Yes, and so are we.' She nodded at the gun. 'That is an absolute last resort, though. I don't want to bring violence to these people, no matter how misguided they are. Apart from anything else, I imagine that firing off several thousand volts of static electricity in a foreign hospital is the sort of thing frowned upon in diplomatic circles.'

'Roger that, ma'am. No zappin' the natives.'

4

An air of hushed expectation settled over the valley of Bles Gabril as the long twilight deepened and shadows crept up the foothills to enshroud the mountain peaks behind. The bellbirds fell silent with the coming night, and in the hospice itself people talked in whispers as they passed each other; even the din in the labourers' tavern muted as the drinkers paused between mouthfuls to peer out of windows towards the head of the valley.

There, a mile distant, where the thread-thin line of a stream disappeared into woods, torches were kindled.

The psyrgeons, robed and hooded against the chill, assembled a group of a dozen patients, some of whom were brought out on stretchers, and, chanting soft hymns, they were led by Frada Corlys along a narrow road which ran by the valley stream. They were followed at a respectful distance by a crowd of silent onlookers, amongst whom were Berylin and Runce, escorted by Matalo Cheyne.

The stream tumbled around the dim shapes of mossy boulders and giant tree-ferns, becoming louder as they climbed higher towards the lamplight which glimmered among the trees. There they found a small lake formed by the stream cascading down a high escarpment, and steeply overhung by curving branches which gave it a cathedral-like atmosphere. The pool was illuminated by lanterns set around it, and a stone platform like a wide, blunt jetty had been built out into the water. At its far end, the stone was hollowed into something resembling a bath, brimming. She tried to observe everything in as coldly detached a manner as possible, but something about the incessant rushing white-water noise made it hard to focus. *Rest*, it said to her, *relax, be healed.* Lamplight reflected from the waterfall's spray in a ghostly rainbow nimbus, which seemed to be out of all proportion to the number of lanterns. Either her eyes were getting used to the semi-darkness, or it was getting brighter.

Buster began to whine, very softly.

Runce was peering at the gauges on the pv-satchel around his neck. 'Something's happening…' he whispered.

'Specifics?'

He shook his head. 'I don't recognise this profile at all.'

A restless murmur of anticipation arose from the patients and the crowd of onlookers behind them.

It was definitely getting brighter. The light was coming from the haze at the bottom of the waterfall. Gradually the haze took shape – grew arms, legs, and a head – until, stepping calmly out from the base of the cascade and across the pool's surface as if it were no less solid than the earth beneath her own feet, there came the unmistakeable figure of a man: hooded, robed, bearded and smiling. He spread his hands in greeting, and Berylin saw that the ends of his fingers trailed off into wisps of iridescent water vapour. At his back, plumes of spray formed the unmistakeable shape of wings.

'I am the Archangel Gabriel,' he said to them in the voice of the waterfall. 'I come in love from the Lord, who brings hope to the despairing, wisdom to the blind, and healing to the sick. Come ye, and be made whole once more.'

She nudged Runce. 'Are you seeing this?'

'Yes ma'am. Walking on water. Very biblical.'

'Look at the surroundings, though. Nothing's changed. That's unheard of. Either the Event had already started and we entered the zone without realising it…'

'…or it's kicked off and had bugger all effect.'

'And look, the people are completely untouched too. Nobody's participating except the sick, and they're remaining themselves. It's like there isn't even a narrative being played out at all. Runce, what kind of dream *is* this?'

'Just so long as it don't turn into something that wants to bite me head off, I'm fine with it for the moment, ma'am.'

One at a time, the patients went – or were helped – up to the glowing figure, who laid a benedictory hand on a limb, a head, a torso; and in the case of those afflicted so badly that they were unconscious or immobile, they were laid in the brimming basin while Gabril blessed the water. With each healing, something effervesced from the patient's skin – their illness, possibly – drifting up in clouds of bubbles, or ash, to evaporate in the air. Berylin watched Soolie climb out of the basin and embrace her mother with smiles and tears, a clear-eyed and beautiful young woman again in the full bloom of health.

'There now,' commented Runce gruffly, clearing his throat a little. 'That's a sight, isn't it?'

'I need to speak to it,' she decided and moved forward through the crowd of onlookers. Buster trotted loyally at her side.

'Ma'am, is that wise?'

'Almost certainly not, so keep your eyes open.'

The healings continued until the figure of the Blessed Gabril started to dim and become hazier around the edges. This apparently signalled the end of the miracle, because the healers stopped bringing patients forward, even though there were many more who could have come. While the figure of the person who dreamed himself to be an angel drifted back towards the waterfall, Berylin saw her chance to get closer without interrupting the proceedings. She dodged through the crowd to the edge of the stone platform and called out to the retreating figure: 'Wait! Please!'

It paused and looked back. From this angle, she could clearly see the wings, which were folded down and melting into something resembling a long cape trailing behind it across the water.

'What would you have of me?' it asked. 'I am weary.'

Berylin's heart thumped with a nervous excitement she hadn't felt since her first work with the DCS. Never had she been anywhere near this close to having a coherent conversation with the author of a subornation. To be this close to actual answers made her stumble and stammer like a child.

'Who... who are you?' she asked. 'Please, name yourself.'

'I am the archangel Gabriel,' it replied. 'I am...'

'No. You are not.' She could hardly believe that she was interrupting it. 'You are simply asleep and dreaming this. Who are you really? *What* are you?'

A shocked silence fell across the lake and the onlookers, and a momentary terror stabbed at her: what if it really was an angel? Would it strike her down?

'I am… dreaming?' The angel's expression darkened with confusion.

'Officer Hooper!' called Frada Corlys in alarm. 'What do you think you're doing?'

She ignored him. 'Yes, you are dreaming. You are asleep, at home in your bed. I need to know where that is. I need to know *who you are*!'

'I am not…'

'Hooper!' Cheyne yelled angrily. 'Step away this instant! You don't know what you're doing! Imbecile woman!'

Runce laid a heavy hand on his shoulder. 'Watch your tone there, sonny Jim,' he said quietly.

'I… am… real…' Gabril was even more indistinct now; a nebulous, agitated shadow.

'No. You are not. This place is real. These people that you've been healing, they're real. I am real. My name is Berylin Evangeline Hooper of the Oraillean Department for Counter Subornation; this is my world, and I order you, phantasm, to *tell me your NAME*!'

Several things happened simultaneously then, so fast that it wasn't until afterwards that she was able to piece together the sequence of events. Frada Corlys lunged at her, crying something about "outrageous sacrilege", but he was intercepted by Runce, who, to make his point clear, shoved quite an ordinary pistol in his face; not the tez gun, but it was enough to cause a panicked stampede of terrified pilgrims. Buster launched a furious tirade of barks at the figure on the lake. In the meantime, something from the boiling shadows under the waterfall howled '*I AM NOT A DREAM!*' as an agitated curl of darkness snaked at her. Instinctively, she caught it, intending to hold the phantasm here and interrogate it, but it was unimaginably strong, and before she could do anything more than cry out to Runce in alarm, it had dragged her off her feet and into the roiling nightmare.

CHAPTER 16

CUT LOOSE

1

There was a moment's disorientation as she fell through a crushing and suffocating blackness, and then she found herself inexplicably struggling awake in a strange bedroom.

Sickly orange light seeped between a pair of curtains, but everything was distorted, as if she were viewing it from underwater. Her movements were sluggish as she struggled with the unfamiliar bed linen – this coverlet felt like it was made of marshmallow – and...

There was someone else here.

She could feel him overlapping her thoughts like she was one of those Kalevian dolls nested inside one another. He was old, confused and frightened. He'd been having the angel dream again – more and more these days it gave him some comfort as the cancer ate away at what was left of his life – but this time something had gone wrong. Something had come back with him, and for some reason he couldn't wake up properly.

Who's there?

'Whose voice is that? Yours or mine?'

Oh dear sweet lord Jesus it's inside of me something is possessing me our Father who art in heaven...

'Shut up! Stop your superstitious babbling, old man, and talk to me!'

...hallowed be thy name thy kingdom come...

'SILENCE!'

Silence.

'Who are you? Where am I?'

Please let me go. I can't wake up. Why can't I wake up?

Berylin could feel the threads of sleep loosening from around her, his voice growing weaker as they did so, and she was seized with sudden panic: was she going to wake up for real, here, in this place and this body? Inside the dreamer? Was this what happened to all those suborned victims who had disappeared? She knew that the adrenaline surge which came with the panic would only awaken her more quickly, but she was powerless to prevent it and raged impotently at him.

'Damn you! You and all your kind! I don't care a whit whether you meant well or not – your dreams are not welcome in our world. Let me go, damn you, *let me go*!'

And then the world – whichever one it was – filled with purple fire tearing over and through her body, and she screamed with two voices.

The shock of cold water slapped her to her senses. She was thrashing in the freezing pool of Bles Gabril – except that there was no angel and never had been. Just a frightened old man dying of a terminal disease and consoling himself with a recurring fantasy that he could heal the sick.

An old man in another world. The Realt.

For the first time in her life, the fact that she was right held no comfort for her, and when Runce dragged her ashore before Frada Corlys and Councillor Cheyne and the other Dravanese, she accepted their recriminations and held her tongue.

2

Runce stood at the stern-rail of the *Spinner* and watched their escort of three Amity warships dwindle behind them. He'd expected to feel relieved now that they were finally out of Dravanese waters, but he found that instead his disquiet was stronger than ever. Something wasn't right.

They'd been kept under house arrest in Bles Marique for four days while diplomatic clatters bounced back and forth between Drava and Oraille. The only reasons they'd been let out were to be dragged before one self-important politician after another to explain what exactly it was they thought they were doing, committing such outrageous sacrilege upon one of their holiest sites, not to mention the unconscionable crime of threatening a member of court with a sidearm. Runce wasn't sure what "unconscionable" meant, but in any case wasn't in much of a mind to explain himself to a bunch of foreigners, especially since at the time he hadn't really been thinking much of anything at all. He'd simply reacted to Berylin being threatened the only way he knew how. He did, however, know enough about how the diplomatic food-chain worked to understand that the only way anybody from the *Spinner* was going home was for someone to get thrown to the sharks – and that was him. He was the one who'd fired the tez at Gabril (or whatever it really was); he was the one who had threatened Corlys. By rights, he should be political fishbait. And yet here he was, free.

'It just don't make any kind of sense,' he said to himself for the hundredth time.

Plainly, some big, nation-moving favours had been traded on their behalf, and he shuddered to think what that implied about their mission.

Berylin hadn't said anything to him about what she'd seen. Nor had she come out of her cabin since they'd got steam up, choosing instead to shut herself away for hours, having incomprehensible philosophical discussions with Harcourt, of all people. He didn't mind not understanding anything of what was in the loop, but being kept out of it altogether made him twitchy and cross, so he kept himself here at the stern and as far as possible out of the crew's way.

3

From Drava, they island-hopped towards the Flats, picking up morsels of rumour and hearsay. Most of this was the standard mariners' fare of sea monsters, ghost-ships and lights in the sky, but the closer they got, the stranger – and oddly, more believable – it became. They heard about holes which appeared without warning in the surface of the ocean to swallow hapless fishing boats and disgorge horrors from the depths; about compasses which spun uselessly and alien constellations which confounded navigation; about a floating, man-made island in the middle of the Flats.

Finally, half-a-day's steaming from an insignificant fleck of land called Danae, they heard from the captain of a merchantman a name which they were able to put to all of this:

Stray.

CHAPTER 17

MOON AND SIXPENCE BAY

1

Bobby's hands were shaking as he drank kaff with Allie in the bright market square of Timini, Danae's single port and only town of any considerable size. He watched the townsfolk coming and going about their everyday business and tried to see it as he had when they'd arrived – what – only two hours ago? How could that be? Far too short a time for an entire world to be destroyed and another created in its place. It must have been a thousand years at least since they'd moored Tatters and stepped ashore. Everything had happened just as Allie had predicted.

At first he'd simply been amazed at the sensation of walking on solid ground for the first time in weeks. Then came the sensory overload of being surrounded by things rising up above him again, where Stray was almost uniformly flat to sea level.

Danae was shaped very roughly like a crescent moon, with white sand beaches on its broad inside curve, and a small round eyot inhabited only by barking sealions between its two points – hence the name Moon and Sixpence Bay. A ridge of hills formed a spine around the outer curve, clustered with red-roofed houses which were surrounded by terraced orchards and narrow fields walled with white limestone. Where the island narrowed to its northernmost point, the ridge tumbled down through Timini's steep, switchbacked streets, lined by tall houses with flat roof-gardens and wrought iron balconies. Allie had moored Tatters a short distance away from town, at a ruined jetty in a sheltered rocky cove – explaining that while she was fairly certain there'd be no trouble with the locals, she wasn't taking any chances – and led him up and along steep cliff paths into Timini itself. Within minutes of landing, Bobby had developed a crick in the neck trying to take it all in. There was so much *up*.

And colour – colour everywhere.

From walls covered in flowering bougainvillea to the boats bobbing like upturned, iridescent beetles in the harbour, market-barrows of tomatoes and gleaming aubergines, men in insanely patterned trousers and women in rainbow headscarves – compared to these, Allie's and his own sun-bleached clothes made them look like ghosts. He helped her trade their mother-of-pearl for sacks of rice and dried fruit at a market which was a riot of colour and noise – surprised to find that everyone spoke good English, though with an accent which he couldn't place – and was so evidently agog that she had to draw him aside and calm him down for fear that he would draw too much attention to them.

'This isn't a package tour,' she warned, half amused despite herself. 'I told you, we're not too popular here. Try not to stare so much. I thought you were used to foreign places, anyway.'

'Sorry.' He pulled himself together. 'I am. It's just a bit of a culture shock, that's all.'

'Understatement of the century, right there.' She waved away a gorgeous young man trying to sell them bunches of grapes the size of golf-balls. 'So,' she tilted her head sardonically at Bobby. 'Still want to find a way out of this awful hell-hole?'

He shrugged helplessly. 'How can I not?'

'Come on then, Mr Frodo,' she sighed. 'Let's get you back to the Shire.'

And that was when everything she'd said on Tatters came true – including the part about how she'd be standing right behind him when the sense of unreality mounted so badly that it seemed to spill out of his head and into the world around him, making the solid ground tip and sway like the small raft on which he'd first awoken, and all he wanted to do was sweep it aside, crash through everything and run, and keep running until he found someone or somewhere he knew. Her hand was on his shoulder as he was about to take it out on yet another confused fisherman – he could feel his fists balling themselves in baffled rage – and that hand was the only solid, sure thing in the world, so he obeyed it and let himself be led away.

The kaff was sweet and scaldingly hot, but it gave him something to focus on. She let him take his time.

'Where are we?' he asked. 'No more bullshit rationing. *Where*?'

'I used to be a doctor in Minneapolis,' she said by way of an answer, 'up until just under a year ago, when I got a bad case of bacterial meningitis. Not that there's any such thing as a good case, you understand, but there you go. That's the problem with hospitals – full of sick people. Do you know what that particular bug does?'

He shook his head, not having a clue what this had to do with anything.

'It causes inflammation of the membrane lining the brain and spinal cord. This is not a fun thing to have. In bad cases it can, amongst other things, put people in comas, which is what happened to me – heavy-duty antibiotics, endotracheal intubation, the works. See this scar?' She stroked the navel-like dimple in the hollow of her throat. He'd seen it but been too polite to ask. 'And then one day I woke up here. Well, not *here*, obviously. Stray.'

'Someone brought you here?'

'No.' She looked at him frankly, but without defiance. *Believe this or don't,* that look said. *It makes no difference.* 'I'm still there. Still in St Justine's Hospice, being fed through a tube and visited occasionally by my grieving family who can't even have the consolation of turning me off because the machines say I still have some brain function.'

'Bullshit!' he laughed reflexively, then reddened. 'Sorry, but…'

'Seb?' she continued. 'The last thing he remembers is just before going out with some friends to a nightclub in Toulouse and taking some pills he bought from a guy he didn't know because his usual dealer was in jail. Silly boy.'

'This is insane.'

'The Lachlans refuse to say anything about who and where they were or what they remember before Stray, so it's impossible to say how they got here – they're certainly not married in the conventional sense – and Joe is simply too young.'

'I thought he was born here.'

'Are you kidding? That pair of old farts? Please. He was found floating, just like the rest of us – just like *you* – so they adopted him "for his own good" and refuse to tolerate any discussion. The only reason me and Seb don't say anything is because it would upset the kid.'

'Sorry, wait, back up a bit. Are you seriously trying to tell me that we are all, that each one of us is lying in a bed somewhere in a coma? And that our minds are all here in this place?'

'I'm telling you what I know to be true. Whether you believe it or not is up to you.' She sipped her kaff and watched him closely.

'And this is all, what?' He gestured around. 'The Matrix?'

'Okay, good, well at least we've got that one out of the way nice and quick,' she said to herself. 'No,' she told him firmly. 'You are not plugged into a machine as a slave to a race of robotic overlords, and you are not Keanu Reeves. You're not that cute, for a start.'

'Thanks for that.'

'This isn't a hologram or a collective delusion or anything like that. This is a real place, and those are real people, and this is real coffee which we're going to have to pay real money for, or we're going to get in real trouble with the owner's really big son. Get it? I don't know how we got here, but I know that here we are all the same.'

'I'm sorry, it's just – it's a little hard to swallow.'

'Then riddle me this, Batman: how much weird shit has happened to you in the last three weeks that you cannot explain in any other way?'

Bobby tried to deny that she had a point but couldn't quite bring himself to do so. His blood, crimson pearls in the sea. The sea itself, seething with billions of fish that first night. The Three Fishketeers, gobbling his blood and coming up to stare at him hungrily for more. Around and around in a circle, and in the middle of it: Sophie, chained to something underwater, touching his hand and saying *You're all here. All of you.*

'Tell me something, Bobby. You got that book of yours? The one you're always reading?'

He brought out *A Tender Death* from the pocket where he carried it. 'Yes, why?'

'Let's have a look.' She flipped through it. 'Nineteen forty-eight,' she read from the copyright page. 'Seems very new-looking for something printed over sixty years ago.' She tossed it back. 'And for someone who claims to be a minor diplomatic flunky from post-war Blighty, how do you know anything about the Matrix?' He couldn't answer that one either. 'You are not who you think you are, Robert Andrew Michael Jenkins. Not by a long shot.'

'So what about these people?' he asked, gesturing around at the crowd in the market square. 'Are they all coma people too?'

'No, they live here. This is their home, not ours. We have no connection to this place. If we were to leave Stray and try to settle on one of the Islands, we wouldn't be able to grow any crops or raise any livestock, and we'd soon starve to death. That's why Marjorie can't grow anything in her flower boxes. The Flats are flat because it's where we live – we made them that way just by being there. Something about not being fully in this world has, I don't know, a dampening effect on it.'

'Like we're sucking the life out of this world to stay alive in ours?'

'Jesus, I hope not. Bad enough that we're somehow responsible for the Tourmaline Archipelago's very own version of the Bermuda Triangle without that little theory getting a hold, so keep it to yourself, yeah? The last thing we need is their equivalent of Ghostbusters turning up to zap us all awake. Incidentally, it's also the reason why you can't get me pregnant.'

'So, silver lining, then.'

'You have no idea.'

'But if all of this is just a big dream, then what does it matter?'

'It matters because how can you say whether or not this place is real when you don't even know if you're real yourself?'

Bobby's brain felt like it was trying to rub its stomach and pat its head at the same time; the only thing he could think clearly were the words *Crash and burn*, which made no sense whatsoever. 'I think I need to go for a little walk,' he decided.

'Fine. I'll head back to Tatters and get her ready. Don't take too long, okay? And don't go doing anything stupid like picking a fight with someone because you think this is all a big dream. That shit I do not need.'

'No, Mother.'

She snorted. 'We can work on your Oedipal hangups on the way home. You *are* coming back with me, aren't you? Did we agree on that or not?'

'I'm not saying that I believe any of this, you understand? But I'm fairly sure that I'm not going to get any clearer an idea of what's going on by sulking around here. So yes, I'm coming back with you.'

'Such touching devotion.'

2

As she emerged onto Timini's stone harbourfront, Allie didn't notice the *Spinner's* deckhands at first because it simply didn't occur to her that anybody could ever be that interested in tiny, threadbare old Tatters and her boring cargo. She'd noticed the steamer itself, of course, as Tatters had arrived at Danae – the hulking steel-hulled trawler with its plume of smoke idling from its stack had been as out of place amongst the local boats as a barracuda in a tropical aquarium – but she'd dismissed it as probably belonging to some regional bigwig doing the rounds and told herself to keep an even lower profile than normal. It was true that the Strays were treated with distrust, but the most that had ever amounted to in the past had been a bit of shouting and pushing. Nobody had so much as pulled a knife on her. The other reason was that Berylin had ordered the crew to dress down in jerkins and tattered crazy-pants like regular fishermen, so as to blend with the local populace, and by the time Allie had spotted their cutlasses and the determined way they were approaching her, it was too late: she was out in the open and committed.

So she did the only thing she could do, which was to brazen it up to them with a big grin and say 'Afternoon, fellas. Nice day for it.'

There were four of them, and they moved quickly to surround her.

'Okay,' she sighed and reached for her purse. 'How much…'

'You are the Stray named Alison, are you not?' said a female voice behind her. Allie turned and saw a young woman, a bit shorter than herself, dressed smartly in high boots, pants, and a man's shirt with the sleeves rolled up. Beneath cropped dark hair, she had a severe beauty which put Allie instantly on her guard. Behind her stood a craggy man with the most outrageous-looking gun she had ever seen strapped to his belt.

'Who wants to know?'

'My name is Berylin Hooper. I'm very pleased to meet you at last.' She put out her hand. Allie ignored it. She put it away again with a small, resigned smile. 'Very well, then. I work for a branch of the Oraillean government tasked with investigating what you might call unusual phenomena. I'd like to talk to you about the Flats.'

She remembered her joke to Bobby barely a few minutes earlier about not wanting a visit from the local Ghostbusters. 'You have got to be fucking kidding me,' she groaned to herself, but she switched on her sweetest smile. 'Have I done something wrong? Am I under arrest?'

'Not at all. It's nothing like that.'

The Hooper woman was lying and not even trying particularly hard to hide it. It screamed at Allie from the stance of the man with the gun and the four goons who were still between her and escape. Even worse, people were stopping to stare. What scared her more than the fear of a physical confrontation was the danger that if by some miracle she got out of this, she'd still be *persona non grata* in Timini and forced to look further afield for supplies in the future. All she could think to do was get this situation out of public view and in the meantime pray that Bobby didn't come back and try something stupidly heroic. At the same time she was kicking herself for not realising that it would come to this sooner or later, and not being prepared for it. She hated having to think on her feet.

'The Flats?' she asked 'Sure, okay. I'll tell you whatever you want to know. I know this great little taverna just around the corner. Why don't we…'

'No. We'll do this aboard my ship.'

Allie knew, with the certainty of a knife in her guts, that if she set foot on board that large steamship, she would never come off it again alive. 'Now wait a second…'

But the conversation seemed to be boring Hooper already. 'Gentlemen,' she waved the deckhands forward. They took hold of her then, and she began to scream.

3

Bobby had stopped on the way out of town to buy Allie a surprise present of a bracelet, which looked like it was made out of iridescent porcupine quills, and was starting up the steeply switchbacked road out of Timini when he heard her screaming for him. If he'd been exploring the market place or the smaller side-streets, he probably wouldn't have heard anything, but the extra height allowed her cries to reach him clearly over the lower rooftops.

For a moment he froze, thinking he'd misheard something – maybe a couple of the locals having an argument. Then it came again. His name.

And he was off at full tilt back down the narrow cobbled street, shoving aside townsfolk and knocking over piles of crates and baskets because the street was so crowded and he was taking corners too fast to care what lay around them, until he skidded out onto the quayside and saw Allie being bundled along by a bunch of men.

Two had her by the arms, with a third leading the way and one more bringing up the rear. Without thinking, he shoulder charged the one at the back, ploughing him straight over the quayside and into a fishing boat full of wicker creels. Consternation erupted; fishermen and traders ran yelling in all directions, clearing a sudden space around the combatants. The two thugs holding Allie kept their grip while the leader ran back, sweeping from his side an ugly but very sharp-looking sword. He raised it high, telegraphing the blow so obviously that Bobby was certain it was a feint and almost did nothing until it was too late. Turned out the guy was simply crap; Bobby stepped inside the sword's downward arc and drove his fist into the man's throat. The sword skittered away, and the thug dropped to his knees, choking.

Odds evened somewhat, the other two looked uneasily at each other.

In a sense, Bobby was conscious of none of this. Muscle memory had taken over, just like when he'd fallen off his first raft and discovered that he could swim – memories earned somewhere else, as some*one* else. Everything narrowed down to the bare essentials: hands, muscles, lungs, the stone under his feet, the positions of the men opposite him. Coma-raft-dream-world be bollocksed, this was something Caffrey knew inside out – a good, old-fashioned kicking.

Who is Caffrey?

But then the two men had let Allie go and were moving, and Bobby had no attention to spare. They tried to flank him, wary now that they had seen how easily he'd dealt with their mates, sword-tips circling. For all that their weapons were basic, unadorned lumps of metal, they gave his enemies a reach which he was going to have to get inside quickly unless he wanted to be skewered from both sides like a spit-roast.

He feinted an attack on one, was rewarded with a panicked lunge, got inside it, grabbed the man's sword-wrist with his wounded hand (*fuck*, that hurt!), and twisted outwards, pivoting the guy on his right hip and driving him arse-first into the stone quay. Bobby followed him down with a knee planted in the middle of his chest and heard something crack inside as the man's skull smacked heavily at the same time, and he was unconscious before he had time to scream. Bobby felt rather than saw the last guy move. He threw himself sideways as the downcut which should have buried itself between his shoulders ended up in the unconscious thug's face instead, splitting it vertically from brow to chin in a fan of blood and teeth, the blow so hard that the blade lodged in his jawbone and wouldn't pull free. While the swordsman was staring in shock at what he'd done to his fallen mate, Bobby kicked his legs out from underneath him and was scrambling to his feet when Allie finished the man off rather elegantly by dumping a basket of fish over his head.

'*ENOUGH!*' yelled a female voice from behind. Bobby whirled, fists clenched, and found himself staring straight down the barrel of a large revolver. The woman holding it was white-faced with fury. The older man with the lunar-landscape face standing next to her was also pointing a weapon at him, but one which looked like a Flash Gordon ray-gun. It was attached by a thick cable to a belt-pack and humming with power. Between them, a small but business-like dog was growling deeply with all teeth on display. He'd been so focussed on taking out the four who had hands on Allie that he'd missed these two, and he kicked himself for the oversight.

'Bobby,' Allie whispered, her eyes huge. 'What do we do?'

'What you *do*,' spat Berylin, 'is you step away from my injured men and get yourselves aboard, or I swear that I will end you where you stand.'

'Do what she says,' said Bobby. 'We'll sort everything out, I promise.' To Berylin, he said more loudly, 'We're co-operating, okay? There's no need for anyone else to get hurt.'

'Is that a threat?' She sounded almost amused.

'If it needs to be.'

'It's a bit late for that, my lad,' growled Runce. Buster barked in agreement.

But before Bobby and Allie had set foot on the *Spinner's* gangplank, a commotion started in the crowd of gawkers which had formed at a safe distance, and a group of men pushed their way through, shouting. Judging by their long wooden staves and baggy cloth hats, they were members of the town constabulary. The largest man in the biggest hat was using his belly as much as his staff to clear a path to the ship, and he swaggered up to Berylin, red-faced and perspiring. He smelled like he'd come straight from a tavern.

'What in goat-buggering God's name is going on here?' he demanded.

'Nothing that you need concern yourself with, Sheriff,' she replied. 'This will be off your dock and out of your hands soon enough. His Majesty King Alexander's Department of Counter Subornation thanks you for your forbearance.'

'Does he now? Well that's just fucking precious of him, isn't it? In case it's escaped your attention, Missy, you aren't in your kingdom now, and you don't tell me a fucking thing about what I concern myself with.' He pointed at Bobby and Allie. 'Jono. Dav. Get them two in irons.' As his men moved to obey, Berylin protested.

'Sheriff, I am empowered by...'

He thrust the end of his staff in her face. 'It's Osk. Serjeant Osk. And you, Missy, are empowered to stick this up your clunge and swivel on it, you snooty bint.'

'Mind your tongue,' warned Runce, taking a step forward.

'Or what, Oraillean?' Osk shot back. 'Picking on a couple of Strays is one thing. Taking on the Amity constabulary will land you in an ocean of hurt. Literally.' He cocked a bulging eye at Berylin. 'Are we going to have a problem with your attack dog, Missy? Either of them?'

With great effort she restrained herself. 'No. We are not. Runce, please take the wounded men back aboard.'

Runce blinked. 'Beg pardon, ma'am?'

'You heard her,' Osk sneered. Runce stared at them both a moment longer, then shoved his way back to the ship, cursing.

'Serjeant...' began Bobby.

'And *you!*' Osk wheeled on him, 'You might be pretty handy with those fists, but the muscles in your head need some work if you think I'm letting you say one buggering thing to me.'

Before Bobby could protest, someone struck him savagely across the back of his head, and the world exploded into black stars.

4

Once the Strays had been manacled and dragged away, Osk turned back to the Oraillean woman. 'I've had clatter messages from Drava about you lot,' he continued and then laughed at her surprised expression. 'Oh yes, we're not so pissingly small and out of the way that we don't hear about stuck-up foreigners swanning around, thinking they own the place. These Strays are scum, to be sure, but they're our scum. If you don't like it, the circuit magistrate will be around to us in a week or so; we'll see what he has to say.'

'Sir,' Berylin answered through clenched teeth, 'I have no intention of waiting a day, let alone a *week*.' She turned on her heel and stalked up the gangplank.

Truth to tell, neither did Osk, who knew well enough that Miss High and Mighty would get her own way just as quickly as it took her to send an enraged clatter to her superiors, who would then shout at *his* superiors, who would then tear him a new one. Let her sweat it. He'd give the Strays as long as he could, if only out of sheer bloody-mindedness. It was the closest thing he had to a virtue.

CHAPTER 18

JAIL

1

Timini was a small town on a tiny island, with little to trouble it beyond some petty theft and the inevitable drunken scuffle, and so the constabulary had no call for an elaborate jailhouse. They occupied a decommissioned pump-house on the town's upper slopes and used a defunct water cistern carved into the stony hillside as their one and only cell.

Bobby fumbled his way to consciousness through barbs of light throbbing behind his eyelids, and he tried to sit up. Fresh pain flared in his skull, and he sank back with a groan. Something was pillowed under his head.

Carefully he explored the back of his skull, wincing as he found a large, wet bump. Plus, the cut on his hand was open again. He was surrounded by the sounds of dripping water. Everything leaked, both outside and in. Trickling through the gaps in his thoughts came memories – faces, voices, a painting? – which used to be his, or should have been, but they faded as awareness grew until he couldn't even be sure that anything had been there in the first place. He was a perforated man. Ironically, his throat was ferociously dry.

Allie sat nearby, arms hugging her knees, watching him. She made no move to help as he struggled up for a second time and finally made it.

'If it's not a stupid question, how do you feel?' she asked.

He grunted something by way of reply. Tried again. 'Where are we?'

The cell was circular, empty except for them, and about the same diameter as the length of the Tatterdemalion. It was open to the sky, blocked with a heavy iron grill. It looked like the day was nearing noon.

'In jail. Which part of "Don't do anything stupid" was unclear to you?'

'The part that included letting you get abducted and raped and killed. Remember that part?'

She hugged her knees tighter. 'I'm sorry. That was uncalled for. It's just – this was precisely, exactly what I did not want to happen. I'm the only one on Stray who can navigate the Flats. Whatever happens to me, they're all going to starve. I should have known this would happen. Everything is screwed, now. *Everything.*'

'Tell me about it.'

'But still. Thank you.'

They were silent for a while, listening to the drip of water and watching the clouds pass by on the other side of the grill.

'Where did you learn to fight like that?' she asked.

'The Bujinkan Ryuku Dojo on Pershore Road in Stirchley.'

'*Where?*'

He shrugged helplessly. 'I have no idea what that means. It just popped in there. I think it's all a bit of a moot point now, anyway.'

The sound of their voices must have alerted those outside to the fact that Bobby was awake, because booted feet approached the grill, and they found themselves looking up at the figure of Serjeant Osk. He hunkered down by the edge and tapped the metal bars thoughtfully with the butt of his staff as he spoke.

'If this were a bigger town with richer people breathing down my neck, you'd both be dead now. Leastways you would,' he pointed at Bobby. 'You,' he directed at Allie, but he didn't finish, just grimaced. 'But I'm answerable to the look my wife gives me when I go home at night, and too many people saw your foreign friend throwing her weight around for me to ignore. Killings on my dock. On *my* dock.' He sucked his teeth and spat through the grill. 'If only it were that simple. So here it is: Miss Hooper wants her prisoner, and she may very well be a nasty piece of work, but she is a nasty *political* piece of work, and I will not put myself in the way of that. I've sent for the magistrate. They're busy, there's a lot of islands, could be a week, maybe two.'

'Two weeks!' Allie protested.

'You hush yourself!' he barked and slammed his staff-butt against the grill. 'Hush yourself there! This is leniency you're getting, Stray. Like I say, too many good people saw what happened for me to take the easiest option, but I will throw you to that woman if you make this worse, do you understand me?'

She said nothing.

'Good. For what it's worth, even a week is too long for my liking. I'd be shot of the whole goat-buggering pack of you if I could. In the meantime you'll be fed and watered. Take this for what it is.' He got up and walked away.

The first thing Bobby did, when he could finally stand up without big flowers of light blooming dizzily in his head, was look for a way out. The ancient water cistern had numerous small pipes and gutters running into it and was drained by an evil-smelling waste pipe in the centre, but none of them was wide enough for anything bigger than a rat to climb through. In one place a ladder of metal rungs driven into the stone wall led up to a hinged hatch in the grill, but the hatch was secured with a huge padlock well out of arm's reach. He pushed, pulled and twisted, but nothing moved. He went through his pockets so see if there was anything he could use, and found that anything remotely of value had been taken – his matches, the small penknife, and the iridescent porcupine quill bracelet. He cursed them for that last one; the idea of Allie's present hanging off the wrist of Osk's judgemental wife made him furious. But it gave him an idea. He hoped that they were simply corrupt and not especially imaginative with it. They'd gone through his pockets but had apparently dismissed the tatty bit of string around his neck with the bits and pieces of beachcomber junk threaded on it, and so had missed Joe's good-luck pearl. He unthreaded it and waited.

Presently a guard came with food and water. He ordered them to stand at the far side of the cell from the hatch while he opened it. Bobby and Allie obeyed. He was a young man, Bobby noticed with relief, with a late bloom of acne on his cheeks.

Eyeing them warily, the guard set down a leather bucket of water and two cups, as well as a plate of bread and dried fruit, and was about to climb back up the ladder when Bobby said, 'Hey, mate. Wait up. I've got a gift for you.'

'Shut up,' replied the guard curtly and continued to climb.

'No, seriously. It's just down there on the floor. By the bucket. You missed it. Check it out – I'm not moving.' He hadn't. He and Allie were both sitting down, doing everything they could to appear totally non-aggressive.

Suspicious, the guard hesitated.

He peered down, caught sight of the pearl, which he had in fact missed, even though it was lying in plain sight on the cell floor, and climbed back down to pick it up. 'What's this?' he asked.

'Payment,' answered Bobby.

'For what?'

'Just thinking about it.'

'Thinking about what?'

'Letting us out of here.'

He laughed. 'You must be crazy. You're going nowhere, Stray. But thanks for this, all the same.' He started to go.

'I have another half a dozen just like that waiting for you,' said Allie. 'Where we come from they cover the bottom of the ocean like sand.'

'Have you got a girl?' Bobby added. 'I bet you do. Someone you fancy, at least. So look, take that and buy her something nice. Get something for her mum too – that always works. I don't know exactly what that's worth in your country but it's got to be at least a month's wages. Then ask yourself how much more you could buy her with ten times that.'

'More like this?' Bobby could almost smell the greed oozing from him. He took a step towards them and raised his staff. 'What's to stop me taking them from you anyway?'

Bobby's return stare was unblinking. 'You're welcome to try,' he said quietly, and the guard hesitated.

'Look, there's no need for this to get unpleasant,' Allie added quickly. 'Obviously we don't have them with us, since you would have already found them. What's her name – your girl?'

'Why?'

'Oh, come on, now, you're just being silly.' Listening to her, Bobby could well imagine her as a doctor, coaxing cooperation out of awkward patients.

'Calla,' he said. 'I'm Jono. I shouldn't be telling you this.'

'That's because you're a good man, Jono. I can tell. The kind of man who just wants the best for the people he loves.'

'Plus you'll be doing your Serjeant a favour; I can tell you that for nothing,' added Bobby. 'He wants that Hooper woman gone just as much as the rest of us. That Oraillean steamer's a pretty piece of kit, isn't she? I haven't seen too much like her around here. So, what, they cruise by every six months or so to remind everybody who's got the biggest stick?'

Jono grunted. 'Something like that.'

'Something *exactly* like that. They pay lip service to the local authorities and they look down their noses at you like they shit solid gold, don't they?' Bobby's heart surged with hope when Jono smiled at that. 'I bet they've even got some of their men in your guard room haven't they?'

'How'd you know that?' Jono asked sharply.

Bobby shrugged. 'Lucky guess. It's what people like them do. They don't trust the little backwater places to do their jobs properly. And I'm sorry, but there's just no way he's going to keep us locked up here for a fortnight making things political for himself. Now that he's been seen to have done the right thing, we're going to have a little accident – I know it, you know it. A fall down the stairs, or maybe I'll hang myself with my own belt. It'll be one of you lads that has to do it, too.'

'Calla wouldn't want that,' put in Allie.

Bobby continued: 'You can save everybody the hassle and skip town with enough to buy yourself a little taverna on another island, and I bet he'd be so grateful that we were gone he wouldn't even come looking for you. He might even wave you off.'

'I can't…'

'Of course you can't,' Allie interrupted gently. 'You need to talk it over with her first and make arrangements. This is all a bit sudden, I know. Just please don't take too long, that's all. Your serjeant was looking pretty nervous when he left us just now. I don't know what he might do.' The note of fear she injected into her voice at the end there made Bobby want to nominate her for an Oscar.

Jono dithered by the foot of the ladder, with one foot on a rung and another on the floor. His face was furrowed with worry, misgivings, and the unaccustomed burden of deep thought. 'I might be back later,' he muttered, and before either of them could reply he rushed up the ladder and locked the grill behind with him with a heavy clashing of metal.

Bobby and Allie both collapsed with relief. He lay back on the stone floor and looked at her for a long moment, as if trying to decide something for himself. Eventually he shook his head. 'No. I just don't believe it.'

'What?'

'You. A doctor. Before Stray.'

'Why the hell not?'

'Based on that little performance you were either a master confidence trickster or a spy.'

She laughed. 'You Boris, me Natasha.'

'I beg your pardon?'

'Never mind.'

2

The remainder of that day was an agonising mixture of boredom and anxiety, which escalated as the sun inched its way across the sky. Allie tried to enlighten Bobby about the shifting tides of alliance and conflict between the dozens of island-states in the Tourmaline Archipelago – but she knew little herself, and that was gleaned only from overhearing market-place gossip every month or so. He gathered that Danae was one of the tiny islands sprinkled like freckles around the larger bulk of Drava, basking in its protective glow even though not technically a part of the Amity, since it was too small to support any warships. Elbaite's historical attempts to crush the Amity had always failed because of the logistical difficulties of holding each of the hundreds of islands as it was captured, until they had changed tactics and gambled their vast resources on the construction of a great deep-water fleet designed not to fight island-by-island, but to cut across the open ocean and strike at Drava directly.

And then Stray had appeared, surrounded by the Flats – a navigational dead zone where there was no wind strong enough to propel their warships, and where strange holes would appear at random in the ocean to swallow vessels into oblivion.

'Holes?' Bobby asked. 'What do you mean holes in the ocean?' Again there was that memory of surfacing, the earliest clear memory he had which he could confidently call his own.

'If we get out of this alive I'll show you on the way home,' she promised. 'Now shut up and listen.'

The Elbaite admirals were not pleased. Committed militarily and economically to a strategy of expansion, they had no choice but to continue prosecuting the war by any possible means, and if they could not navigate their own ships through the Flats, then it was imperative that they find someone who could. Although exactly what an Oraillean steam-ship was doing in the area, thousands of miles from home, was anybody's guess.

'Things are definitely a lot more complicated than I thought,' said Bobby. 'I suppose it's still a strategic asset, regardless of who's got hold of it. So I imagine what they're after is the secret of your little cracker compass.'

She frowned. 'Hmm, maybe. I don't know, though. Something about that Hooper woman doesn't sit right. Did you see her eyes?'

'I can't say I was paying all that much attention, what with one thing and another.'

'She said her job was something about investigating unusual phenomena. And she just – she had a look about her, like one of those hellfire and damnation preachers, you know?'

'Again, I'm not sure that I do.'

'Well I'm from the States, honey, and we've got 'em in spades. Trust me. She's dangerous. She's not after anything strategic, and I don't think she gives a damn about territories or alliances or anything like that. Plain and simple, I think she's just after *us*.'

3

As afternoon wore into evening, they were brought more food and blankets against the cold, but never by Jono, and they debated helplessly whether this was a good sign or bad. At one point Hooper and her craggy-faced major domo turned up to peer down at them. They didn't say anything to Bobby and Allie, just held a whispered conversation while staring at a device which the man carried in a bulky leather satchel, and then they went away again without explanation, all of which only served to fuel Allie's paranoia that somehow this was personal.

Bobby tried not to doze. He knew that it was not a wise thing to do after being whacked on the head, but it throbbed abominably and every time he tried to stand up, waves of dizziness threatened to pitch him over – he thought this must be what a concussion felt like.

It was the last thought in his head before sleep took him.

When he awoke again, it was with the end of a wooden staff nudging him in the ribs. Before he could rouse himself properly to do anything about it, the shaft was suddenly forced across his throat, choking him. He sputtered. Scrabbled. Fear and outrage at what might be happening to Allie didn't help this time – he had a man's whole weight bearing down on his throat.

'I will let you up now,' a voice whispered. Jono. 'Do not cry out. You are safe.'

The weight disappeared, and Bobby scrambled to his feet, coughing. 'Safe? Christ! What the bloody hell was that for?'

'After what you did to those other men, why do you think?'

'Fair enough.' Bobby rubbed his neck. 'I can't help thinking there was an easier way to do that,' he muttered.

'Calla and I have talked. We've agreed to take your offer. Give me the rest of the pearls, and I'll set you free.'

'Give us our boat, and I'll…' but a terrible realisation dawned on Bobby as he looked for Allie.

She wasn't there.

There was a brief, violent struggle and Bobby had Jono up against the cell wall with his staff pressed against his own throat.

'What have you done with her?'

'She…' choked Jono, '…she is with Calla. Safe. If you keep your side.'

'Stupid. *Stupid*!' It was directed at himself, but he found himself with a sneaking admiration for young Jono. He'd have done much the same thing himself.

'Wasting time,' Jono gasped.

Bobby let him go. 'Come on, then.'

'Wait. You were right before – they've got one of their marines sitting outside the main gate.'

'So what are we going to do about that? I have to tell you, I'm not in much of a state to go looking for another fight.'

Jono grinned. 'There's another way around that we use when we want to go for a smoke without the serj seeing.'

He led Bobby to a narrow break in the courtyard wall masked by ivy; they slipped through it and into the maze of cobbled alleys which ran behind and between tightly clustered buildings. In this manner they made it out of Timini and picked their careful way in the dark down the cliff path to the rocky cove where Tatters was moored, with Bobby blessing Allie for her paranoia and praying that nobody had interfered with their supplies. He saw with relief that the sacks and barrels were untouched and climbed to hunt around in the aft canopy for Allie's belongings. It was there: the small pouch which she'd stashed here for fear of pickpockets. In the dark, it felt like there were four pearls left. Not as many as he'd promised. Maybe enough. He gave them to Jono. 'It's all we've got,' he explained.

'Fine, fine,' the guard replied hastily. He was too wired with adrenaline to care, Bobby saw, anxious to finish this business and be gone. *Amen to that, brother*, he thought.

'Allie,' demanded Bobby. '*Now*.'

But she was already there.

Quick footsteps descended towards them down the cliff path: Allie and a young woman dressed in a long travelling cloak.

'Calla!' complained Jono. 'What are you doing? I said to wait…'

'You tied her up,' his lover admonished. 'That was wrong of you.'

'Yeah, what she said,' Allie added drily.

'If you lot are done?' asked Bobby. 'It's been a pleasure doing business with you.' He hopped aboard Tatters while Allie gave Calla a quick hug and then joined him. 'That's got to be the fastest case of Stockholm Syndrome on record,' he commented, wrangling the boom into place.

'She's pregnant,' Allie told him. 'Her parents don't know. They want her to marry some rich merchant's cousin.'

'Can we just go, please?'

They paddled with muffled oars away from the lights of Timini, and when the harbourfront came into view around the edge of the cove, they held their breaths, anxiously watching the dark bulk of the steamship for any signs of increased activity which would indicate that their escape had been discovered. It was slow going, but they didn't dare raise sail for fear that it would be seen against the stars. No lights flared aboard. No voices were raised. The only sounds were distant music drifting from one of the dockside taverns, the gentle slop of water and their own laboured breathing as they rowed their supplies painstakingly out into the open sea.

19

THE FLATS

1

The following morning's chaos began shortly before dawn, when Serjeant Osk marched up to the *Spinner's* gangplank with a group of his deputies, demanding to know what Berylin though she was doing by stealing his prisoners away in the dead of night. Nobody really believed this, of course – especially once it turned out that one of his own men had also disappeared along with his sweetheart – but the noise and bluster did at least allow Osk to save a certain amount of face. The harbour-front was in uproar. There was much indignant shouting and waving of arms as houses and boats were searched without the need for anything as tedious as actual warrants. Elderly maroon-clad matriarchs berated the officers shrilly from their balconies, and children swarmed excitedly along with hysterical stray dogs, each feeding the other's madness.

Runce and Berylin watched all of this from the *Spinner's* foredeck. Captain Mair had ordered all hands to stay aboard for fear of local reprisals – it didn't matter that the only casualty so far had been one of his own crew.

'I doubt this lot could find their arses with both hands,' commented Runce. 'Our runaways could be halfway to Drava by now.'

'The deputy and his girl, possibly,' she agreed. 'But our two? No. They're out there.' She turned her back on the harbour and out at the glimmering horizon. 'They've gone back out to where they belong. The Flats. The hole that they've torn open in our world.'

'Neither of them could have been the suborning phantasm, though, ma'am. If they were, they'd have brought the effect with them. We'd have felt it.'

'Maybe we did, Runce. Did you ever stop to wonder how one unarmed man and a woman older than myself could have taken on that many men and then escaped all the locks and watches put on them?'

'Simplest answer'd be that they're suborned locals themselves.'

She shook her head. 'Remember Bles Gabril? We didn't feel that until we were right in the middle of it. They're subtle, Runce. They're treading lightly in our world to avoid drawing attention to themselves. But it won't work. I've seen where they come from. I've got the stink of it in my nostrils – it's like smoke in one of your horrible officers' clubs. It clings to your clothes and skin. I've been trying to scrub it off since Bles Gabril, but it won't go.'

Runce looked at her sidelong, worried. Her face was pale and shining with perspiration, which he thought had little to do with the heat. She'd long since given up her uncomfortable Oraillean clothes and was dressed in loose shirt-and-britches like one of the crew. Strands of her hair – usually so tightly pinned – had come loose and drifted in her eyes as she stared at the horizon.

'I tell you,' she continued, 'I can smell it out there. He was wrong, the old man. The disease wasn't in his bones – it is in their whole world. They're a tumour in the skin of ours, and they have to be cut out. Now. Runce, go up and order the Captain to set a course into the Flats.

This was an order that was easier given than obeyed.

'Ma'am, you need to understand,' said the Captain, indicating the charts spread out across his desk. The labyrinthine islands of the Tourmaline Archipelago were etched around with depth soundings and indications of reefs, sandbars, and all manner of submerged threats, but more threatening than any of these was the blank white space into which she insisted they turn. 'Island hopping is one thing. A comprehensive survey of an area of open ocean that size would take a squadron of ships weeks.'

'I thought I'd made it clear that I am not talking about a survey any longer, Captain,' she replied. 'This mission was never about establishing the extent of the subornation zone known as the Flats, never mind – Reason forbid – about stabilising it for the blinkered short-term military purposes of a third-world conflict. We are going to put a stop to it for good. And I know precisely where we are going. *Here.*' She stabbed a finger into the dead centre of the empty white space.

'That's as may be,' he grunted. 'I'm not saying no to you, Miss Hooper, but we're going to need resupplying somewhere a damn sight bigger than here – somewhere they have minor things like coal and fresh water, for example.'

'We have just enough to get us there and back. That's all we need.'

Runce could see that the man had tried to be patient and reasonable, but that she was pushing him too far.

'Just enough to perish if the weather turns against us, you mean,' Mair snorted. Not forgetting I've got a dead crewman whose kin need informing and two more injured who I'd rather trust to a sea-cow than the witch-doctors they've got here.'

'Our mission for the King is more important than a few broken bones…'

'*Your* mission for *you*, is what you mean!' He was red-faced and furious. 'My ship and my crew are not playthings for politicians and women!'

'Captain Mair, listen to me very closely,' she said, each word as cold and precise as a piece of oiled machinery, 'because this woman speaks with the voice of the King. I have been given total discretion in this matter by the Department of Counter Subornation, and in case you've spent so long at sea that the salt has dried out your brains, let me remind you of what we do. We stop dreamers from a nightmare world taking over the bodies of your wives, sons, and daughters and suborning them for the foulest of purposes. We clear up the mess afterwards, patch up the bodies and minds, and seal up the holes in the world. We stand on the ramparts of reality and stop the nightmares, and if sometimes in the process we must become worse than any nightmare to do so, then so be it. Because I promise you this, Captain: I am not playing. If you stand in my way and prevent me from doing my duty, then I will see to it personally that you, this ship, and every man aboard never receives another charter, government or private, from Oraille or any other member of the Southern Alliance. I will impoverish them and their families without a second's hesitation, I will revoke every licence and permit you have ever been granted, and after I have this ship impounded and sold for scrap, I will finally see you, Mair, working the remainder of your miserable little life mopping the shit out of prison hulks.

'Now get this ship underway and chase down those two fugitives.'

She strode out of the wheelhouse without bothering to check that her orders were being obeyed.

2

Danae and her sister islands glowed golden in the growing light of dawn, even as they slowly dwindled behind Tatters, creating the dismaying impression that she was making no progress – and even going backwards.

'Are you sure we shouldn't get some sail up on this thing?' Bobby asked.

Allie squinted ahead towards where the sun was still veiled behind the horizon. 'Give it another few minutes,' she decided. 'When the sun's fully in our faces nobody behind will be able to see us for the glare.'

'Sounds like a plan, except for one thing.'

'What?'

'That.'

From Danae a black, accusatory finger of smoke was pointing into the salmon pink sky.

'Shit! Let's get her up!'

'We can't possibly outrun them!'

'We don't need to. We only need to get as far as the Flats. They'll take care of us.'

Bobby looked ahead and thought he could see where the Flats began – a bright strip of mirror-flat ocean – but it was hard to tell anything for certain in the light of the rising sun. They raised sail but, loaded as they were, the going was still agonisingly slow.

He watched a small black speck develop at the bottom of the smoke-finger and grow rapidly. Their patchwork sail flapped and bellied as Allie fought to extract every knot of speed from the slight morning breeze, and he could tell that it simply wasn't going to be enough.

3

On the *Spinner's* compass deck above the wheelhouse, the forward watch raised a yell: 'Sail! Sail!'

Berylin nodded with satisfaction. 'See, Captain? We'll have them before they've gone three leagues.'

Mair bit back a retort, instead ordering a course correction and full steam.

4

It shocked Bobby just how quickly the pursuing ship began to catch up with them; within minutes the speck had grown into a definable shape and he could hear the splash of its bow-wave and the crew calling to each other over the locomotive roar of its engines. Despite the ship's speed, the tiny figures on deck were readying themselves with a cold and professional calm, rather than yelling and brandishing weapons. Barring a miracle, there was nothing to prevent the Tatterdemalion's capture.

He squinted ahead but couldn't see anything which might possibly help them, never mind what Allie had said. The Flats were only a few hundred yards away, with no transitional zone between them and normal ocean. It looked like someone had simply drawn a line across the sea and rolled everything on the other side flat like a piece of tinfoil. But there was still nothing other than empty sky and horizon – nowhere to hide or take shelter when they reached it.

'Nearly there…' said Allie, straining at the sail.

The rowing was petrifying his arms, turning them into useless, cramped, rock-hard lumps of agonised stone which he had to fight to bend. On the foredeck, he saw the woman, Hooper, standing as far forward as she could get, as if dragging the ship after her with the force of her will. She unholstered that strange-looking gun –

all brass and levers with the flex trailing behind – and he was close enough to see cruel satisfaction in her smile.

5

'Ma'am,' said Runce cautiously, from his position at her elbow. 'You're going to tez them straight away? Oughtn't we see if they're suborned natives first? Procedure…'

'Procedure be damned!' she snarled. 'There is no procedure out here, Runce.'

Runce watched the tiny craft and its hopelessly battling crew of two and began to feel a measure of sympathy for them.

6

With barely a few hundred yards separating the two craft, Tatters lunged over the line and into the Flats, and immediately Bobby found the rowing easier, as if the water had lost some essential hold on their hull. Gritting his teeth against the burning cramps in his arms, he hauled at the oars harder, and Tatters shot forward like a greased dart.

The *Spinner* crossed, close enough that Berylin could hear Bobby's grunts of pain as he dragged at the oars.

'Ready the grapnels!' she ordered.

And a hole opened in the ocean between them.

It was not wide or particularly deep, but the *Spinner* ran over it like a speeding carriage hitting a pot-hole. Her bow dipped into it with a sharp lurch that threw many of the crew off their feet. Berylin grabbed the foredeck rail just in time and received a faceful of cold spray as the *Spinner* cut through the other side and wallowed back onto level water. Behind them now, the hole suddenly everted itself in a surging column of water, which collapsed and drenched everyone astern similarly. When it had gone, the surface was littered with bits of flotsam.

'What in blazes was that?' roared Captain Mair from the bridge. There was much running to and fro, but nobody could provide a coherent answer.

'It doesn't matter!' she shouted in reply. 'We keep going!' They'd slowed and lost some of their lead, and she wasn't having that. At the same time, she felt a thrill of vindication. That had been a clear protean effect intended to throw her off the chase. If she'd harboured any lingering doubts, they disappeared entirely now.

Black smoke belched from the engine stack as they accelerated again.

Two more holes opened a-port, and a third appeared on their starboard bow. This last one was much larger, and the spiral vortex which it caused was strong enough to drag the *Spinner* off-course, its straight line becoming a curve.

Berylin stared into its throat, aghast. It seemed to funnel down into the very Abyss, swirling prisms of green and blue darkening to purple and black at some appalling, unfathomable depth. She was paralysed as much by the total unexpectedness of its appearance as the awful destruction it threatened. If the *Spinner* were caught by it, they would all surely be crushed and drowned.

'Ma'am, tez it!' yelled Runce, but she barely heard him. '*Berry!*' he bellowed at her, and the shock of hearing him call her that snapped her out of it. '*Tez the fucking thing!*'

Reflexes kicked in. She aimed the tezlar pistol down into the roaring maelstrom and fired. A gout of steam erupted from where the crackling bolt of purple-white plasma was swallowed, and the hole inverted itself just as the other had done, in a huge water column filled with pieces of debris which swamped the entire deck fore of the wheelhouse.

He staggered towards her, drenched. 'Makes sense,' he gasped. 'We're in an Event, after all.'

'Well, we know what to do about that, don't we? Here, take it.' She passed him the tez. 'I must talk with Mair.'

Up in the wheelhouse, the Captain's eyes were wild. 'What's happening?' he demanded. 'What are those things?'

Seeing the terror and incomprehension in his expression did something to help her regain her poise. 'Protean manipulations of our reality caused by the irruption of an active subornation event,' she replied matter-of-factly. 'Does that help?'

'Damn it woman, this is not the time…'

'It's a dream, Captain. Somebody dreaming in another world and making it come to life in ours. Nothing that Runce and I have not handled a dozen times before. Just get us back on course after that boat and don't worry – so long as there aren't too many more of them.'

'What d'you mean?'

'The tezlar gun only has so many shots before it requires recharging.' Runce had already crossed to the other side of the deck and fired into the vortices in that direction, closing them.

'This is not…'

'This is *exactly* what you signed up for, Captain. Now show some bloody backbone and *resume course*.'

But more holes appeared, on either side, fore and aft. The ocean around the *Spinner* was riddled with them, each spewing its own debris field of wreckage. A large one opened directly under her stern, and for a moment her propeller screw was clearly visible, turning impotently in open air until the ship's momentum carried them past and it bit into water again – but not so far forward that it could escape the water column which erupted, driving her bow deeply down and flooding the deck in sheets of green water. She popped up again like a cork and settled in a cloud of spray.

Navigation became impossible. When the ship wasn't ploughing into vortices or swerving to avoid them, their spiralling eddies slewed her about such that it was the most Mair could do to simply avoid plunging straight into another yawning chasm, never mind following the other craft. There were certainly too many vortices for Runce to handle, and the tez was soon spent closing the nearest and worst-looking ones. Even so, the flotsam belched up by them soon became almost as much of a hazard, with splintered fragments of wood raining down on deck and tangled lines threatening to foul the propeller. Mair had no choice – despite Berylin's curses – but to turn the *Spinner* about and send her wallowing chaotically back into normal waters.

7

Bobby and Allie watched the ship retreat and collapsed into each other's aching arms, relieved and exhausted. The waters of the Flats calmed as quickly as they had risen and were soon their customary preternatural stillness.

'What the hell just happened?' asked Bobby, dazed.

Allie didn't reply but set the tiller, and Tatters drifted slowly towards home.

8

'I woke up, once,' she said, out of the blue. They'd been drifting for some time, regaining their strength. Stray was a small dark smudge ahead of them, and for the first time, Bobby appreciated how insignificant and vulnerable his home was. The fact that he even thought of it as his home, now, was frightening enough.

'I thought you were going to tell me what those things were back there?' he asked.

'I am. Just shut up and listen for a moment, will you? This isn't easy for me to talk about.'

'Sorry. You mean you woke up from...'

'My coma, yeah. Just once. At first I could only hear stuff: nurses, the machines, voices. My mom coming in every day to talk to me about her ridiculous friends and her charity work. I was so excited, you have no idea. I couldn't move or speak to let anyone know, but I think they must have figured it out somehow because they started talking to me directly and getting me to do these bio-feedback visualisation exercises to try and get my brain limbered up again. You know, imagine that you're wiggling your toes, that kind of thing. Trying to build new connections out of the broken wiring in my head. Then one day there was a big bright blur, and slowly that turned into lots of little blurs, and the blurs turned into things and I could see, too.'

'That's incredible.'

'Sort of. I was left with terrible tunnel vision – it was like looking at the world through a toilet roll, you know?'

'Still...'

'You know how in movies when the hero wakes up from a ten-year coma and bounces out of bed all muscled and tanned and goes off killing the bad guys who put him there in the first place? It's nothing like that at all. I was being fed through a tube in my stomach. I was also paralysed down my whole left side. I couldn't... you know, couldn't look after myself. Do you have any idea how demeaning that feels? Couldn't speak properly either. The doctors said they thought with intensive therapy there might have been some gradual improvement but that it was likely I'd need care for the rest of my life. I was a *doctor*, do you get it? I was the one who was supposed to be looking after someone like me.'

'God, how awful.'

'Yeah, well that wasn't the worst of it.' He saw with shock that she was crying now and moved to comfort her, but she pushed him away fiercely. 'You need to hear this!' She sniffed and swallowed. 'I have kids, Bobby. Two boys, Kyle and Sam. Had them when I was too young to know the difference between a gorgeous man and a good one. They're in their twenties now – handsome, clever boys. I told you that voices were the first things I heard – well, some of the voices were theirs, and I didn't recognise them. I didn't know who they were. And when I could see again there were these two strange young men with my mom, fussing over me. I couldn't *remember* them, Bobby. They had to bring in photographs to explain to me who they were. I couldn't remember them being bórn or growing up – that shitty, fucking bug in my brain had turned me into a drooling invalid who needed to be cleaned up by her mother and it had robbed my of my own children. Do you get that?'

Speechless, he could do nothing but watch as she cried and talked.

'I thought, fuck this, you know? I'm not strong or brave enough to deal with this. That probably makes me a coward, but nobody should have to live like that. Nobody. So I let it all slide away – I stopped doing the exercises and trying to talk or remember because I wanted it all to go away so much, and one day I fell asleep and ended up back on Stray. It was a lot easier the second time. I took the coward's way out, I know that, but at least here I can walk and talk and remember my boys.'

'Nobody can blame you for that.'

She wiped her face. 'Nobody but me. Whatever happens to me here – and I'll drown myself before I let that woman have Stray – it's preferable. But it's still just an existence. It's not really what you'd call a life. All of us Strays are living on borrowed time, me more than the rest because I at least had a choice. The thing I wanted to tell you is that since you've been here I've actually started to enjoy existing again.'

'Well that's a relief,' he said. 'For a moment there I was afraid you were going to declare your undying love for me.'

She laughed a little at that and finally let him hold her. 'I may be brain-damaged and terrified, Bobby Jenkins, but I'm not that desperate. The reason I told you what I did is because I don't want you to be under any illusions of what you might be facing if you do decide to wake up. So. You needed to know that. What I didn't tell you right at the start was how I managed to wake up in the first place.'

'Was it something to do with those whirlpool things?'

She nodded. 'I was fishing out past the Up boom when one opened up randomly right next to Tatters. The first Tatters, that is. It was just too strong for me to do anything about, and I fell in, convinced that I was going to drown, but instead I woke up.'

'We call them worldpools. Yeah I know, very funny. What we think is that the worldpools somehow link this place with that place. I don't know if they already existed and we fell through them, or if we created them by arriving here. They pop up in clusters whenever something big from Tourmaline crosses into the Flats – a bit like white blood cells attacking a virus. Occasionally one of the islanders' boats will get grabbed by one, which is one of the reasons they don't like us very much. All I know is that if you really are desperate to get back to the world, jumping into one of those is probably your best bet. When I came back, I found that I had this thing with me,' and she fished out the small plastic Christmas-cracker compass. 'It points to where the nearest one is, or is about to appear. Don't ask me where it came from or how it works.'

'Where did it come from? How does it work?'

'Child.'

'Seriously, maybe something about having gone from there to here and back again has given you a sense for these things, and your mind created that as a result.'

She shrugged. 'It works, that's all I know.'

'So why haven't I seen any of these worldpools before now?'

'How do you think you got here?'

He thought this through, trying to remember what it had felt like, surfacing here, and the rubbish and fragments of flotsam which had surrounded him, just like the debris which had littered the water around the *Spinner*. 'So,' he said, 'the stuff that comes up with them.'

'Dreamwrack. The rubbish left over from when people dream. You know how when you wake up, you're aware that you've had an incredibly vivid dream, but all you can remember are fragments?'

'Yes.'

'Dreamwrack. We use it to build and repair Stray. Same with a lot of the fish around here. You dream, you wake up, and little bits of the dream go swimming off.'

'Wait up. Do you mean that we're eating people's dreams?' He thought about Blenny, Carmen, and Igor gobbling up the bright red beads of his blood and wondered if they were the by-blows of someone's half-remembered dream.

'They aren't dreams themselves – it's like if you get a burning log and whack it really hard you get a cloud of sparks; they're from the fire but they're not the fire itself.'

'This is… this is a lot to take in.'

'Well you just settle back and take it in. We'll be home soon enough. Just take my advice: don't try talking to anybody about it, not even Seb. They won't be able to answer your questions, and they won't thank you for reminding them of where they really are. Especially the Lachlans.'

As Stray grew larger ahead of them, he tried to imagine a small raft with a woman clinging to it being flung out by the upsurge of one of those worldpools and into this pitiless environment – doing it knowingly, willingly – and began to get some idea of how awful the conscious world must have been for her. He didn't rule out the possibility of having a closer look at one of them, but in the meantime she'd said that she was enjoying existence again because of him, and he wasn't about to run away from that.

The sense of homecoming that Bobby felt when he saw the hub of Stray rising from the blue plain of the ocean took him completely by surprise. He saw arms raised in welcome, smiles of greeting on familiar faces: Stuart, Marjorie, Seb, Joe, and even Sophie, standing aloof on the summit. Knowing the names of places and having memories associated with them – *here* I learned how to plait cordage; *here* I dived for kelp and oysters – all flooded up in him quite suddenly and left him trying to help Allie moor Tatters with a strange wateriness doubling his vision. Even his three loyal Fishketeers were there to greet him, darting around under Tatters like dogs welcoming home their master.

Marjorie fell on the fresh foodstuffs with cries of delight while Allie and Bobby distributed presents to the others: a pouch of evil-smelling tobacco for Seb, a bag of marbles for Joe ('Because every boy needs marbles,' said Bobby. 'We tried to get you square ones so they wouldn't roll off the dock but they didn't have any, so be careful with these, okay?'), and a pair of mad Danae fisherman's trousers for Lachlan in a pattern which was as close as they could get to a tartan. In all the excitement, it was some time before anybody noticed the state of Bobby's face.

Marjorie gasped. 'Dear Lord, Bobby, what happened to you?'

He'd done his best to clean off the crusted blood, but there were still several obvious bruises on his face and an ugly purple welt across his throat left by Jono's cudgel.

'Well,' he said, embarrassed, 'there may have been something of a scuffle.'

'Scuffle,' repeated Lachlan, his small eyes shrewd and instantly suspicious. 'Between you and…?'

'Just a couple of the locals.'

'These locals. They wouldn't have been wearing uniforms, by any chance, would they?'

'Look…'

'Oh for Chrissakes, Stuart!' erupted Allie. 'We got attacked, okay? Some foreign woman and her goon-squad tried to abduct me off the street in broad daylight, and Bobby saved me, for which act of bravery the local Sheriff slung both our asses in jail.'

Marjorie's hands flew to her mouth. 'Oh, you poor girl! Are you alright, dear?'

'Fine, thanks for asking,' she replied, still glaring at Lachlan, who was shaking his head in despair.

'I don't believe it,' he groaned. 'I send you off on a simple shopping…'

'Okay, first?' she shot back. 'You don't "send" me anywhere, Braveheart. Second, if it weren't for me, you'd still be eating fish-heads and the fluff out of your goddam navels. Third, *this was always going to happen, Stuart.* I'm just lucky Bobby was with me when it did.'

'No,' Lachlan insisted. 'If we'd kept a low profile, if we hadn't interfered, they'd have left us alone. You must have done something on your last trip to get their attention.'

'You're saying this is *my* fault?'

'You're the only one of us who has any business with the outside world. You tell me.'

'Well Jeez, maybe you're right,' she replied with scathing sarcasm. 'Maybe I shouldn't have dressed so provocatively.' She indicated her threadbare clothes and laughed. 'Obviously I was asking for it.'

'There's no need for…'

'I don't see how this changes anything, Lachlan,' Bobby interrupted. 'The people who live on these islands have known about the Flats for ages. They must have done. Do you seriously think that none of them have ever tried to come looking for you before now? Because you're a fool if you do. The Flats kept you safe today just like they've always done – the only difference is on this occasion it's a little more in your face.'

Seb chuckled. 'Looks like they was in *your* face most of all, my friend.'

'Thanks, Seb. Helpful.'

Sophie, who had been sitting silently at the edge of the conversation, added very quietly, as if to herself: 'Other people are the least of your problems.'

'What's that supposed to mean?' Lachlan snapped.

But she drifted back to her chamber without another word.

Bobby dismissed it. 'Stuart,' he continued, 'this changes nothing if you don't want it to. When the bruises have gone, you can carry on with your little Swiss Family Robinson Crusoe fantasy as if nothing ever happened. Or – and here's a thought to explore – you could try pulling your head out of your arse and dealing with the real world for a change. Either way, I'm going for a drink. Excuse me.' He brushed past and headed for Seb's not-so-secret moonshine.

After that, it was easy to slot right back into Stray's routine as if nothing had happened. Living in such close proximity to each other made it a necessity to let bygones be bygones, and as one day passed after another without any more disturbances from Sophie and no sign of threatening black smoke on the horizon, he began to appreciate what Allie had said about the appeal of not asking questions and pretending that the outside world didn't exist. Far easier to shell oysters and tend the booms and make love to Allie than fret over unanswerable questions about where or who he was.

So he drifted with the days, content for a while, and completely forgot Sophie's parting words.

PART
THREE

PART THREE

CHAPTER 20

HOMECOMING

1

'Sorry, mate, no kids allowed in the bar,' said Barry, and he watched the man in the spectacles look around and down at the boy by his side as if seeing him for the first time.

'Oh, sorry, no,' he said with a little laugh. 'I haven't come for a drink. I'm looking for my sister Vanessa. I was told she works here.'

Before Barry could stop her, Janey – bouncy, helpful, tattooed little goth-girl that she was – piped up cheerfully with, 'She's on a break. She'll be back at one, though. Wow, is this your son? He's big and handsome, isn't he?'

'He's shy,' said the man, laying a hand on the silent boy's head.

'Would you like a bowl of chips and some lemonade while you wait?' she chirped. 'I can serve you in the snug.'

'That would be very sweet of you. Thanks.' His tone was amiable, and his smile easy, but Barry watched his eyes behind those spectacles glancing around the bar, checking out the corners and doorways, the lunchtime drinkers, and himself, seeing that he was watched. Barry held his gaze. The Grange wasn't a violent pub, but he'd learned his trade in the kinds of places where if the bouncers frisked you and found no weapons, they gave you one so that you stood a fighting chance – and every instinct in him screamed that this guy was trouble. Never mind that he had a lad with him.

'We'll just go through and wait, then,' said Spectacles, talking to Janey but looking right back at Barry, and went through into the next room.

'He seems nice,' Janey said as she started pouring a lemonade.

194

'Well done, my girl,' Barry replied. 'You've just earned yourself the rest of Vessa's afternoon shift.'

'What?! Why?' Her face was a picture of dismay. 'I'm meant to be off at two!'

'Because if that was her brother, then I'm the Queen's left tit. Cancel your plans, bab – I've got a phone call to make.'

2

The delivery yard of the Grange was narrow and stacked along both sides with plastic bottle crates, aluminium barrels, and overflowing skips; it backed onto a brick labyrinth of alleyways and service roads between the office buildings, lap-dancing clubs, Chinese supermarkets and multi-storey car parks which occupied the rest of the block, and despite the phone signal being a bit rubbish, it was one place where Barry could be guaranteed that he wouldn't be overheard.

He dialled Vessa's number, cursing when he was put straight through to her answerphone.

'Vessa,' he started, 'it's Barry. Look, flower…'

A hand closed over the phone, hard – unbelievably hard, actually – crushing his fingers against the plastic until something snapped, and he screamed. His fighter's instincts took over, and he swung his left fist up and around, but it too was caught and crushed in a grip impossible for a normal human being. He screamed again and fell to his knees in front of the spectacled man and his boy. Incredibly, the boy was growling. It was the sort of sound he'd only ever heard in dog-fights.

Degan looked down at the man whose fists he held and tutted.

'Barry Ryan Norris,' he said. 'Deputy manager of the Grange public house, cocktail bar and, on alternate Fridays, burlesque club, yes?'

'There's a security camera on this yard, sunshine,' he grunted. 'I suggest you fuck off before I count to three. One…'

'Three,' Degan finished for him and squeezed harder. Something crunched in Barry's left hand this time, and he howled. Blood trickled down his wrist from where Degan held him. 'Mr Norris,' Degan continued, 'believe it or not, I'm not interested in you.' The lad squatted down next to him and made that snarling noise again. Barry couldn't concentrate very well through the pain, but there seemed to be something terribly wrong with the boy's mouth. 'My only concern is to get Vanessa, or Sophie, or whatever it is she's calling herself at the moment, safely back where she belongs. I've been to her flat, but she's not there – now, I could wait for her to get back, which is probably the smart thing to do, but my life is generally quite tedious, and this is the most interesting thing that is likely to happen to me for some time, so I hope you don't mind if I live it up a little.' The hradix, meanwhile, was sniffing at the moaning man and drooling. 'This little tyke, on the other hand, is *very* interested in you. Don't blame him, though. He's had a very long and boring trip down here. You know how kids are.'

The hradix grinned, revealing enough teeth to make a shark jealous. The grin kept on widening, curving up to its ears.

The only thing that Barry could think as he watched its maw widen and come rushing towards him was of an old television ad for toothpaste, in which a little cartoon man's head flipped back a hundred and eighty degrees so he could brush right at the back. *Better get a flip-top head!* babbled his brain, over and over. There were no prayers, no life flashing before his eyes, no last thoughts of his mother – no consolation whatsoever. Just meaningless gibbering and then screaming blackness as his throat was torn out.

3

When Vessa returned from her lunch break via the staff entrance at the rear of the pub, she stopped at the sight of a man – forty-ish, shaven-headed, wearing glasses – lounging by the open back gate. He wasn't particularly large, but he filled his skin in a way that created an impression of compressed power, and her nerves screamed instant recognition.

Hegemony.

'Hello, sweetie!' he said brightly.

'No!' she whispered, faltering backwards.

'Oh, come on, Sophie,' Degan grinned. 'Or whoever you are right now. Are you really going to tell me that you're surprised? Did you actually think that you could hide from us?'

'I'm not… how… but you're not a doctor.'

'That's right. I'm not from the hospital. I'm from a different department – what you might call the 'bring 'em back alive' squad. You've been promoted, sweetie! I'll tell you all about it on the way home. Come on,' he reached to take her elbow. 'The car's just around the corner.'

'No!' She shook him off, calculating how far it was to the door of the Grange and whether or not she'd be able to call for help.

'Not a clever idea,' he advised, as if he could read her thoughts, and it was quite likely he could – or at least, her emotions. 'Not clever at all. Even if you were quick enough, and I'm fairly sure you're not, you know I'd have to kill everybody in there just for having seen me, don't you? As it is…' he shrugged and allowed the yard gate to swing open slightly so that she could glimpse the abattoir beyond, '…there's already been a bit of collateral damage. I get the feeling they're going to be a bit short-staffed tonight.'

'Jesus,' she whispered. 'What have you done?'

She had no choice. All her plans, her careful arrangements to remove any trace of Sophie – all of it had been a waste of time, and everything she'd built up was forfeit. Her mind was racing for anything she could say or use to buy a little time to think. Running was no good; he was bound to be faster and stronger. Calling for help would simply endanger innocent people. Her one consolation was that since Steve had left, there was less danger of dragging him deeper into this. Her mind twittered and flapped like a crippled bird.

Dazed, she let him lead her to a large car parked in a side street. He opened the rear door and she got in, then recoiled in terror and tried to scramble back out again when she found herself sitting next to a solemn-faced child covered in gore.

'Oh my *God*!'

'Yeah, I know,' he grimaced. 'I didn't really think that one through. Maddox's gonna kill me.'

She recoiled, trying to push past him and away.

'Oy, we'll have less of that, thank you very much,' he said and shoved her back in, locking the door. She pressed herself as far back against it as she could, away from the monstrosity which grinned at her and kicked its shoes against the seat in front. The interior of the car was smeared with blood from where it had been climbing around. Degan got in the driver's seat and tossed the hradix a mint, which it snapped expertly out of mid-air and crunched, making happy little hooting noises. 'Try not to antagonise it,' he suggested. 'I don't fancy having to hose what's left of you off the seats.'

'What is it?'

'Easily bored,' he replied, and started the engine. 'So I hope you know some nursery songs, because you're on child-minding duty, sweetie.'

She stared at it, appalled. 'How could you people do that to a child?'

'And we can have a bit less of that, too,' he warned. 'Last thing I want is you being lippy all the bloody way home.'

'If we're not going back to the hospital, then where are you taking me? Who *are* you?'

'I'm the man they send to pick up the confused, the frightened and the lost. When a Passenger appears, there's usually hell to pay, especially if it's an animal like that there.' The hradix, sensing that it was being spoken about, barked. He tossed it another mint. 'I take them somewhere safe and cosy, where they can't hurt anybody, while we figure out who or what they are and whether or not they can be put to any use.'

'But I'm not a Passenger!'

'No, you're not,' he conceded. 'But you have been on the Hegemony's watch-list all the same – or at least you were until you decided to go a-wandering. Somebody somewhere has been very interested in what you might be carrying. Plus, you're not exactly the same girl you were when the doctors took you away in the little van with the square wheels, are you, eh? Vanessa, is it? And now you start making waves, so they send little old me to bring you in and find out what's what. Now, do be a love and shut the fuck up. I'm trying to drive.'

As they drove through the city centre, she wondered how they could pass so many other cars without a single person noticing the blood-covered child bouncing up and down on the seat next to her. Even if they did, what was it that she hoped they would do? Flash their lights? Call the police and have helicopters come flying to the rescue? Nothing like that was going to happen. She watched normality slipping past on either side: first the highrises and dual-carriageways, then the shops, houses, and schools of the suburbs. Soon they would be on the motorway and all of that would be gone forever, along with Steve and Jackie and Barry and every other normal human being she'd come to cherish in the last year and a half of her failed experiment at being real. Not even the Goddess could protect her now.

At that, an awful idea occurred to her, something which might just save her, but at a cost she dreaded to contemplate. But in the end, what choice did she have?

'It's not just me, you know,' she said. 'I mean, I'm not the only one. There's my ex-boyfriend too. He's a Passenger, just like you.'

Degan sighed and flicked a glance at her in the rear-view mirror, and the hradix let out a feral growl of such depth and ferocity that it shocked her into silence.

'What did I say was the last thing I wanted?' Degan demanded. 'Go on, what was it?'

'Me being lippy,' she replied, very quietly.

'Abso-fucking-lutely,' he muttered and focussed ahead once more.

The city continued to slip by. They passed through a no-man's land of budget hotels and motorway slip-roads and then they were on the M5 heading south, and with each passing mile, her heart sank lower.

'Why?' he said suddenly, obviously having mulled this over. 'Why would you volunteer that? About your ex?'

Eager to seize on this, but not to appear so, she manufactured a bitter little laugh. 'Because then you can take us both, and when we get where we're going, and you're the golden boy, I'll have someone who owes me one.'

'What makes you think I'll owe you anything?'

'I've got nothing to lose, have I? You can easily check up on him; there's no point me lying about it. And besides, the bastard walked out on me, so the hell with him.'

'Christ, remind me never to get on your wrong side.'

He hated to admit it, but she made sense. The readings from the Hegemony's buoys had pointed unarguably to her address, but evidence of her relationship with McBride was solid, and it was only an assumption that she was their solitary source. As she said, it was easily verifiable. If she was telling the truth, she'd have earned him some brownie points with Maddox (which might make up for the mess he'd made of the car, if nothing else), and he might very well decide to owe her in return. If she was lying – well then, he'd make sure he had a bit of fun with her on the way home. Not enough to damage her for the Hegemony's purposes, of course. Just enough to teach her to never fuck with him again.

'Okay. I'll play. Where can we find this scoundrel of an ex-boyfriend?'

'He works in a gallery,' she replied and gave him directions.

4

On the short walk from the University's south car park to the Barber Institute, she prayed that the pair of them looked so utterly nondescript that nobody spared them a second glance. There was no reason that they should, but equally there was no way of telling what might be leaking through them from Tourmaline, which might cause people to look again at the shaven-headed man and the frightened-looking woman at his side. It was for much the same reason that Degan had ordered the hradix to sit and stay in the car. There was certainly no point in trying to attract help from any passers-by; it would only get them killed. To all intents and purposes, Vessa and Degan were just another student couple.

They were also ignored by the gallery staff at the little shop kiosk just inside the main door, and the coffee-drinking customers at the tables outside the concert hall, who chatted and laughed as if death were not walking right through them. It amazed her.

They climbed the long sweep of the curving marble staircase which switch-backed to the upper-floor galleries, with Vessa willing Steve not to be there, to be on a break, having a day off, even lying in hospital – anything but here, where he might be tempted into some act of suicidal heroics. Things had finished badly between them, sure, but despite what she'd said to Degan in the car, she still didn't want him to get hurt.

The security station was at the top of the stairs. A man she didn't recognise was sitting at it. Unthinking, she expelled a huge sigh of relief.

'What was that for?' Degan whispered, immediately suspicious.

'What do you think?' she hissed back. 'I'm terrified that you're going to hurt someone.'

He linked his arm with hers and fixed a smile on his face. 'Just so we're clear on this? If you try anything silly, I'll feed you your own kidneys. Okay, sweetie? So where's your ex, then?'

'If he's not downstairs, he must be up here somewhere.'

The corridors of the Barber's upper gallery formed a square, arranged around the two-storey height of the concert-hall, each with a different colour scheme. Straight ahead from the top of the stairs and the guard's station ran the Blue Gallery (art 1800 to 1900), which turned right into Beige, then Red, Green, and back to the stairs. Directly ahead of them, where Blue met Beige, hung She Shall Be Called Woman in glorious full view of everybody who arrived on the upper floor. At the diagonally opposite corner from the stairs, where Beige met Red, was a second security station – just a chair where another guard could sit and watch the two corridors that the guard by the stairs couldn't see. It also meant that Vessa wouldn't be able to see who was sitting there until she and Degan had got all the way to the painting. She led the way forward, just as she'd led Steve's friend Caffrey.

Sophie? she called.

There was no response. They were halfway along the corridor. *Please, I'm sorry. I know I've been a selfish bitch, but I need your help. This man, he's going to take us back to the white coats and the drugs, and I don't think I can take that again. Please, you have to answer me.*

Still nothing. They were within a few yards of the Goddess, and the Beige Gallery was opening up on her right. Her heart stopped.

Sitting on that chair at the far end, doing his crossword, was Steve. He was frowning at the paper; he hadn't seen her.

Don't look up. Please, don't look up. Sophie, where are you?

She was almost within touching distance of the painting now. She had to try to concentrate – no, not concentrate, the very opposite. She had to disconnect herself from the world, reach inwards to the place where Sophie hid and make contact just like when she'd panicked and pushed Neil Caffrey into Tourmaline. But it was impossible to do either when Steve was at the other end of the next corridor and any second he might look up, because then she'd have killed him.

But Degan had already seen, recognising McBride from the picture in her file. 'So that's your chap, then, is it?'

Steve looked up at this loud voice in the otherwise hushed silence of the gallery, and frowned in surprise. 'Vessa?' he called 'What are you doing here? Who's this?'

'Mr McBride, so pleased to meet you at last!' grinned Degan, advancing with his hand outstretched for shaking. 'My sister and I are just having a little family art appreciation time.'

Steve got up, tossed the paper to the floor, and met him halfway. He looked straight past Degan at Vessa. There was only one other time he'd seen her looking this pale and stricken. Her fingertips were trembling inches away from the painting's surface. 'Is this true? He's your brother?' Suspicion darkened his eyes. 'Hey, is this bloke bothering you?'

'Bothering,' mused Degan, and grasped McBride's hand, sensing instantly that he was not a Passenger. McBride didn't have about him that peculiar sense of brimming that a Passenger carried, as if the life-force of the person from Tourmaline – or something about that world itself – was spilling out and over into this reality. 'Tell you about bothering, my man. Piss off out of here right now, or I'll bother your head off your fucking shoulders.' He snatched his hand away and spun back on Vessa. 'And you! What the *fuck* are you…?' but stopped, open-mouthed.

She Shall Be Called Woman was not just moving – it had opened.

The goddess herself had disappeared, and in her absence the hazy golden clouds through which she had been rising shifted and billowed, shot through with the rays of a shimmering, half-hidden sun. The plants and flowers which had wreathed her thighs now swayed in an unfelt wind, even though he could smell the air of that place – warm and humid, like a greenhouse or an aquarium.

Steve recognised it from weeks ago, when Caffrey had gone missing. It was the smell of seawater. And suddenly he realised what he was looking at. He wasn't looking at the sky at all, and Eve hadn't been flying to heaven; she'd been underwater, rising into existence, and he was there too, gazing up through fronds of seaweed at sunlight refracting through the surface. The impression was so vivid that he could actually feel it – the soothing lull of the enclosing waters, the drifting caress of the weed, and he thought: wouldn't it be fine to break the surface and see what colour the sky was in that place? He could search for the missing goddess and bring her back. All he had to do was step forward and kick upwards.

Degan also recognised it: it was the shifting turquoise water of home, and the sight of it filled him with a nauseating mixture of homesickness and terror. 'No!' he whispered.

Then Vessa grabbed him and shoved him as hard as she could at it.

The part of him that was a deck-swabbing grunt in the Elbaite navy fell through and was claimed by the submarine depths, while the part of him that was Roger Simkin bounced off the painting's surface and fell senseless to the floor. The image rippled, wavered, broke up and reconstituted itself into the image of Eve ascendant, as if nothing had ever happened, and all that was left was the smell of brine and a man lying drenched and unconscious on the gallery floor.

Steve was brought back to his senses by the sight of Vessa, who had crouched and was searching through the man's pockets. 'Bingo!' she grinned, scooping up his car-keys. Then she grabbed Steve by the wrist with surprising strength and tried to drag him after her back down the gallery.

After a few unthinking steps he stopped and refused to budge. 'No, stop. What the hell do you think you're doing?'

Before she could reply, the guard from the top of the stairs arrived at a run, wide-eyed and clutching a squawking walkie-talkie. 'What happened?'

'That nutter attacked me,' said Steve, indicating the unconscious man. 'Then he collapsed. Don't ask me, I never even touched him. His friend here,' he indicated Vessa, 'had her hands all over the Watts.'

'Steve…' she started, but he ignored her.

'Sort this one out for medical attention,' he told his colleague. 'I'll get her down to the office and we'll see about calling the police.'

'Right you are.'

'Steve, let me explain…'

He took her by the elbow and marched her towards the stairs, shaking his head in absolute denial. 'No. No way. You're not dragging me any further into this – whatever it is.' It was the taxi all over again, but this time he wasn't getting in.

For her part, Vessa allowed herself to be marched, since he was taking her in the direction she wanted to go anyway. 'What are you going to do?'

'What I should have done the first time you committed criminal damage against a public work of art. I'm calling the police.'

'Do you mean the time I sent your friend Neil into the Flats, or the time after that?' she asked calmly.

'Great,' he replied, still walking. 'You can tell them all about that, too. Add assault and kidnapping to the list.'

She laughed. 'Do you know how melodramatic you sound?'

'Because you, of course, do not in the least sound completely barking mad,' he shot back.

'Help me,' she said, 'and I'll tell you where Neil has gone. I'll even see if I can get him back for you.'

'You'll tell the police, I'm pretty bloody sure of that.'

'Of course I will, but they'll never believe me. You know that. You've seen enough to understand that there is something going on here which people like the police will never believe, even assuming I get anywhere near talking to them. The moment you hand me over, the Hegemony will get hold of me again, and that is precisely why I have no intention whatsoever of allowing you to hand me over.' She pulled free from his grip easily and stood facing him. 'Don't be under any illusions Steve; I'm not begging for anything here. I'm offering you a deal. Help me, drive for me, and I'll help you get your friend back.'

'Sorry, Vessa, it doesn't work that way.' He tried to catch hold of her again, and she slapped his hand aside. She looked closely at him, frowning, as if seeing something for the first time.

'Wow,' she said.

'What?'

'You're really going to do this, aren't you?'

'Do what?'

'This. You're so pissed off because I lied to you that you're going to willingly ignore everything that you've seen, aren't you? You've spoken to Sophie, you've seen a painting come to life – my God, you've even seen Tourmaline. I know you have. But your poor precious pride has been wounded, hasn't it? And you can't possibly let that go, so it's all got to be ignored. I might say that you're a coward and leave it at that, except you obviously haven't given any thought to what's going to happen to Jackie and her boys after this, which makes you a selfish prick into the bargain.'

'Jackie? She's got nothing to do with any of this. Are you threatening…?'

'No, I'm not *threatening*. Don't be so bloody dense. But if the Hegemony can't find me, they'll work down the food chain, won't they?'

'I don't think I believe in this Hegemony you keep going on about. You're just being paranoid.'

'Yeah, see that guy lying over there in a pool of seawater? Just my paranoia. Pride, Steve, can be a good thing sometimes, but I'm afraid that now you're just being wilfully stupid. Goodbye.'

He reached for her a third time, but she was in no mood for him to lay hands on her again. She spun, gathered a handful of his shirt, and cocked her other fist back. 'Swear to God, McBride, so help me I will…'

But he was holding out his cupped hand. 'Give me the keys,' he said. 'I'll drive.'

Degan had left the car in the shadow of some trees, at the far end of the parking lot, to try and avoid casual passers-by seeing the hradix – he'd even cracked the windows an inch and joked about how cruel it was to leave pets in cars on hot days – while Vessa had done her best to clean the creature up with a bottle of water and an old towel she'd found in the boot. But when she returned with Steve, she found that it had shredded the back seat upholstery and made a nest from the stuffing in the rear footwell, and there was no way it was going to pass for anything normal. When it saw her approach it bounced up and down, snapping at the air in welcome.

'Jesus,' he breathed, horrified. 'What's wrong with him?'

'Since you ask, he's possessed by a vicious man-eating reptile from Tourmaline,' she replied. 'And it will rip your throat out unless you give it a mint.'

'That's not funny.' He watched her unwrap an entire packet of extra-strong mints and throw them onto the back-seat. He hradix dove for them, hooting delightedly, and Steve slipped into the driver's seat gingerly, trying not to hear the crunching and slavering noises coming from behind him. As he fastened his seat belt, he became aware of its face suddenly being very close to his own. It was emitting a loose, rattling growl, and its breath stank. Worse, the eye which stared into his own wasn't remotely human; the iris was huge and blood-red. He froze.

'It's not…' he tried to say. 'Not…'

'Not going to hurt you.' She turned to the creature. 'This is a friend, okay? A friend.'

The eye blinked – sideways – and a long purple tongue trailed up the side of his face.

'See? It likes you. Still think I'm being paranoid?'

Steve shuddered and started the engine, trying not gag at the smell of its drool on his cheek. 'So, where to?'

'Ennias.' She was tapping at her phone.

'Oh, him. I have to say, he wasn't too complimentary about you the last time we met.'

'Really?'

'I think his exact words were "silly bint".'

She laughed. 'He'll change his mind and find us somewhere safe. He'll have to.'

'Why?'

'Because he's from Tourmaline, too. He's been living as an exile in this world for years with no way to get home. There are thousands – probably tens of thousands – of exiles here, and I've just sent one of them back. I can send all of them back. Trust me, he'll protect us.'

CHAPTER 21

THE SWARM

1

Degan had always hated the sea.

He hated its easy lies and its sadistic indifference to human suffering. As a child, he'd lost his father and three uncles to it, too young to prevent his mother and sisters from being forced to earn a living by the cocks of foreign sailors, while all he could do was pick their pockets. Meanwhile, the sea glimmered in snatched glimpses at the ends of cobbled alleyways, promising escape and never delivering, while he fought in the shit with the other urchins. And when he was old enough to understand that it was only a matter of time before he was forced to sell his own skinny arse in turn, he signed on with the Elbaite fleet as a bilge-rat and discovered that he'd simply sold it for the King's coin instead – the only difference being that on board a gun-cog there were fewer places to hide – and that taunting glimmer was all about him now, serving only to highlight how small his new prison was. For sure, he'd worked his way up through the hierarchy of shipboard cruelty, but all the time and everywhere, that limitless horizon was in his face, promising freedom which never appeared.

So when he awoke, floating on a shabby raft barely bigger than a coffin and surrounded by that same diamond-lanced blue void, he threw back his head and unleashed a howl of despair.

Sweet Lady of the Islands help him – he was home.

2

Steve and Vessa abandoned the car in a supermarket car park where they spent as much time as they dared buying new clothes for the hradix and cleaning it up properly, before travelling the rest of the way by bus to the address of the safe-house which Vessa said Ennias had given her. It turned out to be an extremely ordinary-looking semi-detached house in a sleepy, suburban street in Hall Green. Nevertheless, they walked past it warily several times before plucking up the courage to approach the front door.

Vessa rang the bell.

'What makes you think you can trust anybody here?' asked Steve.

'Sophie and I lived in a lot of care homes,' she said by way of explanation, 'but when she stopped sleeping we were sent to a sleep disorder clinic. Of course, it wasn't *just* a sleep disorder clinic; the Hegemony keeps tight control on places like that because of the link between dreaming and Tourmaline, obviously.'

'Obviously.'

'Not that we knew this at the time. By then Sophie was unconscious pretty much all of the time, which left me in charge, and I stuck it for as long as I could before deciding to run away. It turned out that the Hegemony weren't the only people with their eyes on places like that, because shortly after I left I was contacted by this man called Ennias who said he could give me somewhere safe to stay. Needless to say I totally ignored him…'

'Why does that not surprise me?'

'… and I ended up sleeping rough for a while. It… well, it wasn't much fun, let's just leave it at that, and he ended up looking like the lesser of several evils, so I took him up on it. I ended up in a house full of exiles in Milton Keynes, and they were the loveliest, most helpful people you could ever hope to meet. So I trust him, yes. I probably owe my life to him.'

They waited.

'So why isn't one of the loveliest, most helpful people I could ever hope to meet opening the door, then?' asked Steve.

She frowned. 'I don't know. He said there might not be anybody in. I'm going to check around the back.'

'Be…' he started, but she'd already gone.

It was evident that the place was well kept; the back lawn and hedges were neatly trimmed, though the patio furniture had a cover pulled over it, and there was no sign of people actually spending time out here. He looked under the cover and found an ash-tray. It was spotless.

Vessa found a post-it note stuck to the back door. *Open Me*, it read.

'Cute,' she commented and, finding the door unlocked, went in.

'It doesn't bother you at all that this place has been left empty with the door unlocked?' he asked. She ignored him.

They found themselves in a bright, spotlessly clean kitchen. On the counter were two carrier bags stuffed with groceries, including a frozen pizza still solid enough, he thought, to have been put there this morning – all accompanied by another post-it inviting them to help themselves. He still couldn't quite believe it was that easy. Checking out the rest of the house he found it to be well-furnished and tidy but utterly devoid of any sense of human habitation: no clothes hanging in the wardrobes, no rubbish in the bins – not even any little flecks of toothpaste on the bathroom mirror. It felt like a show-home or a theatre set. He only allowed himself to relax when he saw that the hradix had made itself another nest in the bath out of cushions and bedclothes.

'Can't we do something for it?' he asked, as they watched it twitching in its sleep. 'Isn't there any way of finding his parents? Missing persons or something?'

'Maybe,' she replied. 'Eventually. We need to get ourselves safe first. There's definitely something human left in it otherwise it wouldn't be able to understand us as well as it does, but even if we did find out his name, do you really think it would be a good idea sending him home in his current state?'

'Probably not.'

They made tea and sat outside in the sun, watching blackbirds squabbling in the hedge. Or they might have been mating – he couldn't tell.

'For what it's worth,' she said eventually, 'I'm sorry.'

'That's actually worth more than you'd think,' he replied.

'I didn't mean to use you,' she added.

'Yes, you did.'

'Actually, yes, I did. But I feel horrible about it.'

'No, you don't.'

She sighed. 'No, I don't.'

They sat and drank tea.

'The problem, Steve, is that I have an over-abundance of self-awareness.'

'Oh, *that's* the problem.'

'You know how most people go through their lives not really sure about who they are, or what they want to do, or what their purpose is in life?'

'Just the little questions. Sure.'

'Well I don't. I know exactly what I'm here for. I've been given a very limited toolkit of responses to fulfil a very specific brief, and that is to protect Sophie, whatever it takes: lying, cheating, it's all good.'

Despite telling himself not to get drawn into it again, he found that he couldn't help himself. 'But I thought you said you were trying to break free of her. You've been trying to make your own life. I thought that was what I was part of.'

'You were.'

'So why the lies?'

'Right, like you wouldn't have run a mile if I'd been totally honest from the start. Which you did, by the way, when I was. I needed you, Steve – all right, so I needed you for me and not for Sophie for once, but that needing you made it okay to lead you on. I'd like to feel sorry for it, and I want to be completely honest with you because you deserve that at least, but the fact is that I just don't. I feel sorry for not feeling sorry, that's what I mean. And I do still need you, because this business is nowhere close to being over.'

Her insistence that she still needed him, despite everything that had happened, made him respond more harshly than he'd intended. 'I'm in this business just until you tell me whether or not you can get Caffrey back, and then that's me done, I'm afraid.'

'Oh, sure,' she scoffed. 'Because you and him were such great friends. Last of the great bromances. You're in this business because you can't keep away from me – face it.'

'You really are that full of yourself, aren't you?'

'I'm trying to be honest with you! I thought that was what you wanted! Sorry if some of it isn't what you want to hear, but I just don't have time for all that he-loves-me-he-loves-me-not bullshit. But alright, have it your way. Let's put that aside for now.' She turned to face him squarely. 'Steve, even assuming I can get him back, do you honestly think that will be the end of it? Come on, you're not that stupid.'

'Again, with the back-handed compliments.'

'No, seriously. What's going through your head? Caffrey has gone physically to a place that people from this world only ever reach in the deepest of dreams, and that makes him valuable not just to the Hegemony, who'll probably want to dissect his brain or something, but also the exiles. There's no way he'll be allowed to go back to a normal life, even if he can.' She hesitated, fidgeting with her mug. 'There's something I haven't told you about the night we… about the night Sophie came.'

'I'll add that to the list, then.'

'When I ended up in the place where she is, I met him. Briefly.'

If he'd thought she'd lost the capacity to surprise him, he was wrong. He stared at her, shocked. 'What do you mean you *met* him?'

'He was there, on Stray. I only saw him for a few seconds. It was all a bit confusing. But I got the impression – no, I'm sure – that he doesn't know who he is. He seems to think he's somebody called Bobby.'

'Maybe you made a mistake. If it was that confusing…'

'No, it was definitely him.'

'But why would he think he's somebody else?'

'I don't know enough about how any of this works,' she admitted. 'It could be that the shock of travelling there in the body, without the protection of being asleep and dreaming; it could have done something to his mind.'

'Done something to his mind. Christ, you're a piece of work.' He sat and watched the blackbirds, listening to the impossibly normal hum of suburbia around him. 'Still,' he reasoned, 'that's got to be some kind of good news. You know where he is, which should make it that much easier to bring him back, shouldn't it?'

'I suppose so, yes. But, Steve, listen to me.' She leaned forward and grasped both of his hands with her own. He stared at them but didn't try to pull away. 'What if there's only Bobby there now, and Caffrey's gone for good? When you add that to the unwelcome attention he's certain to get here, you have to consider the possibility that he's better off over there. Bringing him home might be the worst possible thing we could do to him.'

3

Maddox closed the door of the police holding cell with a calm which belied his seething anger. The empty vessel that squatted timidly on the narrow bench across from him must have sensed it all the same, because it sat very still and didn't say a word. The stink of its fear filled the cell, and his lip curled in disgust. He'd never liked Degan much at the best of times – trusted him, yes, insofar as it was possible to trust a man whose only reason for not escaping was because of the opportunities to inflict pain which Maddox offered – but this thing staring up at him with its big wet eyes was just an affront. He was very tempted to have it destroyed out of hand, but Maddox was nothing if not meticulous, so he ordered the Swarm which he'd brought with him to stand in a corner until it was needed.

He hunkered down in front of the sweating figure and peered at its face closely.

'Are you my solicitor?' Its voice was trembling and faint. 'Because…'

'Shut up,' said Maddox. 'We're going to do this once only, because I do not appreciate having to drive halfway across the country for this shit.'

'I don't understand what…'

Maddox slapped him – only lightly, but he was a big man, and the vessel was obviously in shock, and the effect was like wiping his face with a lamppost.

'On the off chance that I am still talking to Degan and that for some arse-brained reason you have decided to play possum, I am giving you this one chance to stop dicking around and explain how you managed to let the woman get away.'

The vessel blinked at him. God in heaven, it was starting to cry. 'I don't know what you're talking about,' it pleaded. 'My name is Roger Simkin. I'm an accountant. None of this makes sense.'

'You're right enough there,' Maddox growled. Time to face facts: Degan was gone. Discorporeated, and in a fashion which defied sense. Whether you called it psychotherapy or exorcism, discorporeation was an expensive process which took weeks, if not months – it was definitely not accomplished during an afternoon jolly to a bleeding art gallery. 'What were you doing there?' he mused aloud, to the vessel's sniffling incomprehension. He'd pulled the gallery's CCTV and seen the scuffle for himself, but there was nothing about the way that Degan had been bounced against the painting which could explain this – the push hadn't been strong enough for him to have even cracked his head, yet he'd collapsed like a puppet with its strings cut. Nor was there anything in the muddy cow-eyes in front of him to suggest that a part of Simkin's passenger from Tourmaline remained – not even any vestigial memories. It was unusual. Unprecedented. A bit of personal leg-work might be required.

At that thought, his mood lightened. He hadn't been in the field for years. He even briefly considered letting Simkin go – surely, if he remembered anything of the Park at all, nobody would believe him – but then, no.

'It's about being meticulous, old son,' he said, patting the man's damp cheek, and he straightened away to call the Swarm forward.

The suit that it wore seethed as it fought against the confinements of its human shape. It was a unique asset; the combination of factors which had to align properly for a sleeping human vessel to be anywhere near a dormant hive of anything – in this case, what seemed to be hornets – was so rare that only an exceptional circumstance could justify him putting it into action. He carried its queen – or at least, the lump of flesh which the queen possessed – in a sealed metal tube on a chain around his neck, and he could feel it buzzing as it fought to rejoin the others of its kind. The Swarm retained just enough of its vessel's human intelligence to be biddable, once the queen had been identified and separated, and even that process had cost three lives.

'Meticulous,' he repeated. 'From the Latin, that is, *metus*, meaning fear.' Seeing the look on Simkin's face as the Swarm came apart, leaving its human clothes in a puddle and surging towards him hungrily in a cloud of broken flesh and bone, he laughed. 'Now that's what we call ironic.'

When it had finished, the Swarm reconstituted itself and approached Maddox, holding out between a squirming thumb and forefinger something it had found on Simkin which did not belong: a single blonde hair. The wake that it created was so small that only the delicate senses of one of the swarm's insectile entities could have sniffed it out, and Maddox felt vindicated in his choice.

'Find her,' he ordered.

4

There is no awakening so sudden as one caused by something in the same room as you growling.

Steve was conscious instantly, with no awareness of having slept.

Very slowly, he reached for his phone on the bedside table – *3:14am*. He and Vessa had demolished the wine and gone to their separate rooms only a few hours ago, after getting tired of waiting for Ennias to show. In response to his movement, the growl came again. It was at the foot of his bed.

Something was sitting on his feet.

He bunched the top edge of the duvet in his fists, thinking that if he lunged fast and far enough he might be able to trap whatever it was in the bedclothes and either kick the shit out of it or, more likely, run for the door. Then he remembered: of course, the hradix. It knew him for a friend, supposedly. Didn't it?

'Mint?' he whispered, tensing himself to jump.

The hradix hooted softly, and then resumed its low, rattling snarl. Still, that was promising. Sort of. He decided to risk switching on the bedside lamp.

Light flooded the small bedroom, and he tensed again, but still the creature didn't move from its position crouched at the foot of his bed, and when his eyes had adjusted to the brightness, he realised that it wasn't even looking at him.

It was watching something else – something a lot smaller which was crawling up the duvet towards his face.

At first glance it looked like a large grub, or possibly a caterpillar by the way it was arching itself to move forwards, except that it didn't have any legs, or eyes, or feelers, or body segments – or indeed anything which on closer inspection might have confirmed that it was a normal animal. If anything, it looked more like a short length of raw sausage, except that it was purple-grey in colour. And veined. He'd only ever once in his life seen anything like this, when he'd been walking to work one morning and seen a cat which had been run over and killed, lying on the pavement. The force of the impact had ruptured its abdomen and he'd been able to clearly see its entrails, glistening purple-grey in the…

'Mother of God,' he breathed.

The hradix growled louder.

The loop of intestine was joined by a second fragment, this one looking like a shred of raw muscle propelled by half-a-dozen 'legs' made from splinters of pink bone.

That was when Vessa started screaming from her room down the hall.

Both he and the hradix moved at the same time, but the animal inside the boy was faster, and by the time he'd disentangled himself from the bedclothes and swatted the disgusting fragments aside, it was already in her room, barking ferociously.

What he saw when he charged in was not real – could not possibly be real. Despite everything he'd already accepted about the painting, and the Flats, and even the hradix itself; this was so far beyond his comprehension that at first his brain simply refused to accept it.

The air was full of flesh. Dozens, hundreds, possibly even thousands of scraps of human muscle, bone, and internal organs floated like the flakes of an obscene snow globe, circling slowly while more streamed in through the open window. Already many were busy forming themselves into larger clots and ropes of wet tissue which wrapped themselves around Vessa, binding and lifting her from her bed as she struggled, screaming for him to help. But his presence in the room had been noticed. The cloud became agitated. Parts of it broke away and swarmed towards him, buzzing like wasps, and he saw that each piece bristled with barbed shards of bone. He swatted at them, trying to fight his way towards Vessa, but couldn't hope to make any impression on the multitude which was already attacking him. Some simply cut at him, but he was also stung repeatedly on his hands and forearms as he tried to defend himself, and the thought of what they were using as poison revolted him; it burned in great welts. The hradix was going crazy, snatching at the air with teeth and claws, but doing no better. Pain drove him stumbling back into the hall, and the flesh-wasps pursued, stabbing his head, his bare legs, and through the thin cotton of the t-shirt he'd worn to bed.

The shower. All he could think of which might possibly slow them down was the shower. Maybe he could grab a towel and wrap it around his head. That might buy him a few seconds to try and rescue Vessa. His last glimpse was of her tearing at the mask of crawling flesh which covered her face before the door was slammed shut against him, and then something like sinew was wrapping itself around his own throat, and tightening. He fell, cracking his head against the wall, and curled into a ball on the floor, no longer thinking of anything now except trying to get his fingers under the writhing thing which was quickly throttling him. Black flowers bloomed and died in his vision, and he found himself more confused than afraid. *This can't be it*, he thought. *This can't be how I die. It makes no sense…*

There was a high-pitched whining in his ears, and he thought maybe that was what happened when your brain was starved of oxygen and about to die. It grew louder, and at the same time the sense of choking grew less. He found he could breathe. He also found that the stabbing attacks had stopped. The whining grew louder still, hurting his ears, and somebody was shouting: 'Get up, you silly wanker! Get up!'

A hand dragged him upright by the back of his t-shirt, and Ennias' face was in his. 'Stomp it!' Ennias yelled, shaking him. 'Fucking stomp the fuck out of it before it can pull itself together!' With his other hand he waved his phone around – it was that which was making the hideous whining noise – and Steve saw that the bits of flesh were no longer flying but squirming on the floor in obvious pain.

Ennias let him go and began stamping on them, crushing them into the carpet, his boots quickly becoming covered in gore. Dazed, half-strangled, and in pain from dozens of stings, Steve joined in clumsily, even though he was barefoot and the sensation of the flesh-wasps bursting under his heels was disgusting. Ennias kicked in the door to Vessa's room and they repeated the process there, crushing anything which squirmed, until the floor and walls were an abattoir of pulverised flesh and bone.

Then, before either of them could say a word, he hustled them out of the house and into a van, and drove them off into the pre-dawn darkness.

Chapter 22

True Colours

1

'Raft!' Joe sprinted back to Stray along the Down boom as if it were a running track, waving his arms and yelling. 'He's alive! He's alive!'

Lachlan and Allie went out in Tatters and found that this was in fact the case, though only just. Their newest castaway didn't seem to have made any effort to try and survive; he lay on a raft not much bigger than a door with his hands and feet trailing in the water, emaciated, and blistered by the sun. Bobby watched as they towed him back to Stray with an odd feeling of deja-vu, wondering whether they would have enough provisions for an extra mouth and if he would fit in with them or cause trouble – then realised that exactly the same questions must have been asked of himself.

He waited until later in the day, when their new arrival had been fed, watered and rested, before introducing himself.

'I bet you're wondering what kind of madhouse you've ended up in,' he said, shaking the man's hand. It was taken without a smile or much enthusiasm; the fellow looked dazed. Not surprising, Bobby told himself, but there was a wariness about the way the chap seemed to be avoiding direct eye contact that he didn't entirely like. 'Bobby Jenkins,' he added. 'Welcome to Stray.'

'Thanks, pleased to meet you,' replied the other, sounding anything but. 'The name's Degan.'

2

'I thought you said it was a safe-house!' yelled Steve, slamming Ennias up against a wall. His hands hurt like a bastard, and he knew that Ennias could probably break every bone in them if he wanted, but right now he was too angry to care. For his part, Ennias seemed content to take the brunt of his anger. Momentarily.

'Nice to see you up and about,' he commented. 'Cup of tea?'

'What the fuck were those things? What were they doing at your place? Why didn't you *warn* us?' With each question he shook the other man, who continued to bear it patiently.

'Steve, listen, you need to calm down. You're on some heavy-duty pain killers and antihistamines, and they're messing with your head.'

'I'll calm down when you answer my...'

'Plus, you'll wake Vanessa, and she needs the rest; she got the worst of the attack.' Ennias gently but firmly peeled Steve's hands from the front of his shirt, as if he were a child. 'So stop shouting, okay? Now, then. Milk? Sugar?'

Steve subsided and let Ennias make him a cup of tea. Sitting down didn't seem to make much difference to the dizziness he was feeling – it felt like the room was rocking ever-so-slightly to and fro. Then he remembered that he was on Ennias' narrowboat underneath Spaghetti Junction, and that the rocking wasn't just in his head.

Junction Six of the M6 motorway – officially named the Gravelly Hill Interchange but known universally as Spaghetti Junction – was, as its name suggested, a tangle of slip-roads feeding in from numerous other routes and minor local roads, all raised above each other on five levels supported by hundreds of concrete columns whilst underneath it ran two railway lines, the confluence of two rivers, and the junction of three canals. All of this made it an ideal location for Ennias to have moored a short, scruffy-looking narrow-boat called the *Cella*. Steve thought it made perfect sense to find that he lived like a troll under a bridge.

They took their drinks up on deck.

'Let's define "safe", shall we?' suggested Ennias and waved at their surroundings. Vast motorway flyovers curved over their heads in all directions, stacked on top of each other while trees and bushes colonised what open space was left, growing up through the spaces between the carriageways. All of it was mirrored in the canal's perfectly still surface, and despite the constant rumble of traffic all around Steve found it surprisingly peaceful – even the sight of the hradix, which was hunting for pigeons in the maintenance scaffolding which surrounded many of the support columns.

'Funny story for you,' said Ennias. 'A few years ago, a holidaymaker stole a boat he was meant to be returning – he took off into the canal system, repainted it and managed to evade the police for six weeks. Six. You couldn't do that on the roads. From this junction we have access to a hundred miles of waterway in Birmingham alone – with no patrol cars or CCTV cameras. Helicopters can't see shit through all this concrete, even with infra-red. Five minutes' walk that way and you've got Gravelly Hill Station and all points north to Derby. Five minutes the other way is Aston station, then New Street, and you can be in Paris by teatime. Above us we've got eighteen major roads; with a car parked on the hard shoulder under one of those flyovers you can be anywhere from Glasgow to London in a few hours.'

'*Have* you got a car parked on the hard shoulder?' asked Steve.

Ennias winked. 'What do you think? See that scaffolding? I hope you haven't got a thing for heights because if there's any trouble we're up that like rats up a drainpipe. My point is, safety's about having options, not locks. In any event, it wasn't your safety I was most concerned with. It was ours. The exiles.'

Steve laughed humourlessly. 'I love the way you use the word "exiles". Like you're all part of some kind of royal family turfed out of your kingdom by a wicked witch.'

'What word would you like me to use, exactly? Possessors? Demons? Dissociated personalities, like Vanessa?'

'She's not an exile from anywhere. She's… truth to tell, I'm still not sure exactly what she is.'

'That's exactly what she is, McBride, whether or not she admits it. There's no other explanation.'

'So, you're saying that everything about Sophie and the abuse and waking up for the first time and seeing the Watts painting is all a lie?'

'No, that's all true – but where do you think multiple personalities come from in the first place? Why do you think some people wake up from accidents with changed personalities or speaking in funny accents or not recognising their loved ones? Why do you think some people with perfectly happy home lives – two-point-four children and all that – suddenly run away from home or go postal in small country villages? You can say it was abuse or drugs or mental illness, but they're just the trigger factors. The people who wake up one day feeling confused, not recognising the world around them, are us, people from my world. Sometimes we get total control, like me. Sometimes we fight with the original personality, like Vessa and Sophie, even if we were invited in the first place. Sometimes we aren't strong enough and just hover in the background, whispering and shouting; the voices in schizophrenics' heads, desperately trying to escape. You bring us here when you sleep too deeply, and your dreams snare us in ours, like two halves of a piece of Velcro sticking together.

'I was a fisherman before this. Lived in a little seaside town called Candlewick Bay in a country called Oraille. I had a wife, two daughters and a little narrow house with blue shutters. Me and my brothers had a nice old fishing ketch which belonged to our dad, and we ran it in the bay; we didn't make much, but we got by. And then one night, after I'd kissed my girls good night and fallen asleep beside Jessie, a software engineer called Milas Petrovic took the first pill in a course of anti-malaria medication because he was planning a charity trek up Mount Kilimanjaro, and he had the kind of fucked up dreams you usually only get by dropping acid. The authorities in Oraille call what happened a "subornation", which is a nice, lovely, scientific term for what happened. You don't need to know the details. All you need to know is that I was asleep when it happened, and when this guy's dream finished, I was sucked back with it like something nasty going down a plug-hole. I woke up in this body in a council flat in Stoke-on-Trent. Imagine my delight.'

'Jesus,' Steve breathed. 'What happened to this Petrovic bloke?'

'I don't know, and I don't much care. He could be dead. He could be in here somewhere, trapped and screaming to get out, for all I know. What I do know is that I've spent the better part of the last three years travelling around, talking to other exiles, working it out. There are some very interesting people out there if you know the right way to talk to them. Most countries in my world have a branch of their police force or church dedicated to dealing with subornations, and quite a few of them get stuck here. Occupational hazard, I suppose. But this is the first time I've ever met anybody like Vanessa who claims to be able to move between there and here. Most of the people I've spoken to about it say it's impossible and that she's full of shit.'

'What do you think?'

Ennias shrugged. 'What choice do I have?'

'You and me both,' replied Steve.

'Subornation has been going on for as long as human beings have been dreaming, and the Hegemony have been trying to keep a lid on it for just as long. Let's be honest, they were always going to find you. Far better that happen somewhere out of harm's way. Try not to take it personally.'

'Thanks, I'll try,' Steve replied drily. 'But you couldn't have warned us, could you?'

'I couldn't possibly know how they would track you down or what they'd send at you, could I?'

'I suppose not. So what exactly were those things, then?'

'They were an it. A gestalt creature. A swarm. Some poor bastard dreamed himself too close to a dormant hive of something very nasty indeed – from the looks of what they did to you, I'm going with wasps, or maybe killer bees. You're lucky to be alive. You know that thing a few years back, when shopping centres were using high-frequency sounds to scare away teenagers, and then the kids recorded it on their phones to annoy their teachers?'

'Vaguely.'

'Well, it turns out that with a bit of tweaking, swarms of intelligent extra-dimensional insects don't much like it either. Apps, my friend.' He waved his phone at Steve. 'It's all in the apps.'

Steve laughed. 'Well I have to say, this isn't exactly what I had in mind when Vessa told me you were an exile from this other place she calls Tourmaline.'

'What exactly were you expecting?' Ennias seemed nettled by his laughter. 'Tiny winged elephants in cages? Jars of eyeballs?

That sort of thing? Sorry to disappoint you, mate, but I buy my groceries in Tesco and my mugs from Ikea, just like everybody else. The fact that I can do things like this…' and he turned his cup of tea upside-down and drank from it without spilling a drop, '…is only good for getting me unwelcome attention.

'And it's Archipelago. The Tourmaline Archipelago. The whole place isn't called Tourmaline; it's just one small bit of the world. That's like calling everywhere on the other side of the English Channel "Belgium" because that's the only place there you've heard of. Just like this place is called the Realt, because it's abnormal.'

'Us? *We're* the abnormal ones?'

'And the strangest thing about all of this is that despite the evidence all around, you think this is all there is – like you're floating alone in the universe, and that makes you all terribly special and important.'

Steve felt the bruises on his throat gingerly. At this particular moment in time he couldn't imagine feeling less of either.

3

Degan explored Stray with mounting incredulity. He was allowed to roam freely without being pestered by too many questions; for the moment they apparently assumed that he was in shock and getting his bearings, and he saw no reason to let them think otherwise. It wasn't all pretence anyway. Before getting suborned by Simkin, he'd heard of the Flats of course – what Elbaite seaman hadn't? – but like everybody else who'd heard the tall tales of sea monsters and holes in the ocean, he'd expected the secrets at its heart to be grand and terrifying, not threadbare and shabby. How could people have built so much, and out of this garbage? And why here, in the middle of nowhere? For a moment there, this discovery might have seemed worth coming back for, but in the end it was all very disappointing.

He kept in the background and out of everybody's way as best he could, trying to get the sense of how these people worked. The unbelievable shoddiness of their bodged carpentry made him wonder how the whole structure didn't just break apart and float away, though he imagined that they were all very proud of how well they were 'making do'. He spent a while watching the black man and the boy struggling to lash together a framework for one of their shelters – they kept tangling up the rope's leading end with their feet and having to start again – before sheer frustration moved him to intervene.

'Look, coil it like this,' he said, grabbing it off them and flicking it around his elbow with a few deft turns which left it stacked neatly out of the way. He was surprised to find that it actually felt good working a line again after so long. 'And that's just going to fall apart if you so much as piss the wrong way. Ain't either of you ever heard of a shear lashing?'

Seb and Joe looked at him blankly.

Degan sighed, picked up the rope again and showed them.

Bobby watched this awhile and then turned back to helping Lachlan stacking piles of dreamwrack for the fire. 'It looks like the new chap is starting to settle,' he commented.

'He would, if he could curb his gutter mouth,' Lachlan replied, unimpressed. 'It's been less than forty-eight hours. Let's not be in a hurry to give him the keys to the city.'

Mercifully for Degan, they asked him no questions about who he was or where he'd come from. The hints he picked up from their conversations suggested that he should be shocked into a state of amnesia, and he was happy enough to play along. During the evening meal – his second there but the first of which he was properly conscious – their talk was all of weather, currents, the conditions of the booms and the treasures that had been thrown up in the previous nights' dreamwrack, whatever that was. He wasn't expected to join in, and nothing was demanded of him. He'd helped repair a shelter, in return for which he'd been given food, and that simple arrangement seemed to suit them.

Degan distrusted it profoundly.

In his experience no arrangement was ever that simple. There were always conditions and hidden agendas. Dress it up any way you liked – in religious commandments, political alliances or naval regulations – there was always someone getting shafted, and someone doing the shafting. He sat eating his fish stew in watchful silence, seeing the firelight on their happy, empty, chatting faces, and knew that it was going to be the simplest thing in the world to keep them sweet just long enough to find out whose hand turned the wheels around here – and then cut it off.

But he found out who that was much sooner than he'd expected when the beaded curtain parted and Sophie came out to join them, trailing her long chain behind.

It was all he could do to keep from leaping up and gutting her then and there – or running in terror, he couldn't tell which. The stew was suddenly a mouthful of dry fishbones. The fire baked sweat out of his pores, despite the gooseflesh which stippled his arms. He couldn't breathe.

It was her. There was no way it could possibly be her, of course, that went without saying, but it made no difference to what his eyes were seeing: Vanessa Gail. The witch who had thrown him back here like a reject from somebody's catch.

And she looked right through him as if she'd never seen him before in her life. As if butter wouldn't fucking melt.

'You okay, man?' Seb asked, concerned.

'I'm fine, I'm fine.' He manufactured a cough and thumped his chest. 'Just a bone, I think. Pass me that water, would you?'

He drank, and he laughed, and he joined in with the small talk, and later – when everybody was snoring their stupid, complacent heads off – he found a knife and went to have words with the woman who had exiled him in his own world.

4

Sophie was reading a book by her pool, and the flickering light of her lamp competed with its own sinuous reflections on the ceiling beams and walls. She looked up as he came in, and provided a small, polite smile.

'It's late,' she said.

'Oh sweetie, you're good,' he sneered. 'Even with nobody around you're still going to pretend that you've never seen me before. Well you can cut that shit out right now.'

She laid the book aside and got to her feet, confusion and fear in her eyes. 'I'm sorry, Mr Degan, I swear I don't…'

'Send me back!' he barked and drew the knife.

'Send you…?'

'Back! Back to the world, bitch! Back through that fucking painting of yours!'

He lunged and grabbed her by the throat before she could call for help. He didn't have any of the power which had bled through to him from here when he was in the Realt, and he was still weak from his time adrift, but nevertheless he outweighed her considerably. He drove her back against the wall of her chamber, the only thing putting up any resistance being the length of chain which clanked out of the pool link by link after her. He held the point of the knife to the soft underside of her chin.

'Send me back,' he repeated with soft menace, his face inches from hers, his breath stinking. 'I don't know how it is that you're here and there at the same time, and I don't give a fuck. Send me back, or I will gut you where you stand.'

Her lips moved. She was trying to say something. He eased the pressure on her throat slightly so that he could hear better. It was barely a whisper, and it sounded like: 'Wake up.'

'What do you mean, "wake up"? I'm already awake, that's the fucking problem.'

She smiled painfully. 'I wasn't talking to you.'

There was the sound of water moving behind him. Then something black lashed itself around his waist and hauled him backwards with appalling strength, straight into the pool at the centre of the chamber. Water closed over his head before he had a chance to so much as catch a breath, and panic made him gasp a burning lungful of water. He couldn't see anything in the night-black pool except the shimmering brightness of its surface, already impossibly far above him, and he could feel other things wrapping themselves around his thighs, his torso, his arms, his head. Too late, he remembered Maddox's briefing back at the Park. *It isn't from anywhere in either your world or this one,* he'd said. *It's from Between. At the moment we believe it to be dormant.*

It didn't seem to be dormant any longer.

His scream disappeared upwards in a stream of unseen bubbles, and those things were tightening, crushing him as he was dragged deeper into darkness. Then they weren't just crushing, but biting too, scissoring through his clothes and into his flesh like ribbons of razor wire. And even that wasn't as bad as the feeling that something similar had wrapped itself around his brain and was feeding on the terror that it found there, luxuriating in his horror at the violation being inflicted upon him, feasting on his soul as well as his body. Then the blackness was inside him too, and in the end it was everything.

CHAPTER 23

MIND-FORGED MANACLES

1

Bobby was dreaming about earthquakes.

He was back on the quay at Timini, surrounded by Hooper's thugs and watching helplessly as Allie was carried aboard their clunking great steamer, but every time he tried to take a step forward to stop them, the ground bucked under his feet, throwing him off balance. The motion became so violent that it woke him up, but even as he struggled out of sleep, he found that it had somehow followed him. The hammock in which he and Allie lay curled was rocking wildly, as if someone in passing had given it a good hard tug. But everybody else was asleep. Impossible as it seemed, Stray itself was moving. The huge raft was pitching up and down – a movement it had never been designed to suffer, and it was voicing its protest in a loud creaking and snapping of timber.

He fell out of the hammock, Allie a moment later. The other Strays were rousing too, their shouts and cries of confusion coming from all over.

'It's a storm!' yelled Lachlan, his voice high with panic. 'God help us, we'll break apart!'

'Is he right?' Allie sat up, rubbing her head where it had smacked into the deck.

'I don't think so.' Bobby got to his feet – which wasn't as easy as it should have been. It was like when he'd been given the bumps on his birthday at boarding school, tossed up in a blanket once for each year; trying to stand up on that. 'For one thing it's not raining.'

'Then what?'

'Ten to one it's got something to do with Sophie. Wait here.'

'Screw that,' she replied, and staggered after him as he reeled toward the Hub.

2

They found Sophie grimly hauling, with every sinew in her body as tight as cords, at the chain which led from her wrist into the pool – and stopped, shocked. The water was turbulent, as if boiling, and bright red.

'Get out!' she screamed through clenched teeth. 'Both of you! Get out before it kills you too!'

Ignoring her, Bobby grabbed the chain below her hands and added his strength to hers. The chain was as unyielding as a metal bar and thrumming beneath his hands like a guitar string. If he'd ever gone deep-sea fishing he would have recognised the sensation for what it was: something on the other end was fighting back. Something absolutely huge.

Allie moved to join him.

'No!' he grunted. 'Get the others first.'

'NO!' Sophie protested.

'But...' Allie hovered, uncertain.

'Oh Jesus,' he groaned, 'for once will you just bloody *do* it?'

She did it.

Abruptly the chain was dragged sharply left, almost jerking Bobby off his feet, and it ground against the edge of the pool hard enough to splinter the wood. Then it repeated the action to the right, and back again, like a dog worrying at a slipper. It was as much as he could do to simply hold on, never mind pull. How the girl had managed it...

Something wrapped itself around his lower leg. It was dark and thick and muscular; he could see and feel it pulsate as it adjusted its grip – then agony exploded in his calf as teeth on the tentacles's underside shredded his flesh, and it started to drag him towards the water. Sophie shrieked at it in anger, let go of the chain and threw herself on him, wrapping her arms in a fierce bear-hug while he howled at the pain. More tentacles emerged from the water and fastened about the pair of them, exploring. Tasting. But they shuddered as they touched her and recoiled from both – the one slipping from his leg with the wetness of his own blood – and slithered back into the pool.

Then the chamber seemed to be full of shouting people: Seb whacking the surface of the water with a wooden pole, Lachlan dragging at Bobby's arm, Marjorie's face simply an O of paralysed shock, and Sophie clinging to him and moaning into his shoulder: 'Get them out of here Bobby, please get them out of here. It'll kill them all. It'll kill every last one of them, just like before, and I can only hold it, I can't stop it. I can't ever stop it.'

Then Marjorie said – in a very quiet voice which nevertheless seemed to cut through the chaos – 'Oh. Oh my. That's. Well that's quite…'

Something thick and muscular was draped across her shoulders, almost casually, like the arm of an old friend.

She was gone with barely a splash.

'*NOOOOOOOO!*' Lachlan's howl threatened to burst the very timbers around them as he threw himself after her. Seb rugby-tackled him and brought him down at the very edge of the pool, close enough for him to paw desperately at the surface, making awful, raw animal noises of denial.

'Bobby!' Sophie's eyes burned at him. 'They will all die if you do not get them *out of here now!*'

Somehow he managed to do it – limping, bleeding, driving them out of the chamber with pleas and curses and shoves, and then up onto the Hub as high as they could get, as far away from the water as possible, until they collapsed sobbing under the indifferent stars.

3

Towards dawn, an exhausted-looking Sophie joined them. 'It's a bit quieter now,' she said, and sat with her head in her hands, the long chain still trailing.

The others just looked at her.

'It,' echoed Allie.

'The araka. The thing under Stray which none of you believed in. Crazy little Miss Sophie,' she added bitterly.

'Don't you dare say you told us so,' whispered Lachlan hoarsely; his throat was raw with a night's weeping. Joe lay curled in his lap, but he was awake, staring at nothing as his father stroked his hair absently. 'Don't you dare.'

'Sorry Stuart, but I did. All of you. Repeatedly.'

Lachlan closed his eyes and moaned.

'What happened to Degan?' asked Seb.

She hesitated. 'I'm not sure. He was in my room – we were talking – he must have been too close to the pool, or something, because one second everything was fine and the next it just came out and… and took him.'

'Nonsense,' insisted Lachlan. 'I've been in your room plenty of times – all of us have – and nothing like that has ever happened before.'

'It was only a matter of time. I tried to warn you.'

'This is pointless,' said Bobby. He didn't believe a word of her story, but couldn't be bothered trying to force the truth out of her. It didn't matter – the man was dead. '*What* is it? How did it get here?'

'How do we kill it?' added Seb.

Sophie gave a hollow laugh. 'You can't kill it. I'd have done that years ago. The best that can be done is to keep it chained up and out of harm's way. It's been in me since I was a child – in my mind, I mean. It's not a physical thing. At least, not usually, not in the normal world. It is here.'

'Making about as much sense as ever,' Allie muttered.

'It wasn't in me at first. It was in my parents. It's like a parasite that only exists in your mind. My Dad was a soldier; I think he must have picked it up in Afghanistan. It feeds on the pain that it inflicts by making a person do terrible things, and it moves from one person to another when they're dreaming. It was feeding off them for years, and just before I got taken into care it moved into me. I already had Vessa to help me, but we knew it was only a matter of time before it moved out of me and into one of the other kids. We couldn't let that happen. Couldn't kill it, couldn't get rid of it. All I could think to do was stop sleeping and prevent it from getting out. I didn't think I'd end up here, but I did, and the araka came too, chained to me. It wasn't very happy, but after a while it was too weak to do anything about it. I made Stray to live on, and the Flats to keep people away, and Vessa did my dreaming for me, and everything was fine until you people started to appear. And now it's woken up. If you've got any sense, you will too. Go back to the real world, please. I'm begging you.'

'That's not an option for some of us,' said Allie coldly.

'This is our home as much as yours,' added Seb.

'Let it go,' said Bobby. 'Easy. What happened to you is not your fault; whatever this araka thing does when it goes free is not your responsibility.'

'How can you say that? Of course it is, when I have the power to prevent it!'

'Not compared to your responsibility towards the lives of the people around you right now.'

'But you can leave! Haven't you been listening? In case I didn't make myself understood the first time, let's be clear: that *thing*,' she jabbed a finger downwards, towards the base of Stray, 'goes nowhere. I am staying here and starving it until I die, and then I'm taking it with me. If you lot want to stick around and die too, that's your suicide. Don't put it on me.'

'You have the key to the chain around your neck,' he pointed out. 'What's to stop us just taking it from you and letting the damn thing go without your say-so?'

Her hand went to her throat protectively. 'You're a good man, Bobby Jenkins,' she said. 'Degan wasn't. He put a knife to my throat, so I fed him to the araka. You're a thousand times the man he was, but I'll do exactly the same thing to you if you try to force me. Do we understand each other?'

'Yeah,' he replied with distaste. 'I think we probably do, finally.'

'Good. You have your options.' She went back down the Hub to her chamber, leaving them to huddle in the chill, discussing how they might use Tatters to escape to the Islands, and waiting for sunrise.

Dawn, when it came, rendered all of their discussions moot when it showed them a column of thick black smoke from the stack of an Oraillean steamer heading straight towards them.

CHAPTER 24

THE ARAKA

1

Berylin watched the raft grow larger ahead of her, and the small specks on top of its central platform grow into frantically gesticulating human figures, but couldn't summon any empathy for them. Her experience told her that all of its inhabitants would be unfortunate locals suborned against their will, and she tried to put their interests ahead of the visceral need to simply make it go away as quickly and completely as possible. Stray was a gigantic scab on an unhealed wound in her world, a tumorous excrescence which shouted its wrongness at her across the water. The long wooden booms were like metastising tendrils of the cancer, pushing out further and further. They'd start with those, she decided.

She ordered a course correction and instead of continuing straight towards the raft, the *Spinner* began a circuit. She overran the booms without even feeling it, pulverising them into splinters which followed in her wake as she circled Stray. Frenzied shouts and curses came from the suborned, but Berylin ignored them.

Then one of the watches shouted 'Ware! Whirlpools a-port! Ware!' and the crew snapped into the routine which had saved them numerous times over the past day and a half it had taken to get this far into the Flats.

The *Spinner* went into full stop and dropped anchor while the small ship-to-shore dinghy was lowered off the stern. A dozen of Harcourt's electrical buoys were dropped around the ship and the dinghy towed them into a rough circle, connecting them with a thick cable – much thicker than the original one which had burnt out during their earlier field tests – which had been commandeered from an Oraillean signalling outpost engaged in the ceaseless task of repairing the great trans-Antaean clatter network. Harcourt had theorised that the vortices were an automatic and unthinking response to their presence in the subornation zone, like antibodies swarming at an invading pathogen ('As if we were the disease!' she'd snorted, indignant), and indeed it did seem that the more unobtrusively they acted, the less violent were the vortices. Their progress through the Flats was therefore painstakingly slow, but even at best the vortices only left them alone for a matter of hours.

The cable ran back up on deck to a series of huge, improvised capacitors which looked like a row of black beehives, and the dinghy hauled at speed back to the *Spinner*.

And they waited.

She ignored the shouts and pleas from those on the raft. They were not responsible for what they were saying, she reminded herself. They would be restored to rationality soon enough.

The waiting, as ever, was not long.

With a great roaring, sucking noise a vortex nearly a dozen feet in diameter opened just beyond the ring of buoys, with a second appearing seconds later just to one side. Their effect on the ocean nearby started to draw the ring out of true.

'Steady!' Harcourt ordered.

The crew stood on wooden duckboards to insulate themselves from the ship's steel hull, and made sure that they carried no metal objects; several of them were already burned as a result of prior carelessness.

A third vortex popped into existence.

'Contact!'

He threw a lever, the capacitors discharged with a purple flash and a deafening crack, and the vortices everted into three waterspouts which collapsed at a harmless distance. Moments later, dozens of electrocuted fish drifted to the surface. The buoys were reclaimed, the cable re-coiled, and the *Spinner* completed its destruction of Stray's booms before turning towards the raft itself, followed all the while by a retinue of tiny floating corpses.

Numbly, the Strays huddled together and watched the metal ship churn to within hailing distance and stop, loosing a fat black belch of smoke and smuts. At its prow stood a woman in a high-necked uniform – she was scorched in places, static electricity made her cropped dark hair stand out around her ahead like a sea urchin, and her eyes burned with the fervour of absolute conviction.

'I am Officer Berylin Hooper, of the Oraillean Department of Counter Subornation,' she declared. 'By the authority of King Alexander the Seventh, and in the name of all the peoples of this world, I command you to send out to me the dreamer who has caused this abomination.' She smiled, and to Bobby and his friends it was the smile of death itself. 'I have come to deliver you all from your nightmare.'

'What gives you the right?' yelled Lachlan, his face a mask of sorrow and rage.

She continued as if she hadn't heard him. 'Very well. My man will board soon with a sal volatile aerosol spray to determine which amongst you is the dreamer. I understand that you are frightened and confused, but please, violence would be unwise. Whilst I want to return you to your ordinary lives, my commitment is to the common good and I will not hesitate to use deadly force against any of you who endanger that.'

At her command, half a dozen members of the *Spinner's* crew took up positions with rifles on the deck and the upper level of the wheel-house, where Runce stood to direct their fire. Even though the top of the Hub was still slightly higher, Stray had nothing to answer their threat – not even much by way of cover.

'This *is* our ordinary life!' Lachlan retorted. 'This is our home, damn you!'

'I know you believe that to be true,' she replied with something like compassion. 'But I'm afraid it simply isn't. You are fisherfolk and traders with real lives somewhere out on those islands – all except one of you, and as soon as I know which one that is I can end this illusion and return you to those lives. You can't see that now, but you will, I promise you. Trust me.'

'Trust you!' Bobby laughed. 'What happened to you ending me where I stand?'

'I had hoped to do this in a civilised manner,' she responded, and her face turned cold. She raised a pistol and pointed it at him. 'Though that is still an option.'

'Look, wait. Hang on a second.' Allie stepped in front of Bobby, alarmed at the way this was going. 'This is ridiculous. You're right, we don't belong here. But we don't have lives in this world, despite what you think. We don't belong here at all. We're not subordinated, or whatever you call it.'

'Then where else could you possibly be from?'

'We're *all* dreamers.'

Lachlan hid his face. Berylin laughed in utter disbelief. '*All* of you? Really, my dear, think how ridiculous that sounds. Isn't it more likely that it's exactly what the dreamer has caused you to believe? Bring him out to me and I can end this delusion. And even if it were true, all the more reason for me to rid this place of you.'

'But we're not hurting anyone!'

'In the name of Reason, listen to yourself! In the time you've been here nearly fifty individuals from the nearby islands have disappeared in the Flats. Those are fathers, mothers, and children. Gone. You've destabilised the politics of an entire region and drawn neutral countries like my homeland into a petty foreign squabble which may boil over into a full-scale war. And you claim to be hurting no-one? Did you really think you could come here and have no effect? In any event, what you're doing or not doing is completely irrelevant. You could be healing the sick for all I care; it is your very existence which is an affront, and one which I intend to rectify. I will ask you a third and final time: send out the dreamer, and we can end this peacefully.' Behind her, another half-dozen of the crew were readying themselves in the dinghy with ropes and cudgels.

Bobby threw up his hands in surrender. 'Fine!' he shouted. 'You win! I'll go and get her.'

Allie tried to catch his arm. 'Bobby, you can't give them Sophie,' she protested, but he shook her off.

'Why not? I'm certainly not going to die for her, after everything she's done. You heard that woman. We have no choice! I'd rather go with something like a bit of dignity than be herded up like cattle.'

She followed him down the steps of the Hub. When he was sure that they were out of earshot he said to her quietly: 'Of course I'm not going to give them Sophie. What do you take me for?'

'Well what are you going to do, then?'

'Something you're going to like even less.'

2

Sophie was in her chamber, huddled by the edge of her pool and staring into it with red-rimmed, haunted eyes. The chain was taut in her hands and idling around in the water so that it looked for all the world like she was stirring it with a rod made of welded links rather than what was actually happening: that it was taking every ounce of her strength to simply keep it in one place. Every so often the chain would give a swift jerk as if the creature on the other end was testing her, playing her as if she were the fish and it the angler.

Bobby knelt beside her and took her wrists in his hands. He could feel the tension thrumming in them like electricity. Her sinews were metal rods.

'Sophie.'

'I told you. I warned you. Wake up while you can, I said. Now it's too late.'

'Sophie, you have to let it go.'

She looked directly at him, and he saw for the first time how much she desperately wanted to do that, as well as the furious turmoil of dread, pride and hatred which refused to let her. Its power took him by surprise – how could someone so damaged be so strong? 'No!' she rasped. 'Never! Never let it go. Starve it. Kill it.'

'Sophie, it's not your decision any more. It's out of your hands. That Hooper woman is going to send you and me and the rest of us back no matter what we do, and the araka will get loose anyway. You've got nothing to lose. Let it go!'

'NO!' Her mind was set as rigidly as her arms.

He hunkered closer. 'I don't have time for this. I need the monster. I can't help you, and I'm sorry about that, but I can't let Allie get sent back either. I'm not going to allow it. I wish there was some other way of doing this, but I'm all out of options. Help me. Don't make me do this by force.' The string around her neck with the key to her chain was clearly visible and very thin. It wouldn't take much to simply snatch it. He'd have to be quick, though – she was stronger than she looked.

She searched his face, considering and calculating. 'Okay,' she said finally. 'On one condition.'

'Name it.'

She told him.

He paled, but agreed without hesitation.

When he unlocked the manacle from her wrist, she unleashed a cry of such forlorn loss and ecstatic release that everything within hearing – even the araka itself – paused uneasily. Then she collapsed; he caught and eased her down gently, as the chain whipped past them and into the water in a furious bandsaw din so fast that the individual links were a blur. The manacle clattered over the edge and was gone.

3

He went back out to the dock, and to the astonishment of Strays and Orailleans alike, he put his hands up in surrender.

'All right, then,' he called to Berylin. 'I admit it. I am the dreamer. You've caught me bang to rights. Well played, Officer. I will surrender to you aboard your ship.'

Runce's eyes narrowed in suspicion. 'Too easy!' he called down to her.

'Easy?' Berylin shot back. 'Exactly which part of this investigation would you describe as difficult?'

'Then at least don't allow him aboard. Zap him where he stands.'

'Runce, caution is one thing, but I swear you are becoming paranoid. Look at him. He's unarmed, injured – Reason's sake, he's virtually naked. Besides, think of what we can learn from him about the Realt; this is an unparalleled opportunity. It could be the making of our careers.'

'Or the death of us all,' he growled.

'Now you are simply being melodramatic. Bo'sun!' she called. 'Bring that man aboard!'

They sent the dinghy for him, bound his hands in front so that he could climb, and before long he was being marched aboard the *Spinner*, the hot metal of the deck burning his bare soles. A crowd of nervous-looking crewmen hovered nearby clutching weapons, and Runce had made it very clear to Bobby that at the first sign of anything protean he would put a bullet between his eyes and see if he could redream the reality of *that*. Bobby didn't know what 'protean' or 'redream' meant, but he caught the gist.

Captain Mair peered down at him scornfully from the balcony of the wheelhouse. 'So this is the big threat we travelled a quarter of the way around the world to deal with, is it?' he sneered. 'Sorry bloody specimen, if you ask me. Somebody get the doctor to bind his wounds, would you? I'll not have him bleeding like a stuck pig in one of my cabins.'

A crewman moved to obey, but Harcourt stopped him. 'Wait. Let me see him.' He peered at the cut on Bobby's hand and the spiralling tentacle wound on his calf, both of which were bleeding freely. 'Excuse me, Miss Hooper,' he said uncertainly, 'weren't these bandaged up when he was waving to us earlier?'

Bobby smiled.

Their eyes followed the trail of his blood back along the deck to where he'd been brought on board, the smears of it on the ladder which he'd climbed from the dinghy, the spatters of it in the dinghy itself, and the ruby-red pearls of it sinking slowly through the water from when he'd allowed his tied hands to dangle over the side as they'd rowed him over from Stray. They were disappearing, like a string of fairy lights going out one after another, and something massive seethed in the water between the ship and the raft.

Buster raced to the foredeck and began barking at the shadow in the water.

'Get him off the ship!' shrieked Berylin. 'Get him off *now!*'

The shadow in the water glided down the *Spinner's* port side, following the trail of Bobby's blood, and where he had climbed aboard, exploratory black limbs emerged from the water to examine the ship's metal hull. They slithered over the rail and up the superstructure, stroking portholes and testing door handles. Tracking him. Some of the men standing by Runce murmured uneasily.

'Steady, lads,' he ordered, 'it's not after us.' But it was already too much for somebody below. One of the crew jumped forward, yelling at the top of his voice and waving a boat-hook pole which he smashed down on the nearest tentacle. Runce cursed.

All hell broke loose.

The limb flinched, but only briefly, and then half-a-dozen more seethed forward to grab the engineer and haul him screaming into the air, where he was shredded into a bloody mess in moments. The other tentacles exploded into a whipping frenzy, ripping the railings apart and flinging around any objects they could seize on. The force of the araka's sudden fury shoved the *Spinner* hard, rocking the deck and making people stagger for balance. Another crewman fell close, was grabbed by the legs, but managed to get a grip on the railing and hung there shrieking for his mates, two of whom cut at the limb with billhooks and knives until all three of them were dragged in, and the sea boiled a foamy pink. Alarm bells rang, and frantic orders were shouted all over the ship. Mair roared for full astern and the *Spinner's* prop churned as she sluggishly began to obey.

Bobby took advantage of the chaos and ran for the other side of the ship.

Berylin cursed and gave chase.

From the upper level of the wheel-house, Runce ordered a volley of fire into the writhing shapes and was gratified to see them recoil, leaving splashes of stinking black-green blood. He ordered a second volley, and a third, at which the creature seemed to get the message and withdrew completely. Tempting though it was to simply tez the bugger, he couldn't be sure that he wouldn't electrocute half the crew in the process, himself included. He praised his boys.

'Eyes open, lads!' he said. 'If you see it pop up again, don't keep it to yourself.'

Somewhere in the back of her mind, Berylin knew that chasing after Jenkins so closely and so fast was a stupid idea, but something about the way he'd smiled at her when he'd held up his bloodied hands had lit a fuse in her head that she couldn't put out. It had been laid a long time ago and had been getting shorter ever since. She certainly didn't need the force of him barrelling into her from where he'd been hiding around the corner to tell her exactly how stupid it was – but she got it anyway. He shoulder charged her, his heavier weight easily pinwheeling her sideways off her feet, and her left hip struck the gunwale painfully as she flipped overboard.

It was only her reflexes which saved her: her outstretched left hand grabbed the gunwale as she went over, but the pistol flew from her right and was gone forever. She scrabbled for a hold with her now-empty hand, found it, and hung, barely a yard above the waterline. Then slowly she began to to pull herself back up.

'Runce!' she called.

He turned, saw, and pushed past the riflemen to throw himself down the metal stairs to the deck, skidding most of the way, and ran to help her.

'Your gun,' she demanded, once she'd regained her footing. He gave her his revolver without question. 'I'll deal with Jenkins,' she continued. 'Keep the tez and take care of that monstrosity.'

'Aye, ma'am.'

Bobby, meanwhile, had run out of ship. Behind the wheelhouse, a narrow strip of deck extended either side of the ship's superstructure – a long, blocky construction from which rose first the main engine funnel, then a series of hatches, grilles, vents, and finally the main engine compartment. He ducked past a couple of portholes before he reached the very stern, where there was only a raised wooden platform for launching the dinghy, and then the sea. He crouched in the small gap between the rear of the engine room and the platform and tried to catch his breath. The thought of trying to dive clear was tempting, except that unless he could untie his hands he'd drown.

The ship gave a sudden violent lurch. Were they ramming Stray? Strange sounds of groaning metal came up through the deck from below.

There was no time to puzzle it out, because from behind and around the corner to his left, a metal door clanged open. Shouts. An engineer stepped around the corner: soot stained, wild-eyed, with a heavy wrench held high. Bobby pistoned himself upwards and sideways into a clumsy headbutt which connected with the point of the other man's chin, snapping his head back. The rear of the engineer's skull bounced off the wall behind him, and he fell in a heap.

More shouts.

He saw riflemen on the wheelhouse balcony turning in his direction – at least they weren't aiming at Stray anymore, he thought – and that insane woman clambering along the side towards him. She levelled a heavy pistol. Next to him, the open doorway of the engine room was a black hole. Christ alone knew what was in there.

Bullets spat at him, whining off steel.

He threw himself sideways, into the darkness.

The floor of the *Spinner's* engine room was much lower than deck level and reached by half a dozen steps that he completely failed to see, a fact which almost certainly saved his life. He fell, twisting, and landed heavily on his shoulder, aware only that someone had swung something large at him by the reverberating clang it made when it missed and struck a pipe where his head should have been. Winded, all he could do was lie there and watch as the bearded mass of the *Spinner's* chief stoker raised his shovel to drive it down into his skull.

He raised his bound hands feebly. 'Wait,' he tried to say, but all that came out was a pathetic wheezing noise. As last words, he'd been hoping for better.

Then the ship gave another almighty lurch. Screams came distantly from deeper in the ship. A bare-chested scarecrow of a figure – all staring eyes white in a coal-blackened face – scrambled up a set of steps from further down.

'Sir, it's pulled off the main prop shaft!' he panted, too terrified to notice that his boss was otherwise occupied. 'It's peeling us open like a bloody baked bean tin!' Without waiting for a reply he scrambled past them and outside.

The stoker turned back to Bobby, hesitant. Bobby had got to his knees, having recovered his breath somewhat, and he glared at the other man. 'You know what I am,' he said, trying to sound as menacing and mysterious as he could. 'You know what I can do. Run, and I'll let you live.'

For a moment, it seemed that the stoker was going to brain him anyway, but the ship gave another shudder, this time accompanied by the tortured howl of steel plating being twisted. The stoker spat at him, dropped the shovel, and fled.

Bobby was left alone in a room full of pipes, levers, greased brass pistons, and a bank of dials behind thick glass with their needles all trembling in the red. This was probably not a good sign. If the captain had ordered any amount of speed and, as it sounded like, the drive assembly was in the process of being shredded, Lord knew what that would be doing to the boilers.

He began searching for something to cut his hands free, but the blade of the shovel was all he could find. He kicked it around and started sawing through the cord binding his wrists together with its dull edge. As he sawed, he became aware that the floor was now very definitely sloping. They were taking on water. Never mind the danger of getting shot or eaten – if seawater flooded the boilers, the whole ship would go sky-high. Not if, he corrected himself. When.

He sawed faster, trying to ignore the screams and sounds of destruction from below.

The light from the doorway was blotted out.

'You bastard son of a whore,' spat Berylin. 'You've killed us all.'

4

The araka clung to the underside of the *Spinner* like a lamprey, peeling apart her hull plates with its long hunting limbs to get at the struggling morsels of terror inside. It had never felt stronger, nor more aware. As a creature of neither world, but rather the dreaming space between, its entrapment here by the witch-girl Sophie had been, ironically enough, like a nightmare. But the blood of the man Bobby, from there, had given it awareness, and the blood of the people from here had given it strength, and it devoured their souls with just as much delight as it shredded their pitifully frail bodies in the glorious singing light of *I am*.

5

She swayed in the doorway, a gun pointed at him. Not that freakish zap-gun, he noted, but this looked just as lethal. Water slopped over her boots, coming in through the door. The deck must be at sea level. *Jesus, we're going down fast*, he thought. He strained until his shoulders felt like they were twisting free from their sockets, but it did no good. That sort of thing might work in the Saturday morning serials or pulp adventures like *A Tender Death*, he told himself, but in real life rope simply didn't break like that.

'You should have left us alone,' he said, desperate to delay her, even by moments. 'I warned you, back on Danae.'

Her grin was ghastly, a bare rictus in a face drawn tight with madness. 'Yes. You did, didn't you? I suppose this is all my fault, really, isn't it? Time to put that right, then.'

She stepped into the room, wanting to be as close to him as possible when she did it, so that she could properly see that infuriating smirk leave his face when she put a bullet point-blank in his brain. When he suddenly charged at her she was more than ready, sidestepping around him easily as he crashed into the stairs where she'd been standing a moment before. She kicked him savagely in the back of one knee and was rewarded by his grunt of pain.

'Sorry,' she said. 'You only get to do that to me once. You're quite the bruiser, Mr Jenkins, but you have no finesse.'

He came up with the shovel in his hands. He was exhausted, dazed, and it felt like a lead weight as he waved it at her, but at least it was something. 'Just… why?' he said. 'That's all. Why?'

'Why? Because you exist, that's why. Isn't that enough?' She was standing with her back to the stairs which led down into the boiler room; it was full of the sound of rushing water and large objects being tossed around. She raised her pistol, and he got ready to make one last doomed lunge at her when they both noticed something like a thick belt – dark and muscular – which had suddenly appeared around her waist. She looked down at it, at first in confusion, then dawning horror, and back up at him.

'Help me,' she whispered. For a fleeting moment, he even considered trying.

Abruptly, her clothing below where the tentacle gripped her turned red. She shrieked in agony, and with a sudden neck-snapping jerk, she was gone.

Outside, the ship's stern was completely submerged, and her prow pointed high in the air. It made things easier for him, since all he had to do was fall into the water and kick clumsily away as hard as he could. That was where easy stopped; he could just about keep his head above water, but without the use of his arms he couldn't make any real progress. Stray was only several hundred yards away, but it might as well have been on the other side of the world. He thrashed, suddenly furious at the unfairness of it all – at everyone and everything that had conspired to lure him here, keep him here, and kill him here, especially this stupid fucking little piece of rope. He strained again until the tendons stood out in his neck like cables and the water closed over his head and his scream of frustration was a stream of ragged bubbles. But it didn't make any difference. He was going to drown.

And then, miraculously, Joe was there, scooting towards him underwater, waving and grinning around the oyster knife clamped between his teeth. There was something odd about the way he was swimming, but Bobby couldn't spare any attention for anything beyond the fact that his hands were finally being cut free. He clawed his way to the surface, gasping, as Joe appeared next to him.

Joe started to pull him away. 'We have to go! It's not safe!'

Bobby had no breath to reply. He just nodded and obeyed.

They made it nearly all the way to Stray when the *Spinner* exploded. Seawater had finally breached the ship's boilers, and the catastrophic failure of her pressure controls resulted in a blast equivalent to several tons of high explosive, literally tearing her in two. The shock wave pounded the pair of them into the water, and they had to dive deep to avoid the hail of debris which followed.

Burning wood and twisted metal rained down over a wide area, including Stray, the wreckage smashing large holes in the deck and even breaking pieces of it off completely. Tatters was struck by piece of the *Spinner's* funnel and reduced to splintered fragments. Small fires caught in the tinder-dry thatching and destroyed much of their shelter, and whole portions of the Hub had to be simply shoved into the sea to prevent the entire raft burning. By the time Bobby and Joe hauled themselves out, Stray was a scorched and scarred ruin.

Bobby didn't notice much of this straight away. He was too busy lying on the warm wood with his face to the sky, enjoying the feeling of not being chased, hit, shot at, threatened or insulted – and remembering what it was like to be able to breathe. Everything hurt. Again. When footsteps approached he expected them to be followed by helping hands or even the taste of Allie's lips. Not, as it turned out, a dog's low snarl and the click of a rifle's safety catch.

He squinted up at the bald-headed silhouette against the sky. 'Didn't I just blow you up?' he groaned.

'Not entirely, Mr Jenkins,' said Runce.

CHAPTER 25

LILIVET

1

'I'm not sure I can do this,' said Vessa.

Ennias had given her a good day's rest to recover from the Swarm's attack, but he'd made it plain that she was going to have to make good on her claim to be able to communicate with Tourmaline, and soon. She was standing on the *Cella*'s foredeck, hands shoved deeply into the pockets of her coat, feeling cold under the shadow of all that concrete.

'Oh, that's okay,' he said. 'Never mind. I'll just get the car. Do you have a preference about which police station you'd like me to drop you off at?'

'Steady on,' frowned Steve.

'Look, I'm sorry,' she protested angrily, 'but it's just not that simple. For a start, I haven't got the painting.'

'I don't think you need it as much as you think you do,' said Steve. 'You certainly didn't need it that night when Sophie took your place.'

'By the way, ta-daa,' said Ennias, and tossed her a colour print-out of the painting.

She looked at it unhappily for a moment, and then passed it back to him. 'It's not the same,' she said.

'I didn't think it would be. Still, worth a try. Look, the link is in your head, right? The painting is just a switch. A trigger. Maybe it was never meant to be that, but I think if you concentrate on an image of it in your mind's eye and try to feel what you felt those times when the link got made, you can do it without needing the actual painting itself – now that you're conscious of what you're doing.'

Vessa shuddered. 'That's another problem. Those feelings – they're the most horrible ones in the world.'

'Yes, but they're *strong*, and it's strength that opens doors.' He snorted. 'Listen to me. I sound like a bleeding fortune cookie. This is what you've reduced me to.'

'No, I mean I don't think I can make myself feel like that. It's like asking someone to mutilate themselves.'

Ennias carefully tore the print-out into small pieces. 'Then you're no use to me,' he said. 'Sorry to be so blunt, but that's the way of it, I'm afraid. You're too dangerous to me and mine, otherwise. What with the swarm, and your feral kid there, and this Degan bloke – if what you're saying is true – you've taken out three of the Hegemony's assets in twenty-four hours. They might have been mildly curious about you before, but I bet they're just gagging to get their hands on you now, and if you've got nothing to offer me which makes that danger worthwhile, well then.' He shrugged, and tossed the scraps of paper into the canal.

'Okay!' she shouted, and then more quietly, 'Okay. I'll try. Just once. I'll try.'

'Try hard.'

2

She tried to build a picture of 'She Shall Be Called Woman' in her imagination piece by piece – not so much as a literal jigsaw, but more according to the feelings that each element evoked.

...her face, head thrown back, almost featureless except for a yearning to be; her breasts, similarly blurred, little more than suggestions of form swelling outwards from a ruffled haze of chaotic colour, like a husk peeling back for something golden to burst free. White lilies bloom and multi-coloured birds flock at her right hand while clouds stir at her left, and below her is a garden stretching away into hills and a golden sunrise; Vessa thinks of how fine it would be to live in peace in a small place with a garden to tend, and then of her little window-box which she'll probably never see again. Because there can be no peace. Not when Sophie demands. Not when everybody, even the people like Steve who care for her, demand. There is only the fraying apart at the edges when their demands become too much, like scraps of paper floating apart on water, and she gets lost in the pieces and she needs to put a frame

around them all and drag them back together before they disappear and she disintegrates forever. She remembers her first ever sight of the painting – her first ever sight of anything – and how nothing after that ever seemed quite so real, just shadows of the clouds and sky and flowers and birds of another place which...

The hradix was hooting excitedly up in the scaffolding.

'It feels it,' murmured Ennias.

'Feels what?' asked Steve.

'Home.' His eyes were shining.

Steve looked around, but couldn't see anything different. Except, possibly... was the shimmer of light on the canal slighly brighter than before? He thought maybe it was.

Vessa frowned. Her eyes were closed, but she seemed to be staring intently at something. 'Wait,' she said. 'There's...'

'What?' Ennias' face was taut with concern. The hradix's hoots became barks of alarm, and it began throwing itself back and forth in the scaffolding like a deranged chimpanzee.

'There's something... they're fighting...'

'Who's fighting?' asked Steve.

'Bobby... there's a woman... men with guns... and in the water...' Her eyes snapped open in shock, but whatever they were seeing wasn't in this world. 'It's in the water! It got free! Oh Jesus Christ, she let it go and it got free and it's under the boat – don't go down there, Bobby, *it's under the boat!*'

'What boat?' Steve demanded. 'This boat? Us, here?'

Ennias leapt at her, thinking to break whatever link she had created, but before he could touch her, there was a violent concussion in the water astern which rocked the *Cella* and threw them all off-balance. When she settled and the three of them climbed to their feet to look around, they saw a dark-haired woman – half-naked, bloody, and covered in dozens of wounds – floating unconscious in a slowly widening ring of debris.

Steve stared. 'Who the bloody hell is that?'

3

It was almost more than Runce could do to stop his men from executing Bobby then and there – and if truth be told, he wasn't a hundred percent sure that he wanted to. He let them get as far as trussing Bobby up (for the second time, he noted sourly), and marching him to the edge of the raft at gunpoint while the other Strays cursed and pleaded, before his conscience overrode the desire to avenge Berylin's death.

'Give me one good reason why I shouldn't,' he growled. 'Just one.'

'You're trapped here now, just like us,' said Allie. 'Except we know how to navigate out of here. Let us be, and I promise I'll get you safely out of the Flats.'

'Or I could simply shoot you all now,' he returned. 'Return this part of the world to normal and make my own way home by the sun and stars. That would be the simplest thing.'

'Sir…' said Bobby.

'Don't you talk to me! Your talking time is done, understand?'

'…I don't think you'll do that.'

Runce grabbed him and jammed the tez gun's muzzle up under Bobby's jaw. There was a feverish jitter in the older man's eyes, and his throat worked like he was trying to swallow a length of steel cable. 'A dozen men dead in the water and you just keep running that mouth of yours, don't you?' He could barely speak for grief. 'My Berry *dead,* and it just keeps coming. What exactly do you think I'll not do?'

Bobby thought that right at the moment the answer to that question was: *Not much.*

'Kill him and there's still the rest of us,' continued Allie defiantly. 'Are you going to shoot two women, an old man and a child as well? Do that and you may as well not go home at all; and yes, I can see that wedding ring on your finger. What would your wife say if she could see you now? You're supposed to be a *soldier,* for God's sake.'

Slowly Runce managed to claw back his control. He lowered the tez and had his men toss Bobby back to his companions while he stared around at the expanding debris field and wondered what in the name of Reason he was supposed to salvage from this mess.

The job. That was what he was supposed to salvage. Get the job done. For Berylin.

'Fair enough,' he said, turning back to them. 'Let's do this properly.' He took his canister of sal volatile from its belt-pouch. 'We're going to work out who here is suborned, and who's the dreamer – and then I'm going put them out of our misery properly. We'll start with you.'

One of his men took a handful of Allie's hair and forced her head back, and Runce waved the canister closely under her nose. The ammonia stench made her gag and sneeze, but other than that nothing happened. 'That was quick,' the crewman said, letting go of her and standing back hurriedly as if she might explode.

'Quick is just fine,' said Runce, raising the tez gun.

'Idiot!' yelled Allie. 'I told you: I'm in a coma! It's going to take more than a bottle of fucking smelling salts to wake me up!'

'Sorry,' said Runce, looking anything but. 'That's not even close to being convincing.' A high-pitch whine sounded from the capacitors in the tez gun's pack, and he squeezed the trigger.

'You are making a big mistake,' warned Seb, taking a step forward. There were shouts and rifles raised towards him. Runce glanced at him. Bobby tensed himself, even though every muscle in his body felt like an over-wrung dishrag, knowing that he wasn't going to be able to do anything with the momentary distraction other than get himself killed but equally sure that he was going to do it anyway. Allie saw and shook her head urgently. It was all going to go pear-shaped, and there wasn't a damned thing he could do about it.

Then one of Runce's men shouted 'Sir! The boy! Look!'

Everything stopped. Joe was on his feet, and he was glowing.

At least, that was what it looked like at first. His skin had taken on the same nacreous, mother-of-pearl sheen as his eyes, and in the bright early morning sunlight, he shone like a burnished statue rather than a human being. Runce ignored it, continuing to focus the heat of his full scorn on Allie.

'Is that meant to impress me?' he sneered. 'Suborning the boy?'

'Mr Sarge?' said Joe. It was, after all, the only name by which he'd heard anybody address Runce. 'Check your machines. She's not doing anything.'

Runce glanced at the dials on his PV rig. All the indicator needles were flat against zero, which was impossible, given where they were and what was happening. He tapped them and shook the unit, confused. It was tempting to assume that it had been damaged by seawater or the fighting, except he knew that it had been designed to withstand much more severe conditions than either. Whatever was happening to the boy, it wasn't as a result of any human agency – at least, nothing like he'd ever encountered. He felt like he was back in Willoughby Terrace again, aiming his tez gun at a perfectly innocent woman. A rogue swell must have lifted Stray under his feet just then; how else to explain his sudden loss of balance and backward stagger?

But nobody was paying attention to him any more.

Lachlan reached out to the boy. 'Jophiel, please don't do this,' he whispered, hoarse with denial. 'Not after...' but he couldn't finish.

'I'm sorry, Da. He wouldn't have believed any other way.' Joe was thinner now, his flesh becoming translucent and yet oddly brighter at the same time, and then Bobby realised why: it was the scales. The sun shone on the silvery integument that was Jophiel's real skin, revealed now that his human disguise was finally sloughing away. The oddness in the way Joe had come swimming to rescue him also made sense now; gills quivered beneath his jaw. Like sparks from a fire, Allie had said. Except that this spark had created its own fire in turn.

'I was Mama's dream anyway,' the boy continued, even though there wasn't much left of him which was very boy-like. 'We both know that.'

'No. Don't say that. You're my son.'

'I'm less than a dream, Da. I'm a scrap of a dream feeding off someone else's need for something to love. I've been trying to hang on since... since that thing took her, but it's just too hard. I'm too tired. It's time for me to go. I only ever wanted to make her happy. Did I? Did I do that?' Joe's eyes, once the strangest thing about him, were now the most human. The overpowering need to know this one last thing was all that still bound the shreds of his human form together.

'Yes, son,' said Lachlan. 'You made her very happy. You made us both happy.'

Jophiel sighed deeply, as if having been given leave to rest after a long labour, or permission to depart. He kissed his father and walked to the very edge of the raft, but changed his mind and went over to Bobby. The soldiers let him go, drawing back fearfully.

'You've made friends,' said the boy, 'out there.' And he nodded towards the open ocean. 'They'll help you if they can. You've made them strong, but the araka is still alive, and it's a lot stronger.'

'It can't be,' said Bobby. 'It blew up – we both saw it happen.'

Joe shook his head sadly, pieces of his shape scattering in bright fragments which evaporated in the sunlight. His form existed now only as an after-image on the retina, in the middle of which something sinuous gleamed.

'No, it didn't,' it replied, and turning to Runce it added, 'nor did your daughter. I'm sorry – so truly, truly sorry, but there's nothing I can do.'

'She's not...' *my daughter*, Runce wanted to reply, but what was left of the boy had already gone over the side, leaving only the last shreds of its dream-wrought humanity to melt on Stray's deck. A shining, rainbow eel with fins like angel's wings rippling along the length of its body paused for a moment to dance in the warm shallows, and then threaded itself in curving stitches down into the depths.

4

They laid the woman as gently as possible in the *Cella*'s single cramped cabin, where Ennias tended to her wounds while Steve and Vessa hovered helplessly. When he'd done the best job he could, he joined them back on deck.

'And you're sure you have absolutely no idea who she is,' he said to Vessa. She shook her head.

'But you were trying for Caffrey?' asked Steve.

Vessa shrugged. 'He was there. I could see him. But it was all confused – there was a lot of fighting. People running around and screaming.'

'Was someone attacking him? Or her?'

'I can't remember; it's fuzzy. You know when you wake up from a dream which was so clear and you can only remember bits of it?'

'Vessa,' said Ennias, 'when you said "it's free, it's under the boat", what did you mean? What got free?'

Her voice, when she explained about the araka, was so quiet that they could barely hear it. This was the last thing she wanted to tell anybody. When she'd finished, Steve had his head in his hands and Ennias was glaring at her coldly.

'Finally something that makes sense,' he said, and she recoiled from his anger. 'That's why the Hegemony wanted you in the first place, wasn't it? Nothing to do with any link between there and here, because you didn't know you could do that until you pushed Caffrey in, did you? All along they've been after your Passenger – this araka. Something like that… the things they could do with it…' he broke off, shaking his head in disbelief. 'And it's loose out there now, is that right?'

She nodded. 'But I didn't know! How could I have known? I'd never have tried to bring anybody through if I'd known that it was loose. You have to believe me!'

Ennias sighed. 'Yes, there is that, I suppose. As it is, all we've done is gone and plucked some random stranger out of the world. This is completely fucked.'

Steve raised his head. 'Still, it proves that she can do it.'

'Oh, yes!' Ennias' sarcasm echoed off the concrete all around them. 'As silver linings go, that's a corker, isn't it?' He threw his coat on and jumped from the deck to the towpath. 'I've got some calls to make. I need to find out if this has been noticed. All this concrete, though, it plays hell with a phone signal. Do *not*,' he jabbed a finger at the *Cella*'s cabin, 'tell that woman *anything* if she wakes up, and do not let her leave. Got it?'

And without waiting to hear whether or not they'd got it, he was gone.

5

She awoke in narrow darkness. The part of her which remembered being Berylin Hooper recognised the feeling of strange bedclothes from her nightmare at the pool of Bles Gabril, while the part of her which was still araka sensed the weight of water all around – held at bay by only a flimsy steel hull – and remembered its entrapment under Stray by the witch-girl Sophie. Panicked by both, she screamed herself into full consciousness.

Sounds of movement on the deck overhead.

She was in a small cabin. There was barely enough room for the bed in which she'd been laid, with a few shelves and a door beyond her feet, and a curtained porthole above her head. She twisted around and knelt up, discovering that Berylin's sodden clothes had been replaced by a thick robe, and drew the short curtains aside.

The world outside was grey. Scum-covered water lapped a few inches from her nose, with a concrete shore further off, planted with concrete columns which supported a concrete sky.

She was in the Realt. Someone had dragged her into this place that was the source of all nightmare and horror. Dear Reason, she was…

'Alive,' she realised.

There was at least that.

Alive and – something more.

This was a canal. She was in a narrowboat on a canal beneath a motorway flyover. She knew this because Degan knew this and she had eaten Degan and everything of him. More precisely, the araka had eaten him before it in turn had become a part of her – or she a part of it. Impossible to tell. Locked in a killing embrace, the two of them had been dragged here and – what? Fused? Conjoined? Consummated?

The thought appalled her.

At the same time, it was glorious.

Degan had known a great deal about the Realt, it seemed, and specifically about what Passengers were capable of when they arrived here. He knew about a man called Maddox, and a power called the Hegemony, and the tools that they employed to monitor and control this world. She was surprised to discover that far from being trapped, isolated and powerless here, she probably had more options available to her than at home for putting a stop to the curse of subornation once and for all.

A slow smile curved her mouth. She felt the sharpness of her teeth – several rows of them – with a tongue which was no less dangerous.

Correction: tongues. Plural.

That brought her close to panic again. She lurched across the bed to the narrow wardrobe, yanking it open, and found what she needed: a mirror on the inside of the door. Her reflection seemed normal: the same hair, same hazel eyes, same nose that had always been a little too big for her liking. She bared her teeth at herself and found those to be normal too. A bit mucky, perhaps, due to life aboard the *Spinner*, but not the razor-edged points she'd felt a second ago. Was she going mad? Had her subornation into this place broken her mind? If it had, could she be sure she was in the Realt at all? Maybe she was in a padded cell in Beldam, shackled to a wall and drooling. *Angels in my brain.*

Almost afraid to look, she started to open her robe to examine her new body.

'Is everything okay? We thought we heard someone calling out.'

The witch-girl was peering around the door in concern. The araka wanted to leap across and slaughter her on the spot, tear the screaming face off her skull and bathe in her blood as payback for the torment of its long starvation in her mind, but Berylin was more cautious. It was obvious that this wasn't Sophie. Sophie was still in Tourmaline. This was the other, the one that Sophie had conjured into being to trap the araka between them. If anything, it hated her more. But the araka's knowledge was her knowledge now, and it knew everything about Sophie Angela Marchant, having spent long enough tormenting her and being tormented in turn. The girl was far too useful to be wasted on the simple gratification of bloodletting. That would come later.

'Who are you?' she whined. 'What place is this?' She clutched the robe at her throat and backed away to the end of the bed in a facsimile of confusion and fear.

'I'm Vessa, and you're safe,' the other answered, taking a tentative step further into the cabin. 'Can you tell me your name?'

What a question. The simplest one in the world: who are you? And yet for a moment it nearly broke her. She wanted to lash out at it, to destroy it and the woman who spoke it, and she felt her teeth sharpen again. More than that: now she felt things coming alive at her neck, armpits, elbows, groin and knees – wherever she was joined together – and suddenly the answer came to her. She smiled at Vessa with all her teeth, enjoying the way she shrank back in terror.

'Lilivet,' she said. 'You can call me Lilivet, sweetie.'

Before Vessa could scream or do anything like try to push her out of the world, Lilivet bounced her head off the cabin wall so hard that she saw stars.

'Not this time, sweetie,' Lilivet purred. 'You're dealing with the professionals now.' And she slammed Vessa's head again, this time so hard that everything exploded into darkness.

CHAPTER 26

COMPROMISING POSITIONS

1

Steve wasn't having much success trying to coax the hradix out of the scaffolding. It clung and swung from the bars, growling at him, having changed its hands and feet to curved, opposable claws. There was absolutely no way he could pretend it was just some kid gone schizo, but even so he couldn't bring himself to feel afraid of it. It looked like it was trying to revert to its natural form – whatever that was – and when he saw the talons sticking out of the ruins of its school shoes, his guts twisted in sympathy for the poor child that was possessed by it. Still, sooner or later a passer-by was going to spot this 'poor child', and probably get eaten by it. He could hear sirens faintly somewhere overhead on one of the curving slip-roads, and wondered how Ennias was getting on up there.

'Look,' he called up to the hradix, 'if you don't want any of these I'll just have to eat them all myself, won't I?' He crunched a mint loudly. 'Mmm! Yummy!'

It swooped down, snatched one and shot back up into the maze of pipes, grinning. It was playing, he realised. He wondered if there was a ball anywhere on board. Maybe there was a way of encouraging the human personality to take more control.

Abruptly the hradix stopped scampering and froze into an angle formed by three poles, hissing and glaring at him. No, not at him – past him. He turned and saw the strange woman from Tourmaline stepping from the *Cella*'s deck and onto the shore, coming towards him.

'Sod you, then,' he muttered, and headed back down the towpath to meet her. She was still wearing the bathrobe that Vessa had found for her, but it was hanging half open in a way which displayed more flesh than he was comfortable seeing. For all he knew, that was how they were wearing things in Tourmaline this season, but still.

'Morning,' he said awkwardly. 'Are you, ah, feeling any better?'

Lilivet stretched. 'Marvellous,' she yawned. 'Absolutely marvellous. I feel like a new woman.' She laughed, and the hradix whimpered at the sound.

'Riiight,' he said slowly, looking anywhere but at her. 'Um, is Vessa still down there? I need to talk to her about a thing.'

'Oh poor you,' she replied, in tones of great concern. 'You really are still smitten with her, aren't you?'

It wasn't quite the last thing he'd expected her to say, but it was pretty close. 'Sorry? How did – what has she been saying?'

'Nothing. She didn't have to; we've known each other for a long time.'

'Really? She said she's never seen you before.'

The woman shrugged as if it made no difference. 'Figure of speech. It's a pity, really – she never had any genuine feelings for you. She's incapable of them. She's not even what you'd call a proper human being.'

He didn't like the way this conversation was going at all. He'd been expecting her to be confused and disorientated, and possibly even aggressive. Not this – whatever this was. She was still drifting slowly towards him, even though she didn't actually seem to be paying him all that much attention. She was staring at the reflections on the water as if mesmerised, and at her bare feet as they moved on the gravel. The sirens were louder now. Closer. He stepped to one side, planning to skirt a cautious distance around her and head back the *Cella*.

'Vessa?' he called. There was no reply. Her absence was beginning to actively alarm him now.

'I know,' Lilivet sighed, even though he hadn't said anything to her. 'You've followed her all this way, and all it's got you is dead. You and everybody else in this world.'

Steve tried to run.

He got about three feet.

Her araka limbs whipped out, taking him around the torso and throat, and surprising herself almost as much as him. She hadn't known she could be so fast, or so strong. She reeled him in like a struggling fish, thinking that now would be as good an opportunity as any to test the limits of her new capabilities: how much damage they could cause, and how dextrous they could be in inflicting pain. 'I know this is small consolation,' she said as he choked, 'but compared to what's going to happen to the rest of this world, I'm doing you a favour. And don't worry; I haven't killed her. She is going to serve a noble purpose in helping to rid my world of a great evil: yours.' The tip of one tentacle brushed his brow, taking the skin with it, and he tried to scream.

Then the hradix launched itself at her, tearing and biting. In its attack rage, it had shrugged off more of its human shape; Steve saw patches of grey, reptilian skin through the holes in its tattered school uniform. Its hands and feet were all claws, and its jaws looked like they were lengthening even as it bit. Then it was at the woman's face, and she dropped him to defend herself, the pair of them tumbling backward in a pinwheeling storm of limbs and teeth.

Steve scrambled away from the towpath and up the bank, retching for breath, and found his way blocked by a chain-link fence which followed a line of support columns. He remembered Ennias saying something about an escape route up the scaffolding (and where exactly had that useless bastard gone, anyway?), and he ran along to where he'd been trying to coax the hradix down, trying not to hear the awful noises coming from behind him. It sounded like a bobcat being torn apart by a pack of wolves. Halfway up the scaffolding, a stab of guilt made him pause.

It's just a kid. You can't leave it to be killed like that.

He looked back, but it was already too late. Blood painted the canal bank and clouded the water, and in the midst of it a creature of thrashing limbs tore at a small shape too badly savaged to be recognisably human.

And Vessa. Are you going to run out on her too? Just like you did when the Swarm attacked? Just like you did when Sophie came?

He might be able to make those things up to her, but if she were still alive on board the *Cella,* all he'd accomplish by going back would be to give her someone else to mourn. The best he could do was to find Ennias and hope that he had some clue how to fight that thing. He climbed, fuelled by adrenalin and terror, and eventually collapsed onto a maintenance platform attached to the crash barrier of a busy slip-road.

He lay for a moment, gasping, while cars and trucks roared past.

'McBride!' Ennias was running towards him along the hard shoulder. 'What the fuck? I told you to stay with the boat!'

Steve struggled to his feet. 'Where the hell have you been?' he coughed.

Ennias pulled up short, taking in McBride's condition: the mud and blood and marks on his throat. 'Words of one syllable,' he demanded. '*Now.*'

Steve floundered, trying to explain something which barely made sense to himself. Ennias allowed him a second or two of stammering like an idiot before dismissing him. 'Fuck this for a game of tiddlywinks,' he muttered, and headed for the maintenance platform.

'No!' Steve shouted, grabbing at him.

'Ah, so it does speak.'

'You can't go down there. There's something in the woman we found… it's not human. Not even an animal, I don't think. It's got Vessa, and it killed the… the boy. What did we bring back, Ennias? *What the fuck did we bring back?*'

Ennias considered for a moment and then tossed him a set of car keys. 'Get that thing started,' he ordered, indicating a van parked further along the hard shoulder with its hazard lights flashing.

'While you do what? Piss off again?'

'While I see with my own eyes. Or am I supposed to just start trusting you now?' Without waiting for a response he disappeared over the side.

Steve climbed into the van, started the engine and waited as his thumping heart calmed. A line of flashing blue police lights raced along the overpass above this one. Agents of the mysterious Hegemony, if Ennias was to be believed. People like that bloke in the gallery. He looked at the marks on his throat in the rear view mirror. They were real enough. Therefore the thing that had made them was real. Therefore everything that Vessa and Ennias had told him must be true. It occurred to him that he could take off now and put the whole thing behind him. Jackie had been right: he'd been a fool to get involved with Vessa in the first place, and a complete moron to do it a second time. There'd never been any hope of finding Caffrey; he was gone for good, and the hole that Steve had climbed down into to look for him was full of lunatics and monsters instead. Vessa belonged with them – she was welcome to them – meanwhile, he had real people like his sister and her boys who needed him to look out for them. Because if the world really was full of things like that creature, his loved ones needed protecting even more.

His hand was on the gear-stick when he saw Ennias in the mirror, sprinting towards the van. 'Drive!' he was shouting. 'Fucking floor it!'

Ennias leapt up into the passenger seat and sat staring straight ahead, panting, his face pale.

'Where?' asked Steve.

'Just get us out of here. Quickly, before they lock down the motorway. We'll argue about a destination later.'

'Are we going back for Vessa?'

'No. Yes. Later – possibly. I don't bloody know. Just drive, will you? I need to think.'

Steve drove.

2

Within ten minutes of shutting down Spaghetti Junction, the tailbacks were over a mile long. Traffic came to a standstill along the entire length of the Aston Expressway, gridlocking Birmingham city centre, and half an hour later the M6's major junctions with routes west and north jammed solid, effectively immobilizing the road transport hub of the entire country.

Maddox gave a shit about precisely none of this.

He refused to answer a single one of the panicky phone calls from the Highways Agency, police, or government ministers demanding to know what the hell he thought he was doing. He stared, fixated, at the image of the woman in the bloodstained dressing gown which the remote feed was sending to his car. He was parked on the flyover directly above where she sat cross-legged and perfectly serene on the deck of a small canal boat; lying next to her, apparently unconscious, was a second woman who had just been confirmed as Sophie Marchant – or Vanessa Gail, depending on which wittering bloody psychiatrist you believed.

'But we still don't have a confirmed on Miss Butter-Wouldn't-Melt, is that what you're trying to tell me?' he asked, unimpressed.

'Not as yet, sir, no,' admitted Morris, his Ops Deputy, a protocol-obsessed little brown-noser with more OCD tics and twitches than a sleep-deprived meerkat. Working for the Hegemony for too long tended to have that kind of effect on a person; Maddox's personal answer was to channel it into displays of astonishing brutality, but that was by the by. Facial recognition software had so far failed to place the strange woman on a single passport, driver's licence or identification card anywhere in the world – or the bits of the world which had such things – and that worried him.

'What are the wake-sensitives saying?'

Morris called up a report on his tablet. 'There's been nothing active since the m-breach which our buoys picked up, but that was big enough: at least twice the size of Degan's discorp. But even just sitting there she's packing one hell of a wallop – Niagra Falls on legs, one of them said.'

'So what in buggeration is she carrying?'

'Whatever it is, sir, it's big.'

Big. He'd once heard a rumour that one of the North American offices had got their hands on an asset which carried some kind of giant underground worm thing, but that it had levelled two city blocks before they'd been able to collar the bastard. So big was bad. That wasn't what bothered him the most, though.

Neither was it the way she seemed to be totally ignoring the presence of the Lynx helicopter he had stationed overhead and the two fast-response boats manned with snipers in each direction along the canal, or the fact that she'd already shrugged off the effects of a tranquiliser round which would have taken down a horny megalodon. What gave him the crawling horrors was the amount of blood and body parts around her – more precisely, the fact that she'd spelled out his name in them on the boat's roof. There was no way of avoiding the unpalatable truth: he was going to have to talk to her himself.

'Fuck it.'

Maddox got out of the car.

Morris tried to get a stab-vest and a sidearm on him, but Maddox snarled him away. He passed the outer cordon of crowd-controlling ordinary plod, then the inner ring of his own people – not all of whom were, strictly speaking, people – then down to the tow path and the canal.

The woman was waiting patiently, with Marchant an unconscious heap next to her.

'I am Lilivet,' she declared, standing. 'Once of the Oraillean Department for Counter Subornation. Once, also, of the nameless hosts of araka in the dreaming space between worlds. Now of both, and neither, and here also, in this place which we call the Realt.'

'Fantastic,' he replied, unimpressed. 'Since you already seem to know who I am I'll skip all that, if you don't mind, and get straight to what it is exactly that you want.'

She held out her hands, wrists together. 'I want you to arrest me,' she said, smiling playfully. 'I want you to take me to your leader.'

Maddox considered this for a moment. 'Okay,' he said, and waved forward the men with the handcuffs. Pleasingly, she didn't seem to be expecting them to be electrified.

3

Ennias ordered Steve to drive west and out onto the Hagley Road, a busy arterial linking the city centre to the M5 and lined with hundreds of low budget chain motels, bed-and-breakfasts, and conference centres catering to the jetset lifestyles of middle-management executives and travelling salesmen. He led him up the rattling rear fire escape of an ancient guesthouse which might have seen better days as a bail hostel, and into a cramped bedsit.

Steve looked around in dismay. There was a sagging bed, a sink, a television so old that its screen actually curved, and a panoramic view of the delivery yard. It smelled of damp plaster and nicotine. 'What are we doing here?'

'You live here. At least for the moment.'

'Here? Are you insane?'

'Oh, I do apologise,' Ennias replied acidly, 'but all of my better properties are kind of security-compromised at the moment by the feckless idiots I have to keep rescuing – not to mention fucked up with blood and guts. This is the only safe-house I have left.'

'Safe as in safe for everybody else except me, right?'

'That's the one.'

Steve tested the bed's squeaking springs and ran some water in the sink. It was brown and there was no plug. 'How long?' he asked.

'Three, maybe four days. I'm going to find out where they've taken our girl.'

'Screw that. I'm coming with you.'

Ennias gave the kind of sigh generally used when attempting to explain very simple things to very simple children. 'McBride, listen to me. I have to approach some secretive and nervous people who won't say a thing, and they might very well kill us both, if you're with me. The best thing you can do right now is keep your head down here and stay out of everybody's way. Also, at some point in the next twenty-four hours what you laughingly refer to as your brain is likely to go into existential meltdown because of all the weirdness it's had to deal with in the last three days, and it's going to be much better for you, me, and everybody else if that happens behind closed doors. That way you can gibber and scream and wipe the walls with your own shit and nobody has to know. If on the other hand you don't do a complete Renfield,' he shrugged, 'so much the better. We'll talk about insane then.' He lit a cigarette. Steve tried to open the window, but the frame was warped with damp.

'But what about my job?' he complained, thumping at it. 'What about Jackie? I have to let people know I'm all right!'

'Well, you won't be if you try it, and neither will I. Up until now the only reason that the Hegemony might possibly have been interested in you is to get to Vessa, and they've got her now, which means soon they'll know about me. If you pop your stupid head up above the parapets grinning and waving at everybody, they'll come for you – or they'll come for those closest to you – to get to me and the other exiles. Apart from anything else, I've also got to tell my own nearest and dearest to get out of Dodge too. I have absolutely no intention of letting you see anybody I know or care about while you constitute that kind of a risk.'

'It strikes me that you'd be a lot better off just dumping me in a canal or something.'

'Don't think it hasn't occurred. That was a joke, by the way,' he added, dead-pan. 'Probably. But I think you can definitely kiss your career in the arts sector goodbye.'

Ennias left Steve with money, some old clothes which looked like they wouldn't fit him at all well, and a cheap mobile phone which he was told to never under any circumstances use. 'Your tag words for the next seventy-two hours are "low" and "profile", got it?' he said, and disappeared back down the fire escape.

Steve sighed and turned on the TV.

4

Maddox is on the Wall again.

An icy north wind whips over the border-land fells and snaps his prefect's cape behind him as he surveys the day's repair work before him. There is a broken gap in the Wall, and large blocks of limestone lie scattered on the green turf around him. Some are clean and new-cut, lying in neatly organised stacks for the Wall's ongoing programme of construction and expansion, while others are damaged, broken and scorched – already testament to its strength against the incessant Pictish attacks. One would have thought that the rows of barbarian heads on pikes above each of the milecastles would have taught them the futility of attacking the Wall by now – but apparently not. It has become something of a competition amongst the commanders of the milecastles to see who can boast the largest crop of heads. Nobody seriously fears the Picts. The Wall is too strong.

As *praefectus fabrus* of the Second Augustan Legion, he sees to that. He issues orders to his men and they set about their tasks: hammering, chiselling, and cursing the blocks into fitting obediently with their neighbours. The ringing sound of their tools echoes out into the desolate wastes of the fells, and he thinks with savage satisfaction that it is the closest those heathens will ever get to civilisation. He makes it a point of personal pride to inspect each block as it joins the Wall – some are engraved with information about the day's events, and he needs to ensure that everything is organised clearly – but even though he knows that this is not really possible, it doesn't bother him too much, since this is only a dream, after all.

Not a dream in the ordinary sense, of course. Such things are far too dangerous for a man in his position. A "creative visualisation" is how the Legion's psychological analysts described it to him when he first enlisted; a near-lucid imaginative construct designed to provide a framework for his mind to collate and process memories and information from the waking day rather than run the risk of 'normal' REM dreams.

One of his men accidentally drops a block on another, causing both to split. It's Maddox's fault – he hasn't been concentrating on the construction – so he doesn't berate the clumsy soldier, just smiles tolerantly and turns to lend a hand. His men love him. In the back of his sleeping mind runs the understanding that one of the characteristics of non-REM dreams is that they are far less driven by fear and aggression, which probably explains why he compensates by being such an utter bastard to his subordinates in the waking world.

It also helps to explain why, when the woman who calls herself Lilivet climbs casually through the broken gap in the Wall as if she's out for nothing more than a mid-morning stroll, this doesn't bother him too much either. She is wearing very little. Her bare skin – and there is quite a lot of it, he notes appreciatively – is painted in swirls of blue, while curving golded bands decorate her arms, legs, and throat.

She looks around, nodding in approval. 'Well,' she says, 'you certainly proved difficult to find.'

'That's the idea,' he replies affably. 'The Wall wouldn't be very secure if everybody who worked on it started digging tunnels whenever they slept. It also means that people like you can't hijack your way into the brains of people like me through our dreams, which is what I imagine you were intending to do.'

She pouts. 'Now you've gone and spoiled all the fun. I suppose I'm going to have to actually persuade you.'

'Sorry about that. We've been doing this rather a long time. Still, no hard feelings, hey?'

'I suppose not,' she says, and kicks a small fragment of stone sulkily.

He concentrates on putting a few more of the day's blocks in place while she wanders here and there, picking up things, inspecting them and then dropping them again, bored. When he reaches a natural break he sits down on a large block next to her in the sun, enjoying the sensation of the north wind cooling the sweat on his brow. He offers her a drink from his water bottle. 'So,' he says. 'What exactly is it that you wanted? Other than to possess me and turn me into a drooling vegetable, that is.'

'You don't seem particularly threatened by this notion,' she observes.

He shrugs. 'It's a side effect of shutting down the fight-or-flight parts of the brain which cause the dreams that link my world to yours. Besides, I assume that you're clever enough to have a plan B.'

'Are you patronising me?'

'Just a little bit. I think I'm entitled.'

She takes a long drink from his bottle and passes it back. 'This really is a most impressive wall,' she says, in an apparent desire to change the subject. 'I'd be flattered if you would show it to me.'

He is happy to oblige.

'Is it herbal or pharmacological?' she asks as they walk. 'This dream-killer that you use. In the DCS we used nutmeg in our tea. It helped to suppress dreams somewhat.'

'It's a monoamine oxidase inhibitor. A kind of hydrazine, if that means anything.'

At that she begins laughing, hard enough to have to stop briefly.

'What's funny?'

'Sorry, a private joke,' she apologises, wiping her eyes. 'Yes, hydra means something to me.'

'You'll have to explain it to me one day.'

'I'll show it to you in person,' she promises. 'I have come to offer you an alliance. If all I had wanted was to suborn or kill you, I could already have done so a dozen times over.'

'Oh, I strongly doubt that,' he laughs complacently.

'Really? Your countermeasures are designed to work against passengers from my world trapped in the bodies of people from your world, and their control of the subsequent energy overspill between the two realities. But that's not what I am. Not in the slightest. Besides, I would hardly have come bearing a gift, now would I?'

'You mean the Marchant girl?'

'Indeed.'

'What makes you think I have any interest in her?'

'Your man Degan told me. In a manner of speaking.'

'A manner of speaking. Did he also tell you how much I hate enigmatic bloody double talk?' Despite the generally tranquil nature of the construction, he can feel himself becoming rattled. Or it could be her semi-naked proximity which is doing it. 'Why do you think I would value an alliance? What makes you think that I can't simply take what I want from you?'

'Mr Maddox, I know that you believe you are arguing from a position of strength – and who knows? It may even be that you are. You saw what I did to the first person who tried to get in my way, and I'm reasonably confident that I can do much the same with the men you currently have imprisoning me. It might even be amusing to try. But it wouldn't get us anywhere, now would it? I'd be dead, and you would have lost your best chance at obtaining some real power for once in your life.'

'*Real* power? You will let me know when you're getting to within shouting distance of a point, won't you?'

'Explain something to me, Mr Maddox,' she says. 'How is it that you are in command of an operation to control and enslave people with powers that most ordinary humans would kill for, and yet you do not possess any yourself?'

The sounds of stonework cease. The Wall is abruptly deserted except for the pair of them. They've stopped walking. Why in God's name is he still listening to her? She is so close that he can see that her eyes, which he has previously taken to be simply an unusual dark blue, are more unusual still. Their colour shifts between blues and greens so dark as to be almost black, like shafts of sunlight in water at the very limit of visibility.

'Fear, that's what it is,' she continues. 'Fear. Like all tyrants, you fear those whom you enslave. You believe that they are freaks and monsters, not people, and you fear the process by which these people have gained their powers. You might be tempted but you believe that it cannot be controlled, and you fear losing your mind, which is why you hide in childish constructions such as this. I mean really, a Romish centurion on Hadrian's Wall? Bless.'

'A *praefect*, actually,' he mutters.

She ignores him. 'Up until now, you have been entirely right to be afraid. However, I am here to tell you that the subornation process *can* be controlled, because I am living proof, and to offer you the gifts which that control brings. What would you like to be able to do? Fly? Read minds? Burn your enemies at a finger's touch? I can dream an albatross into your soul, or a shaman, or a salamander from the fire-mountains of Isalo. I can put angels in your brain. The Marchant girl is far from being simply a goodwill gift; she remains the key to all of this. I'm offering her to you and much more besides. Turn around, Mr Maddox, and see.'

He turns around, away from the desolate fells, to look over the civilised land of fields and forests that the Wall protects. He sees greater walls than this; he sees strongholds, citadels, and fortresses rising tower upon tower; he sees cathedrals, their hazy spires lost in the very clouds of heaven; he sees thousands of leagues of road stretching from one end of the land to the other; he sees all of this, and he sees that it is his for the building. His for the mastery.

Then he sees the army that she is offering to help him build it, and his sense of duty makes one last feeble stab at resistance.

'The Hegemony will never allow…' he begins.

'I am not negotiating with the Hegemonic Church, whatever its name in your world,' she interrupts. 'I am negotiating with *you*. They have no concept of what I am; neither do the DCS. There exists no protocol to deal with the likes of me. They will order you to destroy me, if you can, and your chance to build all of this,' she sweeps her arm to encompass the vista before him, 'will die too.'

The swirls of blue pigment on her body and the golden bands encircling her limbs are coming alive, writhing across her skin like snakes, and then lifting free to twist and float around her in ribbons of azure and gold like fronds of seaweed and sunset entwined. It is one of the most beautiful things he has ever seen.

'Now wake up.'

Maddox snapped awake and found himself standing naked in the doorway of one of the Park's sub-basement detention cells. His pass-card was in one hand, his gun in the other. He stared at them stupidly as the fog of his dream cleared. Had he been walking? Somewhere distant, alarms were hooting, and Morris' voice was crackling with desperation over an intercom: *Sir? What's happening down there, sir? Can you confirm your status?* but he ignored them both. Morris was an idiot. They were all idiots. *He'd* been an idiot, to think that Lilivet was just another Passenger. Could he confirm his status? It was laughable. His status was *compromised*. Honking great neon letters floating in the sky: *COMPROMISED*, Morris, put that on your clipboard and shove it up your ass. And there was nothing he could do about it.

The shadows inside the cell came alive as something like the gold and blue ribbons from his dream moved restlessly, then drifted out to meet him, darker but no less graceful as they stroked and caressed his skin, coiling around the stiffening length of him and teasing him inside. There he found his goddess; her araka flesh was even more beautiful in reality than it had been in his dream, and he let it enfold him in the bittersweet darkness.

Steve tried to keep a low profile. He really tried.

He spent most of the first twenty-fours asleep or lying in bed feeling like he had a hangover, even though he hadn't touched any alcohol for over a week. He did the crossword. He went across the road to the newsagent and bought an entire book of crosswords and did those too. He watched hour after hour of daytime TV, forcing himself to switch the awful thing off only when he started to develop sympathy with the conspiracy nutjobs who believed that modern broadcast media was a mind-control tool designed to turn the public into drooling zombies – those people, and the ones who wanted to stalk and kill z-list celebs like Jeremy Kyle. He took himself out for walks in parks, and sat in strange pubs nursing pints at solitary tables, and realised that he was now the Lone Weirdo – the one that the other customers looked sideways at either in pity, or vague mistrust, or simply ignored altogether. Despite Ennias' instructions, he tried calling him on the crappy little Nokia, and was unsurprised to find that Ennias' number was no longer in service.

He managed to resist the urge to call Jackie, but on the third morning he wrapped himself up in a hoodie and baseball cap and lurked across the street from her place just to watch her getting the boys to school and herself to work. He reassured himself that she was okay but at the same time felt dirty about it, as well as paranoid that creatures from the Hegemony might be watching her too, and that they would easily notice his pathetic attempts at spookery. He half-expected something which was all teeth and sarcasm to be waiting for him back at the bedsit, but nothing was, so he must have got away with it.

Emboldened by this, he decided to make a quick visit to the Barber Institute. Just a quick glance at the Watts, he told himself, to remind himself of what all the fuss was about. Just one. Looking at himself in the mirror, he thought it highly unlikely that anybody he'd shared a shift with would recognise him; he'd lost weight, hadn't shaved in days, and looked like he was dressing himself out of an Oxfam clothes bin. He might look like a vagrant – but then equally he could just as well pass for an Art student.

When he got there, the shock of finding that *She Shall Be Called Woman* was gone hit him almost like a physical blow.

The huge empty space left by its absence screamed at him. It was filled only by a vague notice of apology, something about the painting being returned to the Tate in London for 'restoration' work. Total bullshit. He was certain that its disappearance was connected to the events on the *Cella*, but there was no way he could find out for sure. When he phoned the Tate he was assured that she was still on loan to the Barber, and when he phoned the Barber anonymously he was given the same line: returned for restoration.

The feeling of impotence this left him with was maddening. Things were happening. Agendas were being pursued. The woman he could still see himself possibly having a future with despite how fucked up everything was might have been kidnapped – if not actually killed – and he'd been sidelined in that stinking fleapit of a B&B while Ennias danced around the sensibilities of his oh-so-precious contacts. If he hadn't simply decided to cut Steve loose altogether, that was. What other conclusion was he supposed to draw from the fact that the man's phone was disconnected? As he himself had so wisely pointed out: fuck that for a game of tiddly-winks. Steve decided to give Ennias until the following morning, after which he would be forced to admit that he'd been screwed over and probably end up doing something very unwise indeed.

That evening he got a text. It consisted simply of two words: *Found her.*

CHAPTER 27

A WALK IN THE PARK

1

'Funny story for you,' said Ennias. 'So there's these two druids, right? It's two thousand years BC, and they're walking through the primeval forests of ancient Britain. One turns to the other and says "I don't know, things just aren't the same these days", and the other says to him "I know what you mean. I remember when this was all fields."'

'That's terrible,' groaned Steve, ducking to avoid a low branch. Ennias was ahead of him on the narrow path, and not making any particular effort to prevent bits of tree from springing back into Steve's face.

'You don't think it's a poignant comment on humanity's eternal and recursive nostalgia for a lost Golden Age?'

'Not really. I think it sounds more like a shaggy dog story with not enough shag to it.'

'Whatever.' Ennias sniffed and forged ahead through the undergrowth.

Somewhere ahead of them, Steve could clearly make out the sounds of the ocean and screaming sea-birds. The problem was, he'd been hearing it for some time – ever since they'd left the car – but because of the closely grown vegetation he couldn't see how close they were getting. Ennias had told him that the non-existent village they were looking for was situated at the edge of a cliff, which was not so unusual since that described most of this part of the East Devon coastline, and he had visions of emerging from a bush into thin air and plunging fifty feet into the English Channel.

The path they were on had been disused for decades and was not very clear at all. They'd ignored one fence signposted with a warning that this section of the UNESCO Jurassic Coast World Heritage Site was currently protected for environmental reasons and off-limits for ramblers under pain of a £5000 fine; then another from Devon County Council Highways Office indicating that the path was temporarily closed due to the danger of sudden and unexpected cliff collapses (although the word 'temporarily' had to be taken with a truck-load of salt since the sign looked like it had been there since at least the 70s); and finally a rusted Ministry of Defense sign which read, quite tersely, "Restricted Area: Danger of Death".

'Okay, that one I believe,' Steve had said, climbing through the barbed wire.

They'd driven south from the Midlands, avoiding motorways and major urban centres and taking hours to find the south coast by B-roads. At Lyme Regis, Ennias had bought him a coffee and a sticky bun at the tiny family-run Dinosaurland Fossil Museum, and under the shadow of extinct sea-monsters had tried to let him know what he was getting himself into.

'It's called the Park. Short for Park Royal Hotel, in a town called Lyncham, which was evacuated forty years ago, after half of it collapsed into the sea. The Hegemony took it over as a processing centre for Passengers.'

'Processing centre,' echoed Steve.

'Yeah, and it's even less pleasant than that sounds. They have very effective ways of detecting the existence of Passengers who arrive all confused and angry, and who lash out with powers that they didn't know they had. I've heard it described as being like the wake of a boat that they can track, but I don't know the details of how it works. They sniff us out and they take us to the Park to see if our talents can be used to help the Hegemony's business. The animals are easy enough to control – it's just carrot and stick stuff. The humans take a bit more psychology.'

'What is their business, anyway?'

'Don't ask me, I'm just visiting, remember? To control the world? Who cares what they want. The point is that they will fuck your life up from one end to the other if they think you've got something they can use, and especially if they think you're a

276

threat. Sad to say, a lot of Passengers are happy enough to work for them at the end of the day.'

'God, why?'

'Put it this way. You've just woken up in a world which is worse than being totally alien because it's so familiar, but you don't know anybody and nobody knows who you are. Worse, they think you're someone else, and they're hurt, angry and confused when you try to explain. They think you've lost your mind. You may not even be fully in control of this body you're in. You panic, hit out in frustration, and cause something freakish and weird to happen which scares the shit out of everyone, yourself included, so you run. You might be sleeping rough for a couple of weeks; you're hungry, filthy, cold, terrified. Then one day a big black shiny car pulls up and a bloke says he knows what you're going through, and he'll offer you a bed, food, and maybe even the chance of finding a way home if you'll come with him and just do a few little jobs, no questions asked. What would you do?'

'Fair point. Naturally there is no finding a way home, is there?'

'Of course not. From that point on you're their bitch. You may even come to like the kinds of things they make you do. If you don't, or you disobey orders, or – worse – you try to run away from them, they have a range of very inventive and painful ways of making you reconsider. And if you don't learn your lesson, well, you're already a missing person as far as the world is concerned, so who cares if you take a long walk off a short cliff?'

'And you know this because?'

'Because I, cunning bastard that I am, escaped.'

'And this is where they've taken Vessa?'

Ennias nodded grimly.

Steve mulled this over awhile, looking around at the fossil exhibits which adorned the walls of the museum. Apparently this part of the world had all been one big tropical lagoon two hundred million years ago. Another few million before that it had been a desert. Who knew what it would be a few million hence? Nothing was certain, not even the very rocks beneath his feet. Maybe it wasn't too much of a stretch to imagine other lands lying alongside his own – not separated by a sea of water, or time, but maybe one of consciousness. Some barrier which was being breached frequently, and in secret. He thought of Lilivet's words again and wondered if one day his world too would be drowned, and under what kind of ocean.

'The woman that Vessa brought through,' he said eventually. 'The one who called herself Lilivet.'

'What about her?'

'She's definitely not human.'

'I think we can take that as a given.'

'Will they have taken her to the Park too?'

Ennias shrugged. 'Most likely. She looked like she wasn't in a hurry to go anywhere. Why do you care?'

'She said something before I…' *ran away*, he sneered at himself '…escaped. Something about how Vessa was going to help her rid her world of a great evil: mine. Do you have any idea what that means?'

'I don't know; does it sound like a good thing to you?'

'Not really.'

'Then finish your cake and we'll get moving– but let's just concentrate on getting Vessa out before we go interfering in anybody's plans of world domination, shall we?'

'Amen to that.'

2

Leaving Lyme Regis, they discovered without surprise that the left-hand turn onto the old cliff-top road to Lyncham was blocked by a large gated barrier which carried signs warning that the road was closed due to coastal erosion and currently undergoing reinforcement works. This seemed to be supported by a roadside portacabin inhabited by several men hanging around in hi-viz vests, but Ennias wasn't convinced, pointing out the lack of any trucks, construction materials, or machinery. They drove past without stopping, left the car in a very pretty seaside town called Seaton and doubled back on foot, hiking up into the woods that masked the cliffs.

A few yards past the no-nonsense MoD sign, the path came out of the trees and turned sharply left at the very brink of the cliff.

Steve staggered slightly under a sudden bluster of salt-laden wind and the expansion of his field of view from a few feet to what was quite literally the edge of the world. Directly below him the ground fell steeply away to a shoreline of sharp-edged limestone rocks against which the sea shoved its glossy green shoulders. Between him and it, seagulls wheeled. Vertigo threatened to unhinge his knees.

Ennias grabbed him by the shoulder, forcing his attention to the left, where the cliff curved back towards them slightly. A few hundred yards away they grew higher, and along the top he saw the shapes of buildings hard up against the almost vertical drop. One in the middle was taller than the rest, and he took that to be the old hotel where, if Ennias was right, Vessa was being held. The cliff-face directly below was buttressed in concrete and sheathed in heavy-duty rock netting. Lyncham, the village which had allegedly fallen into the ocean, looked like it was going nowhere its owners didn't want it to go.

'How can you climb?' asked Ennias.

'That's not funny,' he replied.

'Oh, getting down is the easy bit.' Ennias pointed. Directly below them the sea seethed against white boulders, but further towards Lyncham, a narrow strip of shingle beach appeared. 'Even getting over to that bit isn't so bad. Rock to rock, like stepping stones, hands on the face of the cliff. It's when you're under the village itself that it gets really dangerous.'

'What, and this isn't?'

'They don't patrol this bit. The worst thing that can happen to you here is that you slip and kill yourself. You're lucky it's low tide.'

'No, seriously, you didn't think to bring rope or anything?'

'Fuck's sake, McBride – do you know anything about abseiling? Can you tie any kind of knot which you can guarantee wouldn't come loose? Because I bloody can't.'

'No,' he admitted.

'Then come on.' He turned around and began to lower himself over the edge. Steve watched him closely. It looked like there were plenty of handholds amongst the outcropping stones and tree roots, and he did his best to memorise which ones Ennias was using before he began to gingerly pick his own way down.

His memory couldn't have been that good because about halfway down the rock under his left hand gave way in a shower of earth. He panicked, pinwheeling, with two slim toeholds and a grip on a tree root which he could feel tearing under his weight, so he jammed his hand in the hole where the rock had come from, clawing for a grip, praying not to fall, not to die... and held.

He clung for an eternity, sweating and trembling, while the blustering wind plucked at his trousers and the sea muttered below.

'Oy!' shouted Ennias from below. 'That bloody thing nearly killed me! Watch what you're doing!'

Steve didn't trust himself to spare the concentration for a reply and focussed instead on getting the rest of the way down in one piece.

The boulders at the cliff's foot were green and slippery with weeds, and more often than not submerged, so that he and Ennias were soon drenched from the knees down. It didn't seem to be bothering the Exile from Tourmaline – he was stepping ahead carefully like a chess-master playing hopscotch. Steve was still trembling from his near-fall and chilled by wind and water. He could see the thin margin of white shingle ahead, but that took his eyes from his feet and threatened to make him fall, so he just put one foot after another, trying to avoid the worst clots of weed which tried to tangle his ankles. His imagination played tricks on him; he saw tentacles in the fronds reaching for his legs, and the limbs and faces of half-human creatures in the churning green shadows between the boulders. *What about fish, Ennias?* he wondered. *What makes you think that they haven't found someone with an octopus inside them and set it to plug the gap you escaped through?* But he made it to the strip of beach without being grabbed by anything and sat resting against the cliff-face for a moment, getting his breath back.

'Not bad,' Ennias conceded.

'For someone without any wacky otherworldly powers, you mean?' he grunted. He shook his head. 'This makes no sense, Ennias. How have we not been seen yet? I thought these people were supposed to be some kind of all-seeing, all-knowing super-conspiracy. How have we even got to within a mile of this place? And how are we supposed to get Vessa out?'

Ennias sat down next to him and lit a cigarette. Waves hissed on the shingle just beyond their toes.

'We can do this because everything about the Park is designed to stop the inmates getting out, rather than intruders getting in. Scary signs, men in authority, and the fear of actual plummety death will do that for most people. Trust me, it was nowhere near this easy escaping. Want to see the scars?'

'I'll pass, thanks.'

They sat in silence for a while, getting their breath back. Presently, Ennias stubbed out the cigarette butt on a stone and settled back against the cliff face, gathering his coat closely about himself. 'Right, we wait until dark, when the...'

And the thing which had been watching them from the water struck.

It was like one of those nature documentaries filmed in excruciating slow-motion: an orca launches itself from the shallows to snap up an unwary sealion. But there was no comfortable slo-mo for Steve, and the thing that grabbed Ennias would have given a killer whale nightmares. Its human front half was pale, armless, and diseased-looking, with cat-slitted eyes and a mouthful of finger-length fangs pointing in every direction; its rear half was a muscular tail bristling with spines and striped like a tiger. It seized Ennias mid-calf and was dragging him into the water before either man could do so much as cry out.

This time Steve didn't run.

The only weapons to hand were the rocks around him, so he picked up the nearest and splashed in after the struggling figures, clubbing at the tigerfish-man's head where it was locked around Ennias' leg. The creature lashed back with its tail, sweeping his legs out from beneath him and dumping him into the freezing water, which was already clouded red. Ennias' screams bounced back from the cliff-face, redoubling the sounds of his agony. Steve lurched out, spluttering, found one of Ennias' flailing hands, grabbed it, held, and pulled. The man was choking more than screaming now, as the creature hauled him in a series of vicious tugs. But Ennias' hands were slippery, and Steve couldn't get any purchase with his scrabbling heels on the shingle which just slid away from underneath him.

He was being dragged in too. How could that thing be so *strong*?

With a final, savage yank, the creature ripped Ennias free from Steve's grip, and the last Steve saw was his pale, outstretched fingers disappearing into the black-green gloom.

For moment all he could do was stare at the marks in the sand, trembling. They were all that was left of Ennias – that, and the slim black shape of his phone lying on a stone. He picked it up. The screen was smashed and it wouldn't switch on, so he put it away in his pocket. Just in case. Then – drenched, chilled, and exhausted – he tried to find somewhere to hide. There was no way that the sounds Ennias had been making could have gone unheard; there would be a response team on its way right now – and Christ alone knew what that would consist of. Given how close they were, he probably had less than two minutes, if that.

Voices shouting, distantly above.

Steve ran for the base of the cliff, but a cursory glance at it told him how laughable the idea of hiding was. It was reinforced at the bottom by several feet of solid concrete, above which the rock netting was a wide mesh of heavy-gauge wire, like oversized chain-link fencing, secured to the cliff face at regular intervals by thick bolts and cables. It provided ideal hand- and foot-holds, like one of those hazards on an army obstacle course, and he was able to make surprisingly quick progress up it. Still, by the time he heard the crunch of footsteps running along the shingle and the shout of voices below, he was less than halfway up.

Three figures in fatigues, tactical vests and carrying squat and very lethal-looking submachine guns appeared, nosing around the area of the beach attack.

He froze, flattening himself to the rock, willing the goons down there not to look up and praying that the angle of the cliff face above would obscure the sight of him from anyone looking down. It was a futile hope, and he knew it.

All it took was one goon on top of the cliff shouting down to his mates, asking if they'd found anything, and for his mate to look up when replying: "Nah, there's bugger all down he- *oh Christ, he's on the fucking netting!*", and Steve knew he was screwed.

A surprised face leaned further out from above and looked down at him, accompanied by the business end of another gun. 'Who d'you think you are?' the face asked. 'Fucking Spiderman?'

3

Maddox watched another prisoner transport van unload its shambling, dull-eyed cargo on the forecourt of the old Park Hotel, consulted his phone, and turned to Lilivet.

'That's Belmere Intensive Psychiatric Institution,' he confirmed. 'Eleven souls all told.'

'Excellent,' she beamed. 'Get them under as quickly as you can.'

'At this rate we'll run out of rooms for them all in a few days, even if we treble the occupancy rates.'

'Then we shall put them in the corridors, the kitchens, and the cellars, won't we? And then the road outside, if necessary.'

'Yes, my lady.' Maddox felt sick. It wasn't his own spinelessness in her presence, though that would have been bad enough on its own. There was something else, physically deep in his guts, a sick churning which had been there since Lilivet had fucked him. He wondered if this was what the onset of terminal cancer was like. 'There is one other thing, however,' he added nervously. 'These transfers from acute psych wards all over the country. The Hegemony's systems will register the anomaly soon; it's what they do. Maybe we should…'

'Don't trouble me with petty bureaucratic concerns!' she snapped. 'We are changing entire worlds here, Maddox. By the time the Church has even the slightest clue of what is happening under their noses, our army will be too large for even them to stop.' Turning on her heel, she strode back into what used to be the Ops Room to check on her prize. 'Where is your precious Department now, Jowett?' she continued to herself in bitter, gloating tones, apparently unaware that Maddox was still listening. He held back, trying not to attract further attention. 'I will show you what it means to have an *affinity* with such things, you condescending bastard.'

When she'd disappeared inside, he found Morris hovering at his elbow. 'I really must speak with you, sir,' he insisted. He'd been insisting for the last three days.

'Come on, then,' he sighed. 'You've been moping around the place with a face longer than a suicidal giraffe's. Out with it.'

Morris' head jerked around nervously, looking to see if they were being overheard. 'Sir,' he murmured, 'with all due respect, what the hell do you think you're doing?'

'See? That wasn't so hard now, was it?'

'You've given all-areas access to a being that every one of our wake-sensitives confirms is *off the scale*, and you're letting her shift our assets around like she owns the place. Plus, we've had two *significant* breaches of the meniscus in as many weeks. Eyes are looking in our direction, sir.'

'I know, Morris. I've tried telling her…'

'You've *tried telling* her?!' The look of actual fear in Morris' eyes was enough to shut him up. Not fear of Lilivet, which would have been sensible; it was the kind of shock on the face of someone who'd just woken up lying next to a body, not knowing who they are, how they got there, or what killed them. Morris swallowed thickly. 'Sir, walk with me?'

Maddox allowed Morris to lead him by the elbow around the side of the building and to the rear lawn, which terminated abruptly in the eighty-foot drop to the ocean. 'Do I need to remind you about the scuttling charges, sir?' he asked.

'Of course you don't!' he snapped, irritable now. The nausea in his guts was getting worse.

Morris persisted, getting in his face. He hated people getting in his face. 'Sir, if this gets kicked up to the attention of Regional, and they don't like the way things look, it's one button, no countdowns, and hello, bottom of the Channel. And I can tell you that from my perspective *things do not look good.*'

'Well maybe what you need is a fresh perspective, then.'

Morris' puzzled frown was abruptly punctuated by a small dark hole in the middle of his forehead – and a rather larger, messier one in the back of his skull. Maddox put his gun away, watching Morris' body tumble over the drop to disappear in the waves below. 'Things looking up now, are they?' he asked the corpse.

On his way back inside he stopped by one of the staff toilets, untucked his shirt and examined his stomach in the mirror. Lilivet must have scratched him: there was a long red weal running down the middle of his belly from just below his sternum to just above his belt-line. It was red and itchy – probably infected. He was going to have to do something about that later. He pulled himself together and went to resume his place at her side.

The hotel's large dining room had long ago been retasked as the Park's Operations Room and had more recently undergone another transformation – the cubicles, desks and workstations and had been ripped out and replaced with closely-packed rows of hospital beds. In each bed was a patient from one of the many institutions for the treatment of acute psychiatric illness which fell under the Hegemony's influence, transferred here under Maddox's orders, which – so far at least – had not been questioned. Not that his name had ever appeared on a single document or email. They were all entirely legitimate orders signed off by the middle managers in the appropriate National Health Service Primary Care Trusts, conducted perfectly properly under the terms of each patient's Individual Care Plan. People like McBride who seemed to think that the Hegemony was a huge conspiracy of shadowy, cigarette-smoking men ruling the world from their underground bunkers by brainwashing politicians and dumping oestrogens in the water supply missed the point completely; enough control and surveillance already existed in the bureaucratic systems of the world to render such a super-cabal redundant, even downright obstructive. It was the same with closing Spaghetti Junction – that had been done by a coordinated exercise of relevant Anti-Terrorism procedures across multiple services all the way from MI5 down to British Waterways. Maddox's role was nothing more than a glorified co-ordinator. In a real sense there was no Hegemony at all. Nobody was being kidnapped or coerced, and not a single law was being broken – until the patients were wheeled through the front doors of the Park, that was.

Each was attached to an IV drip feeding them a cocktail of barbiturates designed to induce an artificial coma – the kind of procedure used when dealing with serious head trauma or some forms of neurosurgery, even though nothing of kind was happening here. A handful of nurses moved calmly between the beds, checking the banks of ventilators and EEG monitors which filled the room with mechanical sighs and beeps like a quiet chorus of electronic crickets.

Hanging at the end of the room, presiding over all like an altarpiece, was the Watts painting, *She Shall Be Called Woman.* Two figures were seated and bound before it. In a wheelchair was strapped the vessel which housed both Vanessa Gail and Sophie Marchant – she was only partially doped, and her drooping eyelids flickered like slurred syllables before the painting. In a chair facing her, secured and gagged much more simply with duct-tape, was her lover, McBride.

Lilivet pulled up a chair next to him and sat down. 'I'm afraid that you and I might have got off on the wrong foot,' she said. 'I'll admit, that was mostly my fault. I was a bit… exuberant.' She gave a soft, apologetic laugh. 'I know how this must look to your eyes; trust me, a few weeks ago I would have thought exactly the same thing. But every field agent knows that changeable circumstances demand a flexible methodology, and as I'm sure you're aware, I'm a lot more flexible now.' Her laugh, when it came again, was markedly less sane. 'In any case, I don't expect you to believe a single thing I say, especially when I say that I have no intention of harming you. You're much more useful to me alive. And before you go ranting on bravely about how you'll never help me, let me explain. This young lady here…' She laid a hand gently on Vessa's arm; she moaned and tried to twist away. '…is under a lot of stress. She needs comfort. Support. Strength. The reassurance of someone she cares about who believes in her. Without it, she can't do what I need her to do. You don't care about that, obviously, but you're a decent man, and I know you'll do the right thing by her, at least.'

She turned to Vessa, continuing to stroke her arm.

'Are you in there, witch-girl?' she crooned. 'Can you hear me? I hope so. I wanted to let you know that I'm sending you some more castaways to add to your collection. I'd dearly love to know whether or not the ones I've already sent have arrived; the most feeble minds are the quickest to cross over, but this isn't an exact science, as I'm sure you can appreciate. Still, we'll know when the Flats spread as far as the first island and my new army of Exiles starts waking up here, won't we? I wonder, do you think I could send you enough souls to make the Flats cover the whole of my world? I could bring *everybody* here, and give them all the powers of gods! If in the end I cannot stop your people dreaming, I can give mine that, at least. What fun we'll have then.' She planted a kiss on the girl's pallid forehead and stood.

'Time to let you two get reacquainted, I think.' One of her araka limbs tore off Steve's gagging strip and she swept away, humming an old Oraillean lullaby.

CHAPTER 28

NEWCOMERS

1

In the days following the destruction of the *Spinner,* there had been some heated debate about how to proceed. There wasn't enough room in the *Spinner's* dinghy for all of them, including the four surviving members of the ship's crew and Buster. Sophie flatly refused to move on the grounds that she didn't want to take her subornation zone any closer to human habitation. It crossed Bobby's mind that now she was free of the araka there was nothing to stop her leaving this world for good, but that was her decision, and he'd never press her on it. As for himself, Allie had no intention of leaving and so neither did he; besides, whoever he'd been in the Realt meant nothing to him now. Runce also elected to stay, out of a sense of honour which forbade him abandoning anybody at sea, be they friend or enemy, and instead instructed the crew to take the dinghy back to Danae. With Seb using Allie's little cracker compass to navigate, they left, promising to return with a rescue ship as soon as possible.

At some point during the night following Jophiel's departure, Lachlan disappeared. Despite the watch that Runce had posted, his blanket and belongings were found cold and abandoned in the morning. There was a brief and minor panic over whether the *Spinner's* dinghy was still there, but the surviving Strays knew better. Lachlan hadn't escaped. Quite the opposite: he'd chosen to wake up.

Those that were left behind set about collecting together the largest pieces of Stray's shattered platform, and they had not long finished lashing them together when the first of the newcomers arrived.

There was a surge of water a dozen yards to one side, and a small raft shot edge first into the air, landing with a heavy slap on the surface. A figure clung to it, coughing.

'Well he sure picked a sweet time to come visiting, didn't he?' commented Allie with heavy sarcasm. 'And here's us – we haven't even aired the guest room.'

'What's this?' demanded Runce sharply. 'Where did he come from?'

'The same place we all did,' replied Bobby. 'Come on, let's go and collect the fellow.'

'Why in Reason's name would we want to do that? We know nothing about him. He could be dangerous.'

'Everybody's dangerous here. He'll be in good company. And you're a guest too, remember that.' Bobby tied a line about his waist and tossed the coil to Allie. He dove in but got only halfway to the new raft before its owner began yelling and waving his arms.

'No!' he screamed. 'Keep away! Don't you dare come near me!'

Surprised, Bobby stopped and treaded water for a bit. 'Steady there, old chap,' he called. 'We're all friends here.' He started swimming forwards again.

'No!' the newcomer screamed, even more shrilly than before. 'I won't let you take any more! No more! Never! I'll kill myself first!' He stood up and began gesticulating wildly, making his raft seesaw.

'I know you're confused, but there's no need to…' Bobby stopped again, this time because he couldn't move forward; the rope had tightened around his waist. He looked back. Allie had taken in the slack, preventing him from going further.

She shook her head. 'Bobby, no. There's something wrong with him. He scares me.'

'What's wrong with him is that he's terrified because he's got no idea where he is or how he got here.' Memories of his own first days drifting alone were still close and painful.

'Yes, but look at…'

At that moment another small raft burst onto the surface barely a few yards away and levelled out with a concussion which deafened and drenched him. Allie pulled him back urgently towards Stray, by which time the second newcomer had curled himself into a foetal ball and was rocking back and forth, repeating 'No-no-no-no-no,' in tones of great distress while the first screamed at him to keep away.

'In case I wasn't clear earlier,' growled Runce, planting himself squarely in front of Sophie, 'what is happening to your subornation?'

She stared at the thrashing, screaming strangers helplessly. 'I have no idea!'

'Then may I respectfully suggest that you get one? Fast?'

Over the next hour, there were three more arrivals. One was as incoherent as the first two, one leapt straight back into the water and wasn't seen again, and last actually tried to attack them; they had to drive him off with poles and oars. By early evening, over a dozen had appeared, and Sophie was seriously worried.

'I don't know where they're coming from or why they're here,' she said, 'but I've got a horrible idea I know what effect they're having: whether they mean to or not, they're going to make the Flats expand.'

'I thought it already was,' said Runce. He was sitting on the edge of Stray, polishing the tez gun. Sunset glowed like liquid fire on its brass components, though the charge indicator showed that it was all but depleted. 'It was why we were sent to find you.'

'Yes, well, your mission just got a lot bigger. When it was just me, it wasn't a problem, but then the Lachlans arrived, and then Joe and Allie and the rest, and each time the Flats got a bit bigger. But with so many newcomers arriving so fast,' she shook her head. 'I wouldn't be surprised to find that Danae will be threatened in the next few days. The whole archipelago – who knows?'

'But why would they all appear here?' asked Allie. 'Why would anybody? Why not just pop up anywhere at random?'

'Proximity,' explained Runce. 'Harcourt had a theory. Like a gravity well. Big objects tend to attract smaller objects like a billiard table with a rubber surface – put one ball on and it makes a depression which causes other balls to roll down and join it.' He snorted. 'I told him I thought it was *all* a load of balls.'

'So, like a kind of psychic gravity, then?' Allie suggested.

'No,' said Sophie. 'It's more deliberate than that. This many people so close together can't possibly be a coincidence. Somebody in the Realt is sending them here on purpose, and the link between me and Vessa makes it easier. I think they *want* the Flats to expand.'

'But that's ridiculous,' protested Runce. 'Assuming that there is anybody in the Realt who knows about this place, why would they do that? What could they possibly hope to gain?'

'It doesn't matter why,' said Bobby. 'It only matters that we stop it. If Sophie's right and all these newcomers make the Flats expand enough to reach inhabited land, then they'll drag God knows how many innocent islanders back with them when they wake up. We can't let that happen. Sophie, sorry my dear, but if these people are being sent because you're here, then you've got to go back. I didn't want to say anything before, when it was just us, but this changes our priorities.'

Allie looked alarmed. 'What happens if you go back?' she asked.

'The honest truth is that I just don't know,' Sophie answered. 'Maybe nothing. Maybe Vessa and I swap places, and it all goes on the same way as before. Maybe the Flats disappear, and we all wake up.'

'Screw that,' Allie responded instantly.

'But it's all a moot point, anyway,' Sophie said.

'Why?' asked Runce.

'Because I've already tried,' she answered simply. 'I tried to go back when the first newcomers turned up, but for some reason it isn't working.' She smiled apologetically around at all of them. 'Sorry, I can't leave.'

Allie was on her feet, bristling with indignation. 'What?' she demanded. 'You've been doing what? Why didn't you tell us?'

'Because it's nobody's business but my own,' retorted Sophie.

'Bullshit it is! You can't drag us here to a new life in the middle of fucking nowhere and then just decide to send us all back again when the mood suits you!'

'Allie, I never asked you to come here.'

'Well we're here, and that makes you responsible! I can't go back to that other place! You don't know what it's like!'

'I have a better idea than you know.'

Bobby tried to put himself between them, searching for something to say that would calm the situation, while Runce simply turned away in disgust. Then everybody's attention was claimed by a sudden worldpool which dragged itself into existence directly underneath one of the newcomer's rafts, sucking it and its screaming inhabitant into the green depths. Consternation erupted amongst those nearby, and the water around Stray erupted again into a nightmare of shouting and splashing.

'It would seem that somebody has woken up,' said Runce.

2

Lilivet had grown impatient. She turned to one of the blue-coated medical orderlies who were supervising the induced comas. 'Wake one of them,' she ordered.

'Isn't it a bit early?' queried Maddox. 'It's barely dusk. There's no guarantee…'

'By now the subornation zone should be covering at least half the archipelago – somebody somewhere over there will be asleep, or drunk, or feverish, or in some way susceptible. Do it. Wake that one.' She pointed at random to one of the bed-ridden figures. The orderly hurried to obey.

Reversing the process of a chemically-induced coma in conventional circumstances should have been simple but not necessarily quick – simply withdrawing the anaesthesia would allow the patient to awaken naturally after a few hours, though even hastening the process with other drugs wouldn't have had an instant effect – but conventional medical science didn't reckon with the patient awakening with an entirely new personality which was disorientated, frightened, and capable of lashing out at the fabric of reality around them.

The EEG spiked, an alarm sounded, and the man in the bed spasmed. His IV exploded, and the orderly was flung across the room while tubes and leads rose into the air and thrashed like a nest of snakes. The plaster on the wall above his head cracked, the fractures spiderwebbing outwards.

Lilivet was quick to intervene. She towered over the patient, manifesting her full form in all its glory. Her flesh became armoured in spiked, iridescent plates which tapered in sections to protect even the tips of her many limbs, and rose in a glorious crown over her rows of eyes. She pinned the patient in his bed and bore down on him.

'Name yourself!' she commanded.

He gaped and stammered, terrified almost beyond the capacity for speech. 'Who... what... are you?'

'Never mind that! I gave you an order. Name yourself!'

'I don't... where am... ?'

She lifted him from the bed as easily as if he were a child and slammed him up against the wall. 'Make no mistake, slave,' she snarled, 'I shall soon have thousands more like you – if you are too slow-witted to give me so simple a thing as your name, then what use are you to me?' One of her limbs wrapped itself around his throat and began to squeeze. Her araka senses inhaled the intoxicating melange of his pain, confusion and fear like a narcotic; it rushed into her head, making the lights seem brighter and everything in the room more sharply outlined.

'W... Welan,' he managed. 'Of Toliar. I am a... am a dyer.'

She relented a little. 'Well, Welan of Toliar, the first thing you need to understand is that you are no longer a dyer. You are a soldier. You are the first suborned conscript in a glorious army which will cleanse this diseased world of the dreamers who afflict our own. Fight for me, and when our world is safe I promise I will return you to Toliar. Defy me, and your family won't even have your bones to mourn.' She dropped him to the floor in a trembling and sobbing heap. 'I am Lilivet – your general, your queen, your goddess. Submit to my rule or die.'

Somewhere in all the wet, choking noises she caught the words 'my queen,' and smiled. 'At midnight, begin waking the rest,' she ordered.

The late but not very much lamented Ops Deputy Morris would have been quite dismayed at exactly how much attention the Regional Supervisor for the United Kingdom, Ireland and Iceland was paying to current events. He'd foregone the beaches of Eastern Europe for the tedious necessity of Parliamentary Committee Oversight, and even though none of the politicians or civil servants involved noticed either his existence or absence from proceedings, alerts were being pinged to his phone at such a rate that he had to absent himself and see what the fuss was all about.

He scrolled through the abstracts, and when he saw exactly what colour the shit was that had been hitting the fan on Maddox's watch, he turned pale.

'Christ.'

He sought urgent clarification. Over the next half-hour, he interrogated the data-trawling network to see if somehow, miraculously, it could be a series of impossible coincidences – or better yet, human error. He checked and re-checked. Triple-checked. There was no error. The Hegemony made no error. Data from their psychic buoys and wake-sensitive operatives was represented graphically as a scattering of tiny firefly glimmers across his region, flaring up and dying away just as rapidly; breaches of the meniscus were generally few, sparse, and brief.

Except for that one spot over the Dorset coast which looked like the afterglow of fucking Hiroshima.

There was no question of investigating in person. All that left was damage limitation – and not just to Maddox's facility. There was his own reputation to consider. Questions would be asked about how he'd allowed things to get this far. A report would have to be filed at Interstitial level. This was going to get messy.

Still, not as messy as for the poor bastards down there in Dorset, he thought, and with a certain vindictive pleasure, he called in the scuttling code.

4

'It's got to be you, Bobby,' said Sophie.

'What do you mean it's got to be him?' demanded Allie.

'Vessa won't let me go back. She's too strong. Every time I try to open a worldpool or even see what she's thinking, all I get is an image of that painting. It's very close to her, and it's the single most powerful thing strengthening her sense of self, which makes it impossible for me to even contact her. Someone is going to have to go back first and deal with it before I can do anything. And it's got to be Bobby.'

'Why not one of the others?' She pointed at Runce. 'Why not him? He's got the gun.'

'Because he comes from here; all that will happen is he'll end up trapped in someone in our world.'

'True enough,' confirmed Runce. 'Quite apart from him not actually being too happy about being volunteered to exile himself, thankyou very much,' he added to Allie, pointedly.

Sophie continued. 'If you or any other Stray went – if there were any left, that is – you'd just wake up wherever your body was, nowhere near the painting. Plus, we know how that goes. No, it's got to be Bobby. He's entirely and physically here because Vessa pushed him here – he isn't in a coma and has no body in the Realt to be drawn back to. If he goes back, he'll end up wherever Vessa is, and where she is, that's where the painting will be.'

'And then?' asked Bobby, but he already knew the answer.

'You destroy it, of course,' said Runce. 'Cut the girl's anchor. Let Sophie go back so that she can clear up this whole sorry mess.'

'But he won't be able to come back, will he?' said Allie tightly.

'No,' confirmed Sophie. 'I'm afraid not.'

'Shit. *Shit.*' Allie kicked savagely at a scrap of wood and stalked to the other side of Stray as far away as she could from the others. Bobby followed.

'I suppose it's pointless me asking you to do something selfish and tell the rest of the world to go screw itself, isn't it?' she said, without looking at him.

He shrugged helplessly. 'I made a deal with Sophie, in her chamber – she'd let the araka go on condition that I promise to go back and destroy the painting. I'll find a way to return. There must be other ways between our worlds. I'll find one, and I'll come back to you.'

She laughed shortly, unconvinced.

'You know the thing that scares me the most?' he continued. 'It's the idea of going back and not being able to remember any of this, or you. Whoever I was before I got here – what if he comes back and doesn't give a damn? It's not you I'm afraid of losing, it's *me.*'

She turned, took his face in her hands and looked searchingly into his eyes. 'That's not going to happen,' she insisted. 'You are a good, brave man, whoever you are, and you will remember.'

'I…'

'No.' She laid a finger on his lips. 'Don't you dare say that. Don't give that to me and then take it away again by being a big damn hero and getting yourself all killed. Come back to me. Then you can say it.'

He nodded and kissed her finger instead. Then he went back to where the others were waiting.

'Sergeant,' he said to Runce, 'I'm going to need to borrow one of those swords, if I may. Whoever's on the other side of this thing isn't likely to be pleased to see me.'

Runce tossed him his own. 'I'll have it back when you're done.'

'Yes sir.'

Sophie closed her eyes, and a hole opened in the ocean before them with a roar like a high wind in tall trees.

'I must be out of my mind,' he muttered and jumped.

5

The vortex caught him easily and slung him around its open maw. Looking down into it, he could see only a funnel swallowing itself down into absolute blackness – that and three quick flashes of colour. Even though he was struggling to keep his head out of the water, he looked again to be sure; incredible as it seemed, his three loyal Fishketeers – Carmen, Blenny and Igor – were still riding shotgun, escorting him downwards despite the danger to themselves. Then he had no attention to spare on anything other than remembering Allie. *Hold on to these*, he told himself: *her eyes, her smell, her crooked smile. The feel of her breasts in your hands. The warmth of her around you. Whoever you are on the other side, whatever you forget, don't forget those.*

The worldpool spun him faster and lower, faster and lower as he struggled for air, and as he approached its lightless nadir, he found himself being crushed by the weight of so much spinning water. He'd hoped that he might pass out and be spared this, but it seemed that nature was not of a mind to be that merciful. He could no longer breathe; his lungs burned for air in the screaming darkness which was pulverising every bone in his body. His skull was crushed, shattered and reformed as the funnel narrowed even further, becoming a drainpipe, a drinking straw, a sweat pore, and the essence of him was squeezed out in a thread no thicker than an atom stretching from one end of eternity to the other.

In that elongated moment, he became aware that there was something else here, in the dreaming space between worlds. Several somethings, huge and ponderous, like granite boulders miles across, churning against each other blindly, and yet aware. Aware of him in turn, a miniscule bubble floating between them. Aware and *reaching*…

The pinprick end towards which he was rushing grew just as rapidly, becoming the face of a woman – not the face of… the face of… what was her name? Shit! Think! *eyessmilesmellbreastswarmth* – not her but *She Shall Be Called Woman*, except that now instead of her face being a blur it was very clearly that of Sophie/Vessa. She looked down at him as he approached and smiled in welcome as he fell into her swelling brightness…

CHAPTER 29

RIP TIDE

1

…and onto the institutional carpet of the Park's Ops Room, drenched and gasping for breath.

Strong arms seized him from either side before he could even draw breath, and someone kicked Runce's sword away.

'*Caffrey!?*' Steve barely recognised him – he was bearded, gaunt, dressed in rags and covered in cuts and bruises from head to toe, but still unmistakeably Neil.

'Sorry, mate,' Bobby coughed. 'He's…' and then a fist planted itself in his stomach.

'He's exactly where I expected him to be,' smiled Lilivet, as she watched the guards she had stationed by the painting drag him upright. 'Silly little witch-girl. So predictable.' She lifted his head up by the hair so that he could get a good look at her. 'Hello, Mr Jenkins, remember me?' His expression was priceless. 'Remember *both* of us?' And she showed him her araka face too.

'No…' His voice was a horrified whisper. 'I saw you die… the explosion…'

His dismay was exquisitely delicious, like the sweetly-sour musk of overripe fruit. 'Oh but my dear,' she tutted, 'you should have seen me come *back* again. It's enough to give a sane man religion, wouldn't you say, Maddox?' she shot back over her shoulder. Maddox grimaced. She turned her full attention back to Bobby. 'He's what you might call a true believer. You won't turn him like you did the others. You're good at that, aren't you, Bobby Jenkins? Playing people off against each other? Well, there are no stupid local constables to bribe here, and no monsters to turn loose.' She laughed contemptuously. 'You're not even properly yourself. So what does that leave, Bobby? What tricks have you got to face me with now?'

'No tricks,' said a strange voice, nervous and trembling. 'Just us.'

She whipped around. Bobby looked, and when he saw who it was didn't know whether to laugh or cry.

It was Blenny. Blenny as a man, flanked by the unmistakeably human incarnations of Carmen and Igor.

2

They will help you, if they can, Joe had said. Bobby's rescue squad was – unusual, to say the least.

Blenny was a little guy in a drab-looking suit, with the same protruberant eyes which gave the impression that he was staring around at everything in a state of permanent anxiety – which given the situation, thought Bobby, was entirely justified. Igor was as nightmarish a man as he had been a fish: massively muscled, with a scowling, lumpen face and an underslung jaw full of teeth which were a dentist's wet dream. But Carmen, appropriately enough, stole the show; her flowing, diaphanous fins and tail had become a rainbow of flamenco excess – all she needed was a basket of fruit on her head to complete the outfit. But she, like her companions, was glaring at Lilivet with undisguised hostility.

'Put him down, bitch,' she snarled, 'before I turn your coño to calamari.'

Lilivet laughed. 'This is *it*? This is what you bring against me?'

'Please, you three,' Bobby pleaded. 'Don't do this.'

This seemed to confuse Blenny. 'Um, really? Sorry, we just assumed that you needed…'

Igor simply roared and charged in. Along his arms and down the sides of his neck – and probably all down his body underneath his clothes – points of bioluminescence burst into life as he threw himself at the guards holding Bobby. One was caught by surprise and flung to the side of the room, which gave the other just enough time to try to use Bobby himself as a shield against this unexpected new threat; Bobby elbowed him in the guts and then ducked out of the way as Igor waded in with both fists. Carmen shrieked a high-pitched battle cry and leapt at Lilivet, fingernails clawed to rake at her eyes. Blenny scuttled away along the floor on all fours looking for the sword, babbling 'Oh-dear-oh-dear-oh-dear…'

It was hopeless before it had even begun, Bobby saw. Already the doors at the far end of the room were opening, with armed gunmen pressing through from the other side. Maddox had drawn a pistol and was bringing it around to bear on Igor, who, despite his size, was getting the worst of it from the two guards. Carmen, bless her, couldn't really get anywhere near Lilivet, who was easily able to fend her off and was already wrapping black limbs around her arms. And Blenny was never going to find that sword in time.

Standing before the painting, battered and still half-drowned, he drew his fist back and with every ounce of his fading strength punched through the stiff canvas. Pins and needles exploded in his arm from knuckles to armpit. Pulling out again, grimacing at the pain, he grabbed a handful of canvas and tore a long ragged hole downwards to the bottom of the frame.

Lilivet screamed her denial. It was echoed by Vessa.

And Sophie Marchant awoke as the waters of the Tourmaline Archipelago poured into the world.

3

What streamed through the rip in the painting was not, strictly speaking, water. Nor was it air. It plumed outwards in roiling clouds and streamers which looked like heat-haze, or the shivering refractions of alcohol stirred in water, and since it could not by its very nature co-exist with matter from the continuum called the Realt, the two chased each other about the room in shifting veils and rolling breakers, through which those in the room caught tantalising glimpses of sunlight on the open sea of another world.

More than just the sea. Stray was there, shifting in and out of focus, at one moment close enough to touch, at another barely visible. Bobby saw Runce and Allie standing on the very edge, and knew that they could see him in turn, even though he couldn't hear them; they were waving crazily and shouting something. It looked like Runce was having to physically restrain Allie from leaping into the waters and swimming across the tumultuous breach between worlds to help him.

Wait for me, he urged her silently. *I'm coming back. I promise.*

To those who belonged in the Realt and were firmly anchored there, the sensation of having these veils washing over and through their flesh was delicate but visceral, like the ghost of silken threads drawn through their nerve endings or the faint vibrations of a far-off earthquake felt through fingertips. To others, their touch was cataclysmically powerful. The guards – both of them Passengers working for the Hegemony, and more recently Lilivet – were instantly discorporeated, caught up in the tidal flow of Tourmaline's inundation and swept home while the people who had been their vessels collapsed in shock. Igor went down with them and began struggling to drag himself from underneath.

On the other side of the rip, dozens of worldpools opened simultaneously around Stray as the newcomers surrounding it were the first to be sucked back into their own world. All over the room they began awakening. A cascade of EEG alarms went off in a shrilling din, and the former psychiatric patients started tearing at their restraints – then at their IVs, and before long were staggering out of their beds in a milling, brawling mob.

Lilivet picked up Carmen, who was still thrashing and spitting, and threw her aside as if she were nothing more than a rag doll.

'Don't just stand there!' she screamed at the guards by the door. 'Kill them! Kill them all!' They were hesitating in the face of the flood, but she barely cared. There was no longer any question of trying to secure the subornation, thanks to that bastard Jenkins; all that was left was to avoid being dragged back into Tourmaline like the rest of them. That meant breaking the link between worlds she'd worked so hard to create.

She leapt at Vessa. Bobby, clutching his numbed arm, could do nothing.

McBride, still tied to his chair, threw himself sideways and collided with Lilivet, shoving her into the path of a cloud of Tourmaline's reality. It caught her, slewing her around as if she'd jumped into a raging torrent. Panicking, she clawed at the floor, the walls, the ceiling – anything to keep a purchase on this world.

The part of her which had been Berylin Hooper was as foreign to the Realt as any Passenger, while the part of her which was araka belonged to neither world and so was powerless to act as an anchor – but the tiny amount of Bobby's blood which it had consumed allowed her to maintain the most tenuous of grips in the world.

'Not,' she panted. 'That. Easy.' She managed to brace herself and stood. In one human hand she held Bobby's sword.

'Caffrey, *do* something!' yelled McBride.

Bobby staggered to his feet – but he was too far away and too slow. With a scream of triumph, Lilivet lunged forward, driving the sword to its hilt in Vessa's stomach so hard that it punctured through the back of the chair in which she was strapped. Lilivet leaned forward hungrily, expecting to enjoy the sudden rush of agonised horror which she had been anticipating for so long, but it didn't come. There was nothing in her victim except a sense of grim, satisfied finality.

Because it wasn't Vessa any more.

Sophie grinned in the face of the malicious thing which had caused her so much anguish for so long, and showed it what she had brought through from Stray. The Berylin-part of the thing recognised it and pulled away in sudden, terrified realisation.

'No! He wouldn't!'

Sophie aimed Runce's tezlar gun, even though at such close range she could hardly miss, and fired. The purple-white bolt of energy took Lilivet high in the torso, burning a foot-wide hole clean through and scorching her thrashing araka limbs to blackened stumps, before her charred corpse tumbled brokenly away into the depths.

4

Runce watched her death from the other side of the rip.

'I took care of the monstrosity, Berry, just like you said,' he whispered. Tears were on his craggy cheeks. 'Sorry, lass.'

5

The code sent by Regional activated a series of demolition charges built into the foundations of the concrete buttresses which reinforced the cliff directly below Lyncham. They blew a horizontal gash twice the height of a person and just as deep into the crumbling chalk slightly above high tide level, and running for a hundred yards past each end of what was left of the village. The rock netting shredded like cobwebs as debris puckered the ocean, and the shattering noise drove clouds of cliff-nesting seabirds screaming from their perches. By itself this explosion would not have been enough to drop the cliff into the sea, which was why a set of secondary charges also blew.

These were embedded along the centre of the Lyncham road and were both smaller and further apart. They were not designed to blast great chunks out of the earth, but to perforate it in a long shallow arc which would cut that slice of the cliff out neatly – it and the buildings on it. A dozen geysers of pulverised tarmac fountained upwards simultaneously, in one case directly underneath an ambulance which spun apart in a Catherine-wheel of shrapnel. From the smoking craters, cracks ran across the spaces of what solid road was left, joining the craters together. And widening.

Ahead of the destruction, a large car crashed through the barrier gates which closed off the Lyncham Road from the A3052 to Lyme Regis, swerving to avoid a couple of tourist cars that blasted their horns indignantly at him. Behind the wheel, Maddox didn't give a toss.

6

After everything that had happened, Bobby was surprised at how easy the return to Stray seemed to be. Like a fresh-water spring welling up in an undersea cavern, the waters of Tourmaline spilled upwards after the turbulence of their entry and collected under the ceiling, slowly filling the room from the top down. Where the two realities met, a shifting haze distorted the view of everything on the other side – it was like looking up at the surface from the bottom of a swimming pool. All he had to do was give it a little time, and he could jump up through it and get back to Allie. Or if he timed it right he could leap into the breakers billowing out of the painting and ride them upwards. But it looked like he wasn't going to be given that time.

For a start, Sophie wasn't dead. She was making wet hiccoughing noises and her lips were twitching as if she were trying to say something.

'Jesus, Caffrey,' complained McBride. 'Get me out of this thing, would you?'

'We're going to need to talk about this Caffrey thing, sooner or later,' said Bobby, helping him out of the gaffer tape which tied his arms and legs to the chair.

'Fine. Whatever. Not now.' McBride dashed to Sophie's side and then could do nothing but stare at the weapon jutting obscenely from her torso, appalled at the amount of blood and utterly at a loss as to how to deal with it. 'What am I supposed to…'

The earth shrugged violently, throwing the room into further chaos. Gurneys tipped, dragging tangles of heavy equipment onto the floor. Windows shattered and door-frames twisted. People fell, screaming.

Bobby, McBride, Blenny, Carmen and Igor stared at each other, stupefied.

'What the fuck was that?' demanded Carmen.

'Blenny, go find out,' Bobby ordered.

'Who? Er, what, me?' Blenny stammered, but Bobby ignored him, so he went and did as he was told.

'Igor, the doors. Get these people out. I don't care how. Hurt them if you have to. If you see anybody with guns, hurt them a lot.' Igor gave him a toothy grin and roared off, shoving at the already terrified patients and driving them towards the exit. 'Carmen, we need bandages. There should be loads of them lying around in all this.'

'Oh, right,' she huffed. 'I have to be nursemaid because you imagined me as a woman, yes?'

He looked at her. 'You really think this is the time?' Chastened, she stomped off to scrounge what she could. 'Right, let's have a look at this.'

Sophie was in a bad way. The fact that she was alive at all was something of a miracle. He suspected that it might be to do with the waves of Tourmaline which kept washing over them; something vital about them which was giving her the strength to hang on, but it was really just a guess. 'We can't get her out with that thing in her. We'll probably kill her if we take it out, but I can't see that we've got much choice.'

'No way.' McBride shook his head firmly. 'We need to find one of those medical people and let them take a look at her.' He wasn't at all happy about Caffrey performing his inevitably cack-handed first aid on her.

'See many of them around, do you? Because good luck with that.'

Blenny ran up, white-faced and out of breath. His big eyes were staring. 'The cliff!' he gasped. 'It's collapsing! This entire place is going to fall into the sea!'

'That settles it,' said Bobby. 'Carmen!' he yelled. 'Get back here – whatever you've got, it'll have to do!'

She returned with an armful of bed-linen. 'Is the best I could find,' she apologised.

They wadded the cotton sheets around where the blade of the sword entered Sophie's torso, and Carmen stood ready with another pile to press against her back when it was withdrawn. McBride found the remains of the gaffer tape nearby, and stood behind the wheelchair. He held onto her shoulders firmly as Bobby grasped the sword's handle – and then stopped. He met McBride's anxious stare. 'You ready?'

'Not really. Do you have any clue what you're doing?'

'Not really.' He grinned. It was a ghastly sight.

'Neil, I don't think…'

Bobby yanked the sword out as hard as he could. It came free a lot more smoothly than he'd been expecting; the blade had been buried in soft tissue and the back of the wheelchair was mostly padding. Sophie coughed wetly, and a gout of blood flew from her mouth; it was bright, arterial red.

'Oh-Jesus-oh-Jesus-oh-Jesus…' moaned McBride, as he wrapped gaffer tape around the bedsheets which Bobby and

Carmen were pressing to her wounds. When he'd used the entire roll, he stepped back to survey his handiwork. 'What a fucking mess,' he said, shaking his head. 'We can't carry her like this. It'll just tear her up inside even more. Let's get her onto one of those beds and see if we can wheel her out of here. Maybe steal one of those ambulances.'

Between them they managed to shuffle-carry her onto one of the wheeled gurneys. Igor went ahead of them, clearing their way of obstacles – other beds, fallen furniture, and the occasional distraught patient. Long vertical cracks were appearing in the walls, and there was the sound of heavy objects falling and breaking in distant rooms. Halfway to the doors, the building gave another shrug, and all the lights went out. Blenny gave a little scream. Carmen swore at him under her breath.

There were stairs; they lifted her down them and got as far as the main entrance, but any hope McBride had entertained of taking an ambulance died when he saw what it was like outside.

Beyond a wide forecourt, a low wall, and then the pavement, the road had split along its length in a raw, two-foot wide crevasse punctuated with large craters every few hundred yards. Water from ruptured mains geysered out of it in half a dozen places, and there was a sickening stench of gas. Many of the buildings on the other side of the road – cottages converted into residential and administrative buildings for the Hegemony's more mundane employees – had suffered subsidiary cracks and broken windows from being hit by chunks of asphalt shrapnel. The few vehicles he could see that hadn't already been smashed by debris or partially slipped into the crack were never going to be able to get out of the village. He thought they'd be lucky if they made it the next dozen yards.

'How the hell are we going to get her across that?' He pointed at the crevasse.

'How do you think?' Bobby returned. 'We carry her.'

'That'll kill her for sure.'

'Then she's dead either way, isn't she?'

There was no arguing with that. They slung her arms over their shoulders and staggered out into the road.

It was trembling – they could feel it shuddering like a dying animal through the soles of their shoes. At the very edge of the crack, pieces of debris were still crumbling and falling in. They could see broken pipes, split cables and the gleam of copper wire. If they had any lingering doubts about the truth of Blenny's report that the cliff was collapsing, these disappeared when the earth spasmed once more, the crack widened another few inches, deepened another few feet, and it swallowed more shovel-loads of itself. The ground was definitely lower on their side.

It looked easy enough for a person to step over – just not while carrying another. After a brief debate, Igor took her, carrying her in his arms like a sleeping child and laying her gently to the ground on the other side. The others followed closely.

Bobby turned back and measured his chances of returning to the Rip. In the few minutes since they'd escaped, already the Park Hotel and its grounds had deteriorated. Transverse cracks were spreading backwards from the main crevasse, chopping the slice of severed cliff into uneven chunks, and large parts of the building's façade were crumbling away. As he watched, everything on the other side of the crevasse suddenly dropped six feet in a tremendous, grating roar; he could see now how neatly the explosive charges had cut this thin slice of cliff-top free from the main land-mass. It curved away to meet the edge a few hundred yards on either side and was clearly designed to drop just this bit with the buildings into the ocean. He could still jump down, but he'd never get back up again – and even if he did manage to make it safely inside, there was no way of guaranteeing that that painting would still be upright and the Rip open. Voices from behind him were calling urgently.

'She's dead! Jesus Christ, I think she's dead!'

Turning away from the door back to Stray and Allie was like having a limb pulled from his body.

Igor was hovering beside Sophie's limp body in a state of great agitation, wringing his hands and making small noises in the back of his throat. Sophie's skin was the colour of candle wax, except around her lips, which were a grey-blue. The bedsheet bandage strapped to her front was already soaked with blood. McBride felt frantically for a pulse, and when he couldn't find one laced his fingers together to start giving her CPR.

'There's no point,' said Bobby wearily. He sat on a low wall belonging to one of the deserted cottages, looking utterly exhausted. 'She's gone. Let her go, Steven.'

'We don't know that!' McBride protested and began compressions, even though he knew it was futile.

'Look at her – she's bled out! What do you imagine you're pumping around her?' When McBride persisted, he snapped: 'Damn it all, man! Stop brutalising the poor girl!'

Steve slowed and then stopped. Caffery was right, of course – but it still didn't make sense. How could she be dead? Surely if she were dead he'd feel it more, like something vital wrenched out of his guts, but all he could feel instead was a shocked numbness. It was as if he was back in the hallway of her bedsit on the night he found out about the Cinderella curfew, looking at her lying half on the stairs and terrified that she was dead. As if all of his actions since then had done nothing more than delay the moment between then and now. Life, love – it was all just a holding action and a distraction until the moment you lay pale and unbreathing on the ground like this.

Igor was stroking her hair and making a low keening noise in the back of his throat. He seemed genuinely distressed, but all the same McBride couldn't stand the sight of him pawing at her body. 'Get away!' he shouted, slapping at Igor's hands.

'Back off, man,' warned Carmen. 'We're just trying to help, okay?'

'Yeah, well unless you can bring people back from the dead, it's a bit bloody late, isn't it?'

'Um,' said Blenny, doing a little dance of nervousness in the background.

'I know,' said Bobby. 'We really should be getting a bit further away from here.'

'Um, no, not that.'

'Well what, then?'

'Well it's, um, sort of, yes.'

'Yes what?' he was getting annoyed now.

'Yes. We can. Bring her back, that is. From the dead. Well, not that she's dead. Not *dead* dead, anyway. Just a little bit dead. We can work with that.'

McBride turned slowly, and fixed Blenny with a stare which nearly drove him backwards over the wall. '*What?*'

'She's dreamwrack now. The bits of her are floating apart, but they're still close enough at the moment that they can be brought back together. It's just that she isn't strong enough to do it herself.'

McBride turned to Bobby. 'Is this making any sense to you? Because if your friend here is taking the piss…'

'No, I think I know what he means. Blenny, what's the plan?'

Blenny shrugged. 'Well, like I say, she doesn't have the strength any more, so Igor, uh, wants to give her his.' He gave a tense little smile. Carmen nodded as if this was the most sensible thing she'd heard in a long time.

'His strength?'

'His existence. The existence you gave to us, with your blood, when you fed us. It made us strong enough to follow you and be here, and he wants to give that to her.'

'And what happens to him?'

'He goes back to being what he was.'

'Like Joe?'

Blenny nodded. 'Just like Jophiel.'

'Who cares!' shouted McBride. 'If there's something he can do, just do it!'

Igor did it. He laid his forehead gently on hers and closed his eyes, as if trying to reach her by telepathy, except that where his skin touched hers it continued inward, so that first his brow sank into her brow, then his nose into her nose, his face into her face – until his entire head had disappeared into hers. It looked like he was paying obeisance; bowing not just to her but *into* her. Where they melded, a faint bioluminescence glowed, and as his touch passed her flesh emerged clean, undamaged, and flushed with life – but not entirely the same.

The changes were so subtle that nobody but McBride, who had spent many hours stroking those features lovingly, would have noticed them. Her hair was ever so slightly darker – more auburn than blonde – her nose a little sharper, the softness under her chin a little leaner. They were the features of a woman in her early twenties rather than late teens. This process continued, past their shoulders and arms, chest, torso, hips, knees, legs and finally feet; until Igor was completely gone except for the faint flicker of something silvery disappearing into the gaps between the air, and Sophie awoke with a gasping cry.

Except she wasn't Sophie any more. Sophie was dead, killed taking the araka with her, as she had known it would be in the end, and for a moment Vessa felt the terrible, aching emptiness where the other had always been. This was her body now – wholly and in its entirety – and this was how she had always looked, the only difference was that now it was on the outside. She woke, and saw that Steve was seeing her for the first time as she really was, and that awful void wasn't quite so empty any more.

Moments later the cliff top collapsed completely, disappearing in thunderous clouds of dust, and they found themselves on the brink of an entirely new shore.

EPILOGUE

DREAMWRACK

1

The Sea Life Centre in Birmingham's Brindley Place echoed with the shrieking of children, tinny ocean-themed muzak, and the pervasive thunder of water. It was giving Maddox a headache, but at least that was some compensation for the roiling agony in his guts. He was watching a video of a male seahorse giving birth, and experiencing a mixture of fascination, horror, and an odd kind of sympathy.

The poor creature was latched onto the stem of a plant with its tail and bucking like it was being electrocuted as the contractions started. With each spasm, clouds of wriggling fry – looking like maggots with whip-tails – spurted from the orifice in the top of its distended brood pouch. Hundreds of them. Possibly thousands. It seemed to go on forever, and when it was done, the male collapsed to the bottom of the tank, twitching listlessly.

'I know how you feel, mate,' he murmured. He didn't suppose he looked much better. He knew that parents were steering their children away from him: the crazy-looking tramp in the stinking coat who was munching a hot-dog and getting mustard all over his face. He'd been on the run for days, trying to keep off the Hegemony's radar. Ironically, it seemed that the best way to avoid detection by one of their psychic buoys was to look as much like one as possible. He hadn't washed and barely slept, but in contrast his appetite was prodigious, despite the squirming pain in his stomach. He had no plan and no destination; every time he tried to think through a course of action, his thoughts floated away from each other. The only constant – other than the pain – was the fact that somehow he kept finding himself drawn irresistibly to water. Canals, rivers, sewage farms – it didn't matter.

A sudden, vicious cramp seized his insides. He doubled over, gasping, and dropped his hotdog in a spatter of yellow mustard which looked exactly like pus.

'Oh Christ,' he moaned. He was going to be sick. He had to get out, into the fresh air. Now.

He was also as far away from the exit as it was possible to get. The Sea Life Centre was fan-shaped in plan, with its ground-floor entrance at the narrow end and its attractions rising up and away in a series of switchback turns to the far curving wall, which was where – amongst many other exhibits – the seahorse breeding tanks were on display. From this high vantage point he could look back down over the whole space, and see the crowds of visitors snaking their way past tanks and pools up towards him. Most of them were parents with pushchairs and their orbiting swarms of kids. More fry – human maggots with legs. From here it was an elevator ride down to the underwater viewing tunnel and then out. That was likely to be just as crowded. He didn't dare bring attention to himself by shoving past all those people, not least of all because he was certain he wouldn't even make it as far as the doors before losing his lunch.

Another cramp hit, harder this time, and longer. Sort of like…

'Oh Jesus, no,' he whimpered.

He lurched for the nearest fire exit.

Braying alarms pursued him out into shockingly bright daylight, for all that it was an overcast day, and down the exterior fire escape, more falling than running, to the pavement. Instinctively, he headed for the gleam of open water. The Sea Life Centre was built on the south bank of Old Turn Junction, where the Birmingham and Fazeley Canal met the BCN Main Line Canal, right at the heart of the city's newest commercial and residential developments.

At the edge of the water he fell to his knees, wracked by uncontrollable spasms, and with the last of his failing strength managed to drag himself over the brink. A woman began screaming nearby, but he was able to ignore it in the sudden, blissful coolness of the canal.

His brood pouch split open from the navel, down to his pubic bone and up as far as the joining of his ribcage, and Lilivet's spawn were birthed into the murky waters. There were dozens of them, each barely the size of a tennis ball, and their carapaces were still soft, but they came into the world with the viciousness of their kind fully developed nonetheless, and turned immediately to attack each other. The fratricidal massacre was brief, as Maddox's withered corpse tumbled into the deep silt of the canal bed, and the handful of survivors scattered into the darkness to hide while they grew their armour.

Many of the strongest would perish all the same – in the jaws of the Realt's natural predators, or the propellors of boats, or tangled in rubbish. They were creatures of pure instinct, and the only impulse stronger than those to feed and kill – the one they had inherited from their human blood – was to be conscious. Thus, they crept away into the drains and sewers, hunting for the sweetest meat of all: human minds.

2

The investigative committee set up by the Hegemony's Interstitial Assembly was swift in its investigation of the incident, completely exonerating the Regional Supervisor for the United Kingdom, Ireland and Iceland of substantive culpability in the matter of the meniscus breach at Facility UK187, known colloquially as 'The Park'. Video data salvaged from the operation at the Gravelly Hill Interchange, coupled with witness testimony from the survivors of The Park's enforced closure, supported RegSup UKI&I's contention that the catastrophic breach of the meniscus there was instigated by a female of unknown identity possessing unquantified wake-abilities, who fatally compromised the command of UKFac187's custodian. The subsequent burden of culpability was deemed to be on the Oraillean Counter-Subornation Chief responsible for the investigation and closure of the breach identified locally as 'The Flats.'

When the Regional Supervisor for the United Kingdom, Ireland and Iceland got home late that evening after the final committee session had adjourned, he found that there was a call waiting for him.

'You bastard, Foulkes,' snarled Timothy Jowett.

The voice on the other end of the telephone connection was flat and toneless, despite the anger in its words, because strictly speaking they weren't its words. The voice belonged to a gaunt, shadow-eyed young man who lived in heavily-guarded seclusion on a remote mountain farm in Wales. His twin – or at least, the twin of the Passenger from Tourmaline he carried – was somewhere just as secure in Jowett's city of Carden, a place which Foulkes himself would never see. The twins' existence had been one of the lucky coincidences which the Hegemony had exploited to its full advantage: a unique opportunity to establish a line of direct communication between the two worlds. It was a telepathic back-channel which for many years had allowed Foulkes and Jowett to circumvent the Hegemony's often tedious bureaucracy – but occasionally it had its drawbacks. This appeared to be one such occasion.

He sighed. 'What on earth did you expect me to do, Timothy?'

There was a time lag of several seconds, which was the twin in the DCS relaying his question and listening to the response. When it came, it was in the same toneless delivery. Foulkes hated not being able to hear the other man's voice and the nuances of emotion underneath it. He hated these conversations generally, even when he wasn't getting a mouthful of abuse.

'I expected you to mention the bloody *araka*, that's what.'

'I hardly think the committee would have been interested in a common parapsyte.'

'There was nothing common about it when the God-be-damned thing incorporated and destroyed one of my teams!'

'I have no idea what you're talking about.'

'No? Oh, well I must be mistaken then.' Foulkes didn't have to stretch his imagination much to hear the sarcasm dripping from every word. 'I must have completely misread the clatter message which my man sent from Danae – the one in which he described fighting black tentacles in the water and meeting the same Sophie

Marchant who you declared dead. But never mind. I'll just ask him to clarify the details himself when he gets back.'

Foulkes thought it highly unlikely that Jowett's man would live long enough to be debriefed by his superior. If Jowett thought that the twin was his only contact over there, then he was an imbecile. But he hadn't finished, apparently.

'What I'm trying to puzzle out,' he continued, 'is why you wouldn't tell them about such a common parapsyte in the first place. I mean, why not? It's such a little thing, and you're such a stickler for dotting the i's and crossing the t's. What are you up to, over there? What are you hiding?'

'This conversation has officially become absurd. Goodbye, Timothy.'

He hung up.

Then he called up the images which had been grabbed off the CCTV cameras overlooking Old Turn Junction in Birmingham. Bloody Birmingham again. A man's body floating face-down in the canal, his coat open on either side like the wings of a drowned angel. Enhanced close-ups of the same image, cropped to blurred shapes in the water around him – black stars, or spiders. Dozens of them. What was he hiding? He didn't know. Yet.

3

The hospitality of Serj Osk's home turned out to be as generous as the foulness of his temper had been. It was touch and go whether or not he threw Allie and Runce into Timini's only cell when they showed up on the dock in the *Spinner's* dinghy, had their story not been corroborated by the fact that the Flats had most definitely disappeared – and because of his wife.

Paege Osk took one look at Allie and threw her hands into the air. 'Oh, my dear!' she trilled, sweeping a large maternal arm around her shoulders. 'You will stay with us until a ship can come for you. I will not hear a word against it!' She shot a look at her husband which dared him to contradict her, and so, being a man who knew when a case was hopeless, that was decided.

Their house was large, as befitted the Chief Constable of the island, but largely empty, the little Osks being mostly grown adults with families of their own. As a result, Allie found herself given the pick of the daughters' old clothes – most of which were too small, but at least they were clean. When Paege drew her a bath in a big old tin tub in the scullery, she thought she'd died and gone to heaven, but had to protest when the older woman started throwing handfuls of fragrant herbs into the steaming water.

'Oh no, really that's not necessary,' she said, as kindly as she could. 'Honestly, I'm just glad that it's warm and doesn't have anything living in it.'

Paege Osk shook her head indulgently. 'They are medicinal,' she replied. 'They will help,' and nodded knowingly at Allie's belly.

It took a long moment for the penny to drop. Then:

'What?!' Allie broke into peals of laughter. 'Oh no! No-no-no-no-no. I'm not. You're mistaken. I can't be.'

Paege laid the flat of her palm on Allie's lower stomach. 'I am never wrong in these things,' she said gently. 'All the girls in the village, they come to me. I am always right. Don't worry, it is lovely!' She laid her other hand on Allie's cheek.

'Well I'm sorry,' Allie replied, carefully disengaging her hands, 'but you're wrong on this one. No offence, but there is simply no way I can be pregnant.'

Paege Osk shrugged in a gesture which said *suit yourself* clearer than any words, and left her to her bath.

When Runce returned from Timini's clatter office to tell her that he'd reported back to his superiors in Carden and that a fast ship was being despatched to pick them up, she barely heard him. She sat on the Osk's first floor balcony with a cup of kaff going cold on the table in front of her, idly scratching Buster's head as she stared out at the glittering waters of Moon and Sixpence Bay, but she wasn't really looking at that either. She was seeing in her memory drops of Bobby's blood falling through the water like crimson pearls.

Slowly, her hand went to her lower belly and rested there.

4

'Excuse me, sir, may I sit here?'

The old man looked, up, startled out of his doze. He'd nodded off again in the drifting afternoon light of the Barber Institute's gallery. He seemed to be spending more time asleep than awake, these days, he thought. As if rehearsing. But after all, he was nearly ninety years old; he might be allowed the occasional public kip.

The young man was well dressed, which was a pleasant change these days, and there was something familiar about him – something that he thought he recognised, but it slipped away. *Finally going gaga, you old fart*, he told himself. He shuffled along the wooden bench and waved a hand at the space beside him. 'By all means.'

Bobby sat down. Now that he was here he found that he had no idea how to start this conversation.

The painting opposite them showed a mother and child standing on a rocky shore against a moonlit sky, pointing out to sea where a small fishing skiff was approaching. The interpretation card put it somewhere in Norway; to Bobby it looked just like Moon and Sixpence Bay.

'I used to work here, you know,' he said.

The old man nodded politely.

'Security guard. I must have walked past this one a hundred times and never seen it properly.'

The old man looked directly at him for the first time. 'And what do you make of it, now that you see it?' he asked.

'I like it. It's optimistic. Daddy's coming home; mother and daughter are waiting for him.'

'Funny. That's exactly what I think.'

Bobby reached into the inside pocket of his jacket and brought out a slim brown-paper parcel, then sat fiddling with it, turning it over and over in his hands. 'The day I left, it was in a bit of a hurry. You were here; I remember that. You were having a kip.'

The old man laughed, despite the strange tingle of déjà vu which Bobby's words had caused. 'I tend to do that,' he admitted.

'The place I ended up was dangerous. To say the least. For the first few days I was completely alone, with no food or water or shelter or anything, and I'm pretty sure that I would have died if it hadn't been for you. What you were dreaming.'

'I'm not sure I follow you, lad.'

'Here.' Bobby handed him the parcel. 'It'll make more sense if you open this.'

Somewhat dubiously, the old man pried open a corner of the wrapping until he saw what was inside, then tore the rest away with trembling fingers.

'Oh my…'

The copy of Nicholas Brannigan's *A Tender Death* was battered and dog-eared, having been soaked by the sea and baked by the sun, but still in much too good a condition to be as old as the publication date claimed. When he opened the cover and saw the enigmatic Adriana's inscription and her lipstick kiss, the old man's hand went to his mouth in shock. 'Where on earth…?' he breathed.

'Not on earth, Mr Jenkins. Not really. I wanted to say thank you for what you gave to me, and not just because it kept me alive. I wanted you to have that.'

Robert Jenkins stared at the young man and whispered 'Who are you? Are you… Am I…?'

'No!' Bobby laughed and then swallowed it immediately. 'I'm sorry, that was rude. No, I'm fairly sure you're not dead. As to who I am?' He shrugged. 'Part of me is you – or at least, the younger you that you were dreaming about that day. Part of me is still the me I was when I left. I'm something in the middle, I suppose.'

'But this is impossible.' His gnarled fingers were tracing the outline of the lipstick smudge, as if denying what his mouth was saying.

'Yes, I know, but don't worry – you'll get over it. I also wanted to say that it's an honour, being you.' He turned to leave.

'I was something of a shit, you should know,' said Robert Jenkins.

Bobby paused and looked back. He smiled. 'I think I can probably live up to that.'

'I should have gone back for her.'

'Who? Adriana?'

Robert nodded. 'I was too full of myself. My career – the expectations of my family. We had one weekend in Singapore at the end of the War, and I promised I'd go back for her, but I never did.'

'Trust me,' said Bobby, 'that's one mistake I intend to put right.'

5

'So *this* is what two o'clock in the morning looks like.'

'Vessa,' Steve muttered thickly, 'for Christ's sake will you switch that bloody light off and go to sleep?'

'Grumpy sod.'

But she smiled to herself and turned off the bedside lamp.

ACKNOWLEDGEMENTS

Thanks are due to:

Pam Murphy, one of the bravest people I know, for her invaluable insights into what it's actually like to wake up from a coma; Giles Sutcliffe, for much-needed constructive pedantry; Marie Browne and Paul Merrell for reading and commenting on early drafts; Jon Hansford for correcting my maths; James Lynch for the tiger-fish-man-thing; Tony Quinn for nautical advice; Emma and Anna at Snowbooks; Peter Coleborn and Jan Edwards for encouraging me in this madness; and Mike Watts, Debs Steffen and the cast of Thethem for general therapeutic geekery.

Most of all, to TC, Hopey and Eden, for still being here when I come home from strange places.